The
Merlin
of the Oak Wood

Book Two of the
Joan of Arc Tapestries

Ann Chamberlin

TOR®
fantasy

A TOM DOHERTY ASSOCIATES BOOK
NEW YORK

THE MERLIN OF THE OAK WOOD

Copyright © 2001 by Ann Chamberlin

A Tor Book
Published by Tom Doherty Associates, LLC
175 Fifth Avenue
New York, NY 10010

www.tor.com

Tor® is a registered trademark of Tom Doherty Associates, LLC.

ISBN: 0-765-34499-8
Library of Congress Catalog Card Number: 2001021944

First edition: June 2001
First mass market edition: April 2003

Printed in the United States of America

0 9 8 7 6 5 4 3 2 1

By Ann Chamberlin from
Tom Doherty Associates Books

For Just Joan

Acknowledgments

C'est avec plaisir que je remercie, premièrement en français, tous ceux qui m'ont aidée avec cette œuvre. Mlle. Rachel Hamstead, institutrice de ma jeunesse, m'a introduite au peuple français et à sa langue avec un amour bien sérieux. À Domrémy-la-Pucelle, je me souviens de la propriétaire d'Hôtel de la Pucelle; à Orléans, le personnel de la maison de Jeanne d'Arc; à Blois, M. Eric Gault; et partout, Mme. Josette Melac et ses filles, Sylvie et Annie. Finalement, je remercie Mme. Caroline Malassigne-Donnelly.

In English, I have the pleasure to thank Natalia Aponte and all the folks at Tor who pushed this through. Thanks to Anna Ghosh, to Virginia Kidd, Jim Allen, and especially Linn Prentis, whose long and detailed commentary helped immensely with the rewrites—and when I needed a shoulder to cry on.

My friends Alexis Worlock, to whom this volume is dedicated, and Karen Porcher were always generous with their time and friendship. The Wasatch Mountain Fiction Writers Friday Morning Group was there from the moment this was merely a little glimmer in need of plotting. Among them, I'd like to mention Brenda Bensch and Kathleen Dougherty by name for help far beyond the call of duty. Although we live too far apart, Linda Cook always brought the most interesting perspective to my musings: she named the horse Grison and caught more than one anachronism.

The Marriott, Whitmore, and Holladay librarians never stinted in their assistance.

And of course there's my family. My sons in particular were company on my research trips, drew maps, and bounced ideas. My husband is (sometimes) patient while my mind is elsewhere. My parents introduced me early to France and her people and my in-laws make it all possible.

None of these supportive people is responsible for the mistakes I've made in these pages; they only kept me from making more.

The

Merlin

of the Oak Wood

The Merlin of
the Oak Wood

Mont-Saint-Michel

Avranches

Paris

Brittany

Saint-James-de-Beuvron

Orléans

Blaison

Bourg

English-Controlled
Lands in 1428

Burgundian Lands

Lands Faithful to
Charles the Dauphin

North

Olivia Mitchell 2001

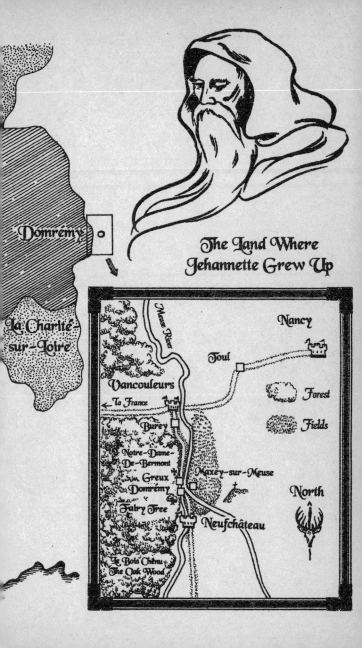

The Land Where
Jehannette Grew Up

Domrémy

La Charité-
sur-Loire

Meuse River

Nancy

Toul

Vaucouleurs

Forest

← To France

Fields

Burey

Notre-Dame-
De-Bermont

Greux
Domrémy

Maxey-sur-Meuse

North

Fairy Tree

Neufchâteau

Le Bois Chênu
The Oak Wood

1

Rich Gold in Stick Hands

BURGUNDIAN- AND ENGLISH-HELD FRANCE,
UPPER LOIRE VALLEY
THE FEAST OF ST. MARY MAGDALENE,
JULY, YEAR OF GRACE 1425

Every step Gilles de Rais took toward the shadow of the Burgundians' castle wall required superhuman effort, the deeds of
legend. Over his head hung the portcullis. In an instant—under
different circumstances—the iron teeth would drop with a
roar, trapping him on the glory side of the gate—isolated from
all his friends outside.

The great maw did not clamp shut. Gilles pressed on un-
impeded by the smoke and dust—of a quiet summer's day in
La Charité-sur-Loire.

No matter that the attack was only in his mind—as yet.
Captain Perrinet Grassart was still Burgundian, the enemy,
gone over to the side of the invading English. His guards were
helmeted and edgy. And the single man following Gilles de
Rais was just an unarmed groom, the noble steed a mule slung
with strong boxes.

Gilles de Rais fully intended to come to La Charité-sur-
Loire again someday and receive a welcome more to his lik-
ing: boiling oil and arrows. Arrows and hot oil were more
honest than the false smiles and chivalry he would need today
to free his cousin held for ransom in this place. His cousin
whom he'd never seen and knew little about. Arrows and hot

oil, he knew how to handle them. They were more honest, even, than the chests of gold coin on the donkey behind him.

He memorized every detail of the castle as he passed with an eye to that future day: the discipline of Grassart's men, their arms. This second gate and portcullis could trap the unwary attacker in its narrow, steep-sided space. It offered no outlet but arrow slits and murder holes so high up, his neck crinked to see them. The defender would rain death down upon the attacker who foolishly let himself get caught here.

Once past that snare, the way turned sharply left, exposing the attacker's sword arm to more arrows, more murder holes. The castle was not new—perhaps two hundred years old. Nonetheless, the best of every defense of the time had been employed. It gave no consideration to gunpowder, but new construction, widening the base outside and here within, said such consideration was under way.

La Charité-sur-Loire would not be easy to take, but Gilles de Rais would take it. After the humilities of this day—and they were only just beginning—he would enjoy taking it.

The expressionless helmets of Grassart's men nodded him across the yard: About twenty horses stabled. Thatched roofs of outbuildings to the south and west, easily fired. A well—that would make the siege much more difficult. Perhaps there was a source somewhere outside the walls that could be poisoned? All it would take would be one good, ripe horse carcass.

A knowledge of a castle's underground works was of little use in a siege, even to the sappers; they rarely got so far. Still, it was a barred window set deep in the ground that next caught the lord of Rais' eye.

A pair of thin, pale sticks waved at him through the bars. There was a sound like the weak mewing of kittens. Gilles took a step or two closer, off his straight line toward the hall, to investigate.

Those weren't sticks stripped of bark to the white wood beneath. Those were arms. And they weren't the arms of fighting men Grassart was holding 'til their cousins showed up with their strongboxes.

These were children.

Peasant children by the rags, though even velvets would have quickly become disgusting in such filth. Braving the incredible stench, stepping yet closer to the dungeon pit, Gilles saw a crowd of them, eight at least, maybe more. It was hard to tell for the shadows, and few seemed strong enough to stand, or tall enough to reach to the window.

Light slanting through the bars fell on one child in particular: a boy of eight or so, with the most beautiful pale blond curls, large blue eyes, and skin so thin and papery white, Gilles could see the veins blue beneath it.

The boy was whimpering for water.

Gilles remembered the well in the center of the keep, glad he hadn't thrown in a horse carcass—yet. He ran for the brink and hefted up a bucketful. He found the bucket chained to the coping. He yanked. He drew his sword and, with no mind for the keen edge he'd rubbed into it that morning, gave the chain a couple of good whacks. Sparks flew; nothing else. He even tried the spell for metal Père Yann had taught him, though he had no time to think of Yann now.

Gilles decided he wasn't calm enough to work magic. Nothing happened, but he couldn't stop for that. At a loss for anything faster to do, he threw aside his sword, cupped his hands, and swept all they could carry, dripping across the yard. There was no thought in his mind but water, as if the thirst were his own.

His groom tried to stand in his way, yelling something at him, very pale and nervous. Sight of this man made Gilles remember the goblet he had had packed along with the gold in his chests. He was at the mule instantly, unpacking a morning's work in an moment.

He filled the goblet at the well and carried it to the dungeon grate.

The sight of rich gold in that shaking, thin white hand struck him so strongly that he froze, wondering what artist he could hire to capture the pathos of it. Only then did he recall his cousin, Georges de La Trémoïlle. Only then did he let the warning hand on his arm grow firmer.

The little twigs waved the empty goblet at him for more. He took it, but his groom very easily worked his fingers free of the stem.

"Come, my lord. Leave it," the man said, begged. "There's nothing you can do for them. The fortunes of war. Surely your lordship understands that."

Gilles recovered his senses. The man was right. The moment he'd drawn his sword against the well, Grassart's men had drawn theirs against him. They had him cautiously encompassed within a tightening circle, these brutes wiped faceless by their visors. In a moment, he'd be in the dungeon with those children.

The idea had appeal—to touch that boy's golden hair. But he had come for Cousin Georges. His cousin, his own flesh and blood—although he couldn't remember having met him before—must be kept in similar straits or worse. If he broke the gloss of chivalry, gave the enemy any excuse to put him in that dungeon, Gilles de Rais could help nobody, not even himself.

With a great sigh, Gilles' sword found its sheath. He followed where the groom's arm led him.

But he would return to La Charité. By God, by *the* God, he swore it. Burn the man alive who kept children hostage without food or water in his *donjon*.

And take his gold back again. With usury.

Gilles left his nervous groom to guard the coin and the mule and took a broad flight of stairs up into the hall. For a moment, he stood in the doorway open to the warm air, letting his eyes get used to the dim light barred with shafts of dust. The coo of pigeons came at him, and the thick male stench of a garrison. No woman saw the reeds replaced and freshened. Gilles sniffed like a wolf on the hunt, then picked out two lords sitting across the large space at the high table with a lavish meal spread between them.

"Monseigneur the baron of Rais, sire de Laval, and . . . no, lord of . . ." A young page pressed into service as a herald stumbled on the titles until Gilles brushed the boy aside.

The fellow at the table with the greatest presence, that huge, white pork of a man, Gilles decided, must be Grassart, the captain of La Charité. The Burgundian captain's name had reminded him of the word "grease" since he'd first heard it less than a week ago: goose liver crammed for the table. Gilles made the man as shallow a bow as he could, forced strength and calm into his voice.

"Monsieur Grassart, I am Gilles, lord of Rais. For the sake of family honor, I've come to ransom my cousin, Georges de La Trémoïlle, whom you hold captive here at La Charité."

"Ah, welcome, Gilles, welcome," the man said, waving greasy fingers toward a chair.

Gilles hesitated, taking offense at this familiar use of his given name, yet unsure what he could do about it. Before he could make up his mind either to sit or to draw sword, the man went on.

"*This* is Perrinet Grassart, captain of La Charité."

The greasy fingers indicated the lesser man. With straight, dirty blond hair and loose limbs, he looked nothing so much as like the straw figures peasants set up in their fields at this season. Gilles had already decided he could ignore the man. Taking the castle appeared easier and easier.

"My good, generous—" The speaker paused in his listing of the commander's qualities to hum appraisingly. "—captor."

The speaker chuckled, though Gilles had done everything in his power to conceal his surprise at this word.

"Yes, Gilles," said the pork. "*I* am your long-lost cousin, Georges de La Trémoïlle."

2

Silk-Hosed Thighs the Size of Hogsheads

———•◦•———

"God's Bones," bellowed the huge mountain of a man, tossing yet another bare-gnawed joint into the growing heap beneath his chair. The hounds couldn't keep up with him. "How long has it been since I last saw you, Gilles?"

Gilles couldn't remember the time, only the years this fellow had been named to him as one of the glowing lights of his dwindling family. Because he knew La Trémoïlle nearly doubled his own twenty-one years, he dreaded the answer.

"I do believe you were in swaddling when I last visited your dearly departed parents at Château Blaison."

Gilles had expected to feel shame, and he did. But for some reason he couldn't explain, a warm sentiment salved the hurt when he thought of those times. Binding that swaddling had probably been his dear nurse, Guillemette la Drapière. He spared a very fond thought for that woman's son Yann, too, and wished, beyond all rationale, that that twisted, half-mad priest were with him in this pass. If ever there were anyone of less use in a battle, whom he less wanted as witness to his shame, it was his milk brother. Yet Gilles found it difficult to shake the thought. No doubt because the present alternative for attention was so disgusting. And all the while, the children starving in the dungeon out in the yard.

"God's Bones." La Trémoïlle shook his porcine head as another joint hit the floor. "How time flies."

The young lord of Rais took the seat offered him, but refused any of the dishes shoved in his direction. He liked fine food as well as the next nobleman, perhaps even better. But he'd been knighted at sixteen and the five years of almost solid campaigning since allowed him to tolerate other victuals well enough. It certainly had its advantages over returning to Château Champtocé and having to face his wife.

And not the least advantage of a warrior's life was the love of Roger, the fair young sire de Bricqueville.

Gilles stole another glance at their host, who regarded the two cousins wryly. Grassart seemed determined to add nothing to the conversation, as if others' family quarrels were his greatest entertainment.

Gilles said, as carelessly as he could, "You and Monsieur Grassart seem to have had a very merry time of it."

"Grassart's a fine soldier, a fine commander."

"A man would have to be a bumpkin not to catch such a slow-moving target as yourself, cousin."

La Trémoïlle said nothing in his concentration on his next mouthful.

"Not cousin of the first degree," Gilles muttered, with real relief. "Both blood and wit are much watered down between us."

Perhaps I go too far, Gilles told himself immediately. The pig was very powerful, very rich—once. He may be again. Peasants, I understand, are very fond, very proud of their household pigs. Why else would I have come so far to bail out such a man? He is also kin; no man can keep his own honor while some portion of his blood rots in captivity. And surely some respect is due seniority. Even if that seniority has learned no wisdom over time.

But Gilles, the lord of Rais, was unused to holding his tongue for anyone. He'd already decided he didn't care what Grassart thought of him. A man who held children captive.

"Good friends, are you? You and your—captor? Excuse me. I nearly said 'host.'"

La Trémoïlle lifted his tankard in Grassart's direction.

The reason why this cousin hadn't been around much since his childhood, why he'd known him by name only, leaped to the front of Gilles' mind. "I'll wager you two were as close as thieves in the old days. Before you switched colors. When you were bumping around in Burgundy's wallet together."

"Yes, cousin. Monsieur Grassart knows as well as anyone that I did once find favor with monseigneur the duke of Burgundy."

"High favor, I hear."

"Yes. I have the talent—if I say it myself—of becoming indispensable to the great ones of the earth. But why should I endure the humility of captivity here and now if I were not a true servant of the Dauphin?"

"I can think of at least one good reason," Gilles said.

La Trémoïlle raised a single thick, grey-flecked brow, stiff as boar's bristles.

"My fourteen thousand *écus*," Gilles elaborated.

"The sum hurts you? How can that be? You've been the richest man in all the family since you were orphaned at the tender age of eleven. Richer with your marriage to Madame de Thouars." Gilles didn't like the lewd tone in that statement. "And bound to become richer still when your grandfather dies. Well, if it does cause you pain, I'll make every haste to pay you back. Indeed, I shall. I'm not without resources myself, as you know. Though they are mostly encumbered at the moment."

"Encumbered, yes." Now Gilles laughed, once, quickly. "I did not know you before this day, but I'm beginning to see it would be just like you, coz. To give yourself into Grassart's hands, then plot with him to split the money half and half when, after a month or two of merry feasting together, I finally brought the sum to you."

La Trémoïlle chuckled, to dismiss the notion. Gilles did not join him. Then he decided there was no better way to thumb his nose at Grassart than more open politics. Let the spies see your numbers, when they're great. It might scare them off.

"Why do you persist," Gilles said to his cousin, "in calling his majesty 'le Dauphin'? His father is dead these three years almost. He is by the grace of God . . ."—by the grace of *the* God, the lord of Rais thought, and the grace of Père Yann— ". . . King of France, Charles the seventh of that name."

Captain Grassart spoke up now, very tersely, as if assuring them this first time he did not mean to make a habit of it, whatever the provocation. "Charles Valois is not, my lord de Rais, King of France. By both treaty and blood, young Henry of England is."

La Trémoïlle smiled at his host, as if agreeing with him. "Monsieur Grassart has so often and so kindly pointed this out to me during my stay with him. Until Charles is crowned and anointed in Rheims cathedral like all his ancestors before him, he is not even King of the tiny town of Bourges where he holds out."

Gilles remained silent, confessing the truth of this. Revealing his strength to the enemy had not worked this time. Indeed, it had ricocheted back to him. Why, he'd left Charles in Bourges himself not two days ago. Two days' ride and he was already far beyond what the "so-called" Dauphin could claim as his own, even in hours of great optimism.

"The big difficulty"—La Trémoïlle's voice took on deep sermon tones—"lies in the fact that England holds Rheims."

In response to a cough from Grassart, their Burgundian host, La Trémoïlle amended his statement: "England *and* her Burgundian allies with whom I, dear coz, was hoping to treaty when I was, unfortunately, captured. Three years since his father's death and the boy has made no progress toward that end."

Gilles didn't like the inflection in "the boy." He himself was younger than Charles by a year and more. "You have the honor of a weasel" was all he could think of to say.

La Trémoïlle only laughed. "I've honor enough. This isn't the first time I've been a prisoner, you must know. The English took me at Agincourt. That set me back a few *écus* as well."

And there've been a half dozen switches of sides in between, Gilles thought. Always captured, never wounded.

Aloud, he said, "A clever man, you're telling me, will keep himself in balance with the other side?"

"Exactly."

La Trémoïlle was beginning to sound like Gilles' milk

brother Yann, with all this talk of balance. Why Père Yann again?

Gilles ran his finger around the rough wood board between them. He watched his cousin bury his nose in Grassart's goblet and come away with rich purple on the shaved but still-dark bristles of his upper lip.

"You know, after this debacle, you'll have little credit at Charles' court when I get you back," Gilles warned.

"Is that God's truth?" The older man did not hide his irony.

"Why don't you stay here and save me my ransom gold?"

Gilles caught Grassart's eyes lighting up at this mention of "gold," like dangerous sparks in the midst of the straw. Of course this is why the Burgundian captain had kept his cousin like—well, like a lord, while he let the peasant children rot.

It was La Trémoïlle who answered. "You forget, my dear young cousin. Burgundy handed Boulogne over to the English without so much as a 'by your leave.' *My* fief of Boulogne. I will not stay with such wretches until I get it back. On that I give you my word."

For all your word is worth, Gilles thought before he said aloud, "Ergo, back you trot to the King. Even when I tell you you have many enemies at Bourges?"

"Such enemies I can deal with. See if I cannot. The Dauphin's a fool. I can work with that boy easily enough. Once rid him of those damned courtiers. Tanneguy du Châtel. Pierre de Giac. Upon my oath, I hate Giac."

"For no other reason than that he holds the post of King's favorite and chamberlain, which you yourself covet."

"Then there's Monseigneur Arthur de Richemont."

La Trémoïlle's tone as he spat out this name on the list made Gilles frown. Gilles himself fought under Count Arthur de Richemont, the scar-faced brother of the duke of Brittany. And no matter what his private feelings may be, no man likes to hear his liege lord debased.

Gilles worked for calm as he stopped his cousin's list of enemies before he heard any more. "So you'll replace them all—with yourself?"

Perhaps the best way of countering his cousin's plans was

by making him reveal them all now to the enemy Captain Grassart. If the two of them hadn't made these plans together, over a cozy goblet of wine.

"You catch on quickly, Gilles de Rais."

Gilles remembered the goblet in the shriveled hand out in the yard. He felt his own thirst, the child's thirst, but he resisted the hospitality offered him once more.

"Well, yes," he said. "I'd say there's enough of you to make four or five other men."

La Trémoïlle took no offense at this reference to his size. He rather enjoyed it with a hearty laugh. "If you stick close to me, boy, you just may follow on my horse's tail. I have no son, you see. Poor, dear Jeanne never had the health to give me one."

"No. You married her for Boulogne, not for heirs."

"Yes, about as full of *amour* as your own match with the heiress Madame de Thouars."

Gilles was silent.

Captain Grassart added another word from the side, as if in the broadest of generalities. "A man can adopt an heir, when he will and when he has no other."

"And I couldn't have had a son more like myself than you, Gilles de Rais." La Trémoïlle spoke boisterously, as if at some new and problem-solving discovery. "Not from my own loins."

Gilles could not resist a glance at those loins—rolling between gaudy, silk-hosed thighs the size of hogsheads—that La Trémoïlle had pushed back from the table. The sight made Gilles shove himself back with more sudden violence and get to his feet.

"Captain Grassart, you have a child, a fair-haired boy in your dungeons, whose freedom I wish to purchase with no more delay."

Both of them stared at him, eyes wide, stuffed mouths agape, as if he'd suddenly gone mad in their midst.

His sword hand itched. He resisted scratching it on his hilt, but he knew the feeling. Magic, Père Yann always called it. Your magic on the battlefield, Sire Gilles. Though why he should be thinking of Père Yann so far from that wizard's haunts he could not tell.

But so it was. Magic. In a way.

"I have horses waiting down at the abbey," Gilles went on to the stupefied pair. "Monsieur Grassart, I have fourteen thousand *écus* in my strongboxes. What is your price for the fair-haired child? And if you insist on my taking this tub of lard along as well, that's part of the cost of doing business. I confess from the start, you'll get the better of the deal."

First Antiphon

A Weft of Black-Robed Figures

THE ABBEY OF THE HOLY CROSS, LA CHARITÉ-SUR-LOIRE

Gilles de Rais, this milk brother of mine, was anything but clannish toward the great nobleman with him. His long-lost cousin was clearly disgruntled that he had to dismount to take this alleyway down steep stairs that led from the castle to the abbey at this point. Georges de La Trémoïlle was in no better mood than the monstrous, excitable, and silver-rigged stallion he had to lead, not the sort of mount one expects a newly redeemed man to own.

Gilles de Rais spared no care or patience for either large creature. My heart sank, weighted by the lengthening shadows of abbey wall on one side, pitched-roofed houses on the other, and the sight of Gilles returning between them. He would not give up the small charge he carried—incongruously in his battle-strengthened arms—to the retainers, nor to the now-unburdened donkey.

All this time, all the goods and hope my milk brother had set out with, and this was his prize? The single child he carried now in his arms?

I should have gone with my milk brother, should have made my presence here in La Charité known to him earlier. Grassart must have seen the lord of Rais' eagerness in a flash and taken him for everything he had. The great sorrow was that Gilles' face told me he considered he had won a bargain. He never would make a profitable trader.

But now that I had waited so long, I could wait longer. Under the rim of my cowl, I watched Gilles stride with his burden into the abbey's guesthouse. I watched the flurry of activity: servants running out, Brother Herbalist and Brother of the Infirmary scurrying in. I waited through the peace of sext, sharing it anonymously with my host brethren in chapel, filling my heart with my own sort of prayer.

It was a Cluniac house, this Sainte-Croix of La Charité. Its brethren wore Benedictine black. My own black robes were not out of place among them, though white linen showed underneath. Christian eyes always saw me as a Dominican: today, a visiting cleric, about some holy errand.

And so I was. Though the holy errand was not Christian.

I was certainly not to blame that Dominic's hounds of God had appropriated the ancient robes of Merlin and druid within the last two hundred years. Deception had been that saint's purpose—he had hoped "the deluded" would bring his inquisition confessions of their heresies so he could root them out—but it was not mine. I wore what men like myself have always worn, a long beard and a tonsure cut, not round, but from the ears forward. If it helped me slip into place in a Cluniac house, that most severe of monasteries—well, I would not hesitate to take what bit of aid the Gods offered.

Then, as we filed out of chapel again, I saw Gilles storm angrily from the guesthouse—for the first time, alone. I left my place as one of the nameless ranks of black-robed figures. I slipped across the priory yard after him to where he halted in his agitation, facing nothing more than a wall draped with roses.

I still didn't let him sense my presence, not at once. I stood quietly beside him, watching fondly how he dragged his fingers through his thick black curls, how the blue mark on his chin twitched with a string of curses. Fortunately, he put no real magic behind those under-breath words or the abbey should have burst to flames around us. I'd seen him do such things before, as an uncontrollable youth.

Adulthood allowed Gilles de Rais to wear a goatee of sharp, clean lines, as if circling his sensual mouth and chin for attention. This bit of a beard did no more than cover the blue mark of the God with blue-black hair he usually slicked with a musky unguent. It was a striking face, beautifully invigorated by large dark eyes. And the goatee helped ease the discomfort many had always felt in the presence of the blue marks of one initiated in the Craft, so openly displayed before, in Gilles' more childish face.

But his whole purpose was not concealment. Around the vigorous muscling of his left calf, even within abbey walls, Gilles de Rais wore a red garter. It contrasted pointedly with the fine black silk of his sleek hose. Many would see in this only the eccentricities of Sire de Rais' peculiar and always-lavish style. But many enough knew it as a sign of a man who has made a contract with the Horned One. Or the devil, as Christians call the divinity in fear of what they do not understand.

Many, many years before, in his country, the English King had christianized the sacred pact as the Order of the Garter. The Prince of Wales' motto *Honi soit qui mal y pense,* "Let him who thinks ill of this be ashamed," did the same. Such dulling of the strong edges of Craft, however, had not served the English forces well when they came face to face with Gilles de Rais, a real Craftsman. In his own dark way. And much as he himself always tried to deny it.

Most folk, having little knowledge of such things, would have to know my milk brother awhile before they began to suspect he was a witch.

As was I.

For my mother had been Gilles' wet nurse. We'd been raised together in the Château Blaison and remained closer to each other than either of us was to his own flesh-and-blood brother. Although I was three years Gilles' senior, that meant less and less the older we grew. And all of this meant even less than the fact that we'd been initiated to the Craft the selfsame day ten years before.

Now I even gazed where Gilles gazed, at the summer-spent roses, a few dark red petals caught throughout the green leaves like drops of spilled wine. And beyond the wall—though I doubted he had attention for the houses of the little town of La Charité as I did, their steep red-tile roofs and tall, thin chimneys. There was a foreign feel to the place, here where a narrow gorge still pinched the Loire and the river had not yet the wide, open floodplain to which I was accustomed.

Even the angle of the sun was foreign, as if it had risen in the north that morning of all the mornings of the world. For the gorge ran north to south, not east to west as the waterway did down most of the rest of its length to the sea. Except again near Ingrandes, the crossing Gilles' grandfather held. And that was an ancient power point, marked by the great standing stone.

Was it any wonder the people here were faithful to Burgundy? Or that I knew I had come to the furthest end of my magic before I entered the realm of another's jurisdiction? If I went any further east, the connection of my feet to Mother Earth would be no more sensitive than any other mortal's. Of what use would I be then, crippled hand, falling sickness, and all?

It was over three years, now, since Meaux had fallen, almost as long since England's Henry had died of the bloody flux. And still the brutal war raged, ravaging France beneath and all around us. Charles the son of Charles the son of Charles was not yet anointed, still no more than Dauphin, a pretender. This in spite of the fact that I had initiated him. Others had his ear. Others who could sway him even over my best magic.

The fact was, I had reached the end of my own Craft. I knew now I would need others before balance and the prophecy came any closer. I needed a coven, that power word. I needed a spark.

Far be it from me to second-guess the Merlin of this neck of the woods, particularly when he was my own teacher, Père Michel. But I needed La Pucelle. We all needed her—that girl whose birth I'd seen, whom the ancient Merlin had prophesied would rise from the Oak Wood in the east—all of France needed her now.

Père Michel had also tutored my milk brother. Though Gilles had never become adept in a Merlin's magic as I had, our teacher had never tired of telling me that he did have magic of his own, an energy dark and powerful. When my priesthood reached the end of its strength, Gilles' warrior nature could come to my aid. And so I had followed him to La Charité.

But seeing the ruins of his bargain, his lack of control even over his own emotions, I had to wonder just what use Gilles de Rais could be to anyone, off the battlefield.

Second Antiphon

The Mystery of the Death of the Martyred Child

"Hello, Gilles," I said at last, when I'd let him get used to my silent presence a bit. When he'd blown off some of his hot anger.

I'd misjudged the glamour spell. Or the depths of his distraction. My milk brother remained difficult to gauge magic for. Perhaps he always would. I managed to startle him in spite of my care. He jumped back a foot or two into a defensive stance and his sword flew right out of its scabbard.

"Mother of God."

He caught his breath and swung his weapon to ease the instant before it cut my cowl. The instant he recognized me. After the fingers of my left hand had flashed a bit of calming magic before his eyes.

"Do you have to sneak around the world like some evil wraith?" Then he grinned. "But I forget. Evil wraith is your sacred calling."

"And not yours, Gilles de Rais?" I joined his amusement.

"Yann, Yann. You devil!" He meant it as a compliment, a term of reverence in fact. His strong arms enfolded me with vigorous affection, the instant he resheathed his sword. "What brings you to La Charité, godforsaken place?"

I didn't begin with what preyed on my mind. Or on my feet, rather. My bare priest's feet had fairly tingled since coming in contact with this land around La Charité-sur-Loire. Who could have suspected this little town would be so important in days to come? Earth always holds something of the future in

Her bones, as She likewise holds the past and the dead. And I was getting better and better at reading it, the more practice I had at my calling.

Then it struck him. "My dear friend. Why, it's a wonder that you're here. A miracle."

I smiled. It was something much more mundane. Just magic. But he gave me no time to say it and was already dragging me toward the guesthouse.

"They say there's no hope for him, the herbalist and infirmarian. They say he's on the verge of death. He can't die, Yann. You must come and—and do something to bring this angel of a child back. The most soulful blue eyes—Yann, I didn't pay fourteen thousand *écus* for nothing."

I didn't dare mention the cousin, and Gilles was filling the abbey yard with his fury.

"Perrinet Grassart is one of these whores' sons who funds his war effort by taking captives and holding them to ransom."

"Lest you want every pious monk in the abbey to know our business, I suggest you keep your tone down. Come."

I slipped my good left hand through his arm and began to lead him across the yard at a more stately pace, one less likely to trip me up in my robes. As priest and sinner in deep confession, we should not raise much attention.

"I thought that was accepted practice," I said. "Taking ransom. Among the chivalrous."

"So it is. A knight counts up his ransoms and adds them to the booty he takes."

"Not every knight in this conflict is as wealthy as you are, Monseigneur de Rais."

"Certainly. I understand how it is. Few of the men—in other companies, I mean, not my own—get paid. Or if they do, only irregularly. They must live off what they can pillage. And, when they haven't taken a rich city in a while, they must— well, they help themselves to what they need from the peasants. You see I am not complaining of knight holding knight or nobleman—I wish Grassart would hold Cousin Georges until his great carcass rots. I am speaking of the taking of noncombatants. Priests. Peasants."

"Ah, the war has been long," I commented, thinking we were indeed bringing the subject around to my design. I had seen plenty of this as I crossed France from Saint-Gilles to La Charité. "A long war. And lacking in purpose. A lot of grinding of wheels, over and over in the same place."

"Sometimes—more and more often these days—the peasants swear they have nothing. They speak truth. Ransacking their hovels reveals nothing. Their skinny forms reveal nothing. 'We have nothing,' they cry. 'Not even to feed our own children.' Well, that's something there never seems to be any lack of. Children. Hungry mouths to feed. So that's what such brigands as Grassart do."

"What?"

"They find a stray child somewhere. Fishing by a stream, playing in a field. They take him."

"What do you mean, take him?"

"Kidnap him. They do the same with adults, too, but that requires more effort. Children are best. They are easily lured. A crust of bread will do the trick. Then the brigands hold them. For ransom."

"But what ransom can the poor parents come up with?" I asked, clinging to my milk brother's arm because I suspected the answer. "The brigands have already discovered that they have nothing."

"You'd be surprised how much folk can come up with when they hear it's their children. And they always have their own bodies. Sisters' bodies. Daughters'."

The thought clearly disgusted him. But not, I suspected, for the same reasons it might disgust others.

"They raise remarkably high ransoms, too, by borrowing from all their friends and kin. When they hear their children are held without food. Without water, sometimes. I saw it in La Charité keep—God, how Grassart gives the lie to this place's name! Two or three in a space no bigger than a campaigner's chest. The parents—some at least, enough—come up with ransoms. Quickly, you'd be surprised. When the thing they'd been complaining about was too many mouths to feed."

"And if the ransom can't be paid?"

Gilles shrugged, but I think it hurt him to do so. "The brats—the angels—die."

I found myself wondering at this concern for children. This was new in my milk brother, whom I'd rarely known to give a second thought to anyone younger than himself, even his own flesh-and-blood brother. Was it part of reaching a twenty-one-year-old's maturity?

Gilles' stride had lengthened with his agitation as we approached the guesthouse door. Though I clung still to his arm, I had to scramble to keep up as we entered. Then he abandoned me altogether, calling over his shoulder as he ran.

"Help me bring more light to this cavern, Yann, and you shall see just how like an angel he is."

I propped open doors and pulled back curtains until we came to a bed alcove at the heart of the guesthouse.

"God's Bones, what's amiss?" La Trémoïlle greeted us as we passed. "I thought we were going to be on the road by now, Gilles, and here it's suppertime. Are we going to be obliged to eat monk's slop . . . ?"

Neither Gilles nor I gave him any answer, but I snatched the lamp from his hand and brought it into the alcove after my milk brother.

I must confess I saw nothing of the beauty Gilles claimed for his prize. Not now, wasted as the child was 'til the bones were covered by only the thinnest parchment of skin. The hair was matted and dull; filth stuck with bits of straw and smelling abominably now covered rags that had been poor to begin with. Sour breath came in slow little gasps, the "soulful blue" eyes rolled back in their sunken sockets. Quickly, I reached for the pulse at the stringy neck.

"Oh, Gilles," I exclaimed, drawing my hand away. He had been cheated indeed. I had been cheated, too. "The monks are right. We are too late. There is nothing to be done for this boy. He's at death's door."

"Cousin de Rais—" grumbled La Trémoïlle, no doubt echoing his stomach.

Nothing but a curtain separated the alcove from the rest of

he guesthouse but I flung it shut in the nobleman's face with
a great clatter of wooden rings.

"Come, Yann." Gilles turned from his concerned gaze to
smile wryly at me. "I've never known you to give up so
easily." He thought I was joking.

"You've met death enough, Gilles, to know it when you see
it. I'm not joking. The boy's already in the hands of the God."

"Why, that bastard!" Gilles' grief exploded. "I'll have Grassart's liver for this. By St. Michel, just see if I don't."

And his sword leaped out of its sheath with a hiss.

"Calm, Gilles, calm," I said, making the magic signs. But I
was not very calm myself. "Why, Gilles, for heaven's sake?
You could have bought another child, one that might have
lived. Instead you let yourself be gulled like a bumpkin in the
market."

"But I didn't want another child. I wanted this one. And he
was worth every sou. I wanted to show the whore's son how
he undervalued, when he charged fourteen thousand *écus* for
my pig of a cousin and, for this beautiful—"

"This beautiful child" moaned and tossed weakly on the
cushions.

"Hush, Gilles, hush. You disturb him."

Gilles was back at the edge of the bed in a moment, his
sword forgotten. "There is hope, don't you mean to say, Yann?
I knew I could not have paid such a price to no purpose."

"I mean, you mustn't shout so. Let's try—let's try to make
the lad's last hour pleasant, at least."

This speech of mine illuminated Gilles' face and mind with
a new project, almost as wild, in its way, as his wish to gut
the commander of La Charité castle on the spot. It was as if
a muse had come to him suddenly and given him the entire
stage piece: "The Mystery of the Death of the Martyred
Child." I couldn't but help remember the time my milk brother
had spent playing women's parts—to great success—with the
traveling Actors of the Bar.

Pushing his head out of the curtain, he called for warm
water and some clothes in his packed chest. He called for more
of his possessions to be hawked. The groom, still wondering

if he must keep the horses saddled, was told to forget the animals until he'd carried out these tasks, which he did.

Gilles soon bathed his prize from head to toe, dressed him in his own finest linen and silken robes. The child swam in them, but that didn't spoil the effect. Then Gilles pressed warm, spiced wine to the thin, parched lips, tried him with sops of the whitest bread softened in milk. He sent for musicians, set scented candles about the room. All this my milk brother did as much as possible with his own hand, as if it were the role he'd longed to play his whole life.

Third Antiphon

A Weft of the Branding-Iron Sun

———

The sun took a path downward from its zenith like a branding iron. All but its heat had vanished from inside the abbey guest-house when my milk brother could think of nothing else to lavish on his dying peasant boy. Gilles settled down to watch unfold the drama that he had so carefully staged, and I sat down with him.

Death held no terrors for me. I was a priest, after all, and more, even, than the Christian, a holy man of my persuasion understands that death must be embraced, celebrated, as much as birth. One is balance, the eternal doorway, to the next. Only the lord of Rais' fascination was a little unsettling. That and the fact that I could see no purpose to this. How could one boy's death out of a thousand matter in this poor, ravaged land of France?

"You know the story of Vauru's tree, do you not?" Gilles asked, whispering softly, after we'd been sitting, watching the death struggle, for a while.

It seemed we'd sat in silence until that point, although a pair of mournful viols drove Georges de La Trémoïlle to distraction beyond the curtain. Within the alcove, I'd listened to the child's labored breathing, the buzz of a fly, and the equally uneasy shiftings of Gilles on the bench next to me. And then there was the sound of my own heart, so strong and vigorous while this child's faded.

"I don't."

I wanted to be silent with meditation, with the sound of that heart of mine, but Gilles seemed to want his drama to have a narration, some meaning he'd as yet been unable to fabricate.

"Vauru?" I repeated, taking on the same low tone in spite of my words. "That sounds like a dog barking."

"Didn't you tell me you were at the siege of Meaux?"

"So I was." Trying to get Henry of England to offer himself as a Sacrifice for France, if he would be her King.

"Denis de Vauru was one who defended the town for the French."

"Yes. I remember the name now. Always spoken larded with colorful English curses."

"When they took the town, the English dragged him all through the streets and then hanged him on a tree outside the walls that had borne his name since before the first siege engines were set."

"No wonder I forgot. I left the place just after May Day. Meaux surrendered, I think, the very next Sunday."

"That is so."

"And I had already done my work there. Confronted Henry, received his rejection. I had to hurry on to find the Dauphin Charles and his father before the year of Sacrifice should spin itself out."

Gilles met my eyes with his dark, intelligent ones. "So it was your hand killed Henry Lancaster in his triumph?"

"You might say that." I turned and studied the shuddering rise and fall of the little sheet-covered chest instead. "I prefer to say it was his own hand, full of pride. His own hand, thinking himself immortal, bending down to scoop up a drink of sacred water."

"I thought such perfect timing was too good to be true." Few in the world would ever know the admiration of Gilles de Rais. It flattered me to hear it now. "Those who fought both with him and against him thought him immortal, too," he said. "And then, young and strong though he was, he dies a neat two months before old, mad Charles of France, leaving naught but the infant Henry VI to follow him."

I tried for humility but found it difficult when the power was not really mine at all. "Half of magic is in the timing," I said. "In knowing what the Earth wants and when, and simply helping Her to it. Like a lover."

"Well done nonetheless, Yann. Well done, I say." He flung an arm about my shoulders momentarily, giving them a squeeze. I felt his craving for his own comfort in that gesture, yet the strange hunger to suffer this scene as none has ever suffered before.

"You were speaking of Vauru's Tree, Gilles, I think?" The deeds of my life had no place when we were celebrating the passage of another. And somehow, yes, Vauru's Tree had something to do with this child who'd probably never been anywhere near Meaux in his brief life.

"A big tree," Gilles said. "Yes."

"Not an oak?" The memory suddenly came back to me. A great oak. By the dark of the moon. In spite of the July heat in the priory yard, in spite of my heavy black wool, a shiver threaded down my spine.

"I don't know." Then he waved a hand, granting a favor. "Certainly. Make it a power tree if it pleases you, Yann. I don't doubt you have that magic after all these years in the sacred grove."

"You are telling me Vauru hanged men from this tree before he himself died on it?"

"There. You know the tale."

"Not all. Tell me."

"Vauru would bring every soul he captured, every laborer in his fields, every cobbler at his bench, every shepherd, every smith, to this tree. 'Pay such and such a ransom,' he would say, 'in such and such a time. Or you shall hang.' "

"As Grassart does with his dungeons." I was sensing the connection now.

"Well, one day they brought word to a young wife that her husband was among the unfortunates captured. 'Adieu,' he'd sent word to her. 'God keep you and the child you carry, for I know you cannot find such a sum by the end of this week so I must prepare to die, and you to live on without me.'

"The young wife was indeed great with her first. Nonetheless, she managed, by applying to everyone she knew to have mercy on her state, to come up with the necessary ransom just one day past the end of the week.

"As quickly as she could, she made her way to Vauru's Tree and there watched with dismay as young man after young man was led to its branches and hanged."

"Puts me in mind of Azay-le-Rideau," I said quietly.

For Gilles de Rais had had a hand in the hanging of the entire garrison there. Three hundred men. As, I suppose, had I, though less willingly. The ruins of the keep had been known as Azay-le-Brûlé ever since. It had been just such a hot summer's day as this, when things could combust of their own accord. Sometimes I thought I could still smell the burning flesh.

"That was different," Gilles exclaimed. "Those were soldiers, Burgundians. Men who had defied the Dauphin—and participated, some of them, in the massacre of the innocents in Paris. From which you just barely managed to save the Dauphin."

"I'm glad you can see a difference," I said.

I was, too. For I remembered that day of horror as the last appearance of Gilles' ghost that had been able to toss pebbles, bodiless, from great heights, to kindle fires and draw blood from dry tapestries. My milk brother had not been bothered by this *daemon* of a disturbed adolescence since. Except I sometimes thought, looking into the flicker of flame in his eyes, that it had entered him on that day.

"You spoke of Vauru's Tree," I reminded him then. "Of the young woman come to rescue her husband."

"Yes." He recalled himself. "The young woman did not see her man among those driven to Vauru's Tree that day."

He recalled himself. And yet, not quite. "She was able to save him, then?" I prodded.

"She took heart and presented herself before Vauru. His men relieved her of her money, more than she could repay if she lived to be a hundred, she well knew. But what of that? She waited anxiously for them to bring her man out to her.

"When it began to grow dark and no one had given her even a sideways glance, she bolstered her courage and tried again, tugging at the sleeve of a passing man-at-arms.

" 'Where is my husband?' she demanded. 'Such-and-such a one.'

" 'Him?' came the reply. 'Why, we hanged him a week ago, the moment the demand for ransom went out. His body isn't even in the tree anymore. We had to cut it down to make room for others, and where you might find what the buzzards and wolves have not claimed, I really couldn't say.'

"Now the woman lost her mind with grief. 'Husband or money,' she cried, not able to believe after all her efforts she could be bereft of both. Ignoring the men who tried to stop her, she ran right up to Vauru again, flinging herself at his feet and begging him to take pity on her condition and restore one or the other to her at once.

" 'Be off, woman,' he said, 'or suffer a similar fate.'

"But she would not. Mad indeed. So he waved to his men to take her, strip her, naked to the waist, and hang her in that same tree by the last of the daylight so all could see. They did not hang her about the neck so that mercifully she might die, but only under the arms, and up among the dead and dying men so that all night long the wind blew their limbs against her face and naked breast.

"Sometime toward the middle of the night, her pains came upon her. She cried out for succor, but though many could hear her, none dared come to her aid. The babe was born, dangling so from his mother. The smell of blood attracted the wolves, and by dawn they had ripped out her belly and eaten them, mother and unbaptized child together."

"Yes, I've heard that story."

The haste in my voice pretended I'd wanted to stop him, only now I knew there was no more to tell. I had had to hear it all almost as much as it had been necessary for him to tell it, as to take his next breath.

"When I heard the story of Vauru's Tree before," I continued, "it was from Armagnacs. Our villain Vauru was then said to be a Burgundian. For the Armagnacs, such deeds belong to Burgundians and the English—to the other side."

Gilles shrugged. "They belong to both sides. The people of

Meaux, many of them, French though they be, were grateful for the arrival of the English at their doors. To spare them from Denis de Vauru."

"You're right," I said.

I said nothing, however, of just how right I knew him to be. For I myself had climbed into the branches of that tree, a perversion of the old tree of Sacrifice. I'd climbed it outside Meaux at night during the siege. Doubtless the haunting spirit of that poor young woman had been among the things that had terrified me so during that climb. For I had cut down one of Vauru's last victims by the dark of the moon. With the body, I'd worked the black magic with which I'd killed Henry V of England. So did bloody deeds balance other bloody deeds in this world grown not much saner, I had to confess, since the death of Charles the Mad.

Fourth Antiphon

The Weft of a Well-Placed Spark

———————

What use was this for the dying boy? Of what use was any of this for France, broken, starved, and dying?

"There are Vaurus on the other side as well." I tried to soothe my milk brother as well as myself after his tale.

"Yes. Grassart's one of them, quiet little sneak that he is. And I wish him to the devil."

"What would you have me do to him?"

Gilles tossed his head at my attempt at a black levity and turned his tear-filled eyes in the direction of the dying boy once more.

"Grassart to the devil and this boy among the angels," he mused.

"We cannot burn this place to the ground," I murmured. "You and I alone?"

My milk brother dragged his hand through his dark curls again as he considered. "Nor would I want to, with those poor children moaning in the dark dungeon. Both sides are equally to blame, Yann. Such is the war we are fighting."

"And to what purpose?"

Gilles nodded.

"The nobility," he pondered quietly. "They call us nobility, but what's noble in what we do? Not a thing, so far as I can see. Burgundian, Armagnac. We both fight for our ancient, noble privileges. As long as they are maintained, it matters not who wins. The death of each of those children is on my head, though I would storm Grassart's keep if I could, if I were here with more men."

"And not under oath of neutrality as you ransom your cousin."

"You think that would stop me? No, it would be a charity to break that vow. Those children—on my head, Yann, do you understand?"

Although his voice remained low, the passion in it was terrible. I tried to calm him. "But you don't kidnap children, Gilles, do you? You don't allow your men to. These are others . . ."

"No, you don't understand. Even when I pay my men, sometimes . . . sometimes the chance to earn a little more so easily is too strong to be resisted."

"But you would stop it if you could," I insisted, whether more for his sake or for my own, I couldn't say.

Gilles stood with a sudden jerk and looked at me levelly with those soulful, anguished dark eyes. His grip crushed my elbow. "Yann, you still don't understand. The reason that dungeon exists where the children are so—" He left me to fill in the words he meant with a deep sigh and a toss of his head—at tears, could it be? "—It's because—"

His eyes left me now, darting desperately here and there for some solid explanation on which to light. We both heard the chant of the abbey's brethren in the choir of Sainte-Croix riding over the violists. The monks cycled into the office of none with all the mournfulness due the celebration of a day sacred to the Magdalene in her sins.

"Because their cries call to me like music," Gilles hissed in his earnestness. "Because I know, whenever I get too close to such things, that I am capable of just such barbarity. Indeed, by waging this war, leading men to it, yes, enjoying it, I am just as capable of such acts against the land—and the cycle of its future—as Grassart, as Vauru, as my cousin Georges in his uncaring grossness, as any of them. Of each little child's death to starvation, each hanging of pregnant women in trees, each death of the old man before his hovel which he tries to defend with nothing but his hay fork—I am guilty of it all. I am as guilty of it as the man who actually lays the blow. Because as lord I stand to gain most from victory, I, as a lord, am most to blame. How can a loving God ever forgive . . ."

His voice trailed off as he stopped to listen to the reading of the Gospel out of the window of the church, propped open for air: "He who is without sin, cast the first stone."

Then Gilles returned to me with sudden force to conclude: "This is a war for devils, Yann. The angels among us all die of horror within the first week." He swallowed and licked his lips for want of moisture. He'd talked it utterly away. "And I am the greatest devil of them all."

Painful as this confession was to hear—and for Gilles to give—I was glad that he had done so. The whole world seemed suddenly to slip into clarity around me. Gilles would always have a struggle to separate the two religions, God from the devil—or God from God. His initiation had been untimely, like the birth of a five-month babe. Yet he hadn't died. Yet his sense of balance, of justice, was keen.

All my milk brother needed, I saw, was a spark, the spark to turn his great evil into divinity. No, I should not say evil, for the Craft acknowledges evil as only too great a straining for good. I'd rather say "dark." Like the dry straw on the floor of Azay-le-Rideau, his darkness waited. Yet, unlike the burned-out fortress, without that spark, Gilles was doomed.

Charles the Dauphin needed just such a spark as well. Indeed, the same spark. And so did I. Then I saw, with a stab of the Sight, the whole broken, suffering land about me from the smoking ruins of Azay to the echoes of the monks' psalm. All lay, kindling and well-seasoned logs together, stacked for the great, cleansing, sacrificial fire.

All that was needed was the well-placed spark. I could not provide the spark myself, though I had helped to lay the wood. I was, in fact, as sapless, dry, and ready to burn as the rest. But I knew where to place the spark and even where to get it. For this I had come eastward, as far as La Charité. But no further. Alas, no further.

No, not yet. But soon. The true spark was coming.

The monks sang. *Gloria.*

And at that same moment, the boy's black-rimmed eyes focused for the first time since I'd entered the alcove. As Gilles had said, they were, even in death, a remarkable blue.

The boy spoke, "I pray—I pray I might do something—something for poor dying France."

Now, I supposed this to be merely the throes of delirium. Perhaps the lad had heard drunken soldiers say such words over and over again as he languished in La Charité keep and he mimicked them with no more thought than a popinjay.

But Gilles would not hear of it. He rushed to the boy's side and, when no effort on the part of either brought forth more words, my milk brother turned to me and said, "This is his last wish, Yann. By God, it shall be fulfilled. But what? What shall he do?"

"I think, rather, you should send for a priest."

"You are a priest."

"A Christian priest, I meant. For last rites. Surely it must be easy enough to find one here in an abbey. I am assuming that is what the boy and his parents would most want. Unless I might serve just as well."

Gilles waved his hand impatiently. "Of course, you'll serve, Yann. And keep the other lot out of here with your presence. But what to do for France? Come on, think, man."

And then it hit me. What I'd been on the verge of seeing all day. All around me the stacked kindling of the world seemed to leap into red and orange blazes like the cage of animals I burnt every year at Saint-Gilles as sacrifice. It was only a trick of the falling sickness—that blessed curse that brought me my Sight—the briefest mirage. But I knew what magic I must attempt.

"It is possible, Gilles, for spirits at this juncture—in this half-world where the boy lies, between the living and the dead—it is possible for them to travel far distances."

"Certainly. I've seen dying men convinced they were at home with their mothers once again. Only too often."

"Well, I suppose a visit to his mother would be of most comfort to the child. To the mother, too, if she is able to sense him."

"But that does nothing for France."

"Just my point."

I shot a glance toward the curtain, to be certain it was as much screen as possible. Then I lowered my voice.

"To the mother's arms is, of course, where the drifting spirit longs to go. To the mother. Or the Mother."

Gilles caught the distinction and eyed me closely.

"But when one is master of certain powers," I continued, "he can send the spirit in another direction altogether."

"Where to?" The sweat on Gilles' face glowed with anticipation.

"Well, I've never tried this before. I'm still not the magician our Master in far-off Lorraine is and I'm not certain it will work."

"Go on, go on," the lord of Rais urged.

"But I've been thinking of a place where, if with his last spark of life this child could go, it would be such a help to France, you cannot think." Help to you—and me—as well, I added in my mind.

"Then you must try it, Yann, at once."

So I did.

And it worked.

Fifth Antiphon

A Weft of Hemlock, Mandrake, Henbane

"No, you stay without," I told Gilles after he'd helped me drag the bed with the dying boy away from the wall, into the center to give me space to draw a circle in the small room. "You may stay within the alcove, inside the curtain, but out of the circle."

"Yann—he's *my* boy."

I found that an odd thing for Gilles to say, but I didn't argue the point with him. "This could be dangerous," I said instead, "certainly to one not used to periodically giving up his soul as my falling sickness has taught me."

I could tell Gilles wanted to be in this scene, to play the part of next of kin with a wrenching pathos, holding the frail white hand to the last. But I gave him a look and he complied.

I drew the circle, then, and set earthenware bowls of herbs from my pouch—hemlock, mandrake, henbane—to smudge at every directional point. Near the boy's head, I flamed a jug of wine mixed with sweet oil and resin. This flared up orange, then settled to a slow, blue, smokeless burn. After that, I sprinkled the salt, scattering it widdershins to turn its power of preservation inside out. The closing heap I accumulated to the east.

"To Lorraine," I chanted. "To the girl. To La Pucelle."

When all of this was accomplished, I pulled up my stool and sat beside the boy, taking his hand. If one of the monks of this house were to peek in, what would he see? A priest, hearing the last confession? Or would he see, in me, death itself, the cowled figure in black robes who sits and waits on every man?

I felt for the boy's pulse, dripping under my fingers as slowly as an icicle from the eaves with a frost settling in again. Because of the mode of his death, his skin was dry. Pinched flesh stayed pinched together and felt almost brittle beneath. Still, contradictorily, there was the slick, cool feel to the hull, the creases and prints that made an individual of him seeming to fade.

As if the boy were rising dough, my finger would leave an impression if I let his hand go. The airy spaces I felt beneath the brittleness of the skin were not the bubbles of yeast, however, but places where the soul had already withdrawn, gathering itself to one place for its exit. I knew the sensation myself, the bubbling at the edge of blackness that was the precursor of my own spells, those little deaths that punctuated my life. I could feel the rising globules now, dancing just at the edge of my vision.

With the control and fearlessness that come of long usage, I gathered the parts of my shifting soul together, circling them first like any enchantment's beginning. Then I sent them off to fill the empty spaces in the boy's body, lest there be any attempt to sift back again. Once there, I began to urge the flecks of his soul along, as sheepdogs herd their charges. The faster he went, with less fear, less hesitation, the less energy he would discharge in the process, the more would be available for me to catch and harness in the final leap.

Then, I felt a trembling. It began with three or four twitches, then grew more constant and firmer.

My own bodily eyes, fixed on the boy's face, saw the change come over him. I saw his lips move in the word *"Maman,"* but there was no accompanying breath to move his vocal cords behind the sound. And his throat was too parched.

I heard the death rattle, once, twice, but then my own eyes rolled up in my head. My limbs went stiff and I felt nothing more than a pressing, a sucking as though through a long, narrow burrow without sight.

"*Maman*," I heard again. But it was the boy's soul crying, without body to back it.

"Yes, this way," my own soul called to him. "This way, you will help your Mother. And She you. Be joined to Her. This, this is the quickest way."

Then we were out. The boy's soul, which I perceived as a sort of grey haze flecked with light, perched at the head of his cot like some bird, staring down in wonder at the abandoned body. I perched beside him, settling a comforting arm around his shoulder, so to speak, as much as two amorphous grey clouds can have arms and shoulders. Some of the bright flecks in each of us shot back and forth, like lightning between clouds.

But mostly I concentrated on the circle, stoking my chant within its invisible boundaries, feeling the building pressure of magic and sharpening the trail of the salt.

"A light. I see a light," the soul beside me said.

Because only his body had been smaller than mine, not his soul, the childishness I continued to hear surprised and somewhat delighted me.

"Like the setting sun," he said. "Calling me. Towards the west."

And I felt his dark form drifting that way.

Yes, this would be the struggle, the point where magic would have to—no, not counteract a natural tendency, for magic never does that. The rigidity of a Christian dogma calls for miracle to sever the normal from the aberrant, the aberrant of which angels—or devils—are masters. Old wisdom merely turns the natural a bit, working what is there to a slightly different level of the everyday spiral of things.

"No," I said. "Not yet, but soon."

I danced my will and the room and his spirit in the same twist as we make by festivities on a Midsummer's night, sunwise now, toward the east. In but a moment, I felt the strain as if I'd danced until cockcrow.

"First you must go eastward." My soul was panting with the effort.

"Towards the dark?"

I had to agree with the lost little tones among the light flecks of his soul. There, westward, there was attraction—

But "Follow the salt," I said. "Come, I'll show you. Dance. Rise. Up first."

I struggled, as much as one weightless thing can put leverage on another, to help him to do so.

Then, he rose, obliquely westward first, but the boundary of the circle caught him. He rose twisting up on the smudging smoke I'd set in that quarter, and that taught him the move.

Briefly, I caught a glimpse of Gilles. He was leaning against the doorjamb before the alcove's curtain, the only figure with the tension of life still in him. That tension leaned him forward, straining to lend our enchantment a hand if he could. But he would not break a magic circle from the outside, that much of a witch he certainly was. And his gaze was fixed on our vacated bodies. He could not see where our true beings were.

Gilles de Rais, like the rest of physical being, had little meaning for me at that moment, in any case. I turned my attention back to the boy's soul.

By the time we had drifted up to the ceiling of the room together, I felt just how strong and powerful a spirit he was, just as I had hoped. I had been pulled upward with him. We— or rather, *he,* myself merely pulled along—hesitated a moment alongside a support beam, up against the rough plaster. But then we were through it. I caught a glimpse of a nest of fledgling martinets under the thatch, but then we were through the thatch, hovering high above the abbey at a level with the clarion bells. Glowing flecks of his slipped from one grain of salt to another as the ring I'd drawn began to spread about us, spiraling, spiraling outward.

"Fine, fine," I said. "Just keep on like that . . ."

But as I tried to extract myself, I found that I could not. Such had been the commingling of our souls as I had lent him courage to try out his new strengths, and such was the strength of his young soul, robbed of so much life but joyful now with the strange, new game, that I could not pull away.

And he, he skipped from one grain of salt to the next. As

a child may skip from square to square in a hopscotch scratched on flagstones, a hopscotch, that, when the time came to turn around and skip back, went instead on and on. Fanciful new configurations tempted him, up and down, side to side, but now definitely eastward. On and on.

For the circle I had drawn expanded and continued to expand. First it was the size of the walls encircling La Charité, then the ring of cleared, farmed lands in every direction. Then, over the dark canopy of forests, the white-etched blue of the furthest horizon extended one great O in all directions.

That boy's spirit, shown the way, had strength enough—all the strength of a full life cheated—to carry me along with it.

Sixth Antiphon

The Weft of a Maid in a Red Kirtle

We traveled thus, the air flowing past like water over stones, scraping over my spirit with the speed of our flight. A rushing like waters filled what senses were left to a senseless form as the breadth of France spread out below.

Then, as the sun lowered, we left the familiar, left France altogether. Mountains began to rise beneath our flight, dark and thick and fragrant with fir forests. We came at last to the clearing and fields around a small village, and here we alighted, just as the bells sounded vespers from the village church. It was as if we were no more than notes within that sound.

Five or six of the village children were coming home with their day's charges, goats and lumbering cattle. Most of the children carried willow whisks as scepters of their office, but they had little cause to use them. The beasts moved on their own, the cattle lowing with the discomfort of their full udders, knowing the way even better than their guardians.

It was not so hot in that place as it had been on the Loire. There'd been a little rain in those mountains during the day, and the wet fields and woods, now that the clouds parted an instant for sunset, were invigorating. One girl among them could not resist. She was twelve, maybe thirteen, short for her age, dark and squarely built, wearing the bright red wool kirtle of all girls not yet of a marriageable age in that country. She could not herd her life to the same dull pace as the others.

"Come on," she called to the rest. "I'll race you the shortcut through the woods to the meadow at the edge of town."

"Ah, *non,* Jehannette," complained two of the youngest, tired with their day's work. "You know you always win."

But three others were game. Leaving the easy herd with the youngest, one called, "Here are our places, ready, set—"

And they were off, bare feet bounding over the narrow path, through ferns and over fallen logs like the wild things of nature they were.

The girl, Jehannette, having tucked her red skirts up above her knees, proved faster than any of them, even the older boys, who cursed and swore in her wake as she ran on and on. Soon she was quite out of sight of any of them, and it was then that I gave the dying boy's spirit the nudge it needed.

Fortunately, I found myself able to pick out my flecks of light from his now, enough to separate, though part of him may flicker in my soul to this day. This enabled me to maintain my vantage in the air overhead, just at the level of the crowns of the great trees. I watched him materialize, angelic face, silken clothes, and all, and step out from behind an ancient beech, just in the running girl's way.

"Watch out!" she cried, and stumbled to her knees in her attempt to stop herself.

She scrambled up, unhurt, but ready for a scrap.

"What do you mean, getting in my way like that? You did that on purpose." Her fists clenched, half raised from her sides. And she knew what to do with them. "Who are you, anyway? You aren't one of us. You aren't from around here."

Her French was so thick with her own accent that I feared the boy could not understand her. Or, if he could, that she would not understand him in her turn.

I could feel him faltering below me and pressed her name "Jehannette" to him. Still he faltered. I could see tree trunks striping through the insubstantiality of his body. Could she?

"*Maman,*" I urged him then.

After that, he never faltered, knowing just what he must say in his clear *tournois* accent. The accent surprised me a little, for La Charité was not so close to Tours. But who knew where Grassart may have raided? It is true, I think, what they say, that the dialect from around Tours is the purest—the most angelic, even—in all of France.

"Jehannette, Jehannette," he said. "Come at once. Your Mother needs you."

Jehannette took a threatening step forward. Then she blinked at him, probably noticing how small he was and his otherworldly pallor. She thought better of her attack and blinked again.

"Your Mother, Jehannette. Please . . ." The boy's spirit was giving out with the strain. It faded, voice first, then appearance, and swirled back up to my arms.

Jehannette blinked again, staring in disbelief at the place under the tree where he had been and rubbing her right side as if the running had given her a stitch.

The other children came crashing up to her now, and then ran by, calling out, "Ha, Jehannette. We shall beat you easily this time."

"Go on, win," she said, turning quickly on her heels and striding off in the direction they'd just come. "Go on without me. My mother needs me."

The others exchanged very telling looks. "Jehannette. Odd as usual," they said, and went on without her.

Together, the boy and I watched the girl come upon her mother drawing round loaves out of an oven on a wooden paddle and shoveling them onto the table. The door to the bake room stood open to catch the sun's last rays, and flour and dust motes danced in that light.

"Good heavens, girl, what's become of the cow?" the mother cried. "I don't hear her bell out in the yard. Where's the milk bucket?"

"She's safe. The others are bringing her along and I'll milk her when she gets here. You wanted me?"

"I want you to be out with your duty, not always handing it to others like you do."

"But you sent that pretty little boy to me in the fine silk clothes—"

"Now, what boy in silk clothes is going to run errands for a poor woman like me, I ask you?"

Jehannette opened her mouth to say something else, then closed it quickly again. She blinked once or twice at her mother, dusting her grown woman's green kirtle with flour-covered hands. Then Jehannette turned back and retraced her steps, slower this time, oblivious to the rain-washed beauty around her, thinking hard.

The boy had meant the Mother of us all, of course, not that poor, overworked woman at her thick pine baking table. He'd meant Mother Earth, with his sharpened vision of those lying between worlds. But there was no way to stop and explain this to the girl. The magic of the boy's spirit was dying, its exertions pushing him even faster into the next world. I had to hurry back while his strength lasted or be left unspirited myself.

In time, however, it would make sense to her. I knew it. The time was not far off.

———————

9 came to myself in the stifling alcove in La Charité, the boy dead on Gilles' pallet beside me. My milk brother had only heard the boy's last words and seen my spelled state, which he was used to. This satisfied him that the last request had been fulfilled.

Later, as I rode to Bourges with Messires de Rais and de La Trémoïlle, crossing the line over which Burgundians glared—and Armagnacs scowled back—I thought again of how all the kindling of the kingdom lay stacked for the fire. Only the spark was needed for the Sacrifice to be complete.

I felt no despair as I had coming the other direction the day before. I knew that, clear across France and beyond, there was just such a spark.

In Lorraine, there was a Maid . . .

3

The Caul

The dark was warm and close, for Jehannette and her younger sister shared a bed squeezed into the same room where their mother's bake oven stood. In winter there wasn't a cozier room in the house, keeping the heat and the fragrance of the day's baking. The smell was enough to make a belly full.

On this summer night, however, it was uncomfortable. Too hot to sleep, even naked, on top of the covers. The girls had their single window open, through which they could peek and catch a glimpse of the church across the way. But it was no wider than it was long, in order to get through the thick stone wall. Jehannette could hear one mosquito after another buzzing in to find her naked skin.

Her three brothers—soon to be only two, when Jacquemin married—slept in the larger room and their parents in the great bed in the front room. All was silent from these corners, no coughing, no shifting of hay mattresses. And in this room, Catherine's breath came slowly and evenly. Wickedly, Jehannette had forced the younger girl to take the side closest to the oven, as she sometimes made her switch back again in winter. Still, Catherine had no trouble going to sleep. Catherine had an easy conscience, hence an easy life.

And Catherine never had strange things happen to her.

Like being born with a caul. In the dark, Jehannette could

feel the presence of the blue woolen sash, kept always on the shelf above her head when she took it off at night. Sewn into the sash was the membrane, dried now like parchment, that had covered her face at birth. If the midwife had not known instantly what to do, tearing the veil with her fingernails, Jehannette never would have taken her first breath. But the midwife also knew that the caul must be carefully kept, buried with it's owner, even. And during life, it would make its demands. Against this, Jehannette's parents had had a special ring made for her, engraved with the names "Jhesus" and "Maria," which she wore all the time.

Catherine slept. Catherine had no ring strangling her finger, no woolen sash over her head. Catherine never had strange things happen to her when she went out to weed their father's garden. As Jehannette had had today. Just as the midday bells had thundered down from the church. On a fast day.

Ever since it had happened to her that noontide, Jehannette had been very quiet. So quiet that her father had commented on it at supper.

"So? What's got into our Jehannette? Decided to grow up and be a young woman, have you?"

But instead of laughing with him, she had only been annoyed. For she'd been trying to make the Voices she'd heard come again. If I move this way or that, very carefully, she thought, they will come. She didn't dare answer her father, or speak to anyone, lest her own voice come on top of the whisper she was listening for.

It had been the same, a month or so before, with the angel-boy. He had never returned, court him with her mind as she tried. Somehow she knew, however—was it because she'd been able to see through him, as if he were made of mist?— that he and today's Voices were connected. As if the boy had come and taught her a new game. Which now she had to play alone.

Then, besides the quiet sitting and hard looking into shadows with which she'd hoped to make the boy return, she'd talked to people about him. People besides her mother, who'd let her know there'd been something odd about his appearance.

"Did you see a boy around? No, not Armand, not Paul, not

my brothers. A new boy. I don't know his name. Blond and pale. Dressed like a little lord. With a strange accent. Like an angel."

When they hadn't laughed right out loud, they'd certainly looked at her oddly. Never mind any boy. They didn't like what they saw when they looked at Jehannette, Jacquot d'Arc's daughter. So she'd stopped talking about it. And so, today, when just a Voice had come—and a light, to the right side—she hadn't said a word. To anyone.

And yet, lying here in the dark, yeasty night, she felt that if she didn't speak to someone, she would burst.

"Catherine?" she whispered.

No answer came but the slow, deep breathing at her side.

"Catherine, I heard Voices today."

No answer.

"About noon. In the garden. I was there, hoeing the cabbages—and—and they came."

"What do you mean, Voices?"

Catherine hadn't actually said anything. She slept quietly on. Jehannette asked the question of herself. And then answered it.

"I don't know. Just—a Voice. Deep. And rich. Like distant bells. Like the sleepy humming of insects under cabbage leaves. And the sound—the sound of growing things."

"Growing things don't make a sound. What nonsense you talk!"

"I know. But that was what it sounded like."

"A light, too?"

"Yes. To the right. Like the glint of sun on cabbage leaves. Only brighter."

"What did the Voice say?"

"It said—But sometimes it seemed there was more than one Voice. Just one at first. Then, more. Like several bells, ringing together. Or echoes, layering one upon the other. The song of a garden full of insects and a tree full of leaves rustling overhead."

"But what did it say?"

"It said, 'Jehannette.' "

"How did it know your name?"

"I don't know. Then it said, 'Daughter-God.' "

"Daughter-God? What does that mean?"

"I don't know."

"It must have meant goddaughter. *Filleule,* as we say, when we speak proper French."

"That's not what it said. I think it meant what it said. This is not a Voice that makes mistakes."

"It was Jean Lingué."

"Jean Lingué?"

"He would call you goddaughter."

"Not so deep a voice."

"A woman, then?"

"Well, yes, so deep. As deep as dirt, yet as light as air."

"It wasn't Sibylla, whispering through the shrubbery?"

"No."

"Or Jehannette, Thiesslin's wife, for whom you were named? Or Mother Agnès? They are also your godparents."

"Half the village is my godparents. Poor Papa, trying so hard to make a family with some sort of ties to this place, if we couldn't have aunts, uncles, cousins."

"But was it man or woman?"

"No one in the village. Not so—not so human a voice. It wasn't even the angel-boy. Though I felt somewhat the same afterwards."

"So what did the voice say?"

" 'Jehannette. Daughter-God. Be good.' "

"That's it?"

"Yes."

" 'Be good?' "

" *'Sois sage.' Sage* is the very word they used. Like an old sage woman."

" 'Be good.' That's it? But that could have been anyone in Domrémy. They all always find something to scold you about."

"Only it wasn't. It was myself—but outside myself."

"Be good, Jehannette. Everyone always says that to you."

"And never to you. They never have to, to you, Catherine."

"Jehannette, Jehannette, wake up. You're dreaming."

This was not the Catherine of her imagination, nor herself talking to herself. Her sister had wakened and was gently nudging her in the dark.

"It's all right, Catherine. I'm awake. I was awake before."

"No, you weren't."

"I was."

"I heard you talking. You were talking—strangely, Jehannettte. You must have been dreaming."

Jehannette wondered just how much Catherine had heard. It was on the tip of Jehannette's tongue to tell the whole, to share the burden of it.

But then her sister said, "You must try to be good, Jehannette," so like a grown-up.

The words of sharing froze in Jehannette's throat.

After a moment's hesitation, she reached over and embraced the soft, sweaty little body next to her, but soon shifted back again as the heat made contact too uncomfortable.

"Be good. *Sois sage.*"

People had been telling her that as long as she could remember, and now here was her little sister telling her the same thing. She'd expected it, of course. When she'd been three years old and she'd learned, vaguely, that her mother was to have a new baby, supplanting her, she had wept an entire winter's evening and could not be comforted.

"What is it, Jehannette? What is it?" they'd all asked.

Finally she'd been able to tell them what the horrible aching was: "I am not good enough for this new baby sister."

And they'd laughed and told her that of course the baby, brother or sister, would love her, admire her because she'd be older. "So be good now and stop crying."

And she'd tried.

It was true, what they'd promised her. Catherine loved Jehannette more than she deserved and Jehannette loved Catherine. And yet, always with a lingering unease, unease quivering on guilt. Guilt that it was not enough, that it never could be enough.

Now—now, here had come these Voices and this light, telling her the same thing, "Be good." She ought to be angry with such messengers who had nothing new to say and wouldn't tell her *how* to be this "good" they were all so anxious about. Which never seemed so very "good" to her.

But no. She must keep these Voices secret. Even Catherine must know no more than she had accidentally heard. For though they said much the same as everybody else she knew, there was that "Daughter-God." That was different, a topsy-turvy thing that had made her shiver in the hot garden. It made her shiver now in the dark bake-oven room.

That was a promise. When her Voices told her to be "good," they meant something quite different from the rest of the village.

She reached up and gently touched the woolen sash where her caul lay safe, then rolled over to sleep. If she listened, someday, soon, they would tell her. Until then, it was her secret, a secret between her, her Voices, and the angel-boy.

4

A Wool Merchant from Piccardy

———◆·◆———

THE SIEGE OF SAINT-JAMES-DE-BEUVRON ON THE
MARCHES OF BRITTANY
EARLY MARCH, LENT, YEAR OF GRACE 1425

That summer had come and gone. Autumn and winter, too.
Another campaign season was beginning its abuse of the land.
And the men of the land. Gilles, the lord of Rais, remembered
the boy he had bought in La Charité. Sometimes. When his
spirits were low. But what was the use of that money, that
little life? Even of the magic that had sent him off?

A hundred boys must have died similar deaths in the
meantime. And men, old and young. And women . . . Gilles
couldn't separate one death from another much in his mind
anymore. Even the campaigns were running into one another.
This drizzling rain was like so many others.

Once he had fought because he'd thought there was a purpose. Weaving spells full of dreams, dreams full of Holy
Grails and resplendent knighthood, Yann had made him think
there was something worth fighting for here.

"The Land," Yann always said. But what did that mean?

For every pace of land Gilles de Rais took back, the English
gained another someplace else. They'd done this dance together so long, he and the *goddam* commanders were old
friends. Why, last Christmas, he'd obliged the earl of Suffolk
by sending his best viol player across no-man's-land for the
English holiday celebration. And Suffolk had reciprocated

with the gift of two haunches of venison and a boar's head.

None of his peasants would appreciate the violist's skill as Suffolk had. They hadn't the taste. Gilles had more in common with his adversaries than the folk he sometimes said he was defending. This war that had been hacking at France for decades, what was it more than a joust between friends? No doubt the English had wives they didn't want to go home to, either. Magic, land, La Pucelle. What did any of it matter? Gilles lived this way because he'd done it so long he knew no other.

And the angel-boy in La Charité, like so many others, had died in vain. Or, touching as Gilles had found the boy's death at the time, it had been no more than yet another entertainment for one of his class.

And now, here were the Scotsmen, striding up through the pouring rain toward his tent. They wanted to join the tournament as well.

Walter M'Ilveyne, the Scots' commander, was, like most of his followers, a huge, wild man. Gilles had seen Scotsmen fight. Having no finesse of either arms or skill, they depended on brute force behind their clubs and axes fueled by a sort of bestial courage.

Faced by M'Ilveyne's shoulder-length locks, Gilles grew conscious of his own, longer than was the fashion for French soldiers. He wondered, not for the first time, if he shouldn't get some barber to clap a bowl on his head and cut his hair off high, above the ears, like any other self-respecting French fighting man. He soon dismissed the notion. Père Yann always said, "Your hair's part of your magic."

"Like Samson in the Bible?" Gilles had asked him once in jest.

"Very like," the mousy little priest had replied in all earnestness.

And in his heart of hearts, in a way he couldn't quite explain, Gilles knew this was true. The same could be said for his goatee, also more trouble than it was worth under siege conditions. And for the black armor that could become a soup kettle on the fire some summer days. And for his red garter.

But this was not the time to be thinking of Père Yann.

Unlike Gilles, the Scot obviously never washed or combed his hair. Instead of musk, it was sprinkled with twigs from last week's bedding. The walk in the rain enlivened its animal smell. And, as for color, it seemed a sort of grey. But that might just be dirt on anything from tow white to brunet to a true veteran's shading.

The Scotsman's face was much abused as it must be in men from the north, such strangers to this land that the sun burned their pale skin. It frayed off their noses and forearms in summer like strips of leather. For all of that, the Scotsman didn't seem old enough to be grey—except from dirt. And the small, random braids holding the hair away from his face had been there so long that they'd grown to a hand's width of straightness from the roots.

Gilles fought back his distaste as well as his boredom in consideration of the boost a troop of Scotsmen would give the fray. If one had to play the game, one might as well play it seriously. He held the flap aside, a cold, heavy weight, and invited M'Ilveyne into his tent. A second Scot materialized out of the mist behind him, and Gilles let him in, too, in spite of the start his appearance gave.

"My clansman, Hamish Power," M'Ilveyne introduced his companion.

This was an older man, rotund with settled life. A streak of grey, true grey, arose quite vividly at one temple among the dark chestnut hair—better tended and in the style of a French merchant—before disappearing under a twist of woolen cap.

"Hamish?"

Gilles repeated the unfamiliar sounds. He did it as an unconscious digression from the formality of greeting, because the moment he met Hamish Power's blue eyes, all assumed dignity vanished from them. The air of a retail shop jerked off this second Scotsman as if he reacted to the prod of a pin.

"Yes. Same as St. James of this place," Hamish said.

Gilles blinked, struggling to understand the transformation he'd seen, or thought he'd seen, a truth beneath the outward form. His ears were little help. They recognized less in common with the Scots' pronunciation of the French St. Jacques than with what the English called the place, Saint-James-de-Beuvron. And Hamish Power jerked again.

"My clansman used to be in the wool trade in Piccardy—until the English came," M'Ilveyne said. As if that explained everything.

"You are welcome," Gilles said with a nod.

He thought, however, that the business of soldiering couldn't suit Hamish Power well. Neither did the surname, for that matter, which Gilles recognized as the English for *puissance*. *Puissant* Hamish was not. Burly and red, like most of his kinsmen, like a badger, yes. But that nervous tic jerked his left shoulder up to his ear about once every two minutes. More when he was anxious. This must prohibit him from being much use with any weapon. He would jiggle arrows and drop bucklers. Besides distracting any man near him.

Gilles certainly found himself distracted. He had to keep looking stiffly in the other direction until his neck muscles ached. This after jerking his own head two or three times in Hamish's direction in response to movement he had always before associated with an assassin's knife.

"Did your men get settled well enough in this weather?" By such talk, Gilles strove to thank Walter M'Ilveyne for his timely arrival before the walls of Saint-James-de-Beuvron.

M'Ilveyne did not take the seat Gilles offered him right away, however, but turned his back to brazier and burning lamps. He stood still at the tent flap and refused to close out the cold. Even when Gilles pressed a goblet of wine into the great fist, he would not come away. There was nothing to see out there. The walls before them rimmed with watch fires barely glimmered through the soupy grey.

"What are our numbers?" M'Ilveyne asked.

Had the man forgotten their earlier conversation? Or perhaps the barbarian simply couldn't add. "Your force brings our numbers up to about fifteen thousand."

Closer to, at their own watch fires, Breton men were roasting fish. Gilles was glad some intrepid souls had made that catch, perhaps going so far as the sea to do it. Of course, it was Lent, and everyone had had just about as much fish as they could bear. But supplies were running low on this side of the siege. And the fish gutted, green twigs threaded up in place of their spines, then set tail downward about the rim of the fire, would be very welcome.

"A pair of those for Commander M'Ilveyne," Gilles called out to his men.

"But of course, my lord," came the reply from the darkness.

Even that promise—the juices catching in the slashes the men had cut in the scales, the splashing of seawater over the whole for flavor—didn't make the Scot less skittish. Gilles looked anxiously at his goblet, certain his guest's hand could snap the encrusted gold like a twig.

"What number do you make the defenders?" M'Ilveyne asked presently.

"Seven hundred, no more."

But they'd already had this conversation, been over the opposition and the lay of the land. Was the Scot afraid? Belying his race's bravery that usually bordered on mindlessness? There was no reason for that. Just look at the numbers. Gilles sought to assure him with his tone and a wave of his hand.

M'Ilveyne was not assured. "But the Earl of Suffolk is not far off?" If he couldn't add, he probably couldn't subtract, either.

"At Avranches. Less than a day's march," Gilles had to confess.

"With how many men?"

"No more than fifteen hundred. We still outnumber them almost ten to one. And—at least to my knowledge—no man has escaped from Saint-James to go running for relief. We'll take these walls and be safe behind them before Suffolk knows what happened."

And Suffolk and I will laugh about it the next time I send him my violist, Gilles thought.

M'Ilveyne muttered something that, with his heavy accent rolling with r's, Gilles could not make out. Then he realized it must be "Verneuil." A year and a half ago in this tug of war, the Scots, fighting alongside the French once again, had suffered terrible losses at the battle at that place on the Norman border. The Scots had sworn—by the ground in which they hoped to be buried—to neither give nor take quarter on the day of Verneuil. But the battle went so poorly that not one of the corpses had gone home to their ancestral ground. The Scottish commander standing before Gilles now must be calculating that Suffolk would have to be drawn to Saint-James and every one of his men slaughtered by Scottish hands to revenge that day.

So M'Ilveyne was going to take this siege seriously. Very well, Gilles would try to do so, too.

Gilles knew the old adage, "the enemy of my enemy is my friend," had never been truer than in the case of this "auld alliance." The Scots fought as if they had wives and children at their backs, even though some of them could understand every English word. They were very useful for spying and cross-examination of prisoners.

There was the Day of Baugé before Verneuil, Gilles considered reminding his guest. At Baugé, Frenchmen, heavily supported by Scotsmen, had wreaked havoc on the English in their turn. Even killed the duke of Clarence, King Henry's brother and, at the time, heir.

But Gilles remembered that Père Yann considered Baugé more holy rite than battlefield. The duke of Clarence, in Yann's view, had shed his royal blood to fertilize England for another Sacrifice cycle. It was no use suggesting that the blood had fallen, that time, on the wrong soil. Nor that wild Scots' axes were hardly sacrificing instruments. Any more than it was worthwhile pointing out to this man before him—whose hand was too big for a goblet, his gut probably likewise for the effects of a delicate Anjou vintage—the eye-for-eye balance of previous battles.

"Just last month, before you came, we set out from the Breton swamps of Ste.-Anne and from the outpost of the Mont-Saint-Michel," he told the Scotsman instead. "Pontorson was the first *goddam* outpost we came to. It was one day's work to take it and kill every Englishman within."

Gilles didn't mention what he suspected, that not every man

who'd felt his sword had been English. A Frenchman or two of the occupation had no doubt come in his way.

"But that's just the beginning," Gilles went on. "Now that Arthur de Richemont is *connétable* of France, the old tale of two English gains for every one of France's is about to end. There is an old prophecy, you know, about a King Arthur of Brittany who will rise like Arthur of old and conquer England . . ."

Gilles let his voice trail off then. He realized the Scot was not listening. Perhaps it was the barrier of imperfect language. Gilles got more the feeling, however, that the prophecies that so inspired him meant little to Walter M'Ilveyne. The Scots would fight the *goddams*—the English—like barbaric demons. But other motives fired them.

M'Ilveyne turned from the door at last. He turned, not toward Gilles but toward Hamish Power, whose unsettling presence Gilles had been trying to ignore. The two men exchanged a few words in their incomprehensible language. Then M'Ilveyne pushed his goblet, hardly tasted, into his host's hand.

"Won't you take a seat, my friend?" Gilles offered once more, swinging the goblet in the direction of a camp chair.

M'Ilveyne gave him a smile. An odd sort of smile, Gilles thought, as if not at him but at something beyond. Then the Scotsman gave a stiff bow and went out into the night.

Before Gilles could wish all barbarians to the devil, a nervous shift from Hamish Power reminded him of that barbarian's presence.

"You must forgive my clansman," Hamish said, and ticked. It must be the years spent in Piccardy, but this man's French was flawless, if oddly accented. Yet he had let his clansman do all the talking—what there'd been of it.

Gilles felt himself shrugging in a mimicry of the man's defect. He fought violently to suppress it and turned away, setting the goblet on his camp table—for want of other business.

"I've Seen his death, you see."

Hamish's words were plain enough, but Gilles couldn't imagine what they meant.

"I've the second Sight. That's how you say it in French?"

Gilles jerked a nod.

"Ever since we arrived here, I've seen the grey haze about him."

"And you've told him this . . . this . . . ?" Gilles wanted to say "nonsense" but restrained himself.

"I felt I must."

"I suppose the grey haze leaves him if he's away from Saint-James?"

"Perhaps, yes. We haven't tried that."

"You'll be leaving us, then?" Gilles felt as if speaking this had set a grey haze on his own heart. Which was ridiculous. He'd been set to wage this battle without any Scots. Let the barbarians come and go as they wished. Attackers still vastly outnumbered defenders.

"Nay. Walter will stay and fight. He's no coward. Still, knowledge like this can't help but unsettle a man."

"Indeed," Gilles said, and watched Hamish give another violent jerk.

"I don't think my kinsman would care for himself," Hamish pursued. "It's the number of other men I also see under that pall."

"Other men? Who? How many?"

Hamish added a shrug to the next jerk. Gilles could hardly tell one from another. "Many. Scots. And your Bretons, too."

For a moment, Gilles felt a sick knot in his throat. His lover, Roger de Bricqueville, was here before Saint-James. Many other men who'd followed him faithfully all these years.

"I hope to God you don't go around telling them," he said, trying to choke down a nervous laugh. "We won't have a man left by morning if you do."

"No. I've told only Walter." The man ticked. "And now you, monseigneur."

It took Gilles a moment to get his next words out. Was he brave enough to stay? Could he, like M'Ilveyne, go up to the walls again tomorrow if he knew? If he didn't labor under the sublime delusion that this was all a game. That death might come to another but never to him. Not to Gilles de Rais.

The man ticked.

Hell, maybe Gilles didn't even believe this hocus-pocus. Yann's Sight he had reason enough not to doubt, but this man . . . Charlatans came twenty to the sou. The Scots had trouble figuring the hard facts of numbers of the sides spread out before them.

"And?"

"And, monseigneur?"

"What do you See for me?"

The Scot's eyes studied him, bright for a moment. As if taking his measure for a new wool cloak. Or a shroud. Then he ticked.

Gilles' heart ticked. Was he man enough to take the truth?

"I did not like what I Saw, my lord. When I first saw you this afternoon." The man ticked. "Standing in such a way that the wall of Saint-James seemed to swallow you whole."

5

The Skirl of Pipes through the Fog

———•+•———

Whirr, thwack. Whirr, thwack.

That Englishman's arrow landed not three paces behind him. Nonetheless, Gilles yanked off his *bascinet* the moment he felt himself beyond reach of the missiles thrown from the walls of Saint-James-de-Beuvron. That was the thing with siege fighting. Once the attackers had settled down in their cordon, a commander could come and go with the rise and fall of responsibility.

Then, too, siege warfare never truly ceased, either.

Gilles tossed the helmet to his trailing page without even a glance at the lad to see if they connected. He would have heard the clatter of hard-forged steel on rock if they had not.

Instead, he heard the thwang, thwang of his own archers, doggedly going on without him. Spates of quiet in between shots assured him they weren't wasting arrows; they waited for something to move, either fog or figure on the walls, to give them some something to shoot at.

He heard his gunners, too:

"Here, hold that mirror up more. There's no sunlight getting into the barrel. I can't see a thing," said one voice, recoiling a deep and eery echo from the mouth of his bombard.

"There's no light getting into the barrel because there's none to catch in this godforsaken fog," countered the other, holding up a mirror, but not using it to look at his own smoke-grimed face.

Catching sunlight to fire their explosions? Gilles liked to

keep his distance from this mystery. Especially since Hamish Power's words that first night.

No. Don't think of that.

With no annoying crash of his helmet—indeed, with no helmet at all—Gilles could concentrate on the other, unearthly sound. He had taken the noise, from his place at the front of the perimeter, to be only the lingering ring of the last bombardment within the suffocating iron shell of his *bascinet*. The sound was clearer now, but no less eerie.

The back of his neck prickled. If this was the effect of the Scots' war pipes gone into mourning on him, what must they mean for a man born within sound of their skirl? What haunting memories must each drone, like swirled mist, dredge up?

Gilles shed the padded-leather, close-fitting coif that cushioned his skull from armor. Weather like this dampened the coif's collected years of sweat and stale musk. The smell could make a man despise living in his own stinking, accursed, forgetful skin.

This morning's sight of half Saint-James' northwest corner tumbling into the moat in response to one of his gunner's blasts had removed a lot of other considerations from his mind. But he shouldn't have needed ghosts to help him remember what the slow mourn of the Scots on their pipes meant.

Shaking out his hair whipped beads of sweat into his eyes. They stung and brought tears, which joined with the fog to blind him. But he kept walking toward the sound.

Even on this day in the first week of March, Gilles could feel his cheeks sweating like a horse's flanks after the morning's exertions. Damn, if only Giac would come through. If only Gilles had arrows enough to raise a dark cloud and take advantage of the tower's collapse.

But now he was thinking in magical images again. That would bring him back to Yann, who always said he, Gilles de Rais, had his own dark magic. Well, Yann was far from Saint-James-de-Beuvron and, no, Gilles de Rais was just a man. He could not do anything on the battlefield without supplies.

And thinking of magic brought his thoughts back to Hamish Power's dark words.

Gilles mopped at his face with his hands, but they were wet, too. Nothing could avoid mud, and perspiration from his shoulders and armpits had seeped all the way down to his wrists under the bands of dark metal that encased his arms.

More than armor weighted his step as Gilles stopped going down from the fortifications and began to climb another slight slope over rough, shrubby ground. But his pace made the boy scramble and his own hinges squeak. They were stiffening again in this cursed air, too salty, though almost half a day's ride from the sea. He would yell at the page for negligence with the oil can—but not now. Now they were too close to the source of the noise.

Gilles waved the page off. The lad fled gratefully.

The stone took solid form out of the fog first. It might be the stone itself, or perhaps St. Benoit, trapped within its hard, grey surface, that was moaning.

But no. Here, at the foot of the ancient standing stone, the priest had consecrated ground. Here the Scots were piping their commander M'Ilveyne to his rest in this place so far from home.

Gilles knew that, for a Scotsman, to be buried far from other sleeping clansmen was one of the greatest of curses. They took their oaths by it: "If I don't do such-and-such, may my bones rot far from such-and-such a place." And now this most faithful of men had come to this.

Less than a week ago, the burly Scot had marched his men out of the fog to join the fighting. Their extra shove had quickly sent the *goddams* reeling back behind their walls. And then, yesterday, a shard of rock from an English cannonball shattering nearby had ricocheted up under M'Ilveyne's belt and leather cuirass. Balls and bowels had gone with it. An ugly way for a man to die, and M'Ilveyne had been conscious to the end, an hour or more afterward.

And yet here they were, Scots and Bretons, foreigners besieging the English together on French soil without a Frenchman in sight. Besieging—and dying. Gilles knew—no, he hoped—there were Frenchmen fighting elsewhere, closer to their Dauphin, along the Loire. The plan had been for Richemont and his Bretons—and now the Scots—to pinch in from Brittany, from the north and west, the French from the south, keeping the English busy and divided.

Gilles was, however, beginning to have his doubts.

Charles' chamberlain, Pierre de Giac, had promised more men—and supplies, lots of supplies—to join up with his allies' maneuver before Saint-James was ever engaged. There was still no sign of it. Not a good portent for the start of this season's campaigning. The men were hungry and running out of arrows. Gilles felt alone in this fog. Except for Walter M'Ilveyne.

But M'Ilveyne was dead.

His men had spent the night in a rowdy, almost jovial sort of grief Gilles found he couldn't join, with its phenomenal drinking and high firelight. But he owed the man this, at least, to be present at the interment.

Gilles drew as close as he could, until the long, hollow sounds of the pipes gave pain—as perhaps they were meant to. The pipers, three of them, stood at a distance, their backs bristling with drones like so many weapons. The drones were draped with black, like so much pall around a dead lord's high seat. The bags under their arms kept the fleece of the sheepskin, the sound like a lamb that had lost its dam. Perhaps most effective of all was the drum, also muffled in fur of a darker sort, fox or bear. It accompanied the tunes almost imperceptibly because its slow, heavy thuds seemed to match a mourner's heartbeat exactly.

The Scots had their camp followers. But though women's wails could sometimes be heard in the pauses between pipe sounds, like their echoes, there were no women here among the mourners. Eight bearers carried the coffin, oddly made of wickerwork—like the cages in which Yann burns the animal sacrifice at Midsummer, Gilles thought. The rest of M'Ilveyne's men followed in two files, then to the drummer's beat parted themselves around the open maw while the coffin was lowered.

Gilles knelt behind, stopping only for a moment to wonder if he could squeak to his feet again later without the boy's hand. He unsheathed his sword and stabbed it into the ground before him like a cross. He thought a fellow knight of the Round Table could not receive greater honors from Gilles, sire de Rais.

Words were said in the Scots' own tongue, more music played, then the shovels began. The dirt first made a rattling, hollow sound on the wicker. Then the sound grew firmer and more deadened.

Gilles saw that each of the mourners had brought a small round pebble with him. At the end, as they made to part, each man dropped his stone beneath St. Benoit's great stone until they formed a shin-high heap at M'Ilveyne's head. This reminded the lord of Rais of an old custom his milk brother liked to follow, at tombs and crossroads. Gilles found a pebble of his own before he creaked to his feet and went to join it to the pile at the end of the flow of mourners.

Was it just the rite that made him think of Yann? No. A priestly figure in black lingering across the newly mounded earth caught his eye. He looked again. The face within the cowl turned toward him, gave a slight half smile in his direction. The figure kept its right hand carefully concealed within the looping sleeves. It was. It was Yann.

And next to Yann, bending his great height down to him, was Hamish Power. The man who had seen this death before it ever happened.

The man who had seen Saint-James' walls swallow Gilles de Rais.

Since that night in his tent, Gilles had learned more of the man. He'd been unable to turn away any time he heard the name "Hamish Power" mentioned. Hamish had a way with animals, and men said any strap or harness he mended was likely to fray again as soon as steel. Hamish had moved his family from Piccardy to Tours with the advance of the English. Hamish had a daughter of marriageable age; a couple of men were vying for her father's favor, whatever the girl's own opinion might be. Others had their doubts about a connection to such a family.

Everyone acknowledged Hamish had a tic. And Hamish had

been known to See deaths since he was a child.

Whatever such a father-in-law must be like, Gilles knew this was the worst of skills to have shadowing a body of fighting men. Even if Hamish did go among the men shouting, "Fight on. Ian MacDonald, you will not die today. Push, push into the thick of things." What of the men to whom he said nothing? But Gilles hadn't known how to get rid of the fellow without adding more credence to what he Saw.

Now, here was Yann, bringing his own Sight, no doubt.

Gilles strode as quickly as reverence and his own hesitation might allow around the mound toward the Man in Black. Seven, eight months ago they'd sent that poor dying boy's soul to "La Pucelle." And what had happened? Nothing. Nothing but the death of another good man like M'Ilveyne.

Hamish or no Hamish, Gilles de Rais had a bone to pick with Yann le Drapier.

6

Tight Heat under a Loose Sleeve

Before he got halfway round the misting soil of M'Ilveyne's grave, Gilles felt his arm caught in the grip of a studded gauntlet. The gauntlet belonged to Roger de Bricqueville, his companion-in-arms, his lover.

"What is it, Roger?" Gilles heard his own voice prickle as soon as he'd allowed himself to be dragged far enough away from Yann, Hamish Power, and the grave for speech.

"My lord le comte de Richemont would like to counsel with you as soon as possible," Roger replied. He'd heard the annoyance and was trying not to look hurt.

Gilles looked down into those mist-grey eyes, remembered times he'd made them reel and grow almost black with love. He is still one of the loveliest men I've ever seen, Gilles thought, admiring how sweat and mist plastered the Norman-blond hair to one remarkably pale and clean-shaven cheek. I ought to invite him to my tent again. It's been a while, and for no other reason than that the war wears on me. I will. Soon. Tonight.

But this thought also called to his mind the fact that Roger knew Yann. Gilles had sent them together on a spying mission near to this very spot four or five years before. It was thanks to Roger's intelligence that the sieges of Pontorson and now Saint-James had so far been as successful as they had. The friends the young Norman had made and renewed on the nearby Mont-Saint-Michel, nineteen knights holding out on that island in the middle of the bay, had been the best reinforcements the Bretons had yet seen—not counting the Scots.

And Yann had friends on the Mont as well. Witch friends, including the woman Gilles might consider milk-sister-in-law, if the Craft thought in such terms. What was her name? Ah, yes, Pieronne. That would go far to explaining Yann's presence in the neighborhood.

Come, Roger. Here's Père Yann. Surely you remember. You two must have old times to discuss together. Come, I'll stand you the drinks if you'll forget Richemont for a moment and come to my tent.

Gilles thought of saying this. And of keeping Roger in his own tent afterward, when Yann had left them, drifting off into the mist again. But Gilles didn't. A knight never put off a call from his liege lord. That was clear from the tales of the Round Table.

Yann would keep. And Roger might help to keep him. Besides, another glance across the grave told Gilles Yann wasn't quite ready for milk-brotherly interruption yet. He didn't stand beside the grave alone, after all, waiting for Gilles to feel his presence as usual, but with one of the Scots. Were Yann, that one–time linen merchant, and Hamish Power discussing the market price of fleeces? Not very likely.

The Scot's words about Saint-James' walls curled through Gilles' mind again.

He supposed Yann might have quite a lot to say to a man like that, now that he thought about it. And maybe "Power" meant something else as well.

Gilles felt a twinge that his milk brother should have business with any other. This was enough to propel him into stride alongside Roger. Gilles had other things to do, too.

But Hamish had spoken of seeing a grey mist around his clansman fated to die. And now that man lay dead. The entire world around Gilles was misted now. He shivered—and looked quickly back to Bricqueville. God, what did the Scot see when he saw Roger?

"What does our seigneur want?" he asked.

"You'll have to ask him yourself, Gilles."

"Ah, secret strategies, I suppose."

For even more intimacy, in case Yann kept one eye looking over the grave, Gilles flung his *vambrace*-weighted arm over Roger's shoulders. The young man flinched, nearly gasped aloud. Gilles remembered.

"By St. Gilles, I am sorry, *mon ami*. Your arm? How goes it?"

Roger shrugged, but Gilles guessed the young man was gritting his teeth. Ah, the dear. He always would do foolhardy things. To win my love, Gilles knew it. But the greatest heat he felt at this thought was coming off the young man beside him. The sweat and pallor were not all his natural attractions. Roger was in fever.

He'd been caught by a stray arrow in the fleshy part under his right arm. He'd been working on the guns, those two stubby, banded English monsters. Roger had captured them himself several years ago—with Yann's help—and taken them to the Mont-Saint-Michel through a rising sea, from which stronghold they'd afterward been dragged to Pontorson, then here to Saint-James at the start of the siege. This history made the young man possessive of his booty, careful of their slightest need—and careless of his own skin. He would not stay behind the wooden barriers that were swung down for gunners' protection as they loaded, swung up again for firing. He would take off his *vambraces* to free up his movements.

Gilles had taken a look at the wound while the blood was still fresh. It had seemed clean enough, hardly more than a graze, the arrow sunk into the ground behind without a jog to its arc. Gilles had ordered Roger to rest for a while, to stay back from the lines and, if he must keep moving to prove something, to serve as messenger between Gilles' camp and his commander's.

Now Gilles tugged at the young man's sleeve for a look. When even that movement made him suck at his teeth in pain, Gilles let Roger do it himself. The sleeve he wore was very loose, but the arm was stiff and hot. Roger didn't uncover it past the elbow, where the linen binding began. He didn't need to. Gilles saw red streaking the pale skin almost to the wrist.

"The *goddams* are rubbing their arrows with shit," he exclaimed.

Roger nodded, pain giving him a glum silence.

"Well, we've got to do the same. To those few arrows we have left. Don't forget to remind the men. Especially those whose bowels are suffering from this lousy food."

"Yes, Gilles."

But what was Gilles thinking? He couldn't send Roger on any more errands. At this rate, the young man would lose his arm before the week was out. He'd be lucky not to lose his life.

"Well." Gilles smiled, trying to convey bravery between the words. "You take care of it. Guess I'd better go see what Richemont wants."

Roger nodded. "I got your horse saddled and ready to go. This way, Gilles."

Gilles had to be grateful as he took his *bascinet*, then the reins from the little page who held them. They switched places, Roger holding the horse while the lad groaned as he helped to swing Gilles' full armored weight up into the stirrups. No, even if their love didn't have the bloom that once it had, Gilles couldn't afford to lose this Roger de Bricqueville.

He gestured to the page to follow him on Roger's horse. "No more running messages for you, Roger. Get to your tent and take care of that arm."

Roger managed a heat-glazed smile and the formal address they used when they teased each other. "Yes, my lord."

Turning the horse to the mist suddenly made Gilles put the pieces together. He turned back, ignoring the horse's snort of disgust.

"Oh, Roger."

"Yes?"

"You know, Père Yann is here."

"Père Yann?" Roger's voice lightened.

"You remember Père Yann?"

"Of course. How he went among the *goddams* camped before the Mont-Saint-Michel. And magicked them all out to sea. How could I forget?"

Gilles had heard the tale, over and over, but still didn't believe it. Seeing the sudden animation in his lover's face went far to removing the doubt. "Right."

"Père Yann is here?" Roger's voice threatened to float away.

Perhaps it was just the fever. But Gilles didn't like how the young lord of Bricqueville's face had lit up at the mention of Père Yann. Ridiculous to think anything of it. Yann had Pieronne, not to mention the scores of women he serviced on a good Midsummer's Eve as the Horned God, the other, desperate cases he saw year in and year out.

"You didn't see him?" he said. "Up by the stone as we buried poor M'Ilveyne?"

I wonder if Yann didn't let himself be seen, Gilles thought. By anyone other than me. And the Scot, of course.

Gilles went on: "Get Yann to look at that arm of yours. I'm sure he'll know something to do you haven't tried yet."

Roger was already scrambling off into the fog faster than Gilles could rein his horse in the other direction. The damp fog closed around him like a second suit of armor, choking him.

7

Saltpetre Dashed with Amber and Quicksilver

————◆————

Gilles got something of a start every time he stepped into the presence of his commander, as he did now, bowing into the tent, *bascinet* in hand. Out of sight, Gilles built up a picture in his mind of the man who deserved his allegiance, something along the lines of a minstrel's King Arthur of Britain: tall, powerful, blond. A beard, perhaps, and ancient armor emblazoned with the red dragon.

Count Arthur de Richemont let the image down with a jolt. Though strong as an oak, he was dark and wiry, sitting on the edge of a chair of crisscrossing wooden slats that could fold in on themselves for packing. There were hours, days even, perhaps, when present concerns made the count forget the pain he had suffered at the battle of Agincourt more than ten years ago. But no one looking at him could forget. Puckered skin, black and strangely pale, showed the places where the links of his aventail mail hood had been hammered right through the flesh of his left cheek. The scars had healed poorly. The count of Richemont probably couldn't have grown a beard even had it been the fashion, even if he'd wanted to.

But the field where Richemont had suffered was the same where Amaury de Craon, Gilles' beloved and still-mourned uncle, had died, where he lay buried in a common, unmarked pit. There had been a golden hero from myth, an Arthur of Britain Gilles de Rais could follow, though this man before him had the name and the post as his commander.

Gilles understood his own actions well enough. There was

a shiver down the bend of his obeisance, a shiver of something not quite right in his service to Arthur de Richemont. This was a man who, apart from the shadow cast by fate on his own cheek, cast no shadow of his own. A strangely shallow man, and fearful—of what, Gilles couldn't say. But Gilles served him anyway. It was his sworn duty, but that wouldn't have stopped him. Gilles understood that he was in love with a knight's duty, unworthy though the object may be.

For Amaury's sake.

Gilles took a breath to cover a sigh, completed his bow, and said, "You sent for me, my lord?"

Richemont did not give any welcome, did not invite Gilles to sit. He kept the expanse of camp table and the baton of his office, the *connétable* of France, weighting a heap of dispatches, between them. He also fingered the heavy golden cross hung from a chain around his neck. Well, one couldn't blame a man who'd suffered as this one had. Let him have his zeal toward any faith that had brought him through.

Over the cross, Richemont looked up darkly and said nothing, forcing Gilles to speak again.

"You've heard from Giac?"

"I have."

"Well?" As an afterthought, he added, "My lord?"

"Good news could be shouted from sentry to sentry. Not this."

"I expected as much."

Gilles dropped his eyes and raised a hand to rub his chin. Then he dropped this, too, remembering what his goatee concealed. Richemont might think the blue initiate's tattoo mocked his scars, earned in quite a different manner. If he didn't know it for what it was and think it out and out witchcraft.

Richemont said, "The supply train was—how shall I phrase it?—misdirected."

"Misdirected?"

"As we speak, it seems to be somewhere between Bourges and La Charité."

"La Charité-sur-Loire?"

"I don't know another."

Gilles could hardly stifle a laugh. It was either that or weep. Well, this explained the *connétable*'s dark mood. Serious news indeed, and requiring immediate decisions. But who could think straight in such heavy air? Perhaps it would help to lighten the mood.

Gilles said: "I've made an oath to take La Charité someday. I mean to teach that Grassart the taste of my sword. For how he humbled me over the matter of my cousin La Trémoïlle."

"You need to be there to do it, not a month's ride away."

Gilles did laugh at that. "How can Giac hire such idiots? Men who can't tell east from west, their heads from their asses?" Richemont did not join him.

"The way I read it—" Richemont touched the dispatch lying open on the table between them. The paper rocked toward him on its crease. "The way I read it, Giac himself is to blame."

"What?"

"He thought other, *French* forces deserved the relief more."

"A curse on him then," Gilles burst before he thought.

Richemont got to his feet and stepped to the back wall of the tent, as far as he could from Gilles in the confined space. Gilles tried to read the scarred features as he did so, but the count turned his back too quickly.

"I might be tempted to echo you," Richemont said. "But I think your curse has more effect than mine."

Now Gilles' hand did go to his chin and his heart to his throat. What did the count of Richemont mean by that?

Levity had not been the right tack, so much was certain.

"So what are we to do, my lord?"

"We have enough for two more charges." Richemont still did not face him.

"And I think my Roger ran out of amber and quicksilver this morning."

"What is the meaning of that?"

The *connétable* turned with violence. In spite of himself, Gilles flinched and instantly dropped his hand to grip the crest of his *bascinet* instead of his chin. "My Roger." Carelessly, he'd said it. But Roger de Bricqueville was his man, in his troop, head of his gunnery. What of it? He'd said nothing of "lover." Richemont might call the lord of Rais "my Gilles." Of course, he never would.

There must be something else wrong with what he'd said. He strove to find it.

"Amber and quicksilver, my lord? Roger mixes it in the black powder."

Gilles did not like the look his commander was giving him. As if he were a pile of dung.

"They are not necessary ingredients. And very costly."

"Roger has the recipe on the best authority."

"What authority?"

"A certain alchemist, sir, who—"

"Alchemy? I thought I smelled black magic here."

Gilles felt his pulse race and did all he could to calm it. What were those damn calming signs Yann always used on him? "Not in the least."

"Plain saltpetre, that's all you need, in six parts to two of charcoal and one of the sulphur."

"I usually leave the guns to Bricqueville, my lord."

"Mixed in the field, of course, because the charcoal settles within the bag in shipping."

"Yes, sir."

"You see the tumble of stone we've brought down on this side?"

"I saw it, my lord. Excellent work."

"No black magic required."

"We have a hole about as large on our side. Quicksilver and amber cannot hurt."

"Except that they cost an arm and a leg, which we on campaign, with that—that Giac backing us, do not have. Not to spare."

Gilles nodded.

Richemont opened his mouth to say more, then closed it. Gilles wondered what this retreat might be. Something in preparation for a greater pull back? Because, as he thought about it, what else were they going to do, without powder, without arrows, and all the food rotting in the damp? They'd have to strike the siege, save the guns, and pull back to Pontorson. Unless—

"We might get more saltpetre," Gilles suggested.

"Where?"

"There's a monastery near Rennes, isn't there, that keeps a compost heap where they cook up saltpetre? We could send to them."

"I have."

"And?"

"They will only provide if my brother backs the order with his word."

"And Duke Jean will not?"

"My brother remembers only too well the part the Dauphin played in the treacherous attempt to overthrow him."

"Charles had nothing to do with it."

Richemont shrugged. "His councilors, then. Who may as well be the ruler himself."

"Roger might put up the money. To keep his hungry guns fed."

"Bricqueville? Bricqueville, whose lands are still in English hands?"

"But not far from here. When the fog lets up, you can almost see Bricqueville from a high point near Saint-James."

"That young lord has already got the moneylenders to forward him everything he can on such hopes of return."

"When they see how close we are to Bricqueville, they will lend more. If we batter down the walls of Saint-James, we will be that much closer."

"But how will we batter down these walls without more saltpetre, eh?"

Gilles took a breath. He'd broached this subject before and been repulsed. But, *in extremis*—

"There's always my fortune."

"You've put up three-quarters of what's running us now," the count of Richemont scowled. "You'd go bankrupt for this—cause?"

Gilles heard only too clearly how the *connétable* nearly set the word "lost" before "cause." This was the man who'd had a dagger come at him through a visor slit on the field of Agincourt—Where Amaury—

"Gladly, my lord."

"Why, for the love of God?"

Gilles sought for a way to explain. Amaury, witchcraft, Yann's knighting of him that had even included a vision of the Grail, a sorcerer's prophecy. He could mention none of these. Even Roger he must tread carefully around. What was a thing Richemont could understand himself? What moved a man without a shadow pushing him?

Before he found it, the *connétable* had let the cross fall down upon his breastplate with a clunk and began to speak again.

"Well, it doesn't much matter what your wishes are—or mine. You're all too extravagant with your estates. Even yours, Sire de Rais, cannot last forever if you keep taking them to the moneylenders as you have recently, for that grabbing cousin of yours. For amber and quicksilver."

What is the use of having lands if I can't spend them on what I want? But Gilles had presented this argument to his liege lord before. Richemont had countered even such sensible reasoning. Although at the moment he couldn't remember what the logic was, Gilles decided to keep quiet.

"As your liege lord, with an interest in your estates, I forbid you to do it anymore."

"Your servant, my lord." With a stifled sigh, Gilles bowed. "Then what are we to do?"

"You do have saltpetre left?"

"Yes. A little. The men were shaking it into the corner of the lead-lined casket in order to get the last crumbs. I think they got three small, charge-size canvas bags when they'd mixed it."

"Order them to make up the lot."

"Tonight? By torchlight?"

"If your men are careful, you should have no loose sparks."

That would be black magic, indeed, Gilles thought, and promised to keep himself far away from it.

"The last of your charges should go off tonight, also by

dark. That will give Saint-James' denizens something to have nightmares about."

"But how to aim the guns in the dark?"

"Just leave them aimed as they were. The walls won't have moved."

Well, maybe Roger would understand such mysteries. If he weren't too ill of his wound. "But why not wait until first light?" Gilles asked.

"Because I have other orders for first light."

Something in the tone made Gilles suspect his love of service for service's sake was just about to be tested.

8

Flesh Hammered with Mail

———◆———

Wary, Gilles didn't immediately nibble the bait offered him about orders for the morrow. "So, without Giac's supplies, this siege will fall silent," he said.

"That's so," the count of Richemont replied.

"To the besieged within the walls, silent guns usually mean the besiegers are about to storm."

"Exactly. That's why we must storm before the defenders realize the true state of our supplies, before the guns have been silent too long. Before there's chance for relief from Suffolk in Avranches."

"Tomorrow morning?" Gilles felt himself staring at the *connétable* but couldn't help it. He felt his pulse race as if he were charging the breach right then.

"I've already ordered my men to finish up their munitions, stretching them through the dark, as I've suggested. We must make the breach as large as ever we can, but go easy on the arrows. We'll need every one of them for the storming. Keep by one charge, to open up what the *goddams* may try to patch up overnight. Fire that as soon as you've light to see. The first sight of the sun over the eastern rise is your signal. Attack."

Gilles nodded, taking it in, trying to see victory in his mind's eye. He failed. "Will the men storm with the breach only half opened, hungry and discontented as they are?"

"They must," Richemont said. "We have no choice."

"And what is your action?"

"I will do the same thing on this side. We need a third

company, waiting in the reeds by the pond, ready to press in at the gate the minute one or the other of us get it open."

"Who will lead that?"

"I thought—young Bricqueville."

"Impossible, my lord. His wound is festering. I don't know—" Gilles swallowed. "I don't know if he'll live."

Richemont stroked the cross down on his breastplate. "That is in God's hands."

"Amen."

Though he amened them, Gilles didn't like something he read under the *connétable*'s words. Something like, Well, such a death is all such a man deserves. A man who's let himself be used like a woman. Could it be?

Gilles didn't want to think in that direction anymore. He said, "Never mind. Leave it to me. I'll have the two forces deployed under—under someone. I do have the Scots."

Richemont nodded. "I'll let you get to it, then."

"Thank you, my lord. May Saints Michel and Denis be for us."

Gilles bowed to go, but just as his spurs clinked on his smart turn, Richemont called him back.

The *connétable* was seated again, thoughtfully stroking his ravaged cheek.

"My lord?"

"Have I ever told you? Of Agincourt?"

"No, my lord."

Gilles felt a chill creep like a cat up his spine. Would the *connétable* actually trust him so far? When Richemont hardly trusted him to run one end of a siege, and that only because it was his own money and troops. Now this, an even greater trust?

Amaury? Would he speak of Amaury?

Still fingering the cross, still looking away, Richemont began, quietly, his voice in that far distance he could hardly see.

"One moment I was advancing, yelling to the charge, battle-ax flailing. The next, a blow—I assume it was a mace, to get such a swing behind it—came out of nowhere. It took me—here." Tenderly, he touched the left side of his face. "I heard the metal of my helmet crumple like only so much paper in the angry scribe's fist. The blow knocked me off my feet and into the field's churned-up mud."

The memory flamed the *connétable*'s face like fire from the blackened coals of his scars.

"I found myself in this helpless position blinded by sudden darkness. The mace had burst the buckle fixing my *bascinet* to my back plate. The headpiece had slipped forward, over my eyes.

"Because I was stunned and slow to rise in slippery, mud-weighted armor, a second attacker—or perhaps the same—overcame me. The *goddam* kept me down easily with a heavy boot planted on my chest. Then—then he went for the visor."

Richemont paused, struggling with the memory. No brash soldier's bravado here.

And all the time, Gilles was thinking—Amaury. Something like this, Amaury suffered.

"The spot most vulnerable to his dagger," Gilles suggested with sympathy.

Presently, Richemont found himself able to continue. "Thanks to God and His saints, the mace had also jammed the hinges. When my attacker found he couldn't pry them open, he thrust his blade through the eyeslit. I heard my own nose snap like so much kindling. But he missed the eyes he was looking for. Then body after body of my comrades fell on me, and I knew no more."

Gilles winced in appreciation of that black world of unspeakable pain, where mud and Richemont's own pooling blood had threatened to drown him. When he looked again, Gilles read the blows Amaury must have suffered in his commander's face, blows that did not go awry. And he flinched to have such ravagement be the liege lord he must follow instead of the golden hero of the ancient tale. Instead of Amaury.

In humble encouragement, he said, "You were, my lord, one of the few Bretons with honor enough to put in an appearance in that lost French cause."

"Yes. Myself. And your uncle Amaury."

"You—you saw him then? Knew him? Knew his fate?"

"His was one of the corpses that fell on me."

Richemont shuddered within the shell of his breastplate.

More, tell me more, Gilles begged with his eyes.

"Anyway, the conditions of my captivity were not conducive to rapid healing. And so . . ."

"Yes, my lord?"

Now, suddenly, the *connétable*'s eyes met his. They were blue, Gilles noticed for the first time. Blue and shallow, like a stream with no shadow.

"I think you are in part responsible for my release from English hands, Gilles de Rais."

"It was only my duty, my lord. My grandfather was the one who actually crossed the Channel to negotiate, as you know."

"While you, a much younger man, stayed behind and led the defense of our duchy, my brother the duke languishing in a prison of his own. How old were you then?"

"Sixteen, my lord."

"Sixteen." Richemont nodded, considering. "And won your spurs in the process?"

"Your house has always shown me great honor, my lord."

Gilles inclined his head again. He could not remember his knighting without a glimpse of the black magic Yann had brought to him at the same time. He didn't think that was something his commander should be allowed to read in his eyes.

"So I owe you something. I can't just—" Richemont made a wiping motion with his hands, as if trying to cleanse himself.

"My lord?"

"Why do you do it?"

"Why, my lord?"

"What drives you to such deeds?"

"A man does what he can—with God's help. And one's liege lord, of course, commands the utmost—"

A slow shaking of the scarred head cut Gilles short.

"You know, as long as Henry of England was my captor, neither you nor all your kin could have won my release."

"I—I suspect that's true, my lord."

"He even set it down in his will, while he lay dying like that, so young, so unexpectedly. 'Do not let Arthur of Brittany go for any sum.'"

"So I'd heard."

"And why was that? Why me more than any of the hundreds of others, all nobles, he captured at Agincourt that day?"

"Henry believed the prophecy."

"Prophecy?"

Might as well mention it now, since he himself leads that way, Gilles thought. But carefully.

"The great Merlin spoke of 'the once and future King,' my lord. Arthur, like Arthur of old. A King who will return and conquer England. Push England from France if not further, that's how I interpret it. I think England's Henry interpreted it that way, too, and so we could not win your release while he lived. Not until his heirs came along, with other concerns on their minds."

Carefully, Gilles curbed his tongue there. He wanted, how he wanted, to give this commander of his the full vision as sometimes, with Yann, it had struck him. He wanted to speak of a King like in the ancient tale whom he, Gilles de Rais, could serve with deeds such as he longed to do, such as he knew himself capable of. With his whole heart, until death. And beyond. A King Arthur for his Galahad.

True, Yann spoke a little too much of a girl, this Pucelle. But Gilles found himself very doubtful any female could command devotion in a nature such as his. There was the duchess of Brittany, Richemont's sister-in-law, whose favor Gilles had worn when he'd led the Bretons in those battles when he was sixteen. At sixteen, it had served him to serve her. In place of the Amaury he could no longer have. But even at sixteen, he'd understood his own nature, the nature Amaury had forged in him in the white heat of passion. The duchess had served, as Arthur de Richemont served now. Easier when he didn't have to face those scars directly.

"Merlin?" Richemont said, fondling those scars thoughtfully.

"Yes, my lord."

"You think *I* am prophesied in some heathen—some sorcerer's black book?"

Gilles laughed awkwardly. "I only meant, that's what Henry thought."

What had he said? How much? He scrambled back through his mind to remember. Henry, Henry, then—But Henry, as we all know, had refused to die as Sacrifice himself. That was the thought Gilles found most firmly implanted in his mind. But those would be Yann's words, not his own.

"I tell you I am not," Richemont growled with fierceness. "I am not your Arthur."

"I—I know that, my lord." And he did, too, as he looked away from those shallow blue eyes.

"I am a Christian, and like the former Arthur only as far as he was Christian—if he was, indeed."

"Yes, my lord."

"And as for black arts—and buggery, too, for they're much the same . . ."

Gilles couldn't help himself. His blue-marked chin shot up and he stared straight into his commander's face.

"I won't have it."

"Yes, my lord."

"Sometimes I look the other way. God and his blessed saints know, long months of campaigning are not easy. Whores or captive women—I don't like my men indulging there, either. But at least that's not against nature. I can't think God can forgive—the other—so easily, and I hate to think I'm leading men to their deaths with such sins on their heads.

"As for your uncle Amaury de Craon," Richemont went on.

Gilles had not imagined his stomach could churn worse. Now it did.

"I saw him the night before Agincourt." Richemont snorted a little laugh. "We outnumbered Henry's English so much, I guess we all were a little careless that night. A little free with the wine. Almost felt like celebrating, before the fact, you know."

Gilles nodded, dumb.

"But I saw him, Amaury de Craon. Through the drizzling

rain that was turning the battlefield to deathly mud behind us. I saw your Amaury. Among the fires and the tents. With his—with his catamite, his boy-whore."

A rush of light filled Gilles' brain. He saw it, too. Saw his beautiful Amaury again—with another. He didn't blame him. Amaury would have taken him to Agincourt, if he could. As his page. As his lover. But the night before, Amaury, feeling death close, feeling the witches' curse heavy on him, had taken comfort—

"Such sin—God could not turn a blind eye to such sin."

"No, sir," Gilles found himself saying before his light-blinded head caught up with his service-trained tongue.

"We outnumbered them two to one—much as we do today, at Saint-James. God could not let even such numbers win. No wonder Giac's supplies go awry. That is God's hand, do you deny it?"

Gilles shook his head, trying to clear it.

"Your Amaury's evilly spent seed churned that killing mud for us. And his dead flesh, lying on top of mine. Shot right through the eye. In the mud. On the field. That made my flesh creep. More than waking to taste a ring of my own mail with my own blood on it in my mouth and three teeth gone."

The *connétable* spoke in the merest whisper now, the breath hissing through those missing teeth. "God sends the victory to those who deserve it. I know that. I know He will. Tomorrow morning. At dawn. Do we understand each other, Sire de Rais?"

Gilles couldn't get the words out until he'd swallowed twice. "Yes, sir."

"Dismissed," Richemont snapped.

And Gilles left the tent.

9

The Lure of a Golden Glow

———————

Gilles' ride from Richemont's camp on the south to his own on the other side of the besieged stronghold took nearly an hour. It hadn't seemed nearly so long going the other direction.

Even the shortest way had to circle a large pond made even larger by damp tailings of wetland. There was, besides, the Avranches highroad to skirt. If there were relief—English relief—this was the way it would come. All of this territory would be his responsibility come the storming, come the morrow.

And he was fighting for a commander who expected, if there were any justice in the world, he would die in the fray.

By the time Gilles returned to his own camp, the sun was already setting through a spume of fog. Not even streaks of yellow tinted the mother-of-pearl colors. Gilles gave the necessary orders to his men, stripped down to his padded leather brigandine and a cloak, ate food so tasteless he couldn't remember it.

Then, when he could no longer resist, he went at last to find Roger de Bricqueville. That young nobleman's tent glowed like the thin horn of a lantern lit against the gloom. It drew him like a moth.

"Ah, Gilles," Roger greeted him, his grey eyes glittering with delight. So different from Richemont's. So deep. So accepting. "You made it back."

Stripped of his shirt, Roger lay propped up on his cot. The warmth that filled Gilles at the sight made him wonder if this was the very flame that drew him. Roger glowed, the few lamps and brazier light striking the planes and shaped shadows of his chest as if he were the source of illumination. The soft down of golden hairs supplied a sheen, and Yann's sponging seemed to lay a slick of sweet oil over all.

So was this magic Yann's? For Gilles found the patient attended by Yann, Hamish Power, and the strong smell of healing herbs. But the young patient's fragile beauty made Gilles de Rais not altogether relieved to have extra hands in the tent that night.

To hell with Richemont and his piety. To hell with the whole campaign. Later, when Yann's magic had healed Roger enough for other ministrations . . .

But then the sight of Yann hovering made Gilles recall the beautiful angel-boy of eight months ago. He thought his milk brother might despair of Roger's life. And desire La Pucelle more. In which case, would he send another dying spirit eastward?

Gilles caught up the corner of one camp stool and drew it close.

"So? What news from my lord Richemont?" Roger asked. "Any word of supplies?"

"Every sentry asked me that, all the way there and all the way back. They've forgotten the *qui-vive* altogether."

Gilles caught the flinch in Roger's eyes. He promised himself he'd moderate his tone.

"If too many more get sick with the bad food, the cordon won't be worth much," Gilles said, trying to put his resolution into practice. "The same is true if they run out of weapons to back their challenges."

Gilles stole a glance at Yann, then at Hamish, jerking at the edge of the lighted circle of the tent. Their movements seemed to be lifesaving, not necromancy. He turned back to Roger.

Roger beamed with gratitude at the simplest thing. No matter the dispatch, Gilles de Rais could please him by delivering it himself.

"This is what Richemont wanted you for?" Roger asked for more. "To tell you such news? What of Giac? Does my lord chamberlain send no word at all?"

Then Gilles told him the whole. Or at least to the point where they were ordered to storm at dawn.

Gilles watched the healers as he spoke. Hamish ticked over a kettle on the fire as if the heat made him bubble. Yann cut fouled linen away from Roger's arm, with amazing care for one who had only one good hand himself.

Roger, trying to ignore the process, pressed Gilles, "We're not to use quicksilver in these next few charges?"

For all Gilles' good intentions, Roger flinched again. Perhaps it was the nursing. Continuing to work without a word, Yann had moved the wounded arm in order to get a basin of water out from under it.

Gilles tried to keep his eyes averted from the business. The red of the exposed arm grew yellow, even black toward the wound's ragged edges, puffing with pus. It was difficult to avoid the sight when the other half of the tent was dominated by Hamish Power's round, jerking shape. And when no smell of garlic pounded with yarrow could mask the smell of poisoned flesh. Wound and Scot were like stern emblems of mortality, like a church wall carved with the Final Judgment, the part representing the Damned. Yann would say, "What is light without shadow? Life without death?"

Gilles didn't like to look at such things, however. Not on church walls, not even when they contained things he loved. Not when Yann suggested, "But you are shadow yourself, Gilles. That is your calling. And very needful is it to the Craft as well."

Proud and willful he might be. And a lover of the sin of buggery. But who did not have his sins? Scripture itself said, "He who is without sin . . ." Gilles de Rais always tried to be good, whatever the temptation. And confessed afterward, too, of course.

"Richemont's gunners don't use quicksilver in their black powder," Gilles told his young friend.

Hamish pressed his long, dark *houppelande* with its bagpipe sleeves through the golden glow of the tent between them. The Scot had taken the basin of water floating Roger's putrid blood from Yann's hands. Gilles averted his eyes as it passed.

He tried to close his ears against the sound of it sluicing out behind the tent.

Roger, bless him, was the one who spoke to ease the situation, when pain allowed him voice again.

"They don't use quicksilver?"

"No amber, either. He says the shots fire just as well without."

"But the alchemist—"

"Perhaps a little too full of magic for milord the count," suggested Hamish, softly reentering.

Gilles looked at the Scot sharply, but the man concentrated more on assisting the surgery.

"It's true," Gilles confessed to Roger. "You know how Richemont cowers from the curse of heaven for every misdeed while on campaign."

But Roger would not be brushed off. "He knows then? Or he suspects?"

"What should there be to suspect?"

Wincing against the pain, Roger moved enough to display what had, until that moment, been concealed within the pillows at his back. The mark on his shoulder blade like a bruise, as if a hoofed beast, a Stag, had kicked him there.

"That you and I are initiates, Gilles."

Gilles couldn't help himself. He had to give his chin a rub. And he felt it. The power passing from man to man and mark to mark around the circle of the tent.

"You brought me to Père Yann yourself," Roger continued. "I went willing enough, because I loved you. Because I was jealous of how you always spoke of this milk brother of yours. Until I learned the mysteries and understood there was nothing to be jealous of."

Gilles didn't like Roger speaking of such emotion before any priest, not even Yann. He bit his tongue and looked away from his milk brother's business with herbs and the wound.

"There is no sin in the way God makes a man," Yann said, not looking up. He was at the brazier, lifting the lid off a small pan so the fragrance of boiled herbs steamed the enclosure. "And no sin when God initiates."

"Yet we must hide it," Gilles protested.

"From men like monseigneur le *connétable,* yes. From men who are just a little too Christian. Then, yes, the sacred must be secret."

Yann caught the handle of the saucepan up with a corner of his black robes and passed it to Hamish. Hamish used his own billowing sleeve to carry the pan out. There was the sound of more draining out behind the tent. Yann splashed some cleansing wine on the blade of his knife and held it to the flame of the nearest lamp.

Roger, refusing to look that way, spoke to Gilles instead, his voice full of sympathy when he was the one about to go under the blade. "But the count was wounded and captured at Agincourt, wasn't he? The same field on which your uncle Amaury died."

"Yes."

Why deny it? The look Roger gave him when he tried to escape his glance revealed another, deeper sort of jealousy. Gilles sometimes wondered himself. Did he only love Roger because he was blond and young and a knight as Amaury had been? Did Roger sense that? Did this golden flesh stand now for something he could no longer have, that lay moldering in a mass grave beneath the fields of Agincourt? What if this flesh, too, were to rot, as it threatened to do now, before his very eyes?

"You can't forget your uncle, can you, Gilles? Any time you see the scars on Richemont's face—"

Roger then drew in breath as the knife blade made its first cut into rotting flesh. Yann offered the young man a strap of leather for between his teeth before he cut more. Roger nodded gratefully, but then whimpered hoarsely, "If Gilles would hold my hand . . ."

Gilles took the hand. Then, feeling the crushing pressure Roger exerted upon this sign of friendship, even before the worst of the pain began again, he set his other hand on top of the clasp. Gilles couldn't distinguish the fevered pain in the young, grey eyes from the throes of love. He saw the flash of Yann's knife again, saw a spurt of yellow-green matter and the smell filled his nostrils. Roger's writhing, the pressure on his hands that grew almost brutal. These, too, were like love.

Gilles said, speaking desperately, "Richemont told me, in no uncertain terms, that if I'm going to throw money away, I must at least do it on decent saltpetre."

"There," Yann said, and slid the knife with a decided ring into the bowl Hamish held. "No more knife."

Gilles had felt the strength of his friend's grasp slipping, and the pallor of the usually golden face showed he had almost gone into swoon. Nonetheless, Roger grinned bravely at this news. In barely a whisper, he asked, "What's wrong with the stuff from Rennes?"

"You haven't tried it, have you, connoisseur though you be?"

Roger shook his head as if to clear it of faint more than to answer the question.

"The monks there live on cider, of course, like all good Bretons. The best nitre composts are pissed on by wine drinkers."

Yann reclaimed the saucepan of herbs from Hamish and looked with warning over the still-rising steam at his milk brother before he made his next move. As the hot poultice hit his sick and bleeding skin, Roger caught his breath and grabbed with renewed fierceness at the hand Gilles had begun to withdraw.

When a sympathetic catching of his own breath passed, Gilles concluded, "Alas, but we're dependent on the French for monk piss as well as every other damned thing."

The most painful of Yann's ministrations was over. A deep breath or two soon set Roger to rights. Hamish traded positions with Yann and began to bind the poultice to the wound. He worked the clean, white linen with remarkable skill.

A deep breath or two set Gilles to rights, too, and he could get on with the relics life had given him to worship instead of Amaury.

"There," the Scotsman said at last. And it seemed to Gilles that some spelling with the hands went along with the conclusion. Though perhaps it was just a return of the tic after what had seemed a quietude. "You rest a bit, man, and you'll soon be fit as rain."

But that was just the point, wasn't it? Gilles thought. Roger was not going to be allowed much rest. Not with the orders Richemont had given.

10

Fate Read in Bloodied Water

Gilles saw Yann and Hamish exchange glances over the potion
they were mixing. Then Yann approached the bed again, bear-
ing a bowl of steeped hyssop and willow bark to dose the
patient. He drew up the other stool and came down to Roger's
level. Roger drank the potion, burying his thoughts along with
his nose in that diversion, bitter though it was.

When he came up for breath, Roger said, "This third company, waiting in the reeds by the pond?"

"Ready to run in the gate the minute one or the other of us
gets it open," Gilles said.

"Who will lead that?"

"Richemont asked for you."

Gilles hoped the honor would rouse his friend, even if he
couldn't accept it.

Yann offered the bowl again and warningly shook his head.
Gilles considered the pallor of the face before him. Did he
hear Yann's thoughts? The boy's not going to lead anything
for a while.

Gilles nodded and stole a glance toward the fourth man in
the tent. "It's got to be the Scots, then."

"By God, I don't like that." Roger didn't consider Hamish
at all in his exclamation.

"I know. Without M'Ilveyne." Gilles crossed himself and
the others followed, using the sign of the Stag.

"Not only that, but not one out of two understands French.
The communication lines between us and Richemont are long

as it is. Then to splice it with men who might misunderstand . . ."

"We've got to get those walls between us and any force from Suffolk. We're easy quarry out here."

"Perhaps Hamish could lead the Scots in the storming," Roger said. "And set our Bretons beside the pond."

Gilles looked with surprise at the Scotsman. Jesus, the man looked more the shopkeeper than the man-at-arms. He did understand French. But his red, open face, displayed no favor to the idea.

As if choosing his words carefully, Hamish said, "That cannot be. Père Yann and I must away this very night."

Ah, yes, those with the Sight would clear out, like rats leaving the burning building. And how to get the men to fight if they knew their magicians were gone?

"Well, I won't leave," Gilles said, glaring back at Hamish, daring him to see a deadly mist. "I can't."

Hamish nodded compassionately.

"But will you take Roger with you?" Gilles asked.

"Gilles, I won't go," Roger said.

"You will if I have to tie you up and send you. You're too sick to fight. You can survive to avenge us another day."

Gilles met Hamish's eyes again. There, old man, he dared those eyes. Do I guess aright? You See Roger's death as well as mine. But I mean to thwart that Sight of yours.

"We cannot take Monseigneur de Bricqueville, Gilles," Yann said. Though he was pressing Roger to take another sip, he spoke as if the young man were not present.

"Even trussed?"

"We go on foot."

Gilles shoved back his stool and stood up. "What supplies and arms the *goddams* have left in there, we could use them, too," he said, veering the subject to something at least he understood. At least he could command. "And time to rebuild the walls a bit would go down well besides. I don't see another way, do you?"

Roger couldn't either. "I will stay, Gilles. I will fight."

"You will guard your guns until we're ready to bring them within the walls."

"Yes, I can do that."

If the fighting got so fierce that the guns were threatened, a sorely wounded man wouldn't stand much chance.

"And I will lead the Scots myself."

Another glance sparked between Yann and Hamish.

Hamish said, "Up the tumble of the wall. Yes, that will be well."

"I didn't ask for your opinion in matters of warfare," Gilles snapped.

"You can believe what Hamish says there, brother," Yann said soothingly. "He has a great gift of power over fibers and the product of the loom."

"That has nothing to do with storming a fortress."

"Hamish has in fact," Yann added, "been initiated. A different rite, being in Scotland, but one of us all the same. He's consented to be one of our coven."

"Fine. I had never had any plan to quibble with your coven, brother. But leave the fighting to me, if you please."

"I will go and acquaint my countrymen with tomorrow's plan before they settle into sleep," Hamish said. "I'll tell them Bluebeard is to lead them. That will please them. You'll find them brave enough, Monseigneur de Rais. Brave enough, even, for you."

"But hold off a minute, Hamish," Yann said. "Just a minute more."

The tent flap dropped—with the Scotsman still within the circle of Roger's tent. Even as he did, a great boom shattered the night beyond the safety of the thin canvas walls.

"Well, that's one of your charges." Roger laughed at how he had flinched, how they all had flinched. "We have one left and the one in the morning."

Gilles felt his own heart still racing from the shock. "A curse on Pierre de Giac."

He turned with sudden violence upon his milk brother, who stood silent, unmoving in his long black robes.

"So, speaking of covens, where's this Pucelle of yours when

we need her, hmm, Yann? Eight months ago you did some very black magic to get her here and still no sign. Is she hard of hearing, perhaps?"

Yann smiled patiently. "She just needs time."

"Well, time's not something I've got much of, this night before Saint-James."

"Our spell worked, never fear."

"So well you will try another?"

Yann glanced from Gilles to Roger, then back again. The potion was sending the patient to sleep. "Not with Monseigneur de Bricqueville, if that's what you're afraid of."

"Not good enough for you?"

"I need him. For other things."

"For your coven."

"Yes. I must have a coven. When the Maid comes."

"We all may be dead and buried before that."

"What we did in La Charité, Gilles, it opened the door for her. How long it may take for her to step through that door—that's another question."

"And I don't suppose you can give her another little shove from behind?"

"That wouldn't be wise."

"At least not with material for your precious coven."

"She's got to do it on her own, or she wouldn't be La Pucelle."

"Well, I can't wait on the whims of any woman any more than I can on the incompetency—the greed, I suspect it is—of some self-satisfied chamberlain. A curse on that Giac, I say."

Yann stroked his beard—grown thick, dark, and chest-length—thoughtfully for a moment. Then he said, "Perhaps Pierre de Giac could use a little firmer cursing than your idle words, brother."

Gilles was not ignorant of all this statement might mean. He stole another glance toward Roger. It seemed a healing sleep, anyway, no soul-wrenching trance. Hamish—well, Hamish, twitching off to the side there, seemed every bit the sorcerer in this low, golden lamplight.

"Oh, yes. At least a nudge in our direction would be most appreciated."

Yann nodded. "That is what we mean to do, Hamish and I, when we set out tonight. I thought we'd like to do it at a little closer range. At what Giac thinks is safe haven, at Charles's side in Bourges. Wouldn't you agree?"

"Hold on a moment there," Gilles said. "You don't mean to take one more good Scot away from me, do you? One who at least speaks French? Who was going to say such brave things to his men about Bluebeard? And on the very night before this great battle? The odds are such that I wouldn't mind a little hocus-pocus on my side tomorrow morning."

"And your commander? What would Arthur de Richemont say to 'hocus-pocus'?"

"He need never know," Gilles promised.

Yann sniffed and stroked his beard. He'd gotten to his feet and did not now sit down. "Tomorrow's fate is already sealed. I read it in the bloodied water from your friend's arm there."

That certainly sounded ill. Hamish was up, too. What had once been the wool merchant in him seemed to have faded.

Then Gilles felt it. What the two sorcerers must have felt all along, what they had been working on. Within the circle drawn by Roger's lighted tent, the powers evoked by burning herbs had passed from one magician's hand to the other until a great cone of power had arisen. Gilles realized now that that was what had drawn him to the place, that he had seen it even without, but had not recognized it. He saw that the four of them, working together, each in his own way, had caused this. What would the power be if their four were multiplied by three plus one? No wonder Yann's craving.

Yet the back of Gilles' neck prickled with resentment. Just as it always had when they'd been children and Yann had understood some point Père Michel had been making and he had not. At such times, Gilles had always thought, Well, who cares for your magic after all?

Yann said, "There is nothing more we can do here."

Just when Gilles was beginning to feel it! Who cares?

Then Yann seemed to catch a look from the Scotsman that

Gilles missed. The priest reached into the bosom of his black robes and withdrew two small leather pouches.

"Before we came to your friend this evening, Gilles, Hamish and I made these."

"What are they?"

"Talismans. We will leave you one each; you and Bricqueville there."

"Oh, that's comforting." Gilles couldn't stifle his sarcasm.

Yann met his eyes—and this time there seemed no brotherhood at all. "I can't very well have either one of you die, just when I've found the thirteenth man for my coven."

Yann tossed Gilles one of the pouches. Gilles wished his brigandine had a wallet attached, to cram the thing away unobtrusively. Yann bent over the sleeping Roger and fastened the second pouch about his neck. He pulled the blankets up as if the lord of Bricqueville were a child, then he turned to Hamish, a question in his eyes.

Hamish squinted, then jerked a nod.

"Good," Yann said. "The mist that clouded Bricqueville's person is gone. This wound will not kill him before the walls of Saint-James."

Both men turned to Gilles and the Scot knitted his brows together in a scowl.

"Put the talisman on," Yann ordered. "Hamish has to See."

Grudgingly, Gilles obliged.

The Scotsman's face cleared. "Gone," he said, then amended the diagnosis. "Mostly gone."

"Good," Yann said again. "Wear that, Gilles, and you'll leave Saint-James alive. You'll live to see La Pucelle and help her when she comes. Now, Hamish, before we set off towards Bourges?"

"A harangue to my countrymen. Which is the least I can do for them, if we cannot make talismans to go all round."

"You'd spare me, Hamish Power, before you'd spare your own clansmen?" Gilles asked.

"I think you'd like to come along, Sire de Rais," he said instead. "To meet the commanders and say a word or two of your own?"

Gilles stood staring back at the shoulder ticking up into the placid, ruddy face. In that time, with quick gestures, Yann blew out all lights but the warming brazier and, releasing the earthly powers back to their haunts with muttered words, broke the circle.

The three men stepped out into the night, which hit them like a cold, wet blanket. Under this cover, Gilles tugged at the talisman. The knot refused to give. He tucked it underneath the brigandine then. What group of men, especially strange men, could take confidence from their new commander if he wore such rubbish?

Or what commander could lead if he trusted to such things? And not deep black magic of his own?

11

Bluebeard's Charge

———◆———

They charged the wall at dawn. They needed no ladders, for the last two cannon blasts had brought the ashlar down in a great fall of stone they could scramble up. The way was unsteady, but impossible for the English defenders to topple over from the battlements. The Scots followed Gilles five abreast, shouting their own barbaric war cries, raked with the urge to avenge their commander.

The skirl of pipes and throb of drums propelled them on, not mourning now but screaming, roaring. It was hard to tell the cries of the instruments from those of fallen men, and Gilles never turned to make certain of the difference.

As far as he could tell, not too many were falling. He and the men closest to his heels were already halfway up the fall of rock before the smell of burning things began to mingle with the rising mist and mortar dust in his lungs. The *goddams* had had kindling ready for days but Richemont's plan had taken them by surprise. They'd only set it afire when they had realized Gilles and his men were storming.

Still, the *goddams* were no cowards and they were fighting for their lives. They were also not hurting for supplies. Their arrows and spears never let up, growing thicker, heavier in their deadly song, leaving the sound of the bagpipies far below, as the Scots neared the top. And, near the top, the bolts came from three sides as well as from their friends behind, who were giving what cover they could, though limited to two quivers a man.

"On, for St. Gilles and Ste. Anne!" The lord of Rais encouraged as any commander must.

And the Scots shouted back something that was as close as their barbaric tongues could get to "Bluebeard!"

Gilles had stuffed his gauntlets into his metal-studded swordbelt for a better grip. Along with the buckler, they weighted his right side now, in counterpoise to his empty sheath. His hands stung with scrapes, set his teeth on edge with their limey grit. Even through the slits in his *bascinet,* the dust mingled with sweat and blinded him. His armor was squeaking wildly now, deafening him as he forced it to move, to keep moving. The joints were freezing up again, the stone powder of the wall combining with the salt and damp in the air.

Rocks began to shower down as the English pried apart their own wall to keep Gilles and his men from it. Privy offal, boards studded with rusty nails. Finally came the burning kegs.

The kegs were filled with resin, sulphur and horses' hooves, set afire. The smoke stole breath with one lungful. The resin spattered and hissed as it spilled out and hit the rocks just over Gilles' head, smoked as it cascaded by. But by the time the defenders had got it hot enough to be of use, Gilles and his men were at a level to see where they lugged the kegs. There was enough room on the rock face, unlike on a ladder, to press out of the way of the tumbling, spattering waterfall, to knock the smoking containers away.

One man didn't move fast enough and got a shoe full of resin. He was hauled off screaming, along with the few casualties—still remarkably few—to other weapons. But the climb continued.

"St. Gilles!"

"Bluebeard!"

Before he was quite winded, Gilles found himself with no more rubble for his handhold. In front of him rose the remains of the wall, about three feet of it, and on the rim he saw the shadow of boot leather, dancing warily. He saw the arc of a pike swinging downward. The glint of its blade in the rising sun blinded him.

Before the pike connected, he got one good swipe at the boot leather with his sword. He felt the blade bite, sink, bite again until it hit bone. There was a scream—one among many—and the boots vanished backward off the wall. The pike head merely caught his *bascinet* a glancing blow, set it ringing, then jumped off his crest harmlessly toward the sky.

Other boots, metal-banded ones, came at once to replace the leather. But Gilles saw these coming, saw how they teetered on the unlevel edge with less grip than leather.

Gilles set his sword just so, and the man walked into it, the point slipping under the place where the *tasse* plate buckled on the man's left hip. Gilles gave a push that began with a curl of his toes and shot through every fiber. He felt the buckle snap. The blade did not sink in, no more than a graze. But the man lost his balance and, with a grunted "God damn—" followed his comrade over and out of sight.

No other feet replaced these. Gilles hoisted himself to the rubbled wall.

"Bluebeard!" The men were roaring that name they'd given him.

He balanced quickly along the wall to the right, toward the postern. He exchanged a few blows with a third *goddam* where the battered stone began to climb to solid battlement. But the ashlar had broken away evenly here, putting the smoothness of a courtyard beneath their feet. The man was an archer, his chest armed only in a brigandine of fustian-padded plates. His quiver spent, he was less a fighter hand to hand. Gilles met his eye and saw the look pass through him. It was the look of a man who might kill at a distance, but who cannot kill another when he's close enough to sense humanity, even at the cost of his own life.

With a frisson of pleasure, Gilles considered the challenge of going after the two forefingers on the man's right hand. That would assure he never fired his deadly bolts again. After a parry or two, the lord of Rais tired of this attempt, however, saw where plate joined plate in a row of uneven stitching over the man's heart. He went for that instead. It was every bit as effective as the fingers.

Now Gilles found himself on the parapet. It was his favorite place to be in any castle.

"Bluebeard!"

Even as a child he'd enjoyed nothing more than to make his elders gasp with panic to see him perched there, swinging his legs out into space, little more sustaining him than what held up the eagle.

He swung the tension out of his sword arm, shoved back his visor for a better view, and filled his lungs with the heady air of a height. His pulse raced. He could feel the glow of life in his cheeks. In fact, he thought, most of the time he felt dead compared to times like this.

The mist—and now the rising smoke and dust—obscured much of the view. He could just barely see to the cordon, to the guns where Roger waited, nursing his wound. Gilles checked on the progress of the Scots. The rock fall, like a heap of salt, was peppered with them. He gave them a shout of encouragement.

Those who didn't need their lungs for other things shouted back. "Bluebeard!" Shouting gave their feet a spring and erased their fear. All along the fall, men sprang forward.

Then Yann's talisman, the small leather bag full of the-Lord-knows-what, lumped in a pool of sweat on Gilles' breastbone. He hadn't been aware of the thing since the moment Yann had given it to him and he'd slipped the cord thoughtlessly over his head. Don't think of it, he'd told himself. How could a man fight his best if he doubted for a moment the success of the campaign? Or his own invincibility?

Now it beat like a second heart. He could smell it, too. No doubt this was just the odor of some herb, released by his own sweat.

But it reminded him of his childhood. Of when he'd perched high on some wall and Père Michel alone had not gasped at the sight. Père Michel—or so it had seemed—had only sent out some net of magic that had smelled of the same thing—

The talisman knocked so hard that it carried Gilles two more steps away from the breach. Even as his feet lifted, the stone sloughed away from under them. Some weakness in the structure had needed but his weight to send rock and mortar tumbling with a fearsome roar. One man below tumbled with them, his short Scottish tunic flying up around his waist. Gilles saw him land below and bounce until the pursuing rubble covered his back at an unnatural angle.

"What luck," Gilles thought. And, as the talisman seemed to cool, as his own sweat cooled, he forgot about it again.

Between billows of smoke and haze, Gilles saw he was the only man on this northern stretch of wall. The southern wall was dark with English as they struggled to keep Richemont's charge down. Richemont, however, had not yet gained the crest. The view to the gatehouse before Gilles was clear, along this battlement to the next tower, then down. The defenders had all retreated to that gatehouse. They wouldn't give it up easily. But the turn of the stairs and height would be for him.

He waited another minute, letting three or four of the Scots join him, then went for it. He dashed from crenelation to crenelation, keeping an eye on the tower, its shadowed door and arrow slits. He tried to make his moves quick, catlike but erratic, to throw his watchers off. A sudden yank from the lump within his breastplate made him more erratic still. It sent him crashing into a bend of the battlement—just as an arrow pinged off his shoulder. Another hand's width, with such force behind it, and that arrow would have pierced his armor through the neck.

Pressed hard against the safe stone, Gilles stopped once more to consider. More arrows before he reached the shadow of the archway? Certainly. They were probably sticking in little pots of cow dung even now, getting ready for him. Oil through a murder hole once he reached the arch? Probably. He thought he could smell it cooking. They'd been fighting three hours now, to judge by the sun, just barely showing white through the heavy mist.

The sweet, warm smell of burning oil made him realize he was hungry beneath the constant battle thirst. Hunger drew him toward the tower and made him incautious. He fought against that draw. Perhaps, he told himself, his hunger was only for the next bit of fighting and, if he wanted to survive it, he must go more carefully.

Still plenty of *goddams* keeping Richemont's force down. The stones of this archway? Two centuries old at least. But recently reinforced. If only there'd been more gunpowder.

Nothing for it. The gate would have to be taken. And he would have to take it.

Gilles pressed against the stone yet closer, preparing to use that to push himself away like the shot they were lacking. Just before the fire of the charge lit in his mind, however, he heard panting behind him. Well, the Scots would follow. In the next seconds, they must.

Then a heavy arm weighed his shoulder back toward the rock.

"My lord, look." The Scot rough-hewed the French words out of the burred panting in his throat.

Gilles looked. Far below and toward the north. A troop of mounted men had appeared at the bottom of the Avranches road.

"Christ," Gilles muttered.

"*Goddam* reinforcements?" The Scot could not conceal a tremor in his voice, even with exaggerated gasps, deep under his ruddy beard.

"I can't imagine who else would be coming up from Avranches," Gilles said lightheartedly. "Now, if we were on the south side and saw the same thing, we might think Giac got something right . . ."

The men in the tower had seen the column, too. Cheers went up. Damn, now they'd fight all the harder.

"We've got to have these walls or we'll be hacked to pieces." Gilles said it, pulling on his gauntlets and replacing the visor over his face. Then he shoved himself away from the safety of the crenelation.

Three arrows pinged off his armor, one after the other. A fist-sized stone connected, left a dent over his right temple that continued to bruise him with every step. Other missiles made his feet unsteady, even when they missed him. Then the man behind him screamed and fell heavily.

But Gilles de Rais reached the cover of an overhang within the arch. A ribbon of boiling water hit his back. It heated the metal plates like a crêpe sheet ready for the housewife's batter, but failed to find a crack as he stepped quickly out of its way.

Two of the Scots were with him now. How many *goddams* faced them in the shadows, he couldn't tell. He saw a gleam here, there. How many? Nobody stepped out to give him a clue. They were waiting for him, light-blinded, to come into the dark and find out.

He worked his kidskin gauntlet on the snakeskin of his sword grip, sweat making all three skins one. The talisman was a heavy presence on his heart and lungs. He was conscious of another weight, too, lower down. What was it about killing and danger that always did this to him? In hip guards, too, which gave precious little room for such dalliance. Until he'd sunk his blade again and again into pulsing entrails, he'd quiver, unsatisfied. In search of a lover, as it were.

This thought sent his gaze over the fortress wall. The mounted men were closer, pressing near a gallop now. Across the road, down in camp by the guns, the wounded and other followers had seen the horses coming, too. They were closer to the road. They must be able to read the banners of the approaching force, read their futures—short ones—in them. Terror sent them scrambling like ants in a kicked-over nest.

In the midst of them all, Gilles saw Roger. "Lover," said both mind and body. The fool was busy with his precious guns, loading them on their carts and yoking the oxen. Gilles knew him by his favored right arm. True, if the guns fell into English hands—and if the *goddams* had extra powder on pack animals trailing them—the safety of Saint-James' walls for Gilles' men would crumble in an afternoon's work.

He heard the clink of armor within the tower before him. A whispered command. The thud of heavy feet on stairs. Going up or down? He couldn't tell. Still, nobody came out to greet him.

"All right, you bastards. All right," he muttered, more for his own sake than for their English ears.

Gilles gritted his teeth, held his breath, and dove into the dark tower.

12

Kilted in Orange Flame

One deadly slash dented his breastplate. He saw the next two blows coming at him only in time to catch them high, weakly, near the point. Then his eyes adjusted well enough that he could catch them firmer, nearer the grip, and so drive the *goddam* back over the ladder pit he was guarding to the far wall.

Gilles spared a glance for the eight or ten steps of a narrow ladder the pit revealed. That's where he must go to open the gate for his Bretons waiting by the pond. But he couldn't leave this man at his back. Gilles leaped the pit after him.

Perhaps one of the Scots could take the ladder. Except that clangs and grunts behind him told him a *goddam* had come out of the shadows to oppose each man.

Then Gilles felt himself rattled, from the point of his *sabatons* to the hollow crest of his *bascinet*. The fellow he was duelling couldn't have caused such a jar. He was weakening with every blow. Had someone attacked him from behind? From behind and near the floor? Gilles couldn't spare attention to look. He'd exchanged three more blows with his man before he realized what the rattle was. He knew what it was—the floor-shaking growl of winches and chains as the postern drawbridge dropped. But for the life of him, he could not imagine what it meant. Why would the enemy open his own gate?

Gilles let his opponent get a blow in under his guard. It hit him across the left shoulder so hard, the buckles on the pauldron snapped, sending this steel guard bowling, ringing across the floor and into the far wall.

Had it been his right arm, Gilles might have lost his sword. As it was, his shoulder now exposed, he went spinning after his armor himself, landing with a crash against the sill of an arrow slit.

Through the narrow shaft, he saw *goddams* pouring out of the tower below him. He saw them falling with incredible ferocity upon the Bretons, *his* Bretons, waiting for him by the pond. The Bretons had been so certain of success that they'd failed to conceal themselves as well as they might in the canebrakes. Certain their friends on the Avranches road would be with them soon, each Englishman fought like twenty.

Gilles' Bretons were taken by surprise to see English rather than he and his Scots come to the gate and invite them in. Though they outnumbered their assailants ten to one, they were letting themselves be cut to pieces. Even in the three gasped breaths' time he watched, Gilles saw two men knocked down into the shallows of the pond and held there 'til their struggles ceased. Others, trying to escape, went further out into the pond until they foundered in their armor and sank of their own weight.

Those who could find solid ground beneath them began to put as much of it between themselves and the fighting as they could.

These were men he knew. Men who'd followed him from one end of France to the other. He wanted to shout a warning to this one, call that one by name, tell him to stand and fight— But the words died in his throat.

He had no more than an instant to take in this scene. Up in the tower, his personal opponent had recovered from the unbalance his blow brought and was on Gilles' back. The *goddam* gave up his sword for his dagger for such close work. The point of this weapon skidded here and there, trying for a chink. It found the exposed shoulder and pain bolted through Gilles' arm down to the fingers. The dagger raked across his neck. And again. It was as if only the flimsy cords of Yann's talisman turned the blade. Gilles was finding it as difficult to get air into his lungs with the weight of the *goddam* on top of him as those wights being shoved into the pond below.

With his good right side and all the strength he could muster, Gilles managed to twist himself round in the tiny gap of the arrow slit. As he did so, he brought his knee up and into the man somewhere between groin and belly.

Suddenly he had space to breathe and more. Not much, but enough. Ignoring the numbing pain in his shoulder, he got his sword point between himself and the man's dagger and kicked the loose sword down the ladder hole before him.

Now it was more important than ever that he get to the winch. But now he must close, rather than open the gate. If he and the Scots could just clear the tower of these few men left to guard it, then make a dash for the south wall to help Richemont over before Suffolk and his men arrived . . .

But there was no time to think further than this blow, the next, against the man before him. The fellow was doomed with only the stub of his dagger to parry with. Gilles' sword found one shallow entry. He withdrew, struck again. The next thing he knew, his point had gone through all thicknesses and found the open space beyond the dying man's back.

"Ah." Gilles sighed as he saw death come. He took the man's last breath into his own lungs, like the gift of a lover.

The sword resisted more coming out than it had going in. Gilles had to let the corpse drop and put his foot on the fellow's neck to free it. He got a *sabaton* full of blood while he cleaned his blade on his victim's sleeve.

The moment he was rearmed, Gilles headed to the ladder pit, only to find a Scot there before him.

"Close it," Gilles yelled at him. Then used gestures. "The winch. Close the gate, don't open it."

This was one of the Scots who didn't understand French. A pox on it. Gilles wasn't certain he'd made him understand, even now. Then a look of wonder came across the man's large, flushed face.

While struggling to comprehend, the Scot had failed to pay attention to the dangers below. Something—Gilles couldn't see what—had given him the death blow in the exposed half of his body, the part below the floor. The ladder grips swayed off the wall, sloughing the Scot off, out of sight.

Gilles looked at the four or five Scots who, having dispatched their opponents, joined him around the perimeter of the ladder hole. What was to be done? They couldn't very well drop below—precariously now that the ladder was gone—to be hacked to pieces one by one by whomever was down there. Their faces looked back at him, empty, waiting for him to fill them with purpose.

Gilles glanced beyond them then and saw the first rungs of a second ladder. He pointed. Two Scots ran for it. Then he realized where the ladder must lead. He gestured the ladder back again. And showed them the kettle of pitch, still on the fire in a stone niche off the platform overhead.

The Scots caught on quickly. He let them do the hot, heavy work while he tore a bit of exposed shirt off a dead *goddam* and used it to bind his shoulder. The pressure stopped the bleeding and allowed him to move it more freely.

Two Scots held the ladder ready, two more heaved the smoking kettle into position, the smoking pitch just at the tipped lip. Then Gilles himself heaved the nearest corpse and sent it slowly, legs first, down the hole on the assumption that *goddam* boots looked pretty much like his own.

I might be fishing, he thought.

The moment he felt the first bite into the inert legs, he nodded to the Scots and over went the scalding kettle.

Screams in at least three voices came satisfactorily up from below. Empty kettle and corpse chased them for good measure, then over went the ladder and two men, one dropping, one stepping, covering each other's backs. Another pair followed right on their heels. Then Gilles took the ladder, a Scot buttock to buttock with him.

His sword struck opposition even before he could see whether it was man or beast. This new opponent danced several rounds with him before Gilles' eyes caught sight of the winch. It remained a tantalizing goal, however, as long as he and every Scot with him were fully occupied. Some had two men on them and the ladder had stopped producing any more.

Gilles' wound surged a sudden, overwhelming weakness throughout his body. His sword grew heavier than the anvil that had forged it and it sank toward the floor. Just at the horizontal, however, a wonderful strength radiated from the talisman on his breast and met the weakness. The forces crashed like ebb and flow meeting at the crest of the wave.

Yann must want this fortress taken. He always spoke of winning the land back from those who didn't belong here. He must, and his magic must work to that end.

Upon this crest of power, Gilles' sword swung and collided with his opponent's neck. He wasn't certain whether head or only helmet shot off the shoulders, and he didn't stop to see. It was enough that the blows from that direction ceased.

Gilles leaped around on the pitch-slick floor, his own feet beginning to warm with what had failed to find cracks yet. He saw a sorely wounded *goddam*, black with hot pitch, dragging himself toward the winch with the aid of a broken-off spear shaft. On his way across the room after him, Gilles tripped up the *goddam* on one of his Scots, gave a sound blow to another skull with his sword.

He kicked the crawling Englishman off the winch——

"Bastard," he exclaimed, and kicked the man again, though he was now far beyond taking offense or feeling pain.

As his last act, the Englishman had managed to cram his spear shaft into the winch's gears and break it off so the thing would be impossible to get out without a mechanic to take the whole mechanism apart.

"Damn, damn, damn," Gilles said, each curse accompanied by an ineffective chop, yank, or push.

"Damn." He turned back to the room. He gazed stupidly at the men still struggling in pairs and threesomes, blinking against tears of exhaustion, pain, and—now, now so close— defeat.

Then Gilles saw an arm at the winchroom's open doorway. The arm tossed in a flaming brand. The ancient wooden flooring, oil-soaked, burst into flame with a gale's whoosh. The smell, so oddly like that of a rich and merry feast, started to choke Gilles even before the first Scot, kilted in orange flame, ran to spit himself on the English sword awaiting him outside.

Gilles felt himself thrown back against the winch by the heat. Now, for a change, the talisman began to pulse cool. But there was no way a bag of smelly herbs was going to get him out of this one by itself.

Gilles felt the floorboards beneath him sag a little as he edged nearer the opening through which the gate chain ran to the level below. At first the sensation churned sickeningly through his stomach. Then, his mind churned.

Quickly, he sheathed his sword and removed his gauntlets, stuffing them into his belt again. He stomped on the wood, heard it crack, stomped harder and felt it give way just as he snatched for the chain and swung his legs out into space.

His left shoulder crumpled with pain as it took his weight. His right hand slipped, sweat on smooth, greased links. Floorboards where he'd just been shot past, eye level. They flowed now with flame as if with golden water, only upward. He felt the blast of their heat through his visor slits. But that was the least of his worries. He was going to crash, and crash hard, on the flagstones twenty feet below.

Then Gilles felt something like a net—like a comforter of eiderdown—spread out from the talisman around his neck and cushion his legs from below.

The fall sent him into a shin-whipping crouch, shook every joint, both in his armor and in his flesh. The sound was like all the crockery shelves in a kitchen toppling at once.

But Gilles quickly straightened, unhurt. He stepped out of the way of falling chunks of flaming ceiling into the sheltering shadow of the gate's stonework and took his bearings.

Behind him was the keep of Saint-James-de-Beuvron, no more hope or safety there. Before him spread the pond, looking like Blaison's castle yard after the fall butchering. Pools of blood floated upon the slime-thick surface of the greater pool. *Goddams* waded in the shallows, dispatching the Breton wounded and claiming their spoils, arms and weapons. He would have to skirt these blood-drunk men without being seen? Impossible.

The hopelessness of it leadened his feet and pressed the air from him in a sigh. He thought it would be a sigh. It came out rather as a whistle, a loud one, shoved from deep under his breastbone, beneath the sweat-sodden lump of leather. In response to the whistle, a horse trotted around the castle's next tower. He was a decent gelding, ready saddled, whose rider must have lost his seat in the fray by the pond.

The horse tripped uneasily, flaring the nostrils in his blue-black muzzle at the billows of smoke pouring from the tower. Gilles whistled again and moved away from the shadows toward the animal.

The gelding calmed the moment Gilles caught his dragging bridle, glad to have a master again to lead him out of this terror. Gilles did, at once.

13

A Sodden Leather Talisman

"At least you saved the guns," Gilles told Roger de Bricqueville as the two plodded along the track away from Saint-James-de-Beuvron and toward the sea. Around them, in no discipline but that made by flight, were fewer than twenty men who'd managed to save themselves. "Well done, Roger."

Roger laughed, releasing tension. "And between us we've a pair of good arms, anyway."

Gilles took that as an open invitation, almost beggary, for his love. He'd have to get his dagger wound properly looked after first, but then—Maybe, yes. Nothing rid a body of the hurt of defeat like good sodomy.

Before he could say anything flirtatious in return, however, he caught sight of the count of Richemont and twenty or so of his men hot on their heels. Gilles let his borrowed gelding drop behind the creaking gun cart until his commander rode level with him. Richemont pulled up short just before, Gilles thought, the spike on his mount's face guard ran his own gelding through.

"I am glad to see you well, my lord." In fact, Gilles didn't think the count looked at all well. The grime and drying blood of the fighting against the south wall streaked his face. Under that, anger pinched and paled his features.

"Why?" Richemont gasped for air from his ride. "Why, for the love of Our Lady and Her mother Ste. Anne, did those damned Bretons run?"

Gilles explained as simply as he could about the approach of Suffolk's men from Avranches.

"That wasn't Suffolk," Richemont said, his jaw beneath the scars very tight. "Those were the men I sent towards Avranches to scout and to see that no English got through to warn the earl. No man did get through. Except fleeing Bretons."

"My lord." Gilles couldn't move his tongue for what seemed a very long time. "My lord. We didn't know. We thought—we all thought—they were English."

"It was a tiny party I sent. If you'd only stopped to count them, you'd have thought nothing of them."

"My lord—" Gilles could think of nothing else to say.

"I wash my hands of these Frenchmen. That damned Giac. Damn him. If he'd sent the supplies, the men would never have been so demoralized that they'd run at their own shadows."

Something like a smile ran crookedly through Richemont's scars and exhaustion. "I am glad, at least, you've saved your guns, Rais. I tried to get down from the wall and save my own, when I saw what was happening. But it was too late. Too few men left to lend a hand. We had to leave them in the trenches where we'd set them. They're lost."

Richemont gave a great sigh and put his hand to his eyes.

"Our camps were too far apart," he said. "I sent you a messenger this morning before light to tell you about the party I'd sent towards Avranches, but he didn't make it through. He died at the pond, I'm told, trying to yell at your fleeing Bretons. Their voices, dying and fleeing, drowned out his own except to the one *goddam* who shoved him under. Now we, like the rest, must make our way deep into Brittany by what safe, small tracks we know."

Brittany is a safebox, Gilles wanted to tell him. Keeping things safe until they can come forward in the proper time and save all the land.

But these were Yann's words, witches' words. Richemont would not care for them. Gilles wasn't certain he believed them himself.

Richemont sighed again. "For your soul's sake," he said, "I'm glad to see you got by with only such a scratch. And your guns. I mistook you, Gilles de Rais. Christ and his saints look after you for all that."

Then the *connétable* set his scar like black slate and swung the baton of his office across his saddle once more. He turned the spike on his horse's head to press on at a rate too fast for talk.

Gilles caught slowly back up to Roger. The look he caught from his friend told him he'd heard it all.

"And just what was all this about Christ and his saints?" Roger wanted to know.

A moment before, they'd been congratulating one another.

"Oh, God. I wish I'd died with those poor Scots in the oil-soaked winchroom," Gilles said.

"Ah, Gilles," Roger sympathized. He patted the breastplate of his own armor. "Your milk brother can work miracles, but I don't think even magic can be everywhere at once."

This reminded Gilles of the sodden lump around his own neck. In a fit of pique, he pulled the talisman up by its thong, yanked it off his neck, out of the knots it worked in his hair. Then he threw it into a passing thicket of shoulder-high gorse.

"Ah, Gilles. I wouldn't do that. Not 'til we reach the safety of the Mont at least."

"You claim deeper understanding of the Craft than I do?"

"Never, Gilles."

"Yann is my own milk brother."

"Of course he is."

"But if this is what my milk brother's magic does," Gilles said, his anger boiling, "I say to hell with it."

"Ah, Gilles" was all Roger could think of to say.

But Gilles found himself talking to Yann out loud, even when the sorcerer was leagues and leagues away.

"So where is your damned Pucelle, eh, Yann? Monseigneur le *connétable* of France, Brittany's own Arthur, sent flying by an English force a tenth its size. La Pucelle? Where the hell is she?"

14

Honey-Colored Hair Wreathed with Daisies

It wasn't quite yet a year after Jehannette had seen that strange boy by the beech tree and he'd told her . . .

But he hadn't told her the most important things. Why hadn't he prepared her?

Catherine's girlfriends had wreathed her honey-colored hair with daisies one last time. Such a crowning, Jehannette thought, ought to have been an older sister's office. She felt sick that she had failed to think of it.

That her Voices had failed to remind her.

Catherine lay like the enchanted princess waiting for the spell to be broken. Her face and hands had the unreal glow of milky glass. Pristine white linen wrapped tight and showed the delicacy of her eleven-year-old form. All signs of the smallpox and fever had miraculously vanished as quickly as they'd come . . .

Catherine, dead. Catherine, who had always been so pretty, so graceful, so good. Catherine who would never have strange boys visit her.

Jehannette found it easier to believe her little sister was simply waiting for the prince's kiss than that she was dead. Even later, after the shovels smeared the whole effect with dirt.

When the procession returned from the graveyard, the

women of Domrémy spread the funerary feast on trestle tables under the maples before the house of the chief mourners. The smell of sausage grease and plum cake sat heavily in her stomach and Jehannette couldn't eat a bite.

"Come, child, you must eat," neighbor after neighbor told her. "It offends the dead not to eat at their passing."

But Jehannette quietly handed the dogs the slabs of bread and chunks of meat pressed upon her and continued to fast. She found herself avoiding the green of women's kirtles even when she knew she should set her own red kirtle among them.

Away from the women were, of course, the men. Jehannette caught her father's eye and expected him to say "Eat more" in his usual way. The laconic words always had an echo to them, as if they came from the past, a past that was very empty and hungry.

And usually Jacquot d'Arc would gesture to his wife to give the older of their two daughters the choicest pieces she had otherwise reserved for him and the boys. Sometimes he ordered her to make Jehannette's favorite foods for no reason at all. And Jehannette would refuse them—for no reason at all.

Except that she knew her father was of two minds. There was the spoken mind that wanted to nourish his daughter.

And there was the silent mind, hidden behind the grey eyes and the pinched mouth. The silent mind knew that soldiers took a plumper maid before a skinny one and a full-grown woman before a child.

Jehannette was not quite certain how she knew this secret, irrational mind of her father's, nor why she felt compelled to play to it. That Jacquot d'Arc did no such thing today hurt her more than she could say, almost more than her sister's death. If *he* would just say it once her gorge might open at last and for good—

But he did not. Jacquot d'Arc stood, rough square hands clasped behind his back as if they would leap to murder if he were not fierce with them, and silently accepted the condolences of Domrémy's men.

"We have all lost a soul dear to us," one was in the midst of saying, "and the frail nature of females . . ."

Even from her discrete distance, Jehannette jumped at the violence with which her father suddenly interrupted the man. And he was staring right at her when he said, "At least Catherine is safe."

"Safe, Jacquot?" the man repeated, as if he thought they must be speaking different languages and not simply different dialects.

"Safe from the dream."

"Dream?" The possibility that grief had turned Jacquot d'Arc's mind was not absent from the word.

"The dream I had. Even before Jacquemin was born, I dreamed I should lose a daughter to the soldiers."

"Murdered in war?"

The neighbor's voice had a certain awe to it now, and he crossed himself. Jacquot d'Arc had come to Domrémy when he was already a man. He did not share the quiet past of the rest of the village. He'd come from a land to the west called Champagne, ravaged by France's civil war.

When men grew bored with their lot, they envied the life they imagined for him. They were naive fools, Jehannette thought.

Jacquot d'Arc himself never spoke of his past in Burgundian lands, in Champagne. But Jehannette knew when that past was playing before his eyes. The flesh under those eyes would turn grey, his mouth would pinch, and she would see him shake with a rage or a fear.

He stood in such a state now.

"To harlotry," Jacquot d'Arc snapped, and Jehannette knew his anger was focused at her rather than at the man to whom the words were addressed. "I'd rather the grave take them both than such a fate. I'd drown her myself rather than—"

"Now, Jacquot. You're overwrought—"

As if flung from a catapult, Jacquot d'Arc turned on his heels from the group of men. Jehannette saw him sweep up the ax as he left the yard and swing it to his shoulder. His long steps gobbled up the path toward the forest. When Jacquot d'Arc came to them again, everyone knew, he'd have chopped more wood than the family could use in a month.

His tortuously neat woodpiles stood as landmarks throughout the common forests, an open invitation to those unable to wield axes of their own. This charity stood as mute testimony to what he could never put into words: the unspeakable past that had left him no other family in the world save this one he himself had founded. And few material goods beyond the woodpiles bleaching like bones in the weather.

"Be a good girl and come and eat something. Dear, sweet Catherine would want you to," urged a voice at her ear. A woman's green kirtle pressed up against her as if it would smother her own red wool. "Your dear sister who never gave anyone a moment's care. Jehannette, can't you be good—?"

It was that word "good" that did it, acted like a spark to the powder. Jehannette bolted. She went in the other direction. She snatched up her distaff instead of an ax. And she did not go nearly so far. But even as she ran away she knew she was more like her father than any other soul on earth.

15

———•————

When the pounding red anger finally cleared her head, Jehannette found herself in the usual place. She sat in the grass that
sloped down to the brook from the straight rows and tortured
weedlessness of her father's garden. Pressing close on either
side of her, the grass bent under its own knee-high weight and
in front, before her outstretched legs, the brook worked its way
through thick reeds toward the wide river. To the right, the
old washhouse was just hidden behind an upstream bend. Usually, the quick laughter of women working over the beating
stones followed their grey water past the wriggle of her bare
toes.

She was glad they weren't there today, though she could
still hear their more subdued sounds and the chink of cutlery
and earthenware floating down from under the maples at the
edge of the yard.

Jehannette could see—over the brook, and less sharply to
the right—cows flicking their tails idly against the flies as they
sought out the shade of the few linden trees. Golden pollen
from the trees drifted through the air along with a blue-black
dragonfly. Beyond, a field of mustard in bloom seemed to
spread the rising roll of land like freshly torn bread. The tangy,
bright color of the condiment stung her eyes long before her
mother's pestle had come into play or even the seeds were
fully formed in their pods.

The larger body of water on the left, the River Meuse,
passed before her view between the willows and thickets of

nettles and blackthorn that framed it. The water was green and capped here and there with white: the blossoms of the water grasses swaying like women's unbound hair under a linen cap in the gentle current.

Just over that river, her father always said with a hiss, were the lands of the "*goddam*-loving Burgundians." The land of this enemy, to her sight, was very similar, almost identical to her own, with cows and fields of mustard and heading wheat strewn with bright red poppies. But to her father's eyes, the Meuse drew such a line that he wouldn't even raise his head to see just how similar the lands, in fact, were. How joined and connected.

Jehannette thought she could hear the heartbeat of her father's ax even from where she sat.

From her father, Jehannette knew the violence that drew the line between Burgundians and "real, Christian folk" like the inhabits of tiny, sleepy Domrémy. Even such a violence had driven her from her sister's funeral feast.

And yet, in her heart of hearts, in the quiet Voices that came to her at times like this—had come to her beginning with the boy by the beech—Jehannette knew there was no real line between peoples at all.

Was this the root of her evil? The deep heresy that would—oh, how she feared it—drive the splitting wedge into the heart of her wood? And her father's?

Because try as she might she could see no real line between the lands. The Meuse was no skin of separation but an artery of blood nourishing both sides equally. Men themselves had drawn this line against all will of heaven, in a rage as blind as that which moved her father when the ax was in his hand. To actually try to make such a cut would bleed the land to death.

The river gave off a mossy, fishy, womany smell to her deep-breathing nostrils. And like a broad-hipped mother, the earth reached herself from horizon to horizon, raising the edges of her green-sown skirts up to the darker greens of forest that ran along the ridges east and west like comforting arms.

From the time the monthly flow first came upon her, a

woman dressed in that dark green of fertility. Wools dyed with the whole yarrow plant and angelica put her woman's power under the protection of St. Michel the Archangel—until widowhood made her turn everything black.

For Catherine's sake, Jehannette had worn a black kerchief, but that was tossed back now and lay crumpled on the grass behind her. She stretched her legs out under their girl's red skirts. Girls in the village younger than she were already wearing green and receiving beaux, had been for a year or more.

"You run too much," her mother told her. "That's very unwomanly. No wonder you are slow to become a woman. Sit, spin. If you act like other girls, you'll become like other girls." And she'd thrust the distaff into her daughter's hand as if she wished to pin Jehannette to the ground with it.

And Jacquot d'Arc would say "Eat more" even when she knew her not eating was a comfort to him.

Demands for discipline hid Jacquot d'Arc's fear for—of—his growing daughter. Knowing that in times of war there was no real safety, any and all could be taken with no excuse or favoritism, his spoken mind said, "Eat, child," and sometimes even threatened to beat her if she did not.

Why did she play to this irrational part of her father's mind? How did she even know about it? Perhaps because, for all the times he threatened her if she would not eat, he never had picked up the whip to her. And she could feel even stronger than words or deeds his look of hope—of final settling and peace, the grey vanishing from around his eyes—every time she took no more than a bit of bread sopped in wine for her supper.

Jehannette felt better when she ate like that, like a bird. She knew the body nature had given her was anything but birdlike. It was short, but not small, tending to the square and a certain peasant stockiness.

That first day she'd felt the edges swelling off the block of a torso that had served her childhood so well—swelling into a woman's form—disgust had made her physically ill. She had been unable to keep more than bread and wine down. The next day as well.

And that had been the day the pale, angel-faced boy had come to her in nobleman's clothes and told her her mother needed her—when she did not.

Jehannette still wondered about that messenger, though he never had reappeared. Indeed, she got the distinct impression that he had died, come to her in his final hour with some desperate message she'd simply failed to understand.

And the more she ate, the less she would understand.

Not long after the boy's appearance, she'd taken First Communion at Father Minet's palsied hands. Father Minet had introduced Jehannette to the notion of fasting. He had told her of the early desert fathers: of Father Theon, who'd lived only on vegetables, and only those he didn't have to cook. St. Anthony lived on even less. Indeed, eating little seemed a prerequisite for sainthood. Father Minet had listed the days the Church sanctioned for fasting: the season of Lent, Fridays, the days of martyrs, Ember Days in the dark of the year.

After old Minet had died, no other priest wanted to come and live in the dangerous borderlands of Domrémy. Yes, there was the molish Père Guillaume Frontey, who stayed buried in Vaucouleurs near the stronghold there and went around the countryside only when things seemed safe. And Père Michel, who had come to officiate at Catherine's funeral, but who usually stayed in retreat in the wooded hermitage of Notre-Dame-de-Bermont.

So Jehannette had learned most of her prayers from her mother, a woman so known for her piety and frequent pilgrimages that people called her Zabillet Romée as if she'd actually been to Rome. Still, for her mother, fasting was no more than an aid in deciding what to have for dinner each night. Jehannette could not much care for a piety that was mere recompense for having married a much older man. A man who couldn't shake off the memory of a first family even when the new and living stood before him.

So when Father Minet had died, Jehannette had added more fast days on her own until the whole calendar was now nearly full. The days of saints that had a special meaning to her. The memory of a day when the world had seemed to explode in her with bliss.

The day the Voices had first come.

Fasting was one way Jehannette made certain that the Voices that came to her could not be devils.

Another was falling to her knees any time she heard church bells, whether the inescapable Saint-Rémy just through the old chestnut outside her own window or the churches of nearby Greux and Maxey from over the Meuse. She could usually hear them as well.

For the Voices did come. They were not the boy again, but similar, leaving her with the same glowing, wonderful feeling. From not eating she had come to this realization: the boy was a precursor to the Voices. A John the Baptist to the following Christ.

The Voices had no name as yet. No face. Mostly they just told her to be good. Which meant fasting. And still they called her "Daughter-God."

Fasting kept the Voices good. Answered their demands that she be good.

Sage. The old sage woman. Was that the Voices now?

For their good seemed very different from the good the folk of Domrémy asked of her.

To her horror, it also seemed different from poor, sweet Catherine's good as well.

Jehannette had nursed her sister, even when her mother had tried to keep her away. She'd spent as much time as she could in the sickroom, hovering over the bed they'd shared even in the first bath of Catherine's fevered sweat. But Jehannette had failed to catch the disease in spite of all her efforts. Was that good? The village didn't seem to consider it so. It wasn't natural. And her father certainly didn't consider it good. He'd rather see her dead and safe. Hadn't he said as much in so many words?

So what did it matter if it kept her in a red kirtle a little while longer? Since she had to wear skirts anyway, they might as well be red. Red eased the haunted grey around her father's eyes.

Jehannette shifted herself within the girth of the blue sash containing the caul. As usual, she wore it tied around her waist, under her kirtle. When she moved just so, the wool rasped on the dried thing within, making a hollow sound. She shrank from it, growing hollow herself.

Then she ignored that constraint. Or rather, grew with it. She stretched her legs and their red skirts again, trying to mimic the spread of the earth around her. And through the center of her being, up and down through her core, she was aware of a strong, eternal stream.

It was something like the flow of women, she imagined. But it did not come and go. It was always there, whenever she stopped to feel for it. Very like the quiet flow of the Meuse, she thought. Sometimes, like now, slow and sluggish. Sometimes, in winter flood, churning at the trunks of trees along the top of the banks that now stood, thorn- and nettle-clogged, higher than a man's head. But never, ever dying. Or letting those who fed on her vanish, either, in their cycle of life and death.

On a pair of benches behind her, at the edge of the funeral and across from the church, Jehannette could hear the old men of the village. She didn't need to see them. They were such a familiar sight. No funeral was required to set them on their benches. Sometimes there were just the three of them, today five or six, favoring their old backs and rheumatisms and fading eyes through the long, summer afternoon.

The old men called each other by the familiar "*tu.*" They'd been boys together. Indeed, there was hardly a soul in the world Jehannette had ever heard them struggle to find the formal "*vous*" for. Strangers didn't come to this place often. Nor did nobility. And now the old men nursed horns of funerary ale cooled by the stream along with their ills and "*tu*"-ed yet another generation into the world of Domrémy.

Little three-year-old Reine's voice had joined the old grumbles. Jehannette imagined the girl standing between the men's benches. Her mother was busy with the feast, trusting that there would be plenty of eyes left in town to watch out for 'Ti'-Reine, Little-Reine.

And there were. The old men were teasing the child now, to the delight of all. In her mind's eye, Jehannette could see perfectly how 'Ti'-Reine must be swishing her kirtle coquettishly as she lisped. "And when my mama finishes at Aunt Zabillet's, she will give me strawberries and cream."

"And why would she want to do such a thing?" one of the old men asked in mock amazement.

"Because," said the girl, as if that word were a decent answer to any question and not saucy at all.

"Because you're good?" prompted another of the men.

"No," said 'Ti'-Reine, lisping, swishing.

"You're not good?" A tone of mock threat crept into the old man's voice, the *sage* emphasized by the whistles around his missing teeth.

"No," said 'Ti'-Reine stoutly, with all the exaggerated wisdom of three years. "Because I'm her 'Ti'-Reine."

The old men loved this answer. Their combined replies and repetitions of the statement mixed with their laughter bounced off the blank face of the church walls, straight to Jehannette's ears. Well she remembered when she'd been the little girl in 'Ti'-Reine's place, everyone's pet. She knew girls who longed for a daughter, just to recapture the time.

Sometimes Jehannette did herself.

"Be good, Jehannette." The Voices came from the walls of the church in echoes. "Daughter-God, be good. *Sois sage.*"

In the presence of the Voices, one small girl on one afternoon seemed but a little thing, but a tiny reflection of the whole. Jehannette felt 'Ti'-Reine's same perfect faith in mother-love for the green, growing mother upon whose bosom her red kirtle rested. But Jehannette's love was bigger than that. Not only she, but every man, woman, and child would have all they wanted—even strawberries and cream for supper—as long as they needed it, for the simple fact that they were all children of the Mother of God.

"Be good."

"The cradles fill no faster than the graveyard," Père Michel always said. He may have even said it today, over Catherine's open pit. Jehannette couldn't remember. And she felt it odd to be thinking of the black-robed hermit now.

Still, she thought of the graveyard, just opposite the old men on the other side of the church. Sometimes it seemed to her that the old men were avoiding the sight, but she knew it was not really so. They were merely counterbalancing the flow of village life between them.

And the rough-hewn crosses and less definite stone shapes of past generations of old men—and women, too—of course. They peered wistfully over the grey wall that sprouted tiny ferns in its cracks. She couldn't see that any more than she could see the old men on their benches. Nor could she hear the quiet teasing that came from the church's other side. But she knew both were there.

She could feel them even stronger now that there was someone of her own lying there. All her life, unlike everyone else she knew, she had never been able to point to any stone in that yard and say, "This was my ancestor, my own flesh and blood." For her people were not from here.

Though she tried hard to feel that they were.

And now they were.

And tonight she would sleep alone in the bed in the bake room.

There was fresh-turned soil now, marking the sleep of her own flesh and blood.

"Daughter-God, be good."

Jehannette stretched herself again, feeling good settle through her like the soil spread out, like water finding its level. She sought for an echoing good under the arch of blue sky, that white clouds only dotted here and there.

Perfect haying weather. Because She is our Mother, She gives us days such as these. Like bowls of strawberries and cream.

And we, because we must bury our dead, must pass some of the proffered bowls by.

Through the blue sky, out from their homes in niches in the tower and under the eaves of the church, shot the martinets. The swift, black shadows grew more numerous now as the day grew longer. Every now and then, one bird would come upon a swarm of insects and shout his find to the others. Their high, excited cries had the rolling quality of thunder, reaching a crescendo then dying back again as they renewed their search.

"The martinet is named for St. Martin," Père Michel always said.

Père Michel again.

St. Martin, a little black-robed god. "To have the birds nest in your eaves is good luck."

Because they eat your mosquitoes? Jehannette often wondered, though never aloud. It seemed too mundane a reason.

"Unlike the blackbird, who is evil luck near the house. The blackbird should be shooed away and her eggs broken."

Evil luck for the blackbird, Jehannette thought, if not for the houseowner.

Why should man choose between the good bird and the bad? Great Mother Earth did not, loved them equally, provided bowls of strawberries for each of her teeming brood.

Though Jehannette had first sat in the shade, the sun was lower now. It sought its level over the hill behind the Bois Chênu and the less-sacred forests beyond that still thudded with her father's grief. The women had begun to pack up the tables and distribute the leftovers, mostly to Zabillet Romée's cupboards.

The new angle of the sun hit Jehannette's arms where she'd shoved the sleeves up to the elbows. The sun was still warm and she loved it. She loved the acorn brown that summer turned her skin, loved the actual feel of the tan happening, like the tingling bite of tannin in the nose. The sun felt as sweet and rich and nourishing as strawberries and cream on an empty stomach.

And it was an indulgence she'd allow herself. She stretched her arms luxuriously to the feel.

And then humming pricked her ear and Jehannette knew one mosquito had escaped the darts of martinets, shaken off the day's hot lethargy, and found her. Still, she didn't move. Still, she stretched out her thin but sun-nourished arm and watched the drifted landing of the lacy, leggy creature. She felt the tiny prick and didn't flinch. She saw the drop of her own blood as red as strawberries.

Jehannette moved less than the cows in the fields swishing against the flies. She tried to be as open and offering as the earth was, plowed for the spring sowing.

She heard another hum. And another. Mosquitoes, like martinets, must have their ways of calling a discovery to their friends. She didn't move, though the state of her arms in hours to come already itched at the back of her mind.

"Daughter-God, be good."

To be good always entailed some bad. Had the Voices told her that as well? Or was it Père Michel? Did the old men on their benches know that? Equal measure, good and bad. Jehannette knew. The man who wished for martinets around his house must not merely break the nests of blackbirds. He must stretch out his arms for the mosquitoes to feed. Most people forgot that. The martinets must also have their strawberries and cream. All life turned and wheeled like the birds through the sky.

And then the blood that merely pricked to her arm was suddenly throbbing in her veins. And the birds were no longer wheeling like dreams at the edge of sleep. They were shooting.

Like arrows. The sky black with arrows, the high, sharp whistle of their flight. And the wisps of clouds in the blue sky were like scales of armor.

Why should she think of arrows? Jehannette had never seen an arrow, certainly not one flying through the air. At most, their feathered fletches—black, martinet feathers? Or the feathers of eagles?—sticking out of a quiver slung on the back of one in a passing nobleman's train. Such an armed man never gave her the slightest glance. Or if he did, he just as quickly looked away again. The back of his armored cap eased her father's eyes. It also told her she was not like 'Ti'-Reine, not like Catherine, and never could be. All the swishing of her skirts in childhood had been an unnatural study. Although, of course, very much what the old men expected when they said, "Be good."

Was it what the Voices expected as well? No, she did not think so.

All that the sight of feathered arrows had taught Jehannette before was this: She did not have the makings of a princess evilly spelled into commonness. Its sight had taught her to avoid the reflection of still water and her image in the side of a pot when she'd finished giving it her best burnish, unlike Catherine, who always loved such things.

So why did the thought of arrows now make the blood pound with such thrill at the temples of her head and on the right side, toward the church? Make the Voices reach the pitch of martinet screams?

"Jehannette . . ."

And then, suddenly, the many shrill Voices shaved down to one, a whisper.

"Be good. *Sois sage*."

Catherine's voice.

16

The Tow-Bound Staff

"Jehannette!"

This was no Voice falling like sheets of light now. It was her brothers, Pierre and Jean, who even on the evening of their sister's burial had chores to do.

"Dreaming again, Jehannette?"

"Where's your distaff, Jehannette?"

"Did Mother not say she'd have your hide if she ever caught you without the distaff in your hand again?"

"Dreaming . . ."

"And if I tell . . . ?"

Jehannette was on her feet and facing her brothers in an instant.

"Oh-oh . . ."

The fear in the older Pierre's voice was not all feigned. The boys, seventeen and nineteen perhaps, had been forgetting their grief in the drink lavishly provided at the feast and they had forgotten more than their grief. Jehannette saw herself reflected in the unsober glitter of those brown eyes. Much as she flinched from what she saw in smooth pools and the sides of copper pots, her image bouncing back from the eyes of an enemy she found irresistible.

She had snatched up her kerchief and her distaff now—she hadn't left it far—though not in the proper up-and-down stance. Truth to tell, she couldn't have used the implement as intended. She'd only taken it up when she'd left the yard because her father already had the ax. She'd abandoned the work as a hopeless tangle days ago, just when Catherine's illness began and her mother wasn't able to help her out of the mess.

Never mind. A pole, even one padded with tow, has other uses.

Tucked up under her arm, it made an excellent lance, and she was on her brothers before they could raise their arms to the defensive—though years of experience with their sister should have taught them better.

The worst teasing never angered her more than an interruption to her Voices.

A little nagging from the corner of her brain said, "But how should they have known? Be good, Jehannette."

"They ought to have." That was the only answer from the red blur of her fury. "Like they ought to know that spring follows winter."

"Ah, stop, Jehannette," squealed Jean as he backed away from her blows.

"We have work to do, even if you do not."

"How can you behave in such an unwomanly fashion?"

"On this day when our Catherine lies dead, no less."

But the references to Catherine and her own unwomanly behavior only infuriated her more.

She left the boys no chance to bend and pick up weapons of their own. This way, that way, this way again, always leaning into the weakest point. It came so naturally to her. Like breathing: inhale coming right after exhale with never any doubt as to what should happen next. Her body sang with the movements, the resistance of the young, strong bodies to her tow-bound staff was better than food to an empty stomach.

Pierre and Jean had turned on their heels and were running now. They no more than anyone else in Domrémy could outrun her and they knew it. But blows to the back hurt less than blows to the face.

She had driven them up the lane now and they were seeking refuge in the barn. Getting backed into a straw-filled corner would not save them. Jean, left below by the older Pierre, quickly clambered up to the loft behind his brother.

Here she paused for a moment, panting, staring at a place

where, in the back seam of Jean's hose, stitching was coming undone. Her stitching, of course, not their mother's. But more than the onerous thought of having to mend that rent, she imagined such a seam running up the back of her legs. Ah, for such freedom when she climbed a ladder.

It's as if I'm just pretending in this red, woolen weight, she thought. Pretending to be something I'm not. And if it were cut free, I could soar—

"Pull the ladder on up after you, Jean." Pierre gasped the order.

But Jehannette had her hands on the rungs at the same instant. It is easier to pull down than up. She yanked the rough-hewn side rails out of the dark opening and Jean had to scramble to keep from being pulled down with them. She tossed the ladder easily against the closest manger. She took a deep breath, contented more than winded.

"You'd let Grison go thirsty for the sake of the devil in you, Jehanne?"

She noted with satisfaction that Jean began his bidding by calling her "Jehanne," without the babying "ette" at the end. But that brother, the younger of the two, would bargain a man out of his own mother and then try to sell the poor woman back again. Playing on her love of all animals, indeed. Especially for the family horse! She had no patience with such tactics.

"Grison won't go thirsty," she assured him. "Though I hope you do."

And with a flick of red kirtle about her heels as she snatched up the distaff now shedding tow, she walked out of the yawning mouth of the barn.

"Taking the horse to water is not a girl's job."

"Mother'll have your hide if she . . ."

Jehannette strode quickly and their voices soon faded behind her. They'd be all right. They were bigger fools and cowards than she thought them if they couldn't find or improvise a way to climb down.

She passed the neighbor's hen run, where, in light growing perceptibly more orange, the black-and-white-speckled birds had left off their day's baths in the dust beneath the chestnut tree. They were discussing the merits of retiring to their roost in sleepy clucks. She crossed the brook on the two-plank bridge, never forgetting the little prayer she recited every time she stepped over water.

Be good, Jehannette.

With a sigh, she retied the kerchief over her hair.

There was an earnest rise to the dirt path now as it led up to the forest of the Bois Chênu. Her father had yet to return from beyond. Perhaps she should go and hunt for him after she'd seen to the horse. But it would be twilight by then. Certainly he'd return on his own.

Saint-Rémy began to announce the late hour with deep-throated clangs of its bell. Jehannette dropped to her knees, by chance just in front of the old stone cross that marked the border between settled village and the wilder places of field and forest. But it wasn't just chance, was it? She said her prayers, trying to summon the revery that had been so rudely interrupted again.

Be good, Jehannette.

She stayed on her knees, propped up by the distaff held like a cross in front of her, until the last of the hour's rings faded against the hillside, from Maxey as well as Greux. Pierre and Jean had had plenty of time to catch up with her if they'd wanted to. They obviously didn't want to risk another beating. She pushed herself to her feet with the aid of the distaff and then, swinging it to her shoulder like a rake, continued on up the cart track that ran along the hem of the wood.

It wasn't far. Grison had seen her coming and begun to nicker happily at her even while she was still upon her knees. He waited for her now at the gate, stumbling impatiently.

Jehannette let the old dappled gelding breathe warm air through his black nose on her hand as she murmured a greeting, then ran her fingers fondly up into his mane. She took the simple length of hempen rope halter and began to lead the heavy clomp of Grison's hooves toward the gate.

Then the temptation was too great—for the horse as well, she thought. She looked around carefully to make certain no critical eyes were watching. Balancing her distaff along the length of her arm above her elbow, she reached back into the mane at the horse's shoulder and pulled herself up onto the broad, sun-warmed back. When she'd rucked her red wool kirtle up to her thighs, she was flesh to horseflesh.

For an instant, she let the idea of men's hose coming between them toy with her mind. Then she dismissed it. She preferred the chafing.

Her knees came too close to her hips to really compass the broad barrel of the back. Her short legs stood out almost straight as if in some sort of ecstatic rigor. Anyone who saw her, she knew, would find the stance comical, if not indecent, and tell her once again that riding could harm a woman's insides. Her insides were already problem enough.

She didn't care. Her toes flexed and unflexed in the air beside Grison's belly. The air up here seemed rare, heady, yet more clean and invigorating than any she ever breathed elsewhere. She loved it, better than anything in the world. She had to close her eyes for a moment to keep from fainting, not because of any fear of falling, but just so the thrill of all the wonderful sensations of power and victory wouldn't overwhelm her.

Be good, Jehannette.

Her head cleared. She opened her eyes and touched her heels to Grison's belly. She took another quick look around for any watchers. When there were none, she turned the horse's head left instead of right. She knew she shouldn't, but she just couldn't resist a little ride up into the woods before she brought him back to water and then hobbled him in the field again for night.

Grison himself had no objections. Indeed, from the instant she landed on his back, he seemed a totally different steed from the usual sleepy thing, older by several good years than she was herself. He pricked back his ears with interest and suddenly held his head with a certain pride. He took breath like some old man trying to suck in his gut for a special occasion and then, with another kick, actually began to move quickly enough that a low whistle came to her ears. The sweat-dampened edges of her funeral kerchief rose up off her neck.

Pines and oaks, especially the sacred oaks, grew on both sides of her now, while in the lower levels of the forest, elder bloomed in pure white umbels. The sun had set behind the close western hill and chills ran down her spine, not so much from the sudden, pleasant cool as from thrill. The panting breaths she took came in little wordless shouts of joy. She lowered her distaff from the vertical of a banner to the horizontal of a lance and took a run at the deepening shadows that flew by her. Her little cries grew into full battle shouts.

And then, abruptly, one of the shadows came alive.

It was hard to say which shied more, the horse beneath her or the heart within. The shadow might have been the angel-boy returning. That was her first thought. He had appeared so suddenly in the shadow between trees. He moved in the same sort of way, a slipping manner, as if between light and shadow, life and death. And there was the feeling of her Voices about him.

Jehannette, be good.

But this figure wore shadow-black and the cowl thrown back from his head revealed the tonsure. Jehannette had not seen clerics enough to know for certain, but she had the feeling the shaving of this head was unusual: forward from a straight line that ran from ear to ear.

Whatever the man's oddities, they could never forgive her own. Sick with apprehension, she slid from Grison's back and onto her knees even before the old horse had quite clopped to a halt and turned into his lethargic old self again.

The figure was Père Michel.

17

Tufts of Linen and Wool among Black, Papery Leaves

"Oh, Father! Père Michel!" Jehannette gasped for breath. "Please, forgive me."

She bowed her head over clasped hands and waited for the blow to fall, a curse at the very least.

None did. When she opened her left eye a crack to peek, she saw that the priest's arm was raised, but not in violence. He was blessing her, at the outset in the normal cross fashion with the first two fingers of his right hand. Then, after a moment's consideration, he did it a different way, with the two outside fingers raised, like some horned animal.

"Serve God, Jehannette," he said.

Jehannette blinked, for he caught the very tone of her Voices. Then she grew afraid, for if he knew, would he take them from her?

"Father, I can explain," she began in a panic. "About the horse, I mean. I was just—"

But what explanation could there be but the miserable truth? Her tongue failed her.

"You like to ride, do you?"

No fragment of condemnation entered his tone. She nodded slowly, staring back in wonder at the kind face with the twinkle of amusement in its dark eyes.

"And to fight, too, perhaps?"

How could a Christian priest possibly want to hear a positive answer to such a question from one of his flock—? Unless the person were on Crusade against the heathen. And a man, too, of course.

But that was exactly the answer Père Michel sought. Even expected. She could tell by the look in his eyes. Jehannette was too amazed to say a word.

"Come, my child." Père Michel reached down to catch her elbow and help her to her feet. "Why don't you and I go sit under that tree and talk about it?"

Jehannette looked back to Grison, hoping for an excuse. "I really have to . . ." she began. But the horse seemed in no danger of wandering off. His placid old self again, he had wandered no more than ten or twelve clomping steps, perfectly content with grass he hadn't snuffled over once already that day. And if he were thirsty, he didn't show it, quite ignoring the nearby well.

Père Michel gestured again to "that tree" with the end of his staff and walked on ahead to take his seat ahead of her.

"That tree." The great spreading beech stood against the darkening purple of the sky at the very rim of the hill, its graceful, rounded crown taller than any around it. A view of all the valley spread out at its feet, south to Neufchâteau, north to the dark spur of Bermont Forest. Across the way east was Mount Julian, which Saint Elophe had climbed to die, carrying his own head in his hands after being decapitated under orders of the Roman emperor Julian the Apostate.

Jehannette always thought it odd that the distant wedge of dark green, which she had never actually visited herself, was called for the villain of the tale instead of Mount Elophe. Almost as if the folk of the Meuse Valley had secretly been glad for the brief respite of paganism under Julian. Perhaps Elophe had been a tyrant in his own, new way. Or perhaps he had been a Sacrifice in a very ancient, very necessary way.

These were strange thoughts. Jehannette laughed at herself. And as the night slowly swallowed these sights, she forgot them. Soon she would be able to see nothing but the few pinpricks of fire- and lamplight that reflected the glory of stars overhead. Still, was it this overlook of her entire world that made people call this tree the Lady Tree? Or others, the Fairy

Tree? Here at the very crest of the Bois Chênu, the ancient Oak Wood.

Did it earn recognition for its beauty? Its age? How no other tree and no plant seemed able to take root in its shade? Was it the mast, the Tree's nuts, even now hanging in pale, tender embryos of the spiny things they'd be in fall? Beechmast made good fodder for swine, for cattle. Even people could survive on it in times of famine, though it made horses sick.

Jehannette looked again briefly, with a thought of care and escape, toward Grison. But the horse showed no interest in what could make him sick and she had to wonder again: Had this Tree kept the inhabitants of this place alive one very lean year, when they had taken beechmast as their porridge? Was that the source of the reverence? Beechmast was the first thing that had appealed to her appetite in a very long time. She wanted to be part of that sanctifying communion with ancient times. If there'd been any ripe nuts, she would have eaten them then and there. Probably so greedily that she wouldn't offer any to Père Michel . . .

She'd all but forgotten him, Père Michel, who sat patiently regarding her now, saying nothing and allowing her mind to roam on these wild, woody paths. But the priest must feel something of what she felt, or he wouldn't have stopped her here. Did he wonder who first set his knife to the bark in a sharp ache to be remembered to the depths of time? Who first tore the edge off her hem and tied it to a lower branch to verbalize a prayer? Jehannette couldn't say. All she could say now was that the limbs as high as she could see fluttered with scraps of linen and tufts of wool among the thin, papery leaves. They shaded growing now to black and indistinguishable, paper from leaf.

Did Père Michel wonder? Or did he, the idea suddenly occurred to her, *know*? She looked away, not daring to ask him. If he was not going to tell her, or say anything to her, why had he asked her to stay here? She turned her back on the quietly seated man and faced the Tree instead.

She touched the trunk with these thoughts, feeling the power of the place. She walked out of the center again and touched the withered fragments of a daisy chain, hanging with other wasted garlands among the lowest limbs. As if the Tree had thorns that had suddenly pricked her to the bone, tears sprang to Jehannette's eyes.

"What is it, child?" the priest asked at last.

"Nothing," she replied, the sharpness for herself rather than for him. "Nothing."

"Jehannette?"

She looked at him, preferring that sight now to any more garlands. Père Michel hadn't moved, but still sat watching her, his staff still across his legs.

"Catherine made that garland," she replied at last. "And hung it when we came at Midsummer."

"As the custom is." Père Michel nodded and continued, as if trying to be helpful. "To lay your cloaks here on the grass, to eat, to dance, to sing in honor of the day."

Jehannette stopped trying to hide the tears in her voice. "Yes, and it was not long after this last time that she fell ill."

"That cannot have been more than two weeks ago."

"No." She dashed at her eyes. "And now she's dead."

"The well nearby is also holy," Père Michel suggested.

"Yes, we tossed wreath offerings there, too."

"The water is said to cure fevers."

"I don't know about that." She turned to him, helplessness bursting from her as anger. "That was the first thing we tried. But for all our flower offerings, it didn't work. For Catherine, it didn't work. And if anyone deserved a cure, it was she. I should have died in her place, I who am wicked and—"

Sobs forced her words to a halt. Père Michel nodded, clearly understanding that her anger was not at him, and forgiving her—of everything, even what he didn't know. His forgiveness made her cry all the more.

"Life is such a gift," he said presently, "that flowers rarely buy its worth."

She wanted to demand just what that was supposed to mean but, on the final wave of tears, the anger was ebbing from her. With it went her strength. She could only sink to her knees against the smooth trunk of the Tree and bury her face against it, framed by her hands. Her tears, she thought, must be sharp enough to carve some symbol in the bark. Indeed, she thought they raised the smell of fresh sawdust.

"And there shall come a Maid out of the Bois Chênu . . ."

She heard Père Michel say this quite clearly, but he seemed to speak as a comfort to himself, not to her. In fact, it was almost as if he didn't speak aloud.

Jehannette raised her eyes quickly, but she was too late to see if his lips moved or not. He was rubbing his moustache in thought and she did wonder how she could have heard the words so clearly with his hand before his mouth.

Clearly? No, it was more than that. The words had hit her with the force of prophecy. She looked about her at the woods so favored, half expecting at least the nobly dressed angel of a boy to return in response to such a saying. He did not. There was only Père Michel. Père Michel—and herself.

She looked up into the branches of the Lady Tree. She rubbed her eyes of tears to see better. The leaves were so dense, she was surprised to see, every here and there, a patch of grey sky shimmering through their blanket. The patches looked like faces to her. Some smiled, but none spoke. They seemed to be the faces of the young people dancing about the Lady Tree on Midsummer's Eve.

Her vision expanded, grew colorful. Generations of them, girls and women in their reds and greens, with stiff sun-bleached linen as a contrast, the men and boys in their woad-dyed blues, exactly matching the colors of poppies in green wheat with the cloud-flecked sky above. And all, all were looped in flowers, down to the eyes with crowns, up to the chin with necklaces. Her soul soared with the remembered beauty of it all. A girl's insides felt as if she needn't stoop to pick flowers then. Her soul could push them through her every pore in reverberating joy. Such feelings were surely what the very earth felt when it split with vibrant spring growth.

Jehannette had eaten, under the Tree, at Midsummer: fried bread pudding. Strawberries. Cream. Just like 'Ti'-Reine's mother promised her own little girl. Jehannette had eaten then until her stomach ached with never a thought of her father's private war.

And then, her brother Jean had had a sieve with a goatskin stretched over it that he had beaten with their mother's kitchen spoon. Pierre had had a whistle on which he lightly skipped from note to note, not always certain of the tune, but always high and sweet.

Catherine had been so flushed with health, so pretty on her little white feet, every movement so graceful, so *alive*. Ah, God, but Jehannette had danced that day. On other occasions, she refused to dance. Her square limbs weren't meant for such display, she knew that. She always felt gross and awkward, especially next to Catherine. But that last Midsummer she had danced, because not to do so had seemed blasphemy, crushing the life within her, asking death to come.

"Death and life are a dance. Always closely intertwined. Where life is the most strong, death is also there."

Jehannette quickly returned her gaze to Père Michel. How had he known what she was thinking? Had he read her thoughts? Or had she read his?

"And bodies not made for dancing," he added as if in confirmation of her unspoken questions—and this time she saw his lips move—"certainly have other gifts. Gifts the world cries out for."

Jehannette laughed nervously and tried to move the subject to less painful ground. "It was so kind of you, Father, to come so far to bury my poor sister."

"We all do what we can, Jehannette, when life shows its underside."

"Of course you would come, for her. Everyone would come for a girl so pretty, so dainty. So *good*."

"Had it only been Catherine, Jehannette, I don't know if I'd have made the effort to come. Others have died of this fever, too, in villages closer to my hermitage at Bermont. Besides, what need have the dead for special comfort, feeling the embrace of our Mother Earth about them? Feeling at last the pain and suffering steeping out of their bodies and into Hers?"

Jehannette had never heard such theology from a priest before. She'd never heard it from anyone before, but it was as if she'd always known it, in every fiber of her being that had ever felt life, and with it, life's pain. She knew he spoke truth.

Then he said, "I came because she was your sister. *Your* sister, Jehannette. Because you still live. And because you are you."

She blinked at him, astonished. New tears crept into the corners of her eyes, the pain of years of wanting to be loved and understood suddenly embraced, soothed, and answered. But she would not believe it. She could not. And to be teased here, where she was most vulnerable, made the suppressed feelings explode within her.

"Don't lie to me."

"I'm not lying, Jehannette."

"You are. Nobody would come for me!" she exclaimed. "A girl who can't spin. Who likes nothing better than to ride and climb trees. Who is slow to be a woman in any way. Who feels the drum of battle in her and who would rather lay about herself with a distaff than . . ."

Jehannette stopped too late, realizing she had taken the distaff up as her lance again and swung it. Père Michel only saved himself by a quick and skillful parry with his own staff. Their eyes locked for a moment, like the strain of wood against wood in their hands.

Jehannette gave in first, letting eyes and distaff sink together. She only waited for breath before she surely must take the horse and go home.

Père Michel broke the silence quietly. "You do like to fight, don't you?"

She couldn't answer.

"And you're good at it," he said, quite merrily.

"Hateful, hateful!" Fury blinded her and she threw the distaff from her toward a chest-high bush. Had the distaff truly been a lance and the bush an enemy, she would have pierced him through the heart. The thought gave her little comfort, however.

"Not so, Jehannette. Say 'wonderful' instead."

He was, indeed, looking at her as if at a miracle. It occurred to her that he might be mad. Hermits sometimes were.

"Aye, wonderful, indeed," she countered. "Like a freak and the devil's work."

Père Michel nodded at this as if she'd said something very wise. "Now, Jehannette. Would you or your parents or anyone find your talents—" He nodded toward the horse, then the distaff-pierced bush fading into the twilight. "—hateful if they came in your brothers?"

"No."

"Of course not. These are violent, insecure times."

"But that's just the point. In a boy, they're fine. In a girl, hateful. Like a crowing hen—first to be taken for the pot—or a pig that can fly."

"Flying pigs are the stuff of legends, Jehannette. Wonderful. And so are you."

"I ought to have died in Catherine's place. Nay, truly." She stopped his mouth half open by the force of her continuing speech. "Like some sort of monster with two heads who cannot live. The devil's work."

"A priest told you this?"

"Yes. Père Minet."

"God rest him. Well, you must learn that I am not like other priests. It's not the devil's work, Jehannette—at least, not the devil as Père Minet meant."

"I don't understand you."

"Surely it is God's work that took your sister—"

"Took good, sweet Catherine?"

"And spared you, from the same bed. Or from the same grinding mill, as the Evangelists say."

"A curse on you for saying so."

Père Michel swallowed. He obviously believed such a curse could in fact take effect. He even made a sign against it, raising his end fingers again like horns.

"I . . . I'm sorry," she said. No one had ever taken her curses seriously before.

Père Michel went on, obviously relieved that she'd released him of the power of her words. "Think, child. I know she was your only sister, and for that I am sorry. For that, I came to be with you. But the world is full of women who can be your sisters. As the world is full of sweet-tempered, pretty girls anxious to do their parents', brothers', husbands' bidding. And the world is full of young men anxious to prove themselves on the battlefield. Such people are the everyday fabric of the world, like sturdy hemp to be worn and worked in and, when old and torn, turned into rags."

"Whereas I am good for nothing."

"Not so practical for every day, perhaps, but you, a girl who can fight—what magic you'd bring to the battlefield. Magic, pure and simple. You are something that happens—ah, but rarely. Like some precious gem holding such power . . ."

Words seemed to fail him at the thought. He'd said he was unlike other priests and she saw now that this was true. No other priest—no other person she'd ever met, in fact—would have told her such things. They settled like softest down about her wearied heart.

And yet she couldn't escape a nagging doubt.

No other priest had ever revered the Lady Tree like this. In fact, Père Minet had forbidden the dances during his days and the people had only started up the practice again after his demise, returning to a holiness that could be pruned but never rooted out. A holiness—or was it, as the dead priest had said, an original sin? Could it possibly be good that Père Michel obviously thought well of this Tree?

"So what am I supposed to do, Père Michel?" she asked. "Run off to the wars? Like my father's seen in his nightmares? It would kill him. Or he would kill me."

Père Michel nodded, thoughtful. "You will know what to do," he said. "In time."

"How?"

"You have your Voices."

He knew. How could he? No one knew. She'd told no one. It was one thing to know about the riding, the fighting. Her name was a byword in the village and obviously beyond. But her Voices. No one knew. No one could know. They were hers.

She was on her feet now, pacing across the uneven ground

in the dark. "How?" she hissed at him. "How do you know?"

"Jehannette, calm. Jehannette, my child, I've known about you—about them—since before you were born."

"How?" she screamed.

"There's an old prophecy. Given by the great magician Merlin in ancient days. That when Mother Earth most needs aid, a Maid shall come from the Bois Chênu."

"La Pucelle." As she said the name, the whole span of her back seemed to crumple in on itself with shivers.

"That's right. Your know the prophecy, then?"

"The story. The myth."

"It is not a myth. Once, I might have thought so myself. But when I look at you, Jehannette, I know—"

"No" managed to work its way out of her strangled throat.

"I was sent to this place, years ago, by my master for this very purpose. To watch for this Maid, to help her. Now is the time. You are the—"

"No! No, I am not a myth. I am real."

"So you are. So is the mark on your neck, the sign the God marked you with from birth."

Jehannette rubbed at the mark. She usually thought nothing of it, since she herself couldn't see it. Even her brothers had stopped teasing her about it long ago.

"How can I be La Pucelle?" she asked. "Do all that the myth says? It's impossible. You might as well say—you might as well say I'm—I'm the Antichrist."

"Yes. So you might."

"Prophecy—no longer. But real." Her back clamped in shivers again. "But I'm good. I always try to be good."

"So you do, Jehannette. *Sage. Sage,* in all its meanings."

"No." She shook her head violently and backed away. "I'm not your Maid. I am nobody's Maid. And my Voices aren't yours, either."

"I have watched you, Jehannette. I heard of your birth clear on the other side of France and beyond. Many, many people awaited your birth, foretold in the prophecy. When I was a child, younger than you are now, I went to Brittany."

"I know nothing of Brittany."

"It is another land, far to the west. Outside France. An ancient land, where ancient treasures of wisdom are kept as in a strongbox, surrounded by ocean's waves. There I studied under a great and wise Master who first taught me to watch for you. And I turned around and taught a pair of young lads who also have to do with the prophecy, as helpers to you, and one of them Saw your birth, told us of it, and I came the moment I heard it. To watch over your growing, Jehannette, and . . ."

"No, no. You have not the control of my life." She knew now, as he said it, that this was the thing she feared most in the world.

"Of course not."

"This is my life."

"Of course it is."

"No, no. I hear you. I hear you calling me a wonder, a precious jewel, and I know. Nobody steals everyday woolens. But jewels—jewels are guarded and kept and fought for and stolen. I would give what I have to no one. No one, do you hear?"

"I hear, Jehannette. I never . . ."

"And my Voices are mine."

"Of course. But they are a gift that others should share."

"No. Others will try to steal them, force them, make them say other than . . ."

"Than your will?"

"By the flight of the swallows, the little martinets, they don't speak *my* will."

"What do they speak?"

"They speak . . ." She'd never put it into words before. They burned her tongue with holiness. "They come from my Lord."

"And who is your Lord, Jehannette?"

"The King. The King of Heaven."

It had grown too dark to see his features, but it seemed Père Michel nodded gravely. "But of course. And all the world with their stopped-up ears waits to hear, Jehannette, what you would . . ."

"No."

She heard her voice pierce the deepening starlight overhead

and the core of her own heart. She was running now, running toward old Grison who started and snorted at her approach.

But Père Michel was close behind her. He'd pulled the distaff out of the slain bush and tried to hand it to her. She planted both her hands firmly on the horse's side instead. If she let go, she felt, her fists would fly at the priest's face.

"Your Voices are yours," he was saying. "No one is trying to take them from you and no one is trying to make them say other than what they say. But if they should tell you to fight . . ."

"No!"

"The world has need of you. This valley has need of you, the wonder of a warrior Maid."

"No!"

She longed to hear the Voices now, to drown out this madman, but she did not. The hermit was talking too much, too persistently. Surely they would tell her to ride, now, if they'd ever told her anything.

She pulled herself onto Grison's back, then reluctantly, ungratefully, snatched the distaff out of Père Michel's hands. The tow was all gone now, a day's full work of carding. Only the bands that had once bound it hung limply from the point. Oh, curse it. She hated carding worse than spinning.

"During the twelve days of Christmas—on a Thursday night—" Père Michel was saying some madness about Christmas. "We do battle then, good against evil."

"Good always wins, I suppose." She turned the horse's head, thinking she knew the answer.

"No. Sometimes one, sometimes the other."

She had honestly meant to be riding away by this time, but his words—again, unlike any priest's she'd ever heard—held her as fast as iron bands. Grison seemed to have grown equally stubborn.

"That's the way of the world," the priest said. "Light and darkness, male and female, life and death, good and evil."

"Like the martinets and the mosquitoes." She couldn't keep from continuing his list in a whisper. She was frantic that the darkness revealed so little of his face.

Only the disembodied voice.

"Come to us then."

"How? How will I know? And where?" She hadn't been paying too much attention. She realized now she'd been too angry.

"You'll know. If it's meant to be, your Voices will tell you and nothing you or I can do or say will stop this will of heaven."

"No." She protested again and dug her heels into Grison's sides.

"Be good, Jehannette," Père Michel called after her.

Just like *them*.

"How can I?" she shouted, but she doubted he could hear her over the pound of horse's hooves down the narrow road. "How can I be good?" And why should I be, since the way of the world is balance and the desire for too much good creates evil in its wake?

The old man was a fool. Yet a dangerous fool, for he knew too much.

And it was very unnerving, for from that day forward, another of the Voices also had a name.

It was, like the archangel, Michel.

18

Black Robes Rimed with Butterfly Silver

———◆———

Yuletide, which had seemed so far away in July when Catherine lay newly dead, came with surprising rapidity. The bad weather made travel worse for armies, which made it better for men of God; the priest came from Vaucouleurs to celebrate the season. Father Guillaume Frontey had not made it by Christmas Day, having too great and too neglected a flock between the fortress and Domrémy. But he did celebrate high mass in the little church a stone's throw from Jehannette's father's house three days later, on the Feast of the Holy Innocents. She, like every other person in the village, attended, after having her soul shriven early the morning before.

In July, she'd thought the intervening months would surely dull the memory of her last conversation with a priest, with Père Michel. But they had not. Then she wondered if she ought to confess one confessor to the other and perhaps that would expunge the memory. But her Voices had held her tongue in the presence of Père Frontey. She'd only been able to say, "I danced under the Lady Tree on Midsummer's Day."

"You and the rest of the deluded village," the priest had muttered. "They call it 'esbattre,' to relax. But it is akin to the Sabbath of the deluded Jews. A Sabbath of the witches."

Then, "Be good, child," he'd said, not even remembering her name after so many others in the past week.

He'd absolved her for fifty *Aves*. She didn't remember what an *Ave* was, but hadn't wanted to cause more trouble by asking him.

Then he'd shifted his stole against the draft leaking through Saint-Rémy's stone walls, squinted his bad, molelike eyes, and called, "Next!"

Neither that absolution nor a mouthful of sanctified wafer had done anything to dull Père Michel's words in her head, "Come, fight with us at Yuletide."

She hadn't seen Père Michel since, but now even her own Voices seemed to have taken up the chant—sometimes. She had no idea where the battle was to take place. That was a good thing. She wouldn't be tempted to go if she didn't know the field.

But, "You'll know," Père Michel had told her.

Four days had passed now since Père Frontey had left to visit other members of his wide-flung flock. The season was passing quickly. It was Thursday now, a week after Christmas, but still within the twelve days of celebration. She'd thought—when Mother's Night, the first night, had hit her with the unnameable urge, the Voices so tantalizing, so persistent in her head—that each day of the twelve must get easier to resist. She'd hoped. But she'd been wrong.

Resist what? She couldn't say. Only the battle drums in her head, drowning out anything else. The cry, "On! Strike! Win!"

All day she'd been unable to sit and spin, although that was what her mother expected and it was a perfect day for it, with a storm blowing in out of the northwest. The distaff would not stay vertical in her hands. Time and again, it dropped to the threat, the parry. It almost leaped of its own accord at every shadow that moved in the day's half light. Her brothers never knew how close they came to getting spiked—for no other reason than that they passed through the room.

Now that supper was over—Jehannette hadn't eaten a thing—she was glad to be able to change distaff for broom. Then she discovered the broom had even more life to it. Every time it caught on the slightest unevenness in the creamy white flags, it skipped up, almost to shoulder height.

Her mother merely credited the jumps and bumps to an extra vigor in her daughter's sweeping tonight.

"Yes, child."

Zabillet Romée nodded and turned to light the wick in the single bowl of oil at chin height to the left of the fireplace. She pulled her chair up close to the golden glow to finish some needlework before damping down the fire and calling it a night.

"The Good Neighbors bless a clean house at Twelfth Night."

Zabillet spoke with a little sparkle in her voice. She didn't really believe in these supernatural visitors. Not honestly, though she was pleased enough to use them to induce her children to good behavior, even now that they were almost grown.

Zabillet might not believe in them, but suddenly, her daughter did, more than she believed in her own life. Something— *something* was imminent, name it what her mother would.

Jehannette swept faster now, trying to work the same methodical pattern she always did, but the broom simply would not let her. And when she reached the door, no hens greeted her to squabble over the sweepings—they'd already gone to their coop on this short, threatening evening. The wind took her little pile of dust and crumbs without her effort. The broom's tight bundle of twigs nearly swept her off and through the yard to the gate with it. Her skirt—still red—billowed like the sails of a windmill going at full tilt. Her breath went before her, riverward.

Throwing every bit of her strength into the effort, Jehannette struggled the door closed—with herself on the houseward side of it. The moment she dropped contact with the door, however, it burst the latch and blew in again. She threw herself against the heavy oaken slats, only to meet with stronger resistance— and a groan. Her father, returned from a last look around at the beasts to see all was secure for the night, was trying to get in and she'd slammed the door right on him. Quickly she yanked it open again—and felt the tug of the night behind him.

"Going somewhere?" he demanded gruffly.

"No, of course not, Papa." Jehannette knew her protest came

too fast. Still too quickly, she tried to change the subject. "I'm sorry. I never meant to shut you out."

Jacquot d'Arc stood in the doorway he would have to stoop to enter, working the mud off his wood-soled boots and panting from his own exertions against the approaching storm. He squinted, eyeing his flustered daughter carefully.

"No matter," he said. "I've been shut out before. Yes, my dear. I've been shut out before."

Jehannette could tell by his tone that she should pay attention. He was telling her more about his past with those words than she'd ever heard, or was likely to hear again. But her urge to sweep him before her with the broom and dive for the gaps of open space on either side took all her effort to resist.

Her father looked at her hard, again, and seemed to comprehend—something, at least. Deliberately, he stepped over the threshold, stooping, and deliberately he turned and closed the door. Then he picked up the beam that stood propped in the corner, so little used that a spider scurried out from behind it into his daughter's newly swept room. He slid the bar to in its brackets across the door and turned to look at her again—no more friendly than before.

"Never mind, Jacquot," her mother said, looking from one to the other with concern her tone tried to cover. "Children are always restless before a storm."

"I think . . . I think I should go to bed," Jehannette said. "I'm . . . I'm a little tired."

"You must finish this bobbin first," her mother said.

"Let the girl go," her father said, never loosing her from the grip of his gaze for a moment.

Jehannette set the broom in its corner and hurried past the open wooden stair to the bake room in the back of the house.

She undressed quickly in the dark, setting the caul's blue sash carefully in its place on the shelf, and climbed into bed. She still hadn't grown used to how big the bed was without Catherine to share it, how empty. How cold on this night when her mother had not baked. She thought of going back out to the main room for a stone wrapped in a scrap of wool to warm her feet. But if she did, she doubted if even her father could keep her from throwing the bar and running out into the night. Every speck of her energy, she decided, must go into keeping herself flat on her back in bed.

The ring on her hand—the ring her parents had given her, etched with the names of Jesus and Mary—seemed to help, pinning her to the straw-stuffed mattress. Jehannette remembered how her mother had told her they'd gotten that ring from Père Minet when she was a baby.

That ring was a strong force. But there was a contrary force in the room, joining with the sound of the wind, to all but send her floating. She determined at last that this must be the woolen sash on the shelf above her head, the sash containing the caul that had covered her face when she'd been born.

"It very nearly smothered you," her mother had always said, and gave the impression that it was an evil thing. "The priest gave us the ring to counteract it, and we passed the birth caul through its counterspell of 'Jhesus—Maria'—while the membrane was still flexible enough to curl so."

But the midwife had kept the caul, telling Zabillet she must guard it with care, that it must go with her daughter to the grave.

"And it will make her one of the Good Folk, teach her to fly."

That's how her mother always reported the sage woman's words. What they might mean, Jehannette hadn't any notion, though they always gave her a vague shiver. She especially shivered when she remembered the time she'd secretly unpicked her mother's tiny, even stitches to take a look at the caul—what was left of it. It was hard to think of it, dry, white, shriveled, except as something for the dung heap. The sloppy crisscross of stitches with which she'd replaced her mother's work would fool no one.

Still, she hadn't gained any notion what the midwife's words might mean.

Until tonight.

Now the voice of the caul seemed to whisper to her, like a leaf in the wind.

She lay listening to the wind and was still cold when she

heard the storm hit. None of her energy, from the first, had gone to warming the sheets. Then she began to confuse the sound with that of her Voices.

"Jehannette, Jehannette. Daughter-God."

Her tiny, head-sized window rattled in its thick wooden frame as it took the first heavy drops of rain. The steep slope of the roof over her head seemed to funnel the blast straight at her.

"Jehannette. Rise. Fight."

She gasped with the effort of keeping prone.

And then, suddenly, it seemed she fell asleep, though how sleep could come through such tension and noisy confusion bewildered her. Besides, she'd never dreamed so vividly.

Still, as in dreams, she found herself unable to move. The force that had tried to lift her from the crackling straw of her mattress before, now pressed her into it. She could feel the network of ropes beneath the sack of straw etching itself into her back. The weight on her chest forbade her any breath but shallow little gasps. Something thicker than vapor infested her lungs, crawled through the shallow gulps of air. In a moment, she learned what it was as each breath coughed out a tiny white butterfly.

A dozen white butterflies, more, began to test their wings in the air about her head. She had no trouble seeing them in the dark, for their delicate white membranes glowed with their own deep sources of blue-white light. Flying together, they looked, in fact, exactly like the caul.

The mist of insects soon rose off her, taking, as it seemed, her breath and soul with them. They fluttered at the window and with their many eyes she was able to peer down into the back alley between her house and the neighbor's barn.

That was when she saw them. The fairies' cavalcade, the Good Neighbors, riding at a steady pace through the narrow pinch of road—coming toward her from the graveyard.

Catherine was the first she recognized. It was the honey-colored hair she knew and nothing else, for the curls grew out of the white bone of a death's head, grinning wildly like lips blown back against the wind. A withered chain of daisies crowned the hair still and her sister's shroud whipped around her like the very source of the storm.

But there were others in the horde, many others, many she knew nothing of, some she remembered more vaguely of Domrémy's departed. Each rode swiftly—none touched the ground, she saw—mounted on some strange beast or other. Some rode pigs, some wolves. Catherine clung to a mane that was the tow of a spindle she'd always known how to harness so well in life. Some needed no more than the long bones of a beast, as dead as themselves, to reconjure swiftness. One rode a fire shovel, one the twisted, blasted branch of a tree, one old woman a broom. Some had even saddled the backs of children, human children . . . Their sound was the howl of the storm . . .

Then Jehannette saw through butterfly eyes that not all the crowd were dead. She'd missed them at first, the live ones, for their numbers were not great, six or seven, no more, in the press of hundreds. These carried torches to help their mortal eyes. The dead, of course, needed no such aid. The mortals were armed with fennel stalk, thick sheaves of it bundled together. Fennel was the smell of the night, that sweetness mixed with the pitch of the torches, the mustiness of the grave, and the sharp bite of the rain.

Jehannette couldn't recognize any of the mortals. Each was masked as some beast: this one a cow, this one wore the bushy tail of a fox. Here waved a goose's feather, here walked a sow, and they danced and squealed and grunted and gyrated like the creatures they portrayed. But she thought she ought to know them. They must be her neighbors, the good folk of Domrémy. And some of nearby Greux had joined them, too, she was convinced, though not many. And who, she still didn't know.

Except the mortal in the lead. She'd missed him at first, but now she returned to that point again and saw him. And recognized at once the black hermit's robes beneath a crown of branching antlers. Père Michel led the cavalcade, torch streaming sparks behind him and, in the other hand, an iron whip.

The tiny window of her room never would have allowed

Jehannette such a wide view of all the party, stretching as it did in a jostling, neighing, shrieking, laughing, clomping train from the fern-topped walls of the cemetery to her own front gate. It was this thought that made her realize the butterflies had pressed through the cracks in the window's thick wooden planks on her gasping breath. They swarmed now over the alleyway and showed her Père Michel striding up to her father's door. He pounded on it with the iron of his whip.

"Jehannette!" he cried. "Jehannette, come ride with us." Again he pounded. Her butterfly light rimed his black robes with silver. "Come fight. Our side needs you. Come!"

Jehannette tried to leap from her bed like a martinet after bugs, and yet, she couldn't move a muscle. There was only the flutter of butterfly wings.

She heard her father's growl, just through the plaster wall beyond her icy feet.

"Who's there at this hour on such a night?"

"It's I, Père Michel. The Horned One. I've come for Jehannette to do Night Battle with us, with all the good folk."

"My daughter doesn't fight."

Jehannette could see her father there, a small figure just struggling into his shirt, struggling for a light. He didn't open the door but peered out of the milky parchment in a window, trying to see something against the dark and the storm. She could tell he couldn't see the dead, he couldn't see his own daughter Catherine. He could see the priest only as a dark blur stuck with antlers. So they stood on either side of the door, the blur of black and the blur of white, offsetting one another.

"She was born with the caul," the dark figure said. "She is the one they call La Pucelle."

"Be off with you, madman."

"Let her decide for herself, Jacquot d'Arc. Jehannette," Père Michel cried against the rain and her father's curses, raising his branching head to where all the little butterflies fluttered on the roof above him.

"Off with you, cursed heathen, or I'll come at you with my pitchfork."

"Your arm and pitchfork would be welcome, too, Jacquot d'Arc, if you'd come."

"I'll see you rot in hell first, horned devil."

"And you the one with the pitchfork. Domrémy hasn't won a single Night Battle these eight or ten years. Our numbers are sorely depleted. We could use you. And your sons."

"You certainly shall not have my daughter. Over my dead body. Over hers, as I live."

Jehannette felt she must in fact be dead, her soul torn in two by the combatting forces that grabbed it by either end.

But then she saw a smile spread across the face Père Michel lifted upward to catch raindrops beneath a fringe of brown deer hide. Her father didn't see, but Père Michel did. He recognized her before she recognized herself, threaded through his antlers like a swarm of butterflies.

19

A Hundred Threadlike Feet Clinging to Antlers

"Ah, Jehannette."

Père Michel's voice was suddenly kind and low enough that her father must hear no more than a murmur. "I knew you would come. Wild horses couldn't keep you away."

That last was a joke. He said it with a toss of his crown—and her, clinging with a hundred threadlike feet to the antlers. The gesture was in the direction of the truly remarkable cavalcade that continued to chomp and howl and cavort at his heels.

Whip held high, Père Michel passed through the company and led them out of Jacquot d'Arc's yard. They turned right into the road and followed it the brief way down toward the River Meuse.

"This way won't do," Jehannette said in a flutter of tiny butterfly voices. "The bridge is too long neglected. Nobody comes this way since the war began and the Burgundians tightened their reins across the road. The bridge's rotted boards will not carry a great horde like this."

"Never you mind about the bridge," Père Michel laughed.

The next moment, the entire cavalcade came crashing after him, down through the reeds and nettles of the bank made unstable by too much water. Père Michel waded in at the edge, struck the surface with the iron tip of his whip, and the river parted. The army crossed on dry land.

The cavalcade from Maxey was waiting for them halfway between the villages. They'd struck their own torches into the mud of a wheat-sown field and their leader, brave in the great horns of a bull, stepped forward to greet Père Michel.

"Come to try for this again?"

The bull's voice was deep but remarkably jovial, Jehannette thought, for a Burgundian. He held "this" aloft. All jostled one another in their attempt to see, striving for the best footing to start. "This" was a ball about the size of a man's head. Its patches of light and dark leather mimicked the bones and hollows of a skull. Wheat seed had been stuffed into its broad stitching, sprinkled with water and allowed to sprout. If this stubble did not make the skull seem more alive, it was the perfect emblem—of course it was meant to be—of fertility.

"I'm surprised you don't just give up," the bull taunted, "since long ago the Lord of Bourlémont granted the relics of St. Catherine to us."

"Never!" cried the combined forces of Greux and Domrémy, who were outnumbered by the mortals from Maxey by at least four souls. Counting the dead, however, the sides were nearly even. And the two sides were companionable about this early banter, greeting these close neighbors that mundane differences had kept apart for a full year.

As their greetings concluded, the men shuffled around until each group faced its own home village. Over the river, Domrémy was completely smudged out by trees and storm and darkness. But everyone knew what he was fighting for without sight.

"Very well." The bull shrugged and, then, tossed the ball down between the two sides.

The battle began with a roar that rang from one side of the valley to the other. There were no rules, no rests, no safety, no quarter. Domrémy's fennel answered bundles of Maxey's. Blows to the mask of the man with the ball were perfectly legitimate, as were gouges to the eyes and tripping into the mud that grew deeper and deeper as the storm howled on.

And the dead fought just as bravely for the fertility of their descendants as the mortals did for themselves. They swung bones—which, true, felt hardly different from the pass of sharp wind—charged on their wild beasts, howled, tore with their grinning skull's teeth and tied the enemy up in lengths of mud-weighted shroud.

At first, Jehannette fluttered, panting, over the field, beating her many wings in terror and confusion. What could she do, in such tiny, insect form as she was? Her real body, the body that wanted to fight, that had fight in its every sinew, lay senseless back home in her bed. And what could such tiny wings and legs do against such burly men, used to hefting hay if not to dealing blows? These Night Battlers probably didn't notice her any more than her father had.

Then she saw Père Michel set upon by six men of Maxey all at once, his protective horns knocked off and trampled in the mud. Without thought, she swept down into the fray. She flapped her wings in one man's eyes, crept up the nose of another, working her way over the acrid sweat between his face and his concealing mask. Seeing a ripped shoulder in one man's tunic, she entered there with thirty-two tickling legs. Then, clumping the rest of herself together, she suddenly burst up and apart like fired powder, blowing the startled men back on their rears in the mud.

"Well done, Daughter-God," Père Michel called. She didn't have time to wonder how he knew to call her that.

It didn't take her Voices—Michel, Catherine, and the other—long to arrive.

"Yes, Daughter-God," they whistled like the wind in her ear. "This is what you were born for."

Even as butterflies, her every move was the perfect thrust to every parry, the best feint to every attack. And her airiness served as a stealthy disguise, even when these people, these folk driven out among the dead on a winter's night to fight, could both see and, more importantly, feel her very well.

Soon her tiny muscles sang with the effort, the red of battle swam before every insect eye, every antenna vibrated with the effort—and the thrill.

"Well done," called the ever-sweet Catherine. "Well done."

"Onward," shouted Michel with a bray of trumpet.

"More, more," said the Other in the patter of rain.

Storm and battle raged all night, but Jehannette herself was hardly aware of the passage of time. She didn't even hear the telltale noise, her tiny heads too throbbing with the screams and batterings of war, of her Voices.

But she did notice when the man—whose swinging fennel, battered now to splinters, she was avoiding with a pretty little dance—suddenly dropped his weapon to the mud. He cried out, "Ah, the cock!"

"Aye, aye, I hear him crow," answered a second, dropping his weapon as well.

"The game's up."

"The battle's over."

"I can hardly believe my own ears," said another. "But I do think it's a Domrémy cock who first stands his guard."

"Old Jacquot d'Arc's bird, if I mistake not."

Jehannette knew it was their cock, by the little growl of a sigh he always put in at the end of his "cocorico." Other cocks answered from here, then there.

"Well, that's the first time in years we've been close enough to *your* village to hear that, old man," bleated a man from Maxey, pulling off a sheep's head mask to reveal the natural grizzled stubble on his chin.

And being closer to one village than another was how they determined the winner.

"Not since old Bourlémont gave *you* the chapel, against all tradition." An old goose-wife from Greux honked this quite personally to the red fox from Maxey, a very young man, as it appeared.

"Yes," bellowed the bull, "I do confess. Domrémy, Greux, you have the best of it this year."

Looking around, Jehannette saw that not a one of the dead remained—unless it were in the mist that had begun to slowly wind up from the field like the shreds of some great and moth-eaten shroud. The storm had ceased, leaving bands of slick silver turning to frost on the furrows. Her butterfly wings shuddered, feeling the cold for the first time.

"I give you twenty paces next year," the bull continued.

"Only twenty paces?" Père Michel demanded. "Say forty at least."

"Isn't it enough that I concede to you?"

"Aye, well done. Well fought, my friend."

"Domrémy has the fertility for the year!"

When the echoing cheers died down, one man from Maxey said, "You won't forget us in your prosperity, Domrémy, will you?"

"Of course not. It's the winner's duty—their honor—to share with the losers."

And another man from Domrémy—Jehannette recognized the voice as Old Gaspar's—said, "We'll be as generous to you as ever you were to us when you were winners."

"Times have been hard," Maxey replied. "The war and all."

"That's no excuse," and "What has some petty war between France and Burgundy to do with Good Neighbors?" Domrémy replied.

Maxey agreed and swore to do better.

In the grey of dawn and the light of the storm sluicing off the horizon east and south, Jehannette saw bloodied heads on each side. One man from Domrémy thought he might have broken a wrist. It was badly sprained in any case, and a bonesetter from Maxey offered to go home with him and take a closer look. Yes, even if it meant crossing the border bridge out of Burgundy.

Then, after bear hugs and slaps on the back all up and down both sides, the people parted with promises to "Meet again next Yuletide" if not before.

Only Père Michel stayed behind, still sitting where he'd dropped at the spell-releasing cock crow. Mud caked him from head to toe except where it ran in rivulets of blood from a gash in his left temple. Carefully, he picked the stag-horned helmet up out of the churned field beside him. One of its tines had broken off, also on the left, perhaps even as it had gouged him in falling.

"Ah, Lord," he said, puffing the breath out so it raised the mud-clotted beard on his cheeks like toadstools. He spoke half to himself, half to the emptiness beneath the horn-crown where his face had been. "I'm getting too old for such sport."

Jehannette spread her wings to the blush of dawn and flew

up to kiss the wound with her many pairs of tiny legs and the curl of her hollow tongues.

"You've a healing touch, my wonderful girl," Père Michel sighed.

But Jehannette suddenly found that, with the battle gone, so was every rivet of her strength. It occurred to her that she had never before seen butterflies at this season, and for good cause. Her wings were tattered and waterlogged. Her thin limbs were growing rigid. Some of her number had even fallen into the clods and were so weighted now that there was no hope that they might fly again. They twitched there, just at the edge of life.

Père Michel saw her distress and quickly forgot his own. "Come on, little one," he said. "Let's get you home to bed, Daughter-God."

He got up and collected every last petal he could find of the membrane of her soul. Then he laid them most gently within his robe where they clung trembling to the hairs of his chest.

Darkness closed over Jehannette and she couldn't see anything more. But she could still feel his life-saving warmth, the pump of his heart and the great bellows of his lungs. She could smell and taste the salt sweat of his exertions.

"You fought very well, Jehannette," rumbled the voice deep from the chest beneath her. "I must credit you with Domrémy's victory this night. I knew you were born for it."

"I am happy to help good triumph," she managed to answer back.

"Ah, but I would not call it good, little one."

"No? I want always to be on the side of good—if I'm to fight."

"Domrémy has won against Maxey."

"That is good."

"The prize is fertility."

"That is good," she said again.

"If the rats are fertile, is that good?"

"I see. Good for the cat, perhaps. Not good for the people."
She spoke thoughtfully, drifting into dreams and remembering

the flight of the martinets and the itch of summer mosquito bites.

"And what is good for Domrémy is not necessarily good for Maxey."

"But I live in Domrémy."

"And are you all the world?"

"No."

"No," Père Michel agreed.

Jehannette wondered if this was her Voice named Michel now or just the old hermit. How closely did she have to listen! Her reeling head didn't want to listen at all.

"The best good is balanced, taking the good with the bad, life with the death, embracing the whole."

"I see," she said.

And thought that, even if it were death embracing her now, she truly did see what the old man meant.

20

The Tug of the Night

Jehannette awoke much later in her own room with her mother
and Père Michel hovering at her side.

Père Michel caught her stirrings of life and said, "There,
you see, goodwife? All will be well with her. You need not
fear to lose another daughter. Not in this bed, in any case."

Zabillet Romée sniffed skeptically at the hermit's words and
bundled another wool-wrapped stone up against her daughter's
toes.

She said, "I never would have called you, Father, if she
hadn't seemed bewitched. Open eyes, staring. But not moving.
Not even to blink or to say a word."

She held a bowl of warmed wine to her daughter's lips and
Jehannette drank deeply.

Zabillet Romée spoke in a hiss over the bowl. "It takes one
witch, so they say, to remove the spell set by another."

"This 'spell,' as you call it, is not unnatural in your daughter. It is brought on by conflict within her soul."

"What conflict?"

Zabillet struggled to keep her voice down, hoping her
daughter would not hear. And although Jehannette would have
gladly taken more wine, her mother pulled the bowl away
suddenly. Hauling Père Michel by one loose black sleeve as
far as she could away from the bed, she let her words melt in
his ear, "What has my daughter done so evil that could cause
such a thing?"

"Not evil, goodwife."

Père Michel felt no compunction to keep his words down. Lying still, almost slipping back into trance again with her effort to hear, Jehannette thought it must be the priest who, by some unnatural means, relayed her mother's words to her as well.

"Say rather," Père Michel continued, choosing his words with concern, "say rather a conflict between two goods."

"The Lord knows I've always done my best to tell her to be good."

"Of course you have, like any careful mother. But what you tell her with the best of will may be at odds with what her own—her own soul tells her."

"She does have a rebellious soul. I've done my best, but . . ." Zabillet dissolved suddenly into tears.

"Consider this." Père Michel spoke in the most soothing tone. "Consider that she was born to fight in the Night Battles with the Good Neighbors."

Zabillet shook her head but couldn't give the gesture words.

"Many are, surely you know that. Born for this, feeling the pull of the Night with every fiber of her being. Yet she stayed in this bed, as she knew a good daughter must. You saw her, lying here. But I saw her, too, out in the field, fighting like a de—Like an angel."

"No."

"Splitting her soul like that, being in two places at once, has caused this long trance. I know folk born with this gift— usually the elderly, who no longer wish to risk their fragile bodies on this pious errand—who lie in bed and send their souls every year. Their trance is not so long, for they have not had conflict with themselves over what they ought to do. Even the younger ones who go in the flesh must usually sleep the exertions off in what seems very like a trance. In your Jehannette's case, you must give soul and body time to find themselves once more after such a wrenching. Truly, you have done so and now all will be well."

"Next year—" Zabillet stammered.

"Next year, if you give your blessing to her going, her soul will not be so—so dangerously wrenched."

"No. I cannot."

"Well, think on it. Pray on it, if you will."

If it hadn't been for the bowl of wine between them, Zabillet's hands would already have been praying. Père Michel caught them between his own and gave them an encouraging squeeze. The mother seemed to gather something from the mingling of their gazes, enough to return her to her daughter's bed and offer her more wine.

"Perhaps it will comfort you more if I tell you—" He considered aloud and then decided. "Yes. I know a young man in France—now become a priest as I am—who is subject to fits much more frequently and distressing than this."

"Say not so here. The mere mention of them might send them into my daughter."

Zabillet was so fierce, she poured the wine faster than her daughter could drink. Wine burned up into Jehannette's nose and she sputtered and choked. Doubtless this confirmed her mother's worst fears.

Père Michel wrapped his great arms around Jehannette's shoulders and helped her to sit up more solidly. Her choking eased in this very unmagical fashion.

"My point in bringing up the case of this boy was to encourage you, goodwife, by helping you to see that what seems to be a curse may in fact be a blessing. By learning to work with his spells, this boy has learned to see with the Second Sight. Good often comes from the seeming bad, that is my point. I wish your daughter could some day meet this boy—well, he is a young man now."

"But if he has entered the priesthood, what good is he to my Jehannette?"

"I'm sorry. I don't know what you mean."

"He's no good to her as a husband, that's what I mean."

"I see. Well, if our Jehannette goes into France, she'll have no need of a husband, I think."

"Go into France? My daughter? Never. Her place is here. France? It would kill her father. Or he would kill her."

"Calm yourself, goodwife. I only wanted to explain to you—"

The priest's eyes glanced over Jehannette's head. She knew what was there. The sash.

"Your daughter was born with the caul, wasn't she?" he asked.

Zabillet shot an anxious glance at the ring on her daughter's finger. "What of it?" she said. "We kept it carefully. There can be no harm in it."

"No harm at all, goodwife. Only to tell you what you must already know, that your daughter is not like other girls."

"She only needs a stronger hand of discipline."

"I saw her birth with that caul, goodwife. Or actually, that boy did, in a fit, when I was by him. There is an ancient prophecy, goodwife, about a Maid who must come from the Bois Chênu . . ."

A deep angry voice cut into the room. "Get out, hermit, with your prophecies of the Bois Chênu." Jacquot d'Arc's great form made the space small and confining. "Put no such ideas in my daughter's head. She's troubles enough without your interference."

Père Michel bowed so his strange tonsure caught the glow of the oil lamp. "I only wish to thank God and Our Lady that she is not cursed and will recover. Twelfth Night is past now and she is out of danger."

The tonsure vanished around the door frame and through the main room, Jacquot d'Arc's glare following it all the way.

Twelfth Night come and gone? Jehannette thought. Then she had been unconscious a very long time, almost a week. Yes, it was true. It was Epiphany. She could feel it in the lightness of her body, the silence of her Voices.

Yet such was the nature of a year that it always swung round again.

21

Pork and Greens Cozy Together

"Is she all right? I mean, can we talk?"

Gilles de Rais could not keep the annoyance from his voice. It had taken more than an hour of pleasantries—which were anything but pleasant—with his cousin Georges de La Trémoïlle to reach this obvious argument against further confidence. To his usual bolster of food in high quantity and quality, Cousin Georges had added a woman. The baggage sat now, trying to find space for herself on the great hogshead of a thigh.

La Trémoïlle caught the creature about her ample waist, visible through the windows-of-hell cut into her fur-edged overdress. His links-of-sausage fingers must have tickled her. She squirmed and giggled—Gilles hated women's giggles in general and hers were even less becoming because she was not so very young. She was past twenty-five, at least, and had seen some heavy use in bed, if not in childbed.

Under his cousin's grasp, she resettled more firmly. "She's fine," Cousin Georges assured him. Putting one fat finger to equally fat lips, he hushed her. "Like the tomb, right, my cabbage?"

She giggled again and nodded.

La Trémoïlle's endearment brought the image to Gilles' mind: if his cousin were a side of pork, his doxy was the vegetable served alongside it. Her over- and underdress were in complementary shades of green. They were not the green of the coven, however, the sacred color of growing things, but of asparagus forced under sand and boiled beyond recognition. They were cozy on the platter together, pork and greens. If his cousin thought they still could talk, he must trust him. But Gilles could get no appetite. He had more at stake here, after all.

"Somebody has to deal with Pierre de Giac," Gilles said.

What in that sentence made the doxy squirm? He thought he'd chosen his words very carefully. Perhaps it was nothing. He would have been uncomfortable on that slippery thigh himself.

She did have a noble air about her. Of course, a man can dress his lowest-born doxy in finery if he's a mind to, but Gilles had the sense it was more than that in this case.

Nonetheless, she was there, and La Trémoïlle was using her—as a shield as well as a whore?

Gilles chose his next words more carefully still. "Giac keeps you from the inner chambers of the King, and the count and me from making any headway on the battlefield."

"So you've come to see me? Not so much for kinship's sake, I take it, but at the behest of monseigneur le comte de Richemont?"

Gilles shifted under the scrutiny of the small, fat-swathed eyes. He had to force himself to keep from squirming like the woman. His cousin's position hadn't improved much since last they'd met, on the impoverished return from captivity in La Charité-sur-Loire. La Trémoïlle still had wayfarer's rooms. True, they were now in Issoudun, the same small town on the Théols River where the vagabond Dauphin held court.

They must have some basis, these rumors that no one was better poised to fall into the position of chamberlain than Georges de La Trémoïlle—if once Pierre de Giac were pried out. How else than by trading on his expectations had La Trémoïlle raised the funds to take the best rooms in the hostel?

Yet he's making me do all the work, Gilles thought. He has yet to risk any such hint in this conversation himself.

Gilles dampened the exasperation boiling in him by looking elsewhere while he silently wished his cousin and the woman might give each other the plague. This was the Hospice of St. Roch, patron of the plague, after all, this place with mildewed walls and tiles missing from the roof even in the best rooms. The brethren were doubtless glad of La Trémoïlle's business in days like these—when the dead of the battlefield clogged the maw of hell leaving none to die in their beds of disease.

As La Trémoïlle—if he hadn't been invited to take a place within the local castle among Charles' favorites—must be glad for these rooms. Local inns—Gilles knew, for he'd had to patronize them himself—were crowded with petitioners and other would-be favorites. And all were unpleasantly close to the dust and stench of looms and tanneries and cattle markets, Issoudun's livelihood when court moved elsewhere.

So La Trémoïlle had his way with the charitable brethren who kept this house. Well bribed, no doubt, they pulled up their cowls and looked the other way when a woman came in to a man's room.

La Trémoïlle said, "You were speaking of Pierre de Giac, chamberlain to monseigneur le Dauphin's household, I believe?"

Gilles wished to God he could have forced La Trémoïlle to say the words. But, by God, the man was stubborn. He'd have to say them himself.

"He'll have to be—put away."

"I agree."

Gilles breathed a sigh of relief. At least that admission came easily enough. "As monseigneur le comte sees it, we must give every appearance of legality, so as not to lose His Majesty's favor."

"For once, monseigneur le comte and I agree." When Gilles hesitated yet again, his cousin prompted, "What does monseigneur le comte propose?"

"Giac must be arrested and tried." Gilles pointedly ignored the little squeal that came from the woman. "But away from here. Some place where the Dauphin cannot intervene."

"True."

"So it will take some—some skill in the arresting."

"That is where we can trust to you, I hope, Cousin Gilles?"

Gilles bowed but said nothing.

"You—and monseigneur—have a plan?"

"We must have your word not to interfere."

"But of course."

Gilles wished he didn't have to ask for such things. He wished he and Richemont could have kept the entire plan in hands they could trust. He took a breath and said, "We must ask you to bribe the guard. To see that the courtiers are elsewhere."

"In return, I expect you will not interfere when the Dauphin offers me the emptied post."

Gilles bowed again. Another—small—concession.

"To every saint his candle," La Trémoïlle said.

There is no saint here, Gilles' mind lashed out. But he kept it to himself.

"We move tomorrow, Saturday night," he said instead. "The eve of St. John of Matha."

"Good. You waste no time."

"We will need the key to the town gates. So the man can be got quickly away."

"Of course. But I can't help you there, my friend."

"Richemont will ask the gatekeeper for it himself."

"How?"

Gilles hesitated. The less his cousin knew, the better.

"I'd like to know how. I don't want to commit myself to a plan that stinks like week-old fish."

"Monseigneur le comte will say he wants to go before dawn to hear mass at Notre-Dame-de-Bourg-de-Théols—outside the town wall—in honor of the saint's day."

"And will that be the truth?"

"That will be God's truth."

"So monseigneur le comte doesn't even have to sully his lips with a lie." La Trémoïlle considered this a moment, a smile on his own lips, then said: "Good. No one would believe that *I* want to go on the pious but decidedly uncomfortable duty of hearing mass before dawn. Nonetheless, for Richemont, it's the most natural thing in the world."

Gilles had to agree, but he didn't like the tone in which the observation was couched. It also occurred to him: How was a man to tell what was right and wrong in this world? If the most pious of men joined with the least, was that a heinous deed? Or merely a necessary one?

"You will lead the arresting force, Gilles?"

Gilles nodded.

"In person? Archers?"

Another nod.

"Good. Once you get Giac, where are you planning to take him?"

"Dun-le-Roi."

"Yes. The King's name in it, but the town owns first allegiance to Richemont's wife."

Gilles nodded, but wondered just what La Trémoïlle was staking on this gamble. Not much, compared to others. Even Madame de Richemont, the duchess of Guyenne, was staking more. Yet who stood to gain the most?

"That guarantees the trial's bailey will be on our side."

Gilles nodded.

"And the verdict of this trial? How soon?"

"That depends."

"On?"

"On what can be brought against him."

La Trémoïlle's face betrayed that fact that he took it for granted that Giac would lose his head. Gilles ought to warn his cousin that the trial, even out of Charles' control, might not go so well as he hoped.

Gilles said: "Embezzling royal funds should be easy enough to prove. But that's not a capital offense. He will rot in Dun-le-Roi dungeon for a while. More, I cannot promise."

La Trémoïlle shook his head as if to say, Not good enough.

And the doxy, she gave another, sudden squeal. As if he'd poked her.

His cousin's next words seemed to come on a slick of grease. "He's a very prudish man, this count of yours."

Gilles said nothing.

"One wonders why he doesn't roast *you* over hot coals, coz, for your sins."

Yes, how did one tell what was good?

"I have some discretion in my sins," Gilles said.

"Oh, and so have I," La Trémoïlle assured him. "So have I.

"I have great hopes for this collaboration," he went on, as if collaboration and sins were the same. "Richemont's prudery is just what we—what I—will find most useful here."

"Never fear. You take care of the courtiers and the guard. Richemont will get the key." Gilles rose to escape, knowing all the while that to leave this room was to enter inexorably into the plot.

"It's not just the key that interests me."

"No?"

"And of your skill, coz, once you've a sword in your hand, I have no doubt, either."

Gilles couldn't quite take that as flattery and still kept the door as his goal. "Well?"

"It should prove a very interesting trial," La Trémoïlle said, "Richemont being present, when he discovers evidence that Giac has dabbled in witchcraft."

Gilles turned back to the room, his hand reflexively on his sword, but there seemed nothing to kill. La Trémoïlle was smiling steadily at him, but so, too, was his woman. It was the sort of flirtatious smile all-too-many daughters of Eve liked to fix upon the lord of Rais. Usually, it turned his stomach. Now, he felt an extra twist of terror to his innards given by the large brown eyes above that smile.

Giac would not do witchcraft, Gilles knew. But there was one who, when last he'd seen him, was just setting out to work witchcraft against Giac.

Yann. His milk brother.

If the court found the evidence of witchcraft—a sheep's heart stuck with nails under the floorboards or whatever vile thing—it might well be Giac's death. But suppose it was discovered where the magic had really come from, that Giac was meant to be the victim, not the beneficiary?

A hard gaze at La Trémoïlle told him this was just what his cousin was hinting. Cousin Georges had covered his own tail, no matter which way the scheme fell out. How was that possible? He'd only just been told of it.

Gilles wanted nothing more than to turn from what he read in that gaze. Much more than he'd ever wanted to turn in terror from a *goddam*.

For want of any better defense, however, he steadied his voice and said, "You have proof? Of witchcraft?"

La Trémoïlle bent his head in his most courtly nod. The glance he exchanged with the woman as he did so gave Gilles a pretty good idea where the proof lay.

"Against Giac, I mean?" Why was he asking so many questions?

"It can be construed so."

It could also be construed otherwise. This woman he had tried to ignore. She held the password. Perhaps she was maid-servant in Giac's household. Perhaps she'd discovered the evidence in her dustbin. Who knew? But she knew something. And she would testify.

That she might incidentally incriminate Yann was bad enough. Worse was the knowledge that La Trémoïlle—and Richemont, for that matter—would consider Yann a price well given to see something more permanent for Giac than a dungeon cell.

Where was Yann? Gilles hadn't seen either him or Hamish Power since the night before the failure of the siege of Saint-James. Usually, he could trust his milk brother to take care of himself. Yann even had magic to spare to take care of others. Gilles pressed the place on his breastbone where the talisman had lain. Empty now. Did his cousin hold Yann somewhere, to be dragged out at the appropriate time during Giac's trial?

The moment Yann was implicated, it was just another half step to deserve a witch's death himself, Gilles knew. But what could he do? The slope of this plot was already too well greased.

And Gilles de Rais was in it up to his neck.

22

A Large Figured Vase among Bed Curtains

———◦•◦———

Issoudun's White Tower dozed in silence, dreaming of its glory days of youth. Its walls were thicker than a man is tall and eight times higher than a village cottage. The White Tower had been built by Philippe-Auguste, part of his defense against England's Cœur-de-Lion. What it would wake to this early morning had nowhere near the same distinction.

The first cocks had crowed—Gilles had been awake to hear them. And, down in the village, bakers and farmers were stirring. But here in the castle, where a courtier's life could burn on by candlelight long after the sun had gone, nobody stirred. Nobody except for Gilles and the ten archers who followed him up the curved stone stair, tiptoe, the glare of their flambeaux covered, swords drawn.

On the second landing, he stopped for wind, lest heavy breathing betray him. There was something about the place and the situation that brought back a memory. As a child, strong authority had caught him abed. Just when he had hoped to begin his life according to the grand plan of Arthurian knighthood by going off to war as Uncle Amaury's page. Armed men—like the very men who followed him this early morning—had torn his Amaury from him. They had sent Amaury off to die and be buried unsung in a mass grave at Agincourt.

Even as he stood catching his breath on this present landing, Gilles remembered cringing on the landing in his father's castle, shivering in no more than a shirt, crying and watching that beloved golden head vanish down the curve of stairs for the last time. Not long after that event, and connected to it, his mother had died. And his father . . .

He shook such thoughts from him. Such a past must not keep him from a future. What he might have beyond this instant. Now that he had rediscovered a course to Arthurian legend.

He crossed the landing quickly, stepping over bad dreams. At Giac's door, he paused, hand on the latch, ear to the thick paneling. He heard an unconscious snore. He glanced at his ready men. They nodded. The latch turned easily.

The first thing Gilles picked for certain out of the sudden blaze of light, curses, and screams was a woman, sleep-naked. He'd never seen a woman in such a state before, unless it were his milk mother from a time he couldn't remember. And a corpse or two scattered along the war road. And the Midsummer rites, of course, though he knew enough to take himself into the woods alone or with Roger before things reached that point. He remembered only too well—or too poorly—things he had seen when, muddled with the hermit's drugs, he'd come from the Earth Mother's womb too early at his initiation. His birth as a man, Yann always said, had been incomplete. He'd seen death instead of life.

Gilles had never spent much time considering such wonders as the naked female. The actual sight disgusted him now as the corpses had done, parts missing, putrid swellings where none ought to be.

I'm in the wrong place, was his first thought, his sword sagging by his side. Women's rooms, as wrong as if he'd burst into the privy—or the chapel.

Then he saw that the woman's leap from bed had been in the interest of saving a large figured vase lest there be a struggle, lest it be knocked from the side table. He looked away, up to the triple orgival arches overhead, streaked with torch-light, and he knew this was a room of state.

Then the man rose up out of the bedclothes. He must have been deeper asleep than his wife. Or had not been waiting, watching in the dark.

"Who's there? What? What do you want?" the man mumbled.

Gilles thought it odd that people surprised at swordpoint often asked things like this. As if they still maintained the right to grant or deny. Or struggled to keep it. Pathetic.

"We're looking for Pierre de Giac."

Gilles was glad one of his men had the presence of mind to keep to business. This man and four others had knives, swords, and drawn bows pointed at Giac's chest, naked but for grizzled hair.

"It's he," Gilles assured them.

"Ah, I'm a dead man."

Giac no longer asked what he could do for the intruders. One weak gesture went in the direction of his wife—to protect, to console, to say "Adieu"?

The woman returned no gesture, no word, no sign of recognition. She hugged the vase protectively in her arms now, cowering behind the bed curtains at the edge of light.

Gilles' men ripped off blankets, dragged bare ankles out of their warmth and into the room's February chill.

"Come on. Move it," they ordered.

And, after one final glance toward his wife, Giac moved without resistance. He thought, perhaps, that that was the last thing he could do for the wife of his bosom, leave her a room as tidy as possible, the vase whole in her arms.

Gilles allowed him a loose night robe and his boots, which slapped awkwardly against his gooseflesh with no intervening hose.

"What's the matter?" Cries were coming from without now. "What alarm?"

"That's from the Dauphin's room," Gilles hissed at the same moment Giac gave one cry: "My Lord. Help—!"

One of the archers quickly put a stop to that with a threatening pull back on his bow.

And from somewhere, out beyond the walls, came La Trémoïlle's soothing voice: "It's nothing, Your Majesty. Stay calm in bed. All is happening for your own good."

Whether calm or not, Charles gave no further protest. Gilles and his men hustled their captive, now gagged and bound, out onto the landing.

The air here did strange things to Gilles' memory again: the grotesque shadows of hustling men torch-splayed against the wall. He was a boy, standing distraught and helpless in a nightshirt once more . . .

But, in this air, he also remembered where he'd seen Madame de Giac before. Without clothes, he'd hardly had time to look at her face, but the landing reminded him.

He almost returned to the room to run her through. He was that certain she deserved it. But killing Giac's wife hadn't been part of the plan. And at the moment, in his distress, Gilles had to cling to the plan.

Madame de Giac had been the cabbage-woman, the whore sitting on his cousin's knee.

23

The Torturer's Black Cloth Hood

———◆———

Gilles de Rais stood as far from the fire as he could, the shutter of the room's narrow window thrown open upon a silent fog. He shivered, but continued to let the damp air coat his face, his hair.

He wished himself back at the English front, a hundred leagues away. There, if a man screamed—his bowels hacked from him by an enemy sword, perhaps—there, it was an honest scream. Not like Pierre de Giac's tortured shrieks echoing through the keep of Dun-le-Rois here.

The screams ended, suddenly, on an ear-piercing note. The silence afterward, clogged with fog, left Gilles' ears ringing. He hardly heard Alain Giron, the local magistrate in Richemont's service and charged with the case, enter the room behind him. The man moved, too, as if he hated to set a foot upon the earth, as if he might hurt Her.

But Gilles was listening for the man and presently, with reluctance, he turned to face him.

Alain removed his hood as soon as Gilles' eyes met his. Gilles had a moment's glimpse of the hollow-eyed apparition, however, a death's head in reverse. And though the man stood fingering the fabric gone limp in front of him, he did not manage to cover all the blood splattering his doublet like a butcher's apron. Giac's blood.

The shiver that ran up Gilles' spine was more than just his back turned to the open window.

Alain had a gaunt, pale face, made yet more skeletal by his

labors. Gilles wondered how such a frail man had the strength to do what he did. And maybe that was the problem.

"Well?" Gilles demanded of him.

"He's out, my lord. Shall we bring him round again?"

"Did he say anything? Did he confess?"

Alain considered, his cheeks pinching and his eyes sinking into their sockets even as he did. "He's offered to pay any ransom and never to come within twenty leagues of the Dauphin again—if you will let him go, my lord."

"That won't do," Gilles said.

Alain considered again and found these words: "He certainly feels guilty about the death of his wife. His first wife, I mean. Making her ride so far over rough terrain when she was with child. And pressing her to eat rye bread beforehand, which the midwives say can be dangerous. But still he swears he had no thought of murder, nor of poison. He didn't even know she was with child, or he never would have done it. It was his child, too, after all."

Something like a catch in Alain's throat might have led one to believe it was his child as well. He recovered himself and concluded, "Or so he swears. A tough nut to crack, my lord, if I may say so."

Gilles remembered Pierre de Giac, naked from his bed, then strapped to the donkey in a loose robe and boots for the long, cold ride from Issoudun. Neither of these images made one think that body had the stamina to withstand even the first sight of the instruments. Why, Gilles had felt no more at the sight of such a body than he had at Madame de Giac's—a mild disgust.

Such reasoning made Gilles consider his own ability to withstand torture. His tough, muscular body could fight in a hundredweight of armor, days on end. It had been his pride and joy as long as he could remember. He sometimes put it through trails that made Roger cringe just to see . . .

And here was stay-at-home Giac . . . Maybe time spent on the battlefield was a hindrance when it came to withstanding the concentrated efforts of the torturer instead of the random evils of war. In war, one could still imagine there was a God, who struck down this man but spared the next—so far, had always spared Gilles and his Roger.

The man with experience of the battlefield could imagine the effect of the torturer's live coals, his tongs, his ropes and lashes, before they ever hit his own skin. In such a world, in the smoky world of the torture chamber stinking of blood and burnt flesh, there could be no God at all. Or, only the torturer, his individuality, his humanity erased to divinity behind a black cloth hood.

When—if—torture presented itself to him, would he, Gilles, the lord of Rais, would he flinch? God forbid—And yet, before he could answer his own question satisfactorily in his mind, Gilles retreated from it and faced Alain once again.

"What about . . . about the other . . . the other matter?" he asked.

"Other matter, my lord?"

Was torture so hard on the torturer that his wits left him as well? Gilles jerked his head toward the expanse of battered oaken table that stood between them, toward the women's white kerchief that was the only thing on that table.

"Ah, the charge of witchcraft," Alain said.

"Well?"

"Also nothing, my lord."

Now Gilles decided he would have to look at the thing, touch it, lest the magistrate, used to reading the flickers of guilt in those on the rack, might see—

Gilles reached out and plucked back the corner of the kerchief, Madame de Giac's kerchief. There it lay, the evidence, a dried red-black lump about the size of a small fist. A heart. An animal's heart, he certainly hoped. A sheep's, or perhaps a goat's. The entire surface of the thing was studded with nails, their square heads making a sort of metallic mosaic, one beside the other.

The thing did not smell, at least, not at a reasonable distance. It was too far gone for that. But Gilles felt it ought to. It reeked of black magic. Not just any magic. It reeked of his milk brother, Yann. He knew as well as he'd known it of the talisman at Saint-James, and that Yann had hung around his neck with his own hand.

"But Madame de Giac found this in their chamber," Gilles insisted. "So carefully she provided the evidence. Against her own husband, no less."

Maybe it's Madame I should bring to the rack, to get at the truth of this business. Gilles almost thought he could read Alain's thoughts running along this line. Gilles hoped he wouldn't say it, though. He had no wish to haul her out of bed. His cousin La Trémoïlle's bed, that would be. The man said nothing close, however.

"The prisoner—" Alain couldn't say Giac's name. Not after torture's intimacy. "He still swears he knows nothing of it. He never saw it before, nor does he know the first thing of magic. By all the saints, or so he swears, he's always been a Christian."

Gilles tossed the corner of the kerchief back over the thing with a studied carelessness. He sighed heavily while he considered what to say next.

"Oh, have a seat," he said at last to the magistrate, whose fatigue—the fatigue of self-disgust—was showing. "And pour yourself a bit of my hippocras. You look as if you could use it."

Alain moved to do as he was told, gratefully. Gilles didn't join him. He didn't even face him for a moment, but turning himself back to the window again, stood rubbing the blue marks on his chin under his beard. The fog outside seemed the best reflection of the state of his mind.

He heard the chair creak with the man's weight, heard a stiff quantity of the mulled wine poured, quaffed in a breath, more poured.

Alain smacked his thin lips thoughtfully and then said, "He just keeps talking about this monk."

Gilles whipped back around to face the room. "Who?"

"The prisoner, my lord."

"Of course, the prisoner. But a monk, you say?"

"He keeps saying the magic must be the work of some

monk he saw lurking around in recent days. A monk in black robes. And in the company of a Scotsman."

"A Scotsman."

Gilles could hardly suppress a groan. So it was Yann. Yann with Hamish Power in tow, of course. The fool. Not only was he a sorcerer, he was a damned fool besides. Damn that Yann. He sets off from Saint-James, promising some hocus-pocus to get Giac out of the way so the war could go on apace. Not only does Yann allow his horrific, bloody fetish to get discovered—by the intended victim's wife, no less—but now it threatens to blow up in their faces like a keg of powder. He lets himself be seen, for God's sake. Has he never heard of such a thing as a glamour spell? It's a wonder Giac didn't add a twisted right hand to his description of the black-robed monk. Point the finger to nobody else in the entire kingdom.

Gilles wondered how long Yann would last under torture for witchcraft. Witches were supposed to have potions that could make them hold out forever, but considering how well this last spell had worked—

Gilles wondered again how long he himself might last. Because once the law got its teeth into Yann, it would only be a moment before it would turn to the next likely culprit, the fool priest's fool of a milk brother. The law was like that, like a dog once he's got the taste of chicken blood. You can't let him loose in the yard again.

"The prisoner keeps saying he saw these two men." The hippocras had untied Alain's tongue. "The monk and the Scotsman, acting quite suspicious—" Suppose it unfroze the gears of his brain as well.

"Giac was insane. He was seeing things."

"Yes," the magistrate mused. "I wouldn't be surprised if the torture turned his head."

"The man is guilty," Gilles thundered. "Guilty as hell. You must get him to confess."

"But, you know, my lord, if the prisoner is innocent, God gives him the strength to withstand what an ordinary mortal could not."

Christ, the fellow actually believed that rubbish. Believed

he was acting as the hand of God to winnow out the truth.

"Go on," Gilles ordered, managing to rein in his voice to a low growl. "Wring it out of him. The moment he comes to, crush him."

Alain looked into his goblet, then seemed to decide that any more drink would unsettle his stomach too much for the task at hand.

"Crush him," Gilles snarled, low in his throat.

And Alain Giron fled back to the warm safety of his torture chamber.

24

Tow through a Spinner's Fingers

White snow twisted through the grey sky like tow through a spinner's fingers. It landed in feathers on the tree stump at the water's edge. Had they been real feathers, tufting the burst of red gore on the old, dried rings, one might have thought a chicken had just been slaughtered.

Tendon and white bits of bone spiked the raw end of the severed hand. It hadn't been a very clean cut, requiring two whacks to get through.

One of Gilles' archers kicked the hand off to the dogs, then went to help bundle Giac into the hempen sack, tying it firmly over the head of the man moaning his prayers.

Pierre de Giac had confessed. He'd confessed to witchcraft: it had been at his own request that they'd chopped the hand off while he was still alive, to comfort him. For, having promised his right hand to the devil, he had no chance of paradise if he died with the limb attached.

Giac had also confessed to murdering his first wife.

The whole thing sounded strangely familiar to Gilles, rather like the tale of Vauru and the victims in his tree. Rather too like.

But Giac had confessed.

After the torture.

Whatever the source of that confession, it was legal. The Dauphin could not complain. Alain Giron, the magistrate of Dun-le-Roi, stood—about to lose his breakfast—at Gilles' side to prove it.

The men finished tying the sack and looked to Alain for orders. The man was incapable. Gilles gave the nod instead and they shoved the struggling but featureless sack off the bank and into the fast-moving river as the snow swirled, stinging, above it.

Giac sank like a rock, with barely a bubble to show where he'd been. A bubble and a small trail of pink where the blood, filtering through the sack, stained the water.

"If he was a witch," Gilles heard one man ask, "shouldn't the water have rejected him? Shouldn't he float? Should we pull him out, an innocent man?"

"No," replied another. Talking helped to cover the crunch of dog teeth on the hand. "If we'd left the hand on, he would have floated. But now he's fine."

"Oh," said the first, nodding, but the wrinkle between his brows said the thought was still too much for him.

Gilles wondered if he'd float himself, if he were tossed in. Garter-removed. Hand removed. Blue-marked chin. Heart.

"If a man's innocent," Alain had explained, over and over, like a prayer, "God will help him withstand, and only the truth will be winnowed out."

Gilles didn't think God would help him, the lord of Rais, to anything. At least, not the same God the magistrate meant.

Well, the first thing he'd confess was that this execution had helped out Georges de la Trémoïlle more than anyone.

———•———

Not long afterward, Gilles stood beside Arthur the count of Richemont as that man, girded with the sword of France's *connétable,* carrying the baton of his office, knelt before the Dauphin. He pleaded, with his usual Breton volubility, that Georges de la Trémoïlle be given the empty place of favorite and chamberlain and control of the royal purse strings, so that the war against the English could continue without any more interruptions.

Pale, nervous Charles got up out of his battered throne and paced on his knock knees, wringing his thin, bony hands.

God, Gilles thought, as he did every time he saw what his

young playmate had grown into. This is all the royalty we have to work with, to beat the English and fulfill prophecy? No wonder we lose at every turn. I doubt Yann has half the magic in his twisted hand that this is going to take. Perhaps I'm on the wrong side after all.

Charles turned and faced them then, his bulbous nose exaggerated by the way the sunlight hit it from the high clerestory in the room.

"Very well, good cousin," he said. "It must be as you say, for I fear I have no choice."

"God help us," Gilles muttered under his breath.

The would-be King's eyes were bright, but not tearful as he said, "But I think you will repent this, monsieur le comte. And I think I know Monsieur de La Trémoïlle a little better than you do, for all your plotting together."

25

The Fox Pelt

THE VILLAGE OF DOMRÉMY, IN THE MARCHES OF LORRAINE
APRIL, YEAR OF GRACE 1428

Physically, Jehannette recovered from the Night Battle
quickly. And lived to fight a second year.

In her spirit, however, she continued as disturbed as ever.
If not more so. Frequently, throughout those months that grew
to years, she found that her spirits carried her down to the
Meuse again. And again. She spent hours looking at the spot
where Père Michel's whip parted the waters—though in the
swelling of rain or the spring thaw, it was impossible to believe that such a thing had ever really happened.

Now she looked off toward Maxey, to the field where the
battle took place. The wheat was coming in, a lush green pelt.
There were many places where the beast seemed to have the
mange, however, places where the sown seed had been unable
to recover from a tumble and wrestle over the multi-patched
ball. And Jehannette was quite certain she could see places
where the fennel had seeded itself in feathery growth among
the grain.

She knew the farmer didn't mind, however. The honor of
having hosted the fight with the phantoms was too auspicious
for his whole well-being.

It was April, just after Holy Week and Easter. Once again
she was standing, considering the spot, when a sudden splashing and thrashing in the water just upstream interrupted such

thoughts. Peering cautiously around a clump of wild plum in white bloom, she found herself face to face with a young man struggling to free a small boat from a muddy bank and a tangle of reeds.

"God save you," he said cheerfully when he saw her.

"And you," she muttered.

"Daughter-God."

At the exact same moment, a Voice whispered through the dry and withering daffodil heads on the bank like a breeze. She whipped around, her back to young man and stream, hunting for the light, the wonderful source.

"Bide a moment, there," he called after. "Don't I know you?"

Jehannette shook her head and took another step up the bank where violets bloomed at the feet of the spent daffodils.

"Of course!" he cried. "You're the girl who fights for Dom-rémy in the Night Battle."

No more Voice. She turned and studied the young man instead.

"I don't remember you." What she really wanted to know was how anyone could recognize her now that she no longer flew on butterfly wings.

An early cabbage moth took flight, disturbed from the grasses at her feet. Perhaps that was the connection, though she herself found it far too tenuous.

"That's good," he said. "My mask was a success, then. Though everyone in Maxey knew me at once. I was the fox."

Vaguely, Jehannette remembered a fox. She remembered crawling around under his unwashed shirt.

"A fox kept running off with our ducks all last summer," the boy chatted on. "So I went out and trapped him in his hole. Then I had this lovely pelt and tail and I just thought, 'Well, that's what I'll be when I go to fight.' So I am. Everyone in Maxey knew me at once. That's what they call me, you understand. Renard the Fox. For my hair, you see."

He took off a dark green and well-worn cap and gave his thick hair a toss. It was, indeed, a very warm chestnut, like the bay of a horse's back in the summer sun. It was, Jehannette could imagine other girls sighing, "his best feature." But whatever she was supposed to feel at such a sight failed to come to her.

"And your name is—?"

She didn't immediately answer, for, urged by a word from her Voices, a debate had begun in her mind.

"Consider the name of your home village, Daughter-God."

"What, Domrémy?"

"Consider how it was named for monseigneur St. Rémy."

"That is so."

"Consider how St. Rémy also gave his name to Rheims."

"What? The great city?" Jehannette almost laughed aloud at her thoughts. "I've never visited such a distant place."

"But you've heard of the cathedral there."

"Yes."

"There the Dauphin must be anointed."

"With St. Rémy's sacred oil?"

"Yes, if ever he is to truly become King of France."

"But city, cathedral, and oil all are out of Charles' reach in English, Burgundian hands."

"And who shall bring him there?"

"Who?"

The Voices faded without answering her. There was some important connection here, but she couldn't quite see it.

"Jehanne," the boy was saying, maddening her with the interruption. "I've heard your name is Jehanne d'Arc. I asked, you see."

"They give me the name Jehannette at home. And my mother's name is Romée. A girl goes by her mother's name where I come from."

"I like that," he said. "Jehannette Romée. A pretty name."

Jehannette thought the comment silly. Jehanne or Jehannette, it didn't matter. It was such a plain name, as serviceable as a good strong hoe. Her brother Jean's name, just feminized. Even though she was their first daughter, even with the caul, her parents had not been inspired by her birth.

"You're from Maxey?" she spoke to him suddenly, moved through inner dialogue.

The young man looked at her as if she were stupid. No doubt that had been a stupid thing to say. He'd already told her as much, but she'd been too distracted to mark it.

"I mean, people from Maxey don't usually come to this bank."

"The more fools they," Renard said.

He was looking at her quite strangely, Jehannette thought, as if indeed he were a fox. And she a duck.

"I mean, we certainly miss a lot by sticking to our own side. That's why I've always liked the Night Battles so much."

"Liked them?" Jehannette had to try that phrasing on for herself. Certainly she had fit into the task as if she had been born for nothing else. But to *like* it was as much as to say one liked to breathe or feel her heart pump. It simply *was,* and life would cease without it.

"You're from Maxey?"

"Well, actually, I was born in Toul. My family moved when I was very young. Too much fighting down at the north end of the valley there."

"My father came here because of the war, too. He came from Champagne."

"There, see?" Renard was exuberant. "Just see how much we have in common, we two."

"The war is horrible and destructive to all. And you, you're from Maxey. I mean, you're a Burgundian."

She felt all her father's unspoken anger against the enemy welling up inside her. All the lust for the fight she'd ever felt came, too. There was room for nothing in her brain but an image of herself going at that firm, tanned young throat with a knife. With difficulty, she kept herself within the bounds of reality.

"Well, you see," Renard scampered on, only partially aware of the light in which his hearer viewed him. "I was out fishing today. First day of the year. Eke out the greens until the main crops come on, you understand."

Jehannette nodded vaguely, mostly to shake the vision from her head. Renard took it as a confirmation that her family, too, was still in something of a fast, though the church calendar said Lent was past and gone.

"Anyway, I just forgot how strong the current can be this time of year and, not getting the slightest nibble and sort of daydreaming, you see, here I am thrown up against the shores of Domrémy and at your mercy, demoiselle."

When she couldn't give his humor the reaction he'd obviously hoped for, he went on, more plainly. "Give us a hand, won't you?"

Jehannette did, mostly because she was used to doing as she was told when men gave her orders, even when her mind was only half present.

One good shove freed the boat easily.

"My, but you're strong," Renard said, wonder in his gaze. "You wouldn't think it, looking at you."

The boat bobbed on the green water, anxious to be off, while Renard lingered, keeping the end of the boat's rope wrapped tight around his fist.

"You did that very well," he went on. "Almost as well as you fight."

"I don't know why you should remember me from the battle."

"How could I not?"

She looked straight into his eyes, liquid brown as they were. What sort of magic was in such eyes that they could recognize a girl in butterfly form? She felt she should be grateful for such recognition. Instead, a worm of unease wriggled in her belly.

"Not too many women join us these days—except for the dead, of course. And those who do usually prefer to cluster round the torches and wave their stalks and cheer. Like that old goose of yours from Greux. But you—Well, you know what they're saying, don't you?"

"No."

"They all say Domrémy never would have won—certainly not two years in a row—without you. I won't soon forget the torment of all those little legs in my shirt, I can tell you. Just when I thought I had a firm grip on the ball and could have run it all the way to St. Catherine's door in Maxey—tickled so I couldn't breathe. Powerful magic, Jehannette. Powerful. My father says—well, you don't care what my father says."

"What does your father say?" Jehannette asked.

"Well, my father fights, too. Always has. He was born with the caul, just like the rest of us. Anyway, my mother doesn't and it drives her crazy to have him off, riding the Wild Ride with the dead and then the days afterwards when he just stays in bed and mustn't be moved or his soul might stay where he left it, with the dead. Anyway, Father pities her and says it would be so much easier if both husband and wife had the calling.

"My mother disagrees and says, 'Oh, so then for three whole days at Yuletide we'd have two helpless souls around the house. And who'd look after the babies in such a household? What about the milking? Feeding the hens? Hmm? That's what I'd like to know.'

"But seeing you on the field and here again today, I sort of think my father's is the best way of thinking. At least, I tell myself, it's worth a try. Is it?" he demanded, twisting his face at an odd angle in an effort to get it between hers and whatever she was staring at so fixedly.

"Be good," said another puff of breeze. She stood rigid, for a moment, listening. But that was all.

"Is it what?" she asked and blinked.

"Is it worth a try?"

She replied, trying for airiness. "Oh, anything is worth a try. That's what my V—I mean, that's what Père Michel always says."

"Does he, indeed? Well, that's just fine. Then I may come and see you sometime?"

"Why would you want to do that?"

"Well, you know, like boys and girls do. Like courting."

"Courting?" Suddenly he had all her attention. She turned and faced him squarely, her mouth open with astonishment until she remembered herself enough to snap it shut and then to stammer, "But . . . but you're from Maxey. A Burgundian."

"It's not a problem for me. If it's not a problem for you."

"You don't understand. I . . . I mean, my father . . ."

"Some people are like that. But I'll talk to him, get to know him. Then we'll see what his thoughts are on the matter."

Jehannette had to agree that this Renard could probably talk anybody—even her father—into anything. The trick, as she saw it, was not to let him get started.

"But I'm not . . ." She swished her skirt before his eyes, not coquettishly but to make its color plain to him.

Renard shrugged, making her think girls in Maxey must be such another species that they didn't have to wear red. Or perhaps not even skirts at all. But that was not the source of his disregard.

"You'll be of marrying age soon enough," he said. "That's plain to anyone who looks at you. And what should be the harm in courting? Or even getting betrothed before? It seems to me, if you're old enough to fight, you're old enough to marry."

Without another word, Jehannette turned on her heels and ran all the way back to her father's yard.

"Come, Jehannette, don't be shy," Renard shouted after her. "You certainly weren't on the battlefield." And then, "Well, I will surely see you. At Midsummer. By the Fairy Tree."

26

Wilted Flowers at Our Lady's Feet

———◆◆◆———

Jehannette felt a moment's pang of guilt for bursting into the peace of the clearing like that. But Père Michel took only a moment to break his trance of meditation in front of the round-faced, painted-wood Our Lady, her child small in comparison, with comically overlarge ears. Père Michel looked up patiently to the clump of wilted flowers Jehannette tossed at his—and Our Lady's—feet.

"Now, what's this?" he asked.

"It was hung on our gate this morning," she replied. Half a May morning's walk to get to this place had not been enough to work the anger—and a bit of fear—off her shoulders. She continued to pace now, back and forth within the narrow confines of the clearing as if an endless road still stretched before her.

"And a very pleasant May bunch it is, too. Made by someone who truly appreciates Our Lady's power and beauty in this month. But different, too. By the cattails and river grass among the hawthorne and wild carrot, I would guess—yes, certainly. This man must have crossed a river to get to your house."

Jehannette stopped and stared at the priest where he sat, totally without care, on the grass of the forest floor. She thrust her fists in tight balls against her hips in an effort to keep her temper to a simmer.

"You know this Renard, this wily fox?" she accused him.

"I know him. In fact, he came to me asking of you a week ago."

Père Michel gestured to a patch of grass beside him. Jehannette refused to take it.

"He came to *you,* asking of *me?*"

"Well, your father will have nothing to do with him. Turned him away at the door with a pitchfork, so I hear. Now, I've seen that side of Jacquot d'Arc myself. I must sympathize with the lad. If your father of the flesh won't talk to him of you, he must come to your spiritual father, I suppose."

"You're no kin of mine if you encouraged him in any way."

"He's a good lad, Jehannette."

"Oh, and I'm a good girl, so we make a perfect match."

"He might come to this side of the river in a month's time," Père Michel suggested. "For Midsummer."

"You told him to do this?"

"Take a look then, when wine and festivities make people easy. See if you can like him."

"I already know I cannot."

"How do you know, Jehannette?"

She kicked at a tuft of grass and didn't answer.

"I don't care to see him hurt, that's all."

"So you encouraged him?" she demanded.

"Not exactly. But he . . . he did seem convinced the dislike was all on your father's part and not your own."

"I thank the little martinets, my father never let him get close enough to have to hear my mind."

"I see. Yes, well, that's what I warned him."

"What did you tell him?"

"I told him my suspicions."

"What suspicions?"

"That you are La Pucelle we've waited so long for and that he mustn't get his hopes up. La Pucelle is—well, just as the name suggests. The Maid. A woman—shall we say?—who has no time for men. The work of her life is too great for— for many things."

"By my life—" Jehannette didn't finish. She slumped heavily down beside the hermit on the grass but turned her back to him, sinking her flushed face into her hands.

When Père Michel continued just to regard her silently, she added, "I wish you'd give up on the prophecy. I've no desire in the world to be your Pucelle. Or anybody's Pucelle." She spoke it into the pressure of her hands, so few of her consonants were enunciated beyond an "h."

"But I think that's what it means to be 'Pucelle.' To be a woman who belongs to no one but herself." He paused, studying her. "And to her Voices, too, of course."

Jehannette looked away. She gave no reply for a very long time. At last, Père Michel broke the silence.

"It seems to me, if you are La Pucelle—if your Voices tell you anything of the sort—you must not keep it secret. It does no good to keep nice young men like this Renard in doubt. And it is no good to keep the world waiting for your gifts either, Jehannette."

She sat up, suddenly very straight, and confronted him squarely in the eye. "My Voices say nothing of La Pucelle."

"Very well."

"They say nothing of mock battles at Yuletide."

"What do they say, then?"

"My Voices want real battles. They want real blood sacrifice. They want me, Father, to fight for France."

"To fight for Charles the Dauphin?"

"Yes."

"Like a man takes a lady's kerchief and fights for her," Père Michel mused.

"Exactly," Jehannette replied. She could feel the glitter in her own eyes. As if the notion of such passive gallantry were the greatest diappointment in her life.

"Poor Renard," he murmured, unable, for the moment, to meet her gaze. "I almost said, 'Poor France.'"

"Don't mock me, Father."

"Child, I don't."

"You are the first I've ever told anything about my Voices—and only because it seems you already knew. Believe me, they will not be mocked." Every beat of the last phrase was clear, precise, and very fierce.

"I would never think of mocking the word of God," he replied, just as earnestly. But the emphasis he gave the words suggested she was the one doing the mocking.

She nodded brusquely, somewhat appeased. "Good. Because you would do so at peril of your own soul."

Père Michel nodded.

"My Voices say I must ride into battle. I must ride into France."

"Then that is what you must do."

"But how, Father? How am I to do it?"

"Your Voices don't tell you?"

"No. I hoped you would."

Père Michel thoughtfully rubbed his beard with its heavy streaks of grey. "I suppose if you just jumped on Grison and headed off over the hills towards the west—"

Jehannette shook her head furiously. "I thought of that. That would never do."

"I'm glad there's some reason in you, anyway."

"My father and my brothers would be after me in a moment. It's only by the best of fortune that they gave me leave to come so far as your hermitage this morning. Besides, a girl, alone, with all that Burgundian territory to cross before France . . ."

Père Michel nodded. "It would take you a fortnight at least."

"Yes, it would never do."

"Your Voices won't protect you?"

"Not if I'm a complete fool."

"I see."

Jehannette knew that anybody else speaking to her with the same twinkle in his eye would have been suggesting that he thought her a complete fool from the start. But things were not so with this priest, and she quite loved him for it.

"You might protect me, Father." She jumped toward him as she said it, landing on her hands and knees in her anxiety. "You might come with me and then I'd be all right."

"Is that what your Voices say?"

"You don't seem too overjoyed with the prospect." She rocked back onto her heels with disappointment.

"I'm an old man, Jehannette. I've seen you raised and that's all I'm good for anymore. That last Night Battle was just about the end of me. I can still hardly walk on my right knee these days."

"So—you can ride Grison."

"You're the one who's supposed to ride into France, remember?"

"We can both ride."

"Grison's too old to carry us both. Besides, he's hardly the proper mount for La Pucelle who must save France."

"Then we must get a second horse."

Père Michel stopped the argument that could have gone on infinitely between her vision and the reality of one who has no such Sight. "Just what do your Voices tell you, Jehannette?"

"Well, recently they've been saying—"

"Yes?"

"The name of Vaucouleurs has been much on their tongues."

"Very well."

"Vaucouleurs is the name of a town?"

"Yes."

"My father has been there once. Not far from here?"

"A day's walk."

"There's a fortress there?"

"Yes."

"And a commander named Bawdy—"

"Bawdy?"

"Well, something like that."

Père Michel smiled. Obviously he knew the man and "Bawdy" must not be such a misnomer.

"Robert de Baudricourt," he corrected.

"That's the man. That's the place."

"Very well, then you should go to him. I think your Voices speak wisely. You're halfway there already. Just continue on up the road as you began. You'll be in the fort by sunset."

"That will not do."

"Why not?"

"I told you. I only have permission to go as far as your hermitage today. If I'm not home long before sunset, Father and my brothers will come looking for me."

"Then you should set off at once. Not a moment to be wasted."

"No. My Voices assure me it will take more than a few hours to convince this Baudricourt. Three times I must ask him, they say."

"To convince him of anything. Your Voices are very wise."

"I need to have some excuse to come this way—for several days. A week, perhaps. My Voices give me no hint. I hoped you might think of something."

"I see." Père Michel studied her thoughtfully. "Well, all right. Give me a while to think about it."

"See that you do," she replied. "My Voices do not have all the time in the world."

Père Michel smiled indulgently and she realized she'd been high-handed. It was becoming quite a fault, thanks to her Voices. Oh, well, there wasn't time to worry about it.

As if avoiding the insistence of her gaze, Père Michel slowly climbed to his feet, leaning heavily on his staff. It was now his turn to pace and he began to do so. But he had not made it halfway across the clearing with a gait that was agony to watch before he turned to her. Light spread suddenly over his face and the bad knee seemed forgotten. Perhaps he had Voices, too. Perhaps that is how he understood hers so well. She must remember to ask him. Another time. Now he was coming rapidly toward her.

"You have an uncle who lives near here, have you not? At Burey-le-Petit, I think."

"That's Durand Laxart, my mother's cousin. I've called him uncle since I was a child. But we do not meet often. It would seem very suspicious if, out of nowhere, I were to say, 'Papa, could I not go and spend a week with Uncle Durand?' "

"Ah, but his young wife, so I hear, is expecting their first child. Very shortly, I think."

"So?"

"So a woman must have help at that time, must she not?"

"I'm no midwife."

"Of course not. She will have her midwife. But women need other help, too. Usually—unless they have daughters of their own or a mother- or sister-in-law in the house—they require some young woman, capable, but without a house of her own to run. Someone to cook and clean and so on so the mother can heal and rest and care for the baby."

"That is so." Though such things had never interested her much, Jehannette was beginning to catch his drift and excitement thrummed in her temples. "But surely my aunt will have made arrangements with another girl by now, one closer to her home."

"Surely she will," Père Michel agreed. "But something may happen to such a girl in the next day or two that makes it absolutely impossible for her to help out. Then she would have to call on her more distant kin."

"Yes!" exclaimed Jehannette, clapping her hands at the thought. "She could fall and break her neck."

"I hope nothing nearly so drastic." Père Michel took a step or two and then stroked his beard. "I would only have to switch knees with her for a little while . . ."

"Can you do that?" Jehannette asked.

"I can. Whether I should or not is another question."

"Of course you should—for my Voices."

"Part of the good, Jehannette, according to ancient wisdom, is that each person should suffer his own pain. He should never try to pass it off on another, either by making that person do the work of his own life or by taking a cure that must injure another."

Jehannette tried to take the lesson soberly, but the thought made her too excited.

"But you could," she insisted.

"Well, let me find out who this woman is first. Let me look at the possibilities. In the meantime, why don't you hurry back home so your father suspects nothing?"

Jehannette was on her feet in a moment.

"If my plan works, you will have word soon enough," he called after her.

And as she ran from the clearing, Jehannette kicked aside the wilted May bouquet without a backward glance. She slowed only a moment as the premonition pressed on her like a heavy cloak. She knew she would miss all Midsummer festivities that year.

27

Dirty Baby Linen

"God's Wounds." Robert de Baudricourt, commander of Vau-couleurs, slammed his gauntleted fist into his heavy council table so the wood shook with the impact. "Send the slut back to her father."

Jehannette flinched. But her Voices insisting, "Daughter-God" made her stand her ground.

"You would do well, monsieur, not to blaspheme when the future of France is in God's hands."

Baudricourt stared at her, dumb for a moment, his fleshy mouth open, pink and round between brown mustache and beard. "And have him give her a thrashing, too."

Jehannette could tell it was only by letting off such thunder that the man managed to keep himself from doing her father's duty for him that very minute.

Uncle Durand, who'd been making a fool of himself, scrap-ing and bowing and rocking from foot to foot behind her, now took her by the elbow and began to try and force her to obey the order.

"Daughter-God, go!" buzzed like a fly in her ear.

Jehannette shook her uncle's arm from hers and took up her own stance again, bare feet apart and firm on the fine parquet floor. Unfortunately, the effect was probably lost under her red kirtle.

"Beware, Robert de Baudricourt," she said.

"Go, go, go!" Her Voices were so loud she could hardly

hear her own words. They pricked at her, a physical, almost unbearable pain.

Her pitch rose, almost to a cry of anguish as she went on, "And all you of Vaucouleurs who neglect my warning. Within this week, you shall rue the day you did not hear me."

Then—then there was silence.

Rubbing her temples, she turned and strode out of the room and the fortress. Uncle Durand scurried behind her like a frightened mouse, no easy feat for such a large man.

"Oh, Jehannette, you shouldn't have done that," he kept saying over and over until she stopped and glared at him. Her pace had already brought them to the edge of Vaucouleurs, that small town that seemed backed against the mountainside like a cat by the barnyard dogs.

"I told you already," she said. "I must do what I do. I am driven to it by my Master."

"Very well, very well," he said, as cowed by her as by the commander. "I don't understand these matters. But I meant that last thing you said. It's one thing to preach repentance and a closer hearkening to God's word. Preachers who do the same thing are a sou a dozen."

"Against which men like Baudricourt can too easily shut their ears."

"That's a great lord's prerogative, I suppose."

Uncle Durand considered, then scurried to catch up with the quick strides her short legs had resumed.

He added: "But it is quite another thing to call down curses on his head. Jehannette, truly. That smacks of witchcraft."

Jehannette shrugged. "I can't help it," she said. "It's what I'm told to do."

———•———

Six days later, as Jehannette gathered up a basket of dirty baby linen to take to the stream to wash, her uncle came running into the house from the fields. It was midmorning; she hadn't even begun to cut bread and cheese to carry out to him for lunch as he made the hay.

"By my martinet, Uncle. What's the matter?"

"I'm taking you back to your father this moment."

"You don't like my work? Yes, maybe I'm not as good a cook as your wife. But I do try and if there's something you don't like, you must tell me and I will try to do better. Anything before you send me back. And then you must let me walk back on my own and not leave your wife and baby son like this."

Uncle Durand finally caught his breath and snapped, "A young woman cannot walk the roads alone."

"Why not? I did coming here."

Uncle Durand glanced anxiously toward the next room, where his wife and baby lay. The sight of such a great, bear-like man trying to tiptoe made Jehannette want to laugh. But she resisted. She stood quietly, trying to look good and obedient while she watched her uncle peer in at his family, find them sleeping, at least pretending to do so, and shut the door—for their own protection.

"Uncle, I don't think—" she began.

He cut her short, the quiet of his voice serving rather to underline his words. "The Burgundians have invaded."

"Burgundians?"

His voice rolled up a level as he threatened to lose control. "I saw them from the fields: horses, banners, men-at-arms. The Burgundians are here."

"Here?"

"Don't play so innocent with me, Jehannette, when it is your curse that brought them."

"My curse . . . ?"

"Did you or did you not tell Monsieur de Baudricourt he would regret the day he didn't listen to you?"

Uncle Durand allowed her a pause in which to answer, but she did not. She turned toward the outside door, which he had not bothered to close on his entry. Light streamed in from the yard, blinding her.

Uncle Durand continued. "You gave him a week. Well, it's been six days. A group of a hundred or so men flying Burgundy's red St. Andrew's cross passed into our valley last night from Champagne and have laid siege to the fortress of

Vaucouleurs. Baudricourt and his men are sitting ducks. All the houses and yards and goods around the fortress these men have pillaged, burned, or taken for their own use. It was poor folk struggling along the road with nothing but the clothes on their backs who brought word to me and others in the fields."

Jehannette rushed to the door, staring up the road towards Vaucouleurs.

When she still made no answer, he prodded her. "Well? What have you to say for yourself?"

"Siege machines?"

"What?"

"Have the invaders siege machines? Cannons? How many archers? Crossbow or longbow?" she babbled in the white heat of excitement.

"Jehannette, Jehannette, whatever possesses you?"

"Here I was thinking I would have to ride into France to fight the enemy, but God brings them to my very doorstep to save me the trouble."

"Save trouble, girl? Can't you see there's been no worse trouble in this valley since I was born? Heaven help us, if we can only manage to survive."

She found she still had the basket of souring linen threaded over her left arm. She had it pressed up against her chest instead of the shield she'd been imagining. She tossed it in her uncle's direction. He caught the basket but also caught her by the elbow and stopped her in her tracks. She tugged against him, but not enough to free herself.

"The time has come. Yes, I must go. You're right, uncle. I must go and fight the Burgundians."

"Raise the siege of . . ." her Voices thrummed in her ears.

She couldn't quite hear their last word for the throb of her own pulse, so when she repeated them in human speech, she said, "Raise the siege of Vaucouleurs. Prove to Baudricourt that I am . . . I am . . ."

She kept staring along the road toward Vaucouleurs, here where it dipped between two banks high over her head with nettles and wild carrot. Where a neighbor's wooden gate let onto the road, the light was brilliant. Behind such a light she could hardly see how rotted the gate was from the damp soil upward.

"I am . . ." She finished her sentence at last in a whisper of awe. "I am La Pucelle."

"Jehannette, are you out of your mind?"

She could hardly hear him for the beat of "Be good, Daughter-God, be good" in her mind.

"You don't mean to fight all those Burgundians yourself?"

"No."

She turned a gasp into a little laugh. Uncle Durand relaxed perceptibly and loosened his grip on her arm. That gesture was nothing compared to the sudden release of the Voices from her mind.

"No," she repeated in a tone of which she felt herself more the mistress. "This small raiding party has come only to teach Baudricourt a lesson. Teach him that he does need me, after all. I must stay put. A hundred Burgundians, you say?"

Uncle Durand nodded, licking his lips against an obviously overdry throat.

"Just a hundred. I must not waste myself on such a petty crew. No. Not for anything less than five thousand. Revelation must not come to anything less."

"You are mad, Jehannette."

"Yes, uncle, you're very right."

She laughed a little, realizing what she'd said, having missed her uncle's last few statements. Then she laughed again. It might very well be true that she had lost her mind. But that didn't change what she must do.

"I must stay here." She turned on her heel off the road and back toward the house. "Now, what was I doing?" She spied the basket where her uncle had let it drop just inside the door. "Ah, the laundry."

"No, Jehannette. I must take you back to your father at once. It's not safe for you here. This is too close to Vaucouleurs. When the siege begins to bore them, when they run out of food and wine and—heaven preserve us—women near Vaucouleurs, it will be nothing for them to come here to Burey-le-Petit. You cannot rest safely here."

"You worry about me? What of your wife and your baby son?"

"Of course, I had thought of them, too," Uncle Durand admitted.

"I am much better able to take care of myself than they are."

"I was thinking. Perhaps I should load them up, too. In the cart, perhaps, with all we can carry. And then go up along the valley and beg your father's hospitality for a while . . ."

"I doubt my aunt is well enough to travel. It was a very hard birth, the midwife told me. We must give her another fortnight at least. And really, she ought to be churched first before making a trip like that."

"Good Lord, Jehannette. The Burgundians will cut our throats in our beds and burn the house down around our ears."

"If that threatens," Jehannette said with another wistful glance between the banks and along the road to Vaucouleurs. It all seemed very peaceful—and bathed in light. "Then, yes, that is the time to move her."

"But what should we do in the meantime?"

Imperceptibly, her uncle had turned responsibility over to her. He did not seem to notice.

"You? You should go back to the field where you were and finish your raking. If your hay is going to feed Burgundian horses, we don't want it to be rotten, do we?"

"But—" Uncle Durand stared at her wild-eyed, unable to say more.

"I'm teasing, uncle," she had to tell him. Then, "You might do that. Or you might go and see if you can't find a woman to replace me. I'm certain one of the women fleeing the siege would be only too grateful for a roof over her head tonight. Once I can leave you with ease in my heart, I will make it back to my father's house on my own. No, you needn't worry about taking me. The Burgundians are all north, right? And the path I must take is south. Besides, I suspect I'll have plenty of company on the road with people from Vaucouleurs.

"I will go to my father," she continued, "and warn him and my mother of the danger in the valley—though I suspect they will have heard from others long before I get there. I will warn him you might be coming, my aunt and the baby, and that we should prepare for you. I will warn all the people on the way. They should make certain their axles are strong and they should think about what they might pack if, at a moment's notice, they must flee."

"Yes, yes, that's very good." Uncle Durand was plainly making his own quick mental list as she spoke.

"The Burgundians entered our valley at its northern point. I suspect we'll all be flushed to the south—to the strong walls of Neufchâteau, I shouldn't wonder."

"As far as Neufchâteau? So far? Ah, Jehannette. Are you certain it will be as bad as that?"

"It's in God's hands, uncle," she replied.

"Of course." Fervently, he crossed himself.

"But we must be prepared for the worst. If that's the sort of lesson Baudricourt requires."

"Yes, of course."

Jehannette spoke almost to herself: "If I am not to lift a finger. Ah, my Master, shall I endure it?"

Uncle Durand turned to the gate in a rush, then turned helplessly back again. "What if I can't find a woman from Vaucouleurs?"

"I'd be very much surprised," Jehannette replied, the laughter staying with difficulty in her chest. "But if not, you might go and see if the girl I replaced is feeling any better. Didn't you tell me it was almost witchcraft the way such a bad knee came on her so suddenly?"

"So it did. With no accident, and in one so young and healthy just the day before." Uncle Durand crossed himself again.

"By witchcraft it might leave her again, just so suddenly."

"Of course. Very good."

He took two or three steps, then turned once more in another blanch of helplessness.

"And you, Jehannette? What will you do?"

"I? I must go back to my new little cousin's linen, I suppose." She was at the basket now, and with a sigh she stooped and hoisted it. "If I'm not to pick up a buckler yet."

Her uncle was gone and she didn't think he heard her next sigh. With her left hand, she reached into the basket slung against her right hip and stirred the contents thoughtfully. The strong yet strangely sweet baby smell released itself to her nostrils.

The next moment, she had pressed the basket to her with all the ferocity of terror. She clung to it as something normal, something working as it should, that little baby boy's bowels and bladder. How safe it was, how wonderful. How full of life.

"And is this as close as La Pucelle may ever come," she said aloud, though only she and her Voices could hear, "to having a baby of her own?"

28

The Silt of People and Animals

The silt of people and animals had been following the Meuse, flowing counter to it actually, most of the day, pressing themselves, their children, and their flocks to their fastest rate. But the greater part of their quickened breathing and pounding hearts was due to constant searching glances over their shoulders.

There, the whole northern horizon billowed with smoke. Vaucouleurs's walls had thwarted the Burgundians. They were not a large enough party to attempt to storm them, so they'd turned their attention to the exposed valley instead. They dawdled on their way, but their destruction was thorough enough.

The villagers fled before them, everything they could drive, push, or carry going with them toward the safety promised by Neufchâteau. As for the rest—well, most of it, they never hoped to see again.

Jacquot d'Arc and his family had set off with a full cart harnessed to old Grison, the milch cow tied up behind. They'd given place in the bed of the cart to 'Ti'-Reine's grandmother in the beginning, to the little girl later, when her little five-year-old feet gave out along the way.

There was no mistaking the way. It was marked by possessions those fleeing before them had picked up as they were leaving home and then decided they couldn't carry, abandoned by the side of the road.

The folk of Domrémy had just passed the road leading to the abandoned castle of the Bourlémonts—the lord and his men being away fighting in France—when the cart's left wheel caught on the rock-hard arc of an old rut. Pierre, who'd been set to lead Grison, gave the straining rump a whisk with his stick. The poor old beast stumbled forward, the wheel pitched up and over the rut and landed hard, too hard for how overloaded the vehicle was. Even over the bleating of the sheep it was her task to follow, Jehannette heard the sickening crack of the axle, the screams of 'Ti'-Reine and her grandmother.

So their cart and most of its contents joined the other belongings beside the road.

"The Burgundians will have my baking trough." Zabillet Romée wept.

"Better it than you," Jacquot d'Arc snapped back at his wife with stern impatience.

She wept silently into her sleeve after that.

Jacquot also yelled at his son for the carelessness that had caused the accident.

"Hell with it," Pierre replied. "I'd rather be fighting the Burgundians than running from them."

Jacquot d'Arc snatched the switch out of his son's hand and laid it hard across the boy's backside. "And that's nothing compared to what the Burgundians'll give you if they catch a fool boy like you," he said.

Pierre struggled between tears and pride. But what could he do, where could he run with his whole family, everything he'd every known, uprooted and on the road south? Finally he said, "Let Jehannette take the horse then. I'll go with the sheep."

Jehannette looked at her father, afraid he'd lash out at her, too. A girl lead a horse? Pierre only wanted someone else to feel their father's wrath and Jehannette's thoughts raced, trying to think how to turn it from herself. Her father met her eyes, looked back to the smoke-draped northern horizon again, then shrugged.

So once they got him unharnessed and 'Ti'-Reine and her grandmother transferred to Grison's back, Jehannette, with a deep breath, openly picked up the reins, still wet with her brother's sweat. Grison breathed a welcome upon her hand, quietly, as if to say, "Let's not make too much of this, my glory girl."

Jehannette swung her small bundle of clothes wrapped in a cloak over the other shoulder and put foot before foot on the road again.

Dusk was falling as the weary folk of Domrémy began the last climb toward the grey stone ramparts of Neufchâteau. A few thin beeches lined the path, choked by the dust of scores of previous refugees. The trees seemed stunted and crippled compared to the proud Fairy Tree at home. Jehannette wondered if this is what happened to people torn up by their roots and planted too close to Neufchâteau's walls to thrive.

They were close enough now that they could see the watch, kindling their fires on the ramparts of the Gate of France. They could hear them, too, calling to one another over the protestations of the tired animals and the crying of the children.

"Good Lord, more of them."

"By St. François and his bones, too, the streets can't hold another soul."

"Where are you from?" the men called down.

"Domrémy," Jehannette's father and the other heads of households answered together.

"Greux," said others they'd traveled with and "Burey-le-Petit." For her uncle, aunt, and the baby as well as many of their neighbors had fled their homes in the north two days before. They'd spent the time resting, telling their horror around Jacquot d'Arc's hearth, until the nearing clouds of smoke made their hosts ready to move on with them.

"We had the folks from Maxey earlier. I guess it's time for these folks now."

The man of the watch gave a shrug as he said this. Jehannette's reaction was nowhere near as careless. So the people of Maxey were here. That meant Renard. But surely Neufchâteau was a big place. She might never have to come face to face with him.

And that worry was wiped from her mind by Grison's stumble.

"Ah, you poor old horse," she calmed him.

His own shoes had grown too heavy for him after all this way. Jehannette gripped the bridle with comforting strength and instantly threw her own weight against the great grey side threatening to collapse. She kept him on his feet and 'Ti'-Reine and her old grandmother steady on his back.

Then she said, "Come on down, now, 'Ti'-Reine."

"No," came the saucy reply.

"Poor old Grison can't carry a big girl like you any more, and, see, we're almost there."

"No."

The little girl wriggled, avoiding Jehannette's outstretched hand, and Grison blew a great sigh of protest.

"Look, there goes your *maman,* on ahead. She will be the first to see the inside of the town."

This brought the little girl slipping down into Jehannette's arms, then scrambling up the hill on her own legs. "*Maman, maman,* wait for me. Your 'Ti'-Reine wants to see Neufchâteau, too."

"And you, Grandmother?" Jehannette asked the old woman. She could not ask her to come down, too, unless she was prepared to carry her on her own back, for the crone couldn't walk at all. "Are you all right?"

The grandmother replied with a nod but she didn't, Jehannette noticed, waste breath for words. Probably too much pain in her joints.

While this had been happening in her immediate charge, Jehannette had also noted further shouts coming at them from the men on the wall.

One of the faceless helmets yelled, "What? You're not going to bring your sheep and goats in here?"

Pierre and Jean were having trouble enough keeping the pig, the cow and the herds together when their exhausted legs and full udders made the beasts think only of home. The combined sounds of bleating and lowing and squealing on the evening air stung Jehannette's own ears with a fear and misery of her own.

She suppressed it, and strained to hear Jean's reply to the man instead. Her brother's head was away from her, however, toward the wall, and the crying animals pressed around him so she heard nothing.

She did hear the helmet on the wall reply. "Impossible. There isn't room, not even for milch cows. No fodder, either. People only. Take them around to the east there. Down by the Mouzon River, before it joins the Meuse. Before the mills, there's pasturage. Yes, it's already quite crowded, but it's the best we have. And our archers will be able to give them— well, some protection, anyway, should the bastards get this close."

The jostling and general confusion, which had exhausted Jehannette's senses all day, now increased as the herds backed up through the press of foot traffic. It did make her wonder how all these bodies could fit into one confined space. Added to the refugees were now people who had ventured out by day—for firewood and greens to add to the cooking pot, or to tend their own beasts—scurrying back to safety before nightfall.

"Give me the buckets, wife," Jehannette's father said to her mother, and relieved her of the yoke she'd carried across her shoulders all day, exchanging her burden for his.

"The boys and I will milk them tonight, once we've got them settled," he went on. "We'll slop the hog with what's more than these buckets will carry and bring the rest back. That'll be something for our supper, anyway."

"But where do we go? Where shall I meet you again? I don't know this town at all. Let me go with you, Jacquot. I'd feel safer with you." During this speech, a glaze of panic came across her mother's eyes and she gripped her husband's sleeve with the one hand she now had free.

Jacquot d'Arc turned from her panic to look northward. A trick of evening light made the Burgundians' smoke seem very close, a shift of the air filled the lungs with its odor—or was it only the stifling proximity of so many fires in Neufchâteau?

Jacquot d'Arc translated his wife's fear, and his own, to fury. "Get into the town, woman. Take your daughter and get safe behind those walls."

"But where shall we go?"

Jehannette saw her father struggled before finding control and clamping onto it. "Go to the house of the Franciscans," he told her. "They'll take you in."

"But everyone I spoke to on the way is planning to go to the Franciscans."

"Only the people without kin in town." Jacquot added bitterly, "Like us."

"Can even the friars have space for so many?"

"You must go and find out, Zabillet." He was almost gentle now with her helplessness. "Jehannette will be a good help to you. The boys and I will come and look for you at the monastery. We certainly don't have money for any inn."

The curl on his lips gave the suggestion there was something not quite right about an inn besides its cost. Something bad for a female. Something like running off with a band of soldiers.

"It must be the Franciscans," he concluded. "We have no choice."

Zabillet Romée swallowed and nodded. She stood by the side of the road, watching the back of her man for a while, then turned to the comfort of her daughter.

Jehannette, meanwhile, had helped the old woman to dismount.

"You see how it is, Grandmother? I must take the old horse to pasture with the rest of the beasts. Sit on this stone by the road. Here, I will give you my cloak to sit on and my bundle to keep. My mother will stay with you until your family or my brothers can come and carry you."

But as she turned to lead Grison after the sheep, the voice from the top of the walls called, "Wait. Where are you going? You, with the horse. You, girl. Yes. I'm talking to you."

Jehannette lifted her head and saw that, indeed, the blank slits of the helmet were looking directly at her. She felt her pulse racing, her mouth gone dry. Don't be afraid, she told herself. Then she realized that what she felt when she craned her neck up at that glinting metallic figure wasn't fear at all. It was—envy. Perhaps even a little scorn that that man should think a helmet and breastplate made him greater than she.

Someday, I will be in such a place, she thought.

Instantly, she told herself she was mad. Or exhausted, anyway, from the long walk.

But "Yes, Daughter-God," she heard her Voices say. Off to the right, in that breathless glint of light like a butterfly in the leaves of that beech.

"For horses, there is room within the gates," the soldier said.

"See, Jehannette," Pierre muttered to her as he swung by, pursuing the tail end of the sheep. "There's a man who knows the value of things. Leave it to a soldier."

Her brother laid his hand fondly on the old gelding's rounded shoulder, felt the animal breathing, still hard though they'd been stopped quite a while now, in great, sad sighs.

"Poor old Grison," he said briefly. Then, tossing his head toward the wall: "It must be getting too dark for milord up there to see very well, if he thinks he's going to ride the poor old fellow against Burgundy. Or maybe he only wants the hooves. To make glue to stick fletches on his arrows, maybe."

"How can you say it?" Jehannette flew at him, fists, flying.

Pierre laughed, held her back the distance of his long arm. "See? Maybe you ought to have brought your distaff along after all instead of leaving it to arm the enemy. Go on, Jehannette. Go on and lead the old fellow in. I'm sure they'll feed him like the very best of their steeds."

Pierre left and Jehannette did as he told her. She was suddenly too tired to fight any more. With her mother, she helped the old woman up on Grison's back. Then they plodded under the city gate and entered Neufchâteau.

29

Tendrils of Red from a Kerchief

The moment they were inside Neufchâteau, the poor old woman had to get down again. Another helmet—or was it the same one?—accosted them and took the bridle from Jehannette's hands.

"Horses this way," he said. "We'll keep him here."

"Good Lord," he went on, after Grison stumbled again. "He is an old sack of bones, isn't he? Oh, well. Orders are orders."

Jehannette's hand still reached for the dear animal. Grison turned his head and snorted as if to say, "You're not coming, too, my glory girl?"

"Take good care of him," she cried.

"Of course, of course," the soldier said, his words hissing within the hollow of his helmet.

"Grison, I'll come and visit you every day. We'll ride, if we can. And soon, soon I'll lead you home to your own pasture again."

Grison whinnied in reply, then he had vanished, around the corner of a building.

There were far too many corners of buildings in this place, Jehannette decided within her next glance around. And all too close together. The prospect was stifling. There was no spot for the old woman to sit with any comfort. The way was too narrow, too filthy with what was not clean dirt. She would be crushed. She stood, bent nearly double in her pain, clinging to Zabillet Romée. Neither woman seemed capable of thought.

"Come, we must find the Franciscans," Jehannette told them.

"Grandmother Marie cannot walk," Zabillet said.

Jehannette ignored her mother and tried to stop a woman scurrying past them with a basket over her arm. "Excuse me."

The woman gave no reply but hurried on.

The next person she tried to stop, a young boy carrying firewood, stopped only long enough to spit across her path and say, "A pox on all refugees."

"Aye, and we shall get it here within your walls," she shouted back at him.

The fellow grew pale, almost dropped his fagots, and ran off beyond another corner, muttering something about "a witch."

"Fool," Jehannette grumbled, but stopped herself from saying more.

She noticed a woman across the narrow way and a bit, standing in stockinged feet on the low stone threshold of her door. She was a broad woman, from her gap-toothed grin to her feet planted widely on the stoop. And she was very red: Tendrils of red sprang out of her kerchief. The flush of her face bled well down to where her bosom strained at the lacing of her chemise. She'd taken off her sleeves at the shoulders to work at some scrubbing or baking, and the linen shoved up above her elbows showed meaty, freckled forearms and more red hair.

This woman had watched the exchange with the wood hauler with open amusement. A St. Christophe set in the plaster wall beside her might have spoken of aid offered to travelers. But with the houses cheek by jowl here, who could say if it was her house after all? A leather tankard dangled from a chain directly over her head. But "We cannot stay in an inn," Jehannette's father had said.

Jehannette wasn't even going to ask that broad grin the way to the Franciscans and make it that much broader with satisfaction.

She went back to her mother and the old woman. "Come on. We'll find it."

The old woman simply could not walk. She seemed to have shriveled even more in this one day. Yet, meager as they were for being all they had in the world, Jehannette and her mother both still carried enough possessions to make carrying her out of the question. They didn't dare drop their things, not here in this place . . .

Before Jehannette had figured out how to solve this problem, 'Ti'-Reine, her mother, and three or four of the other women from Domrémy, including Uncle Durand's wife and the baby, all appeared, returning around yet another corner.

"Ah, good," Jehannette said. "Look, Grandmother. Here come your daughter-in-law and granddaughter. They will have news and help."

"The Franciscans have no room left for us" was their tale. "For men, yes, within their sanctuary. But they cannot allow women into most of the abbey, and the places where women can be are full."

"People, women, children are sleeping in the streets, further up," Uncle Durand's wife whimpered. "They shooed us away from under the eaves of the church porch. The house owners shooed us from their walls."

The infant in her arms was crying. He had soaked through his linen long ago, and the dampness stained far down the woman's green skirt. 'Ti'-Reine had begun to cry, too, in a temper, stamping her feet and calling for her "chou-chou." Her little cloth doll, it seemed, had been forgotten at home in the rush to flee, and the little girl's five years could not compass the loss.

This is the subject of Gospel stories, isn't it? Jehannette asked herself.

"We'll find someplace," she told the women, her mind imagining stables and straw, like the Christ Child's surroundings—where Grison had gone. The mothers probably wouldn't like their children sleeping anywhere near horses' hooves. But surely there must be some sort of shelter there.

She suggested the women with children stay with the crone and the baggage while she and the others hurried off to find the place. It gave her a moment's pause that she was the one still in red skirts and all these women in green were looking to her, waiting for her to tell them what to do. But nobody else was making decisions.

"Those of us who go ought to stick together," she said. Even so, she told herself, I won't have to pass too many of these corners before I can't find my way back again. They all look so alike.

While these adjustments were being made, Jehannette noticed that the red woman under the tankard sign had stepped within for a moment. Someone had called her, it seemed. Before Jehannette could take a deep breath of relief, however, the woman was back, her feet shoved into wooden pattens. These raised her stature a good hand's width above the muck in the street as she clomped across the way toward them.

"Women of Domrémy?" she addressed them.

Jehannette found herself speaking for the rest, hesitant, almost hostile, though the word came out. "Yes?"

"Everyone calls me La Rousse, for obvious reasons." She yanked a strand of red hair further out of her kerchief. "I keep this house here, this inn, the Saint-Christophe, and I'd be happy if you'd come and stay under my roof 'til, God willing, this all passes over."

The other women were already murmuring with relief and thanks before Jehannette could get out the words: "Thank you, goodwife, but we can't afford to pay you."

"Who's talking of any payment?" La Rousse protested.

Perhaps it was just because she'd done the talking—though still in a red kirtle—but Jehannette felt the woman's blue eyes ringed with fair red lashes studying her very keenly. Certainly anyone would want to know the character of strangers she meant to invite into her home, but why study her so much more than the rest? And there was that grin as she did so, as if she knew something . . .

"You brought herds and cattle with you, didn't you?" La Rousse kept bubbling in a busy fashion, just like a kettle on the fire. "Out on the lea? Yes, I'm sure you'll help me and mine put food on the table for those who can pay while you're here and that will be enough."

"Of course, of course." The other women were all speaking now.

"And would I be a Christian, to turn you away at a time like this, babies and all?"

The women were already hefting their loads again and following the way she led. La Rousse herself got a good, firm red arm under the grandmother and fairly carried her after the others across the street.

Jehannette, feeling her legs made of lead, brought up the rear. Hesitating further, she stood a moment on the threshold, rocking her own wooden shoes on the unevenness in the stone.

The inn's interior was already plunged in the coming darkness, but a few candles worked against the gloom of this windowless foreroom. It was hot and stuffy, though no fire burned in the nearest grate, only in a kitchen beyond. There, from the depths of kettles, came heavy, rapid sounds and damp, delicious fragrance. The place smelled, too, of ale, the heaviness of yeast, the bitterness of hops, but it was not a bad smell. Everything underlying this smelled clean enough.

The inn was crowded. In the half-light, as her eyes adjusted, Jehannette picked out many forms. Who were her friends and who strangers? She couldn't fathom it yet.

She heard La Rousse's voice and looked that way, up a steep twist of wooden stair to the right on which the hostess's pattens clattered.

"It's just one room I can offer you, but it is my largest. You'll all have to sleep on the floor. I'll have my lads here move out the rest of the furniture, just to give you more space, and you'll all be together."

"Our men are coming . . ." Zabillet Romée's voice faded as she followed the woman upstairs.

"Well, I'm afraid I've no more room for men. I am sorry, goodwife. They'll be fine, though. Up on the ramparts with the soldiers, if nothing else. We'll send to them, to tell them you're safe. See, now, isn't this fine? Very light. We'll just open the window to get a little air . . ."

The sabots of all of Domrémy's women drowned out the alewife's voice now. Jehannette still stood on the threshold, seeing little of the room yet, seeing nothing but vague, dark shapes shifting.

I must go after them, I suppose, Jehannette thought. The smell of food compelled her and she began a weary step inside. It will feel good to rest—anywhere.

She made the step—then heard her Voices, there, to the right, in the light beneath the stairwell. "Daughter-God," they said. It was faint, as if they spoke with no more than the sound of the dried rush that burned in nut oil there, as if they'd been shut away from her in some coffer.

Or as if, on entering Neufchâteau, she was the one on whom the coffer lid had shut.

"Daughter–God." Though she could barely hear them, they seemed to be calling a warning.

Danger. What danger? Jehannette froze, listening, looking. What could the matter be with a woman like La Rousse? A woman who, out of the kindness of her heart, welcomed strangers in?

Then, under the ale smell, the smell of supper and the smell of cleanliness, Jehannette got a whiff of—could it be?—magic.

La Rousse was a sorceress? Well, such skills often went along with a knowledge of the mysteries of brewing. Ale, in its own way, was certainly potion enough. But why should her Voices warn her, even from a sorceress? Père Michel had his magic, and they never warned her from him. The beech Tree, the magic of Night Battles. These were things they fairly flung her toward.

A young man was helping the women of Domrémy haul their bundles up the steep stairs. They would reach them upward and time after time his head would thrust itself into the stairwell. He'd reach down and relieve them of baskets and bales.

Certainly there must be windows on the floor above, rising over the neighboring houses, catching twilight's last glow. Once or twice, as the head appeared in the opening, Jehannette thought it must be La Rousse herself, having shed her linen coif. The light caught glints of the same sort of red in this boy's shorter hair. What should be strange, ominous, in the fact that this widowed alewife should have a son who'd inherited her features?

The stairwell cleared of climbing forms. She heard many footsteps creaking the beams over her head. She longed to join them, just to have a place to sit for a moment. She took another step inside.

The red boy's head sprang into the light at the top of the stairs again.

"What? No more?" he called. "I would have sworn there was one more woman in Domrémy."

Then he saw her. "Jehannette!" he called. "Come on."

He swung down the stairs two at a time and was at her side in a moment, snatching bundles from her until she felt herself standing exposed, almost naked, without a bundle to hold before her chest.

There was, of course, one other person of her acquaintance who had red hair of just such a foxy hue. It was Renard. Renard of Maxey.

30

Satan's Apple

"I'll keep an eye on the little ones," Jehannette offered, more than a week later.

The mothers were pleased not to have the threat of leaving the merry company anytime soon.

"I'll come with you," Renard offered, stopping her at the bottom of the stairs.

Jehannette felt the women behind them exchanging knowing glances and titters. But his hand on her arm made her flesh creep.

"No. I'm . . . I'm sorry." Something close to panic made the words sharper than she meant. "I must be alone."

And she fled, leaving him staring after her.

The heat grew more intense, not less, as Jehannette made her way up from the kitchen. The tight, dark stairwell crammed with steep, narrow stairs rocked unsteadily in its wooden frame. First her head, then the rest of her emerged into a golden sunlight, blinding after the dark below and still warmer.

Nevertheless, it was good to be free of the chatter of so many women and the smells that stuffed the well, stacked like the stairs: The smells of dinner's boiled cabbage and turnips overlaying the many tightly packed human bodies allowed no refreshing escape to a stream to wash either body or clothes. And these smells overlaid a bedrock stench of ale and of the privy. Many more visitors than it was used to, and no way for the contents to be carted out to the fields in the meantime, both combined had clogged the small wooden cabinet in the yard.

This was Neufchâteau. Jehannette sighed for the thousandth time. She herself had prophesied it, had she not? Prophesied all the Meuse Valley from Vaucouleurs and even Toul sluiced up behind the safety of Neufchâteau's walls, men, women, children, all. But in all her prophecy she had failed to see how stifling she herself would find the place in late June.

Nor that her Voices—which had always been her consolation in unpleasant situations before—would grow dumb in such a place. She had the feeling they were still speaking—a continuous hum like frogs by the brook on a summer's night. But like the frogs, though she knew they were still there— they must be there or she would perish of grief—she couldn't hear them over the day-and-night press of humanity.

Even the sounding of the hours from Neufchâteau's church towers—a sound she had often considered the medium of her Voices, like strings to be plucked by sweet, skillful hands on a lute—served here rather to drum all sensitivity from her brain.

And until now she hadn't realized how dependent she'd become on their counsel during the three years since they'd first made their presence known to her. Their hum, or at least the hope that she would hear more shortly, had become like bone and sinew to her being. She and her family had been ten days in Neufchâteau, and every passing day seemed another day boiling her bones down to jelly. It seemed just as difficult to move as if her sinews had in fact been hamstrung.

The room at the top of the stairs was even brighter and warmer than the hall that led to it. The ceiling's slope, pierced by a dormer, faced full west, the other small window south. Both were open to the noise of yards and street below, but it was still stifling, directly under the press of the afternoon sun. Nevertheless, it was quieter than where she'd come from. Jehannette entered gratefully and shut the door behind her as quietly as she could so as not to awaken the two sleeping occupants.

'Ti'-Reine and Jehannette's new baby cousin were there,

having their afternoon naps. The warm room was thick with the innocent fragrance of infant sleep. Jehannette loved it, and she stood in the sunlight breathing it in for several minutes.

Jehannette didn't sleep well at night. The nights were muggy, the baby woke and fussed and woke 'Ti'-Reine, who fussed. The small inn room was wall-to-wall bodies then. Jehannette envied the men their air. Muggy weather was good mushrooming weather but nobody could take advantage of the dancing white rings in the cool forest shade. Nobody here under the sign of La Rousse's tankard.

In the last ten days—the first night, actually—Jehannette had learned that La Rousse was mother's sister to young Renard of Maxey and Toul, the fox-haired boy from the Night Battles. Her nephew had demanded the favor so that both families would be under one roof. For the past ten days, Jehannette had been obliged to work very closely with the young man's sisters, mother and grandmother.

Zabillet Romée liked the Maxey women. Even La Rousse, who had a reputation—as a brew-wife must—of the morals at her house not being quite what they ought, was endearing in her loud, brash, buxom manner. And only the most wretched soul would fail to be grateful to her for the open hand she showed to so many who had so little. She opened her cellars and smokehouse as if it were Yuletide. Or as if the folk of Domrémy were able to pay more than their disturbed herds' irregular milk and an ailing sheep or goat every other day or so. The result was an ongoing, lively if crowded party. Rather, Jehannette hated to think it, like an extended wedding.

Which is exactly what La Rousse hoped it would turn into. She made no secret about it all, and in the very same raucous terms with which she might discuss such things with her Saturday night regulars.

Jehannette thought she shouldn't mind the teasing. She'd been teased all her life over one thing or another. Perhaps before, when she'd been younger, she'd been happy for any attention. And then, later, she'd had her Voices for comfort. Also, everything people had found to laugh at in her before was something of which she was secretly proud: She was a tomboy. She liked to ride. She had a tinder-dry temper. The fact that at sixteen her kirtle was still bright red.

"I'll show you," she'd always thought prideful words toward her tormentors. "What you criticize in me will someday be a good."

But she simply could not bear with equal grace to have her name joined with Renard's every time she turned around. It was the first thing she was teased for that, the more she imagined it actually happening, the less she could abide the idea.

It was even worse when Renard was present.

With no fields to go to, no fences to mend, no wood to chop, the men hadn't much to occupy themselves. Nothing to do but join the watch upon the city walls where they surveyed the northern horizon for the billowing black and glowing red of fire and tried to decide among themselves whose village was going up now.

"Can it be Maxey?"

"It must be, so close to Mount Julian."

Then trying to put some good face on it, "Well, yes. We did lose the Night Battle this year." And a sideways look at the cause of that loss.

That couldn't be pleasant work, Jehannette had to grant. It wasn't pleasant to have to deal with the men afterward. To be brought the new rumors every night and then to debate them with the women every day.

Jehannette would rather be up on the wall herself. She'd rather give these helpless men something to do and lead them against the Burgundians in person.

So she couldn't blame Renard for his sudden arrivals in the kitchen, not only for meals but many times during the day, as she chopped carrots, as she did the washing up. But she also couldn't keep the tension he brought with him from exhausting her so she couldn't stand and had to beg to go upstairs to nap for a while.

So now she stood in the middle of the hot, bundle-strewn floor, with only sleeping babes for company, and the relief was like the cooling of a sudden breeze upon her fevered skin.

What could be the matter with her? Renard seemed a nice

boy. Boy, she called him in her mind, never man. She'd even liked him well enough—except for his persistence in interrupting her Voices—until this flight to Neufchâteau. Now, suddenly, for all the joking, everything had turned so serious.

Her young aunt and the other girls hardly let her sleep at night for telling her how fine they thought her beau, how handsome, how well figured, how kind, how well placed, how certain to prosper.

"Oh, my Durand's a dishclout to him," her aunt had said—about her own husband, the father of the child she was nursing even as she'd said it.

Why couldn't Jehannette share their enthusiasm? What was wrong with her?

She sighed and sank to the rectangle of blankets that marked her spot upon the floor, between her mother's place and the sleeping 'Ti-Reine. She landed on something unusually lumpy and hard. Rubbing her bruised backside, she sorted among the blankets until at last she withdrew the object. She got it turned right way round—for she recognized at once that this was a thing that had a top and a bottom. It was, in fact, an odd sort of doll as big as her baby cousin if not bigger. It was made from a root of some sort, the lower portion of whose thin body nature had divided into two very human legs. Nature had even given, Jehannette noticed, a third little knob around which were growing tiny little hairs. That, she thought, was much more lifelike than a child's toy needed to be.

She quickly pulled down the smock that had been made for the thing from a scrap of cloth. She noted the rough face that had been carved into the brown root just below the crown, the large, drying, dark green leaves that had been left in place as hair although they gave off a fetid odor. Another scrap of cloth served as a cap.

She was glad someone had finally made something for 'Ti'-Reine to love, for that was what Jehannette supposed it was. With her "chou-chou" back in Domrémy, the poor child had been inconsolable the first nights away. She'd begun to find some delight in Jehannette's baby cousin—whom she mothered as often as they'd let her—but it was good she had something of her own now for the times when only the infant's real mother would do.

Jehannette tucked the doll up beside its "*maman*," loved the beauty of the child's sleeping face, damp with sweat and blue eye-lidded. Then she quietly rocked back to her own space. She lay down and tried to relax.

The worst of the whole Renard business was her father. She'd expected him to side with her, at least. Jacquot d'Arc had been as surprised as she had been at the invitation from this woman "with the misfortune of Burgundian relations." And for a while, Jehannette had held out hopes that he'd refuse the hospitality, rude though that might be, not to mention inconvenient.

But during the past ten days, Jacquot d'Arc had clearly changed his mind about his ancient enemies, the Burgundians—at least about those that hailed from Maxey.

"These are good people." He'd drawn Jehannette aside to tell her this just last night. "The Burgundian troops have been as abominable to them—their own people—as they have been to us. This army has ravaged both sides of the Meuse—they don't care. Maxey was the very first to burn. We've had clear word of it and knowledge that anyone who stayed behind there is dead. And just see how kind and generous these folk have been to us."

She hadn't been able to give him a reply. Not even a straight look in the eye.

Jacquot d'Arc had glanced away. Talking had never been his strength. And here he had no forest to retreat to with his ax.

He shrugged. "Anyway, I've given the lad my permission to court you."

"Papa—"

"I know you're—you're not wearing green yet, but there's no reason why you couldn't court, even betroth, if you'd a mind to. His people have even said they'd take you into their home and care for you and you could learn their ways beforehand. I must say, at this point, nothing would please me more."

"Papa!" she'd cried, her heart breaking.

But because she hadn't been able to say anything else, he'd only looked away and shrugged his heavy shoulders again.

"There's time, of course. There's not much of Maxey to go back to, by the sound of it. No more than of Domrémy, so they say, so maybe it doesn't matter, one way or the other. Only in such a world as this—"

He'd sighed and she'd thought even a tear crept into his eye. He'd turned quickly away and she couldn't tell for sure.

"Anyway, it would be good for someone else to have a care for you. I'm getting old."

And that had been his final word on the subject.

"But I don't need taking care of," she whispered in a too-late reply. "It's I who must care for . . ."

She let the phrase drop, uncompleted. She no longer felt that compulsion, now that she had no Voices to back her.

Perhaps it was all as her friends and family told her. The moment she became a woman, she would come to understand love between men and women and to long for it. But the private fear continued to niggle her: What if she never did become a woman? Where she lay now, a woman's skin seemed so foreign to her. Yes, she could quite believe she was a totally different species. Something so rare, few knew to name it and so give it shape.

Père Michel had named it. La Pucelle . . .

"Oh, Auntie Jehannette."

"Hello, 'Ti'-Reine. Did you sleep well?" Jehannette whispered, trying to show the little girl waking beside her that they must still be quiet for the baby's sake.

But see, Jehannette thought to herself. Even innocent children give me the names of women. "Auntie." She had to admit she liked it very much.

And, as she looked at the sweet, sleep-tousled head—the short, pale brown curls plastered to one side of the child's face, the red marks of bedding in the sweat-softened and plumped skin and the little beads of sweat across the bridge of her pert, upturned nose—Jehannette felt a pang. She loved children. To have one of her own would be so—so renewing was the best word she could think of. Little ones, over and over, always new and unformed, holding out the hope that this time it would be right. This time life would not be as limited as one's self by expectations and personal quirks.

But what if the name of that renewing thing women looked for in their infants was not 'Ti'-Reine or Jehannette or any other name godmothers gave. What if it was La Pucelle? And what if, by embracing the common push to marry and have a child of her own, she would be denying the power of that very formlessness she sought when she pushed herself into the common mold?

"But Auntie Jehannette."

'Ti'-Reine had been chatting at her and Jehannette hadn't been attending.

"What is it, 'Ti'-Reine? We must be quiet so we don't wake the baby. But what is it?"

"You gave me the doll." She said it in the precise, petulant way children use when they must repeat something for an adult who hasn't been listening. Her little lisp exaggerated the effect.

"Your new chou-chou got lost in my bed, sweetheart. I found her—him—" Jehannette remembered what was under the doll's smock. "—And gave him back to you."

"No." 'Ti'-Reine was quite sure of herself. And she continued, with more lisp-slurred precision, the recital of what grown-ups had told her over and over. "My chou-chou is back in Domrémy and we shall not be able to get her until we go home again."

Oh, why did they tell the child such things? Domrémy might burn along with Maxey and how could they give her hope that one rag doll might survive out of all the rest? Honey-coating the truth was the first way parents put shells of despair around the perfect formlessness of their offspring.

When I have a child—Jehannette began to promise herself.

But 'Ti'-Reine went on to say, "This isn't my doll. It's yours."

"I'm too old to have a doll," Jehannette said, thinking that actually she couldn't remember ever having been young enough.

"But you're not old enough to have a baby and until you're old enough to have a baby, La Rousse says, you must play with dolls."

"La Rousse?"

Jehannette snatched the doll from 'Ti'-Reine's offering hand. The violence of the move bruised more of the strange, fetid odor of the leaves into the air. Jehannette felt it filling her lungs and rising like mist into her brain.

"This doll came from La Rousse?" Jehannette demanded of the child, and remembered suddenly that the brew-wife's sordid reputation was not just for harlotry, but for something else besides. Petty sorcery. Casting fortunes, preventing unwanted births—always useful in a tavern—and the opposite. Love charms. It went along with her red hair. With Renard's red hair.

"When?" Jehannette demanded, quite forgetting now to keep her voice down.

"Today. This morning. When *maman* brought me up for my nap, La Rousse came, too, and said she should tuck it into your blankets and then we should have a wedding soon enough."

"And I would have come up later, in the dark, and felt it, perhaps, but been unable to find it until morning after a night of sleeping with it . . ."

Her anger woke up her little cousin and he began to wail, but Jehannette paid no attention. The baby was able to vent feelings in a way she longed to, but had to repress.

She knew the root now. Rare but powerful, pulled shrieking from the ground by full moon. In fact, it was best to draw a protective circle around its crown of leaves when you found it and set a dog or goat to do the pulling, for the shrieks were so horrific that the puller was in great danger of dying at the task.

"Mandrake," Jehannette said the fearsome name aloud, then renamed it the even more dreaded appellation, "Satan's Apple."

No stronger love spell was known to witching women than this root said to grow from the juices that dropped beneath the gallows from hanged men.

Jehannette found herself laughing a little wildly, matching in tone the baby's rising screams. "Well, perhaps that is exactly what I needed to make me normal, marry Renard and live happily ever after in Maxey-sur-Meuse."

But even as she said it, she was on her feet and at the little dormer window. She pitched the root out over the roofs as hard as she could, ignoring the shrill protests of both children now behind her. She was quite content to see the thing lose its ragged smock as it smacked against the thatch opposite, then skitter down into the yard below. There, a sow with ranks of saggy teats began to root at the doll, content because the press of refugees in town had sorely limited her pickings in recent days.

"Well, Neufchâteau pigs shall flourish this year," Jehannette said with contentment equal to the sow's. Only then did she turn and begin to try and comfort 'Ti'-Reine.

"You shouldn't have done that, Auntie Jehannette." The girl was sobbing. "La Rousse has a powerful magic. My mother says so."

"We'll just see if my magic isn't more powerful than hers," Jehannette replied.

Now the mothers had come in shocked haste to save their children and wonder what Auntie Jehannette had done to them. 'Ti'-Reine had to tell the whole tale and the mothers shook their heads for shame.

But the putrid smell of mandrake clung still to Jehannette's fingers and filled her brain. She'd been too long in contact with the sorcerer's root.

Jehannette knew herself bewitched.

31

The Dragon Curling at Ste. Marguerite's Feet

"I want to be a nun."

Jehannette repeated her statement to Brother Luc at the Franciscans' gate. She'd been saying it to herself all afternoon, in a sort of desperation.

But even as she said it, she knew "I want to be a nun" was not what she meant.

Why wouldn't her Voices come and tell her what she meant?

"I am La Pucelle," was what she thought she was trying to say. But even she found that difficult to believe, let alone understand, here in Neufchâteau.

One look at the already-closed face of Brother Luc told her he wasn't going to help her explain it any better. It had been so much easier in the woods of Père Michel's hermitage.

"I've promised myself to God" was the closest she could come within the stifle of these city walls.

Everyone translated that, though not very happily, as, "She wants to be a nun," until she came around to saying it, too.

"I want to be a nun." The smell of mandrake still weighted down her brain.

After all, in the usual framework of the world, if a girl did not become a wife, what else was there for her?

At La Rousse's, in fact, there seemed but the single option, that of wife, and "nun" was not met with much enthusiasm by anyone.

"Then you must look into the life," her father alone had

said, though not as if he truly believed it, either. "You must go to the brethren here, see what they say, and learn what should be done. I can't give you much of a dowry, you know," he added. "Renard is content, but I'm not at all certain the Church will be."

"We are a men's house here," Brother Luc replied, fingering the warts on his chin, as he eyed her closely.

"I know. And you are full of refugees at the moment."

The light impatience of her tone made him raise his brows. "The closest house for women is Courcelles, and it would be impossible to get there through the Neufeys Forest until the Burgundians leave us in peace."

"I know."

"In fact, I worry for the poor sisters at this time, undefended as they are. The life of brides of Christ is not an easy one, my daughter."

Jehannette flinched at that word, "bride," but she found her tongue to reply, "I am prepared for hardship."

Brother Luc continued to look her up and down. She averted her eyes from his scrutiny and studied the Ste. Marguerite beside the door instead. Ste. Marguerite as a shepherdess, the chained dragon curling submissive at her feet. Ste. Marguerite who had consecrated her virginity to God against the wishes of her father, a pagan priest, and of many a lustful suitor.

This wasn't her first time at the Franciscans'. In fact, she'd come to confession nearly every day since their arrival in Neufchâteau, until the confessor had said, "There is such a thing as too much, my child. You mustn't shirk to help your mother."

And, "That is the sin of pride, child, to think you are the cause of this curse of Burgundians upon us."

And when she'd explained the whole situation with Renard, the friar had said, "A daughter's first duty is obedience to her parents. You cannot think that your mother and father want anything but the best for you."

"Of course not." It had never crossed her mind that it could be otherwise.

"And marriage is the curse of Eve upon her daughters."

But confession had been a relief from the press of people and the teasing at La Rousse's inn. And now there seemed no other way to counter the effect of the Satan's Apple she'd been unable to scrub from her skin.

"I want to be a nun," she said again, as if she'd take the house of retreat by storm as soon as any Burgundian fortress.

"Very well," Brother Luc replied at last. "I can take you on a tour of our house, explain our rule to you, see if it is something you could submit to. I must warn you, there are many places I cannot take you. Women may not enter most portions of our house. The brethren must not be disturbed in their holiness by any daughter of Eve."

"I understand."

So he showed her the chapel, cloister, and refectory, no more. But the cloister was enough. In that little piece of nature, forced into rigid blocks of strictly useful, weedless herbs though it was, she saw a butterfly, black and yellow and brown. And in that instant, she heard her Voices for the first time in a fortnight.

"Daughter-God, this is not for you" was all they said.

She bowed her head. "I know."

She found Brother Luc glaring at her, his brows clumped together unhappily. He thought her mad, no doubt, and worried that there were all too many such in holy houses.

He led her on hurriedly. The words "La Pucelle" came after her as if on butterfly wings—until stopped by the harsh shadow of the abbey walls. Like a fortress, she thought, keeping out what is all my religion.

"Thank you, Brother," she said.

She knelt for a blessing on a pebble walk and then went on her way.

———— • ————

That night, Domrémy burned.

Jehannette ignored her mother's warning and went up to watch it on the walls with the men.

Here, Renard finally caught up with her.

"So. Would you really be a nun?" His voice seemed to fortify itself against the worst.

"How can I, with this horror . . . ?"

She stopped herself, realizing that the end of her hope meant the rekindling of his. She longed to follow the arm she flung in the direction of the red glow, like arrowshot, with a battle cry of "Vengeance." But she let it sink down and hid it meekly by her side.

"I must pray about it," she amended her words. "I must pray very hard."

"I will, too."

Renard went away, cheered, and left her alone in the dark. And she did pray, though not in the way he must have imagined she would.

The next day, her prayers were answered.

"The Burgundian brigands have moved off," came the word.

They gave the news a day and a night to prove itself. Then all the refugees packed up their herds and their goods, left La Rousse to her smelly inn and her petty magic, left Neufchâteau and went home.

32

Rectangles of June-Blue Sky between Blackened Walls

———◆———

Domrémy lay in smoky ruins. The very buttressing piers of St. Rémy's church were crumbling, the bell cracked and silent in the apse stripped of every vessel and altar cloth. The black-ened walls gaped rectangles of June-blue sky overhead. The nests of the martinets had been pounded to dust underfoot.

Next door to the ravaged church, Jehannette stood in the doorway of her own home, broom in hand. She was trying to get up the energy to help her mother scrub out every mark of the Burgundians—and there were disgusting ones: feces in the cooking pots, dead and rotting chickens in the baking oven, torn-out parchment in the windows. Writing whittled into the wall which nobody, fortunately, could read. Her family was luckier than most, she tried to tell herself. Although com-pletely ransacked, every stick of furniture broken, fouled, or carried off, their house had not been burned like those of most of their neighbors'.

They would be spending much more time in close quarters with 'Ti'-Reine and her family. These women were all over now, helping with the cleaning up, while their men started the rebuilding of their own home before the autumn rains began. At the moment, all that stood in their lot were four walls hard-ly higher than a man's head. Most of the grain on that side of the village had also burned, standing almost ready to harvest in the fields, and tinder-dry.

'Ti'-Reine was in Jacquot d'Arc's yard, playing. Her faith in her elders had been completely, miraculously justified, for her "chou-chou" was about the only thing that had been saved. They'd pulled it out of the family dung heap, only a little worse for wear.

"At least we still had our dung heap," she'd gloated to her "Auntie Jehannette" merrily. And with only that much hope of renewal—a pile of manure and her "chou-chou"—she had been content.

But Jehannette thought she must still be under the spell of the mandrake. Sweeping the floor seemed the last thing on earth she ought to be doing to counteract the Burgundians. Feeling sick at heart—and also, greatly to blame—she could hardly make her arms swing from flagstone to flagstone.

Just then, her brother Pierre came walking slowly up from the barn. He stopped to greet 'Ti'-Reine with a hand on her curls and congratulations for the health of her "chou-chou." Then, when he could no longer avoid it, he moved on up toward the house until he felt Jehannette watching him, her broom handle still, supporting the weight of both her hands.

Pierre stopped, weak in his tracks for an instant. Then he took another step or two toward her and sadly shook his head.

"It's no use, Jehannette," he said. "I couldn't do anything for him. The old fellow's gone. Poor old Grison's dead."

Her "No" came out a strangled whisper.

She let the broom fall against the door frame, heard it slide and smack the floor behind her, but she didn't care. Well might they say her feet could fly; she didn't feel them touch the ground at all. She passed Pierre and was on her knees in the barn before he caught up with her.

"I tried, Jehannette." Pierre rested his hand on her quivering shoulder, but she shook it off.

Of course he'd tried. The litter of his attempts—old blankets, buckets of hot and cold water, a pile of sundry herbs, only wilted, not dried—were the barn's main furnishings. Although they hadn't burned this building, either, the Burgundians had foddered their horses on the year's supply of hay. They had stolen or broken beyond repair everything else from the old plow to the good-luck horseshoe over the door.

Poor old Grison had not done well in Neufchâteau. Perhaps

it was the bad feed, perhaps it was the crowding with other horses, some of which had not been very well themselves. Jehannette knew she should have seen to him more herself, but there was no place to ride him in the foul city air and many more tongues to wag if she did. Besides, she'd had enough to think about at La Rousse's.

He'd seemed so weak on the march back, they'd had to lead him and had given him nothing to carry.

"Perhaps when he gets to his old barn again," Pierre had offered hopefully.

Jehannette saw it now. These were promises like they'd given 'Ti'-Reine about her doll. To find the old barn in such a state, befouled by strange horses, that had been the last indignity for the old gelding.

"Let me do what I can for him," Pierre had said, another false hope.

Jehannette had let him shoo her off. Cowardly, yes, no doubt it was. But she couldn't bear to watch this best of her companions suffer so and be able to do nothing for him.

Now she lay beside the great mound of grey hide and felt the life within it settling to match the inert ground around it. Grison's remains seemed much smaller than the living creature had been.

Something in Jehannette severed. That's it, she thought. There is nothing left for me in Domrémy now. Nothing can ever reconcile me to life in this village again, now that I have no stolen forest rides to console me. That Grison had been one of only two horses in the whole village did not concern her nearly so much. That he'd been shared and that there were heavy jobs now that could not be done by a dozen households also did not concern her. Only that she had lost the only escape she knew.

She would have to leave Domrémy now. She would have to go to Maxey to marry Renard. Or she would have to—

"Father said we're going to have to eat him," Pierre was murmuring. "There's going to be very little to eat around here for a while and even a tough old horse will fill a belly if you're hungry enough. I . . . I'd better try to see if I can still bleed him a little so the flavor won't be too strong."

Pierre twisted his bone-hafted knife nervously in his hand, hesitant to begin. "I . . . I know how you felt about the old fellow, Jehannette. So . . . so maybe you'd like to go back to the house . . ."

Suddenly, not thinking what she did, Jehannette stood and snatched their father's ax, brought by her brother from the house and hung on a hook, ready for his work. Pierre opened his mouth to say something, to warn her like a child from something sharp. Then he stepped back, staring at her as if she were not his little sister, as if he'd never seen anything like her before.

Jehannette hardly heeded him. Her Voices pulsed through her every vein, the light seemed to have entered her limbs and moved them beyond her control.

"Daughter-God," they said, the crash of spring floods, the splitting of great trees in the forest. "La Pucelle. Go, go, go!"

She stepped past Pierre, who'd flattened himself against the barn wall, as far out of her way as he could. Two great whacks—"La," whack! "Pu," swing, "celle" whack!—the strength of her Voices sang in her arms. The horse's nearest leg lay hacked off at the knee.

She straightened up, facing her brother across the dead body, leg in one hand, ax in the other. Still-warm blood stuck her fingers together and stained the front of her red kirtle as if it were time for her to start wearing green. She'd even smeared a little on her face: she could feel it puckering the skin as it dried.

She held the limb before her and knew it possessed power, transfered from her Voices, through her. Magic. A possession. A spell.

Every panting breath she pulled in shook her whole body. She tried to make the breath catch in her throat, to make the sobs come. If they didn't come soon, she knew her insides would explode into madness.

And then she thought she was indeed mad. She thought she heard the whole tribe of dead horses riding down the road to claim their Grison. The cohort of the dead, riding to do Night Battle. Yes, the death of this dear creature had been necessary. It was right. Now, at last, she was ready to join them! Yes, to fight for the fertility of her people against the jaws of death. Yes—!

But it wasn't night. And it wasn't winter. And the horses on the road were . . .

"It's Sire de Baudricourt and his men," someone shouted from the yard outside.

"I don't know how he dare show his face."

"Come to survey the damage, I guess."

"Hope he gets an eyeful," grumbled another.

"Trying to prove himself brave after the fact."

Still clutching Grison's foreleg, Jehannette hurried up the slope from the barn. The crowd seemed to part for her, though they were too sullen and defeated even to remove caps or curtsey to the approaching men-at-arms. Not knowing what she did, Jehannette found herself in the middle of the dust in the road, barring their way.

The face she knew as the commander of Vaucouleurs came into view, visor shoved back, shadowed by the flutter of red plumes. As soon as he was close enough, she waved the blood-ied horse leg at him.

"Robert de Baudricourt," she shouted.

They could easily have run her down. There were twenty of them at least, all men-at-arms. But the smell of blood of their own kind made the horses falter and skitter backward when their riders urged them on.

From every direction, from every burnt ruin of a cottage, from every blackened field, the Voices screamed like ravens, death birds. Heart-stoppingly close they circled, close enough to see their individuality, crooked feathers in this one's wings, gold on this one's crown.

"Go, Daughter-God." Why should anyone need her to trans-late them? And yet, she must.

"This—" With the wand of the horse's leg she pointed out the deafening surroundings. "This, Robert de Baudricourt, is your fault."

Oh, but that was a lame thing to say. Surely the men had been confronted by the same words a dozen times already on their ride, and probably half of those times had been by a woman carrying, not the severed limb of a broken old horse, but the corpse of a child instead.

Had the folk of Domrémy wanted, they could have presented the corpse of one of their own—one of the old men who used to sit out on the wooden benches opposite the church was still lying on his bier, awaiting burial. When the rest had fled, he'd stayed behind, insisting, "I was born in this house and, by God, I'll die in it." And so he had, at the first Burgundian onslaught.

But Jehannette only waved Grison's leg and sought for the words she must say, the words she alone could say. The words that were different than all the other laments. For these men had ridden through all these other laments unseeing, unhearing, their faces set forward. Their greatest worry was how they could meet this year's taxes to their overlord with this mess to draw from.

"I warned you, Robert de Baudricourt, that you would pay if you ignored my word to you in May, and so you have. So have we, your people, most especially, while you who are supposed to protect us stayed safe behind your walls at Vaucouleurs—cowards."

"Who is this girl?" Jehannette heard Baudricourt ask the man at his right hand.

"I am Jehannette—"

"No," her Voices scolded. "You know better than that."

"I am Jehanne la Pucelle," she corrected herself. "You told my uncle to take me home when I came to you in May. You told him to have my father beat me. Well, I stand before you again, Robert de Baudricourt, and you are the one who is beaten."

"What on earth does she want?" Still the man beneath the red plumes would not address her directly.

"It seems—" The right-hand man swallowed with difficulty, staring fixedly at the swinging limb. "It seems her horse has died."

"She wants another horse?" Baudricourt laughed out loud. "There's not a spare horse to be had in this valley for love nor money, you may be sure."

"Yes, you will give our Daughter-God a horse. And more." Jehannette heard her Voices loud and clear, but she knew that first she must speak other words.

"I have a message for you from my Lord."

"Who is your lord? Not I? Not the duke of Lorraine?" That took him a little aback. Made his face flush the color of his plume.

"My Lord is greater far than you or the duke. My Lord is the King of Heaven."

"Oh, that explains it." Baudricourt's color returned to normal. "The girl is mad."

"My Lord says to you that you, Robert de Baudricourt, are to give me—" Her fingers worked blood into the dear, stiff grey horse hair. "You are to give me a horse, a sword, some armor and a few men . . ."

The start of her list had set the murmurs going among the men-at-arms. They were guffawing now, and the villagers were not far behind their lords in expressing their horror and dismay at the shamelessness of one of their own daughters.

Jehannette allowed them their noise. But as she did, she looked from man to man mounted before her until she was certain each one had seen her eyes. What they saw there quieted them. She was not just one more peasant girl in a red kirtle. She saw that reflected in their eyes. And they fell still enough for her to raise her voice to be heard again.

"You are to give me men, but a few will do. Four or five will be enough, any you can find who are not totally henhearted." They were completely quiet now. "And you are to give me a letter for the Dauphin."

"The Dauphin? And who is to ride into France to deliver such a letter?"

"Why, I am, of course. I and my escort. We shall ride into France."

"Ride into France?"

Baudricourt wasn't speaking now. This was one of his men,

followed by others in a more ribald fashion. Such joking let them regather their courage, shake off what they, for a moment, had seen.

"You? As the whore of what army?"

"Don't you know there are ten—eleven days' worth of Burgundians between this lone outpost and the Dauphin?"

"Haven't you seen enough what Burgundians can do, girl?"

Jehannette said: "I have seen and I am she who must set all to rights. I must get into France, to the Dauphin, and—"

"Orléans," rang in the shooting of martinets overhead.

"Raise the siege of Orléans."

Orléans? Why had her Voices said that word? She wasn't even certain she repeated it correctly, but the soldiers had fewer doubts.

"Orléans?"

"Orléans is not under siege."

"The *goddams* wouldn't dare."

"They'd lose all honor if they did. The duke of Orléans is still a prisoner in England. Since Agincourt."

"Well, if they did," said another, not nearly as convinced of the English sense of honor as his companion, "there'd be nothing else to stop them before they reached the Mediterranean."

"But Orléans, we can thank God, is not under siege."

Jehannette felt her heart sink a little. Had her Voices lied to her? Had she said it wrong? She felt herself a fool, but only for the briefest moment. She could not doubt when her Voices sang.

"Well, if there is no siege of Orléans today," she said, "there will be soon, mark the words of my Lord."

She watched the face under the plumes closely. She could tell Robert de Baudricourt was considering her just as closely, closer than he had done any other grief-mad petitioner who'd confronted him on this outing.

But presently he said, "The girl is out of her wits. Get her out of the way and let's move on."

"Come on, girl, move along." The right-hand man rode up

and addressed her gruffly. His horse skidded nervously and whinnied a protest.

Jehannette didn't move.

Another man came up, a squire following the others on foot. He drew a crop out of his belt and raised it to her. "Get out of the way and let my lord pass."

"My Lord is greater than your lord."

The footman looked doubtfully back to Baudricourt, who nodded.

Jehannette didn't flinch until the crop actually bit into the flesh of her left cheek. Even then she didn't move. She didn't think he hit as hard as he could. But she did feel her own blood mixing with Grison's on her face.

"You will regret that," she gasped, as soon as she found breath. "Third time is the charm, Robert de Baudricourt. Next time, you will do as my Lord commands, would you or no."

The cavalcade began to pick its way around her and she noticed that not a few of the men looked back with wonder— and a little fear. What was that word again that had stopped them so in their tracks? Orléans? What, she wondered, did it mean?

She hadn't time to wonder long. Before the last dust of the departing men and beasts had finished curling about her feet, her arm was caught up in a grip that made her draw in breath in a little gasp of pain.

"What, for the love of God, do you think you're doing?"

Her father wrenched her up by that arm until her face came within a finger's breadth of his. She could see the deep pores on his nose, smell his hot breath. But worst of all was the pinch of anger between his brows—anger, and a horrible fear.

"I . . . I don't know." It was the truth. She'd done what her Voices told her, as they told her, but she herself couldn't say what it meant. She had no better idea than her father did.

"If you think to run away with men-at-arms, I will throw you in the river. I swear I will."

Jehannette said nothing. She was vaguely aware of the villagers widening the circle around her, not coming to her aid as they usually did when tempers were lost. She could only let herself be shaken roughly to and fro until the protests of her Voices blurred, leaving her no defense at all.

Then her father noticed something else. "What, for Our Lady's sake, is this?"

Another yank on her left arm made her lose the grip on what she held in the right. Grison's leg fell into her father's hand. He looked at it. He felt its power. Understanding dawned in his eyes and he threw it from him, off toward the weeds by the river's edge, as if it were a firebrand.

"Spells? You work magic spells against the lords?"

Her father's grasp weakened, but the moment there was no pressure on the bruises he had caused on her arm, they throbbed. She was weaker than he, limp as rags before him.

Because she could not lift her head, she felt rather than saw him look around at the village folk who had formed a circle at a good safe distance about father and daughter. Although she didn't see them, she knew what they looked like. She knew every face, and she knew what coming straight from a survey of their ruined lives must cast upon each familiar feature.

"Your spells are responsible for the lord's helplessness? For this?" her father whispered.

She couldn't deny him.

"Now, by all the saints at once, I will toss you in the river." Her father choked with emotion. "But as worse than a harlot. I'll swim you as a witch."

33

Coming to the Surface Like Good Cream on Milk

"I cursed Baudricourt," Jehannette herself had admitted in the dust of her ruined village. "I cursed him now, but I cursed him before. This destruction is the result."

The entire population had heard her say it, staring at her as if she were a greater stranger in their midst than those Burgundians.

And if they doubted her confession, they had seen her power to silence an entire company of horsed, armed men. With the spell of a horse's leg. That they couldn't doubt.

Jacquot d'Arc had no choice, in the face of such confession and proofs, but to declare that his own daughter must submit to the ancient trial by water.

But that didn't settle the matter. A great deal of discussion around the benches in front of the shell of a church was required, snatched between the more pressing business of setting the community to rights again. A new set of benches was among the first things hammered together on the return from Neufchâteau, however. And, slowly but surely, over the greater half of a week, the debate edged toward some sort of judgment.

"A witch in Domrémy," one after another said, shaking his grey head. "A witch whose curse caused all the Burgundians' destruction from one end of the valley to the other."

And one after another said, "It must be done, of course."

"The swimming?"

"Naturally. The trials that men compose, with judges and

such—those can't be trusted. For men can lie, even in their sworn oaths. But things in nature have more fear of God."

"That is so."

"No more than it would flow uphill can water tell a false-hood."

"Indeed, indeed."

Jehannette went about her work among the women, helping to shovel the ashen rubble of roof and altar out of the church, scrubbing and scrubbing the fire-blackened walls.

Listening.

She didn't notice, at first, that her Voices, after the great proclamation before the men-at-arms, had fallen silent. The voices of the men on the benches filled her head instead.

Even as she listened to the men talking, she never really believed it would happen. The dirt and the work had a way of making things seem normal. She supposed that sooner or later her father would pick up his ax, go off to the wood, and by the time he'd replaced all the logs the Burgundians had helped themselves to, the thing would have passed.

But it did not. If ever there was a time to creep off after Baudricourt to Vaucouleurs and make the third demand, surely it was now, during these days of talk. But the voices she heard as she toiled among her father's cabbages—mere stalk stumps now, for the Burgundians had eaten them all—were only the voices of the village men. And the most pressing work seemed to be that of helping to set Domrémy to rights again. Surely once that was so, they'd stop talking like this.

No one had actually ever seen a witch swum. They'd only heard of it. How, exactly, the trial should be done, nobody knew.

"If she's innocent, she'll come to the surface like the good cream on milk."

With no cow left in the village giving, it was natural enough that their thoughts ran in this direction.

"But I am quite certain it's just the opposite," insisted another. "A normal woman would sink and drown."

"The pure water will reject an evil thing and Jehannette—

if she were a witch, which I still doubt. Our Jehannette? If she were a witch, she'd float."

"In the natural way of things, I don't think you could make a rule. The trial is a special case, marked by the Church."

"But this is just Jehannette, after all. *Our* Jehannette."

"You must admit she's always been a little odd."

"And whose fault is that? We're all her godparents, aren't we? Almost all? Who else is to teach a girl how to be good if not her godparents? If she comes to ill, we're all to blame."

"But she is a little odd."

"Well—yes. But no witch. Or at least—no more so than our old sage woman and midwife."

"Or the hermit, Père Michel, for that matter."

"I'd wager both of them would sink like a stone."

"But if sinking were the sign, why, the innocent would die along with the guilty that came to the top. That makes no sense."

"It has nothing to do with good or evil. A great, fat person ought to sink to the bottom like a stone. Does that mean our Armand, then, is evil?"

"A twiggy person—and no one's skinnier than Jehannette— she ought to float."

"No, exactly the other way round. Don't you remember when we'd go swimming as lads and Armand le Grand, big lump that he was—still is—he floated like so much old, dry wood. Don't ask me why, but it's so."

"Well, you know how grease rises to the top of the soup."

"Yes, so it does."

"It was us skinny lads who had to paddle like the devil just to keep our chins above water."

Any statement like this, innocently enough begun, was always followed by an uneasy silence. The devil, who seemed lurked within every shadow, had been thus carelessly evoked closer still.

Some men even wandered off and tried throwing different things in the slow-flowing Meuse to test the effects. Stones, logs went in. Bundles of grass. Things known to be evil: trapped rats. A litter of kittens that couldn't be fed, tied up in a sack. There were no clear conclusions. Jehannette, listening closely as she went here and there about her work, felt her every movement watched for clues, too.

Still, she found it impossible to believe that such talk was different from what had gone on at the benches before the flight to Neufchâteau, when the church behind them had had a roof. In those days, any man passing the place, his plow over his shoulder, driving his oxen before him, would call out, "What of the weather, Grandfather? Won't that cloud on the horizon grow to give us some rain to loosen the soil for my blade? To sprout the seed I toss in?" Or, if he carried his scythe: "Grandfather, what do your old bones tell you? Will this fair weather hold 'til the hay is made?"

And the discussions that ever followed were very similar to these that concerned her swimming. Two or three sides presented and defended. But from their benches, they could do little about the weather save pray and talk. No more than about the weather did she truly imagine the men of Domrémy would do anything about *her*.

Only the constant presence of her father pacing back and forth before the benches kept the topic alive. He kept muttering things like, "I saw it in my dream. Yes. She will run away with the soldiers. I must throw her in the river before she does such a deed."

If only he'd pick up his ax and go to the wood, she thought, all might be forgotten and return to normal so much the sooner. Once or twice she even tried, by a subtle gesture, to turn her father's notice to that ax by the door. But he would not be swayed. Then she gave up the attempt. It occurred to her, looking in Jacquot d'Arc's haunted eyes of an evening, that if he did pick up that ax, he was more likely to use it on her than to carry it up to the calm and safety of the woods.

That was the strange thing. Even with her Voices grown dumb, even though it was her life they were discussing so distantly, as if she were no longer part of them, Jehannette felt no fear. It occurred to her that she might be wise to go to Père Michel for guidance, while all this talking was going on. In the end, she was too sure of herself even for that. Père Michel had, after all, only told her, over and over, what she now accepted with both hands.

She was La Pucelle.

Losing herself before Baudricourt and all the rest had only infused her with new confidence. What must be must be. She had a mission, and nothing would stop her from fulfilling it—unless she herself drew back in cowardice. This confidence translated itself, in her mind, to a total disbelief that they would ever actually do such a thing as toss her into the river.

Jehannette was convinced. The trial would never come.

And, for all her father's fury, it would not have come. If Père Guillaume Frontey had not arrived in Domrémy.

This waiting and watching had been time enough for word of the matter to travel all the way north to Vaucouleurs.

"A witch in Domrémy," the rumor echoed. "A witch whose curse caused all the Burgundians' destruction."

Père Frontey would not leave the safety of Vaucouleurs and come to Domrémy when there were infants to baptize, the dying to shrive, the dead to bury, children to catechize. But he came for this, the punishment for all his neglect falling on another. He came to lead them through every step of the way. Père Frontey came to swim a witch.

Jehannette realized she could have traveled herself to Vaucouleurs in that time. She could have gone and faced Baudricourt before word ever got to old Père Frontey. But she hadn't. Her Voices hadn't spoken.

And now it was too late.

34

Ribbons on a Branched Pole

It was a glorious day. Never had Jehannette felt the old chapel of St. Rémy so holy as today when the broken arches reached up to embrace the sky. Above its blackened, roofless walls, the light and warmth and sounds of high summer caught Jehannette in an embrace so tight, she felt the breath squeezed from her chest. The renewing smell of greenery even managed to overcome the stench of burning that days of scrubbing had not removed from the ancient holy building.

Jehannette's heart caught in her throat and tears filled her eyes. Such beauty. Sunlight pouring from a sky of perfect blue coated her skin like warm, fragrant oil. A barrage of martinets shot overhead, whirring to her in their joy. Their greeting reminded her of that given to the divine King: "Noël, Noël, blessed be she that comes in the Name of the Lord." Did her Voices sing with them?

What came to her was not a great, booming thing, but—a great multitude of tiny, little things. The crunch of pebbles beneath her feet, the working of sunlight on her skin, the touch of wind springing to her face. A butterfly. An invitation to every vein and particle of her own being.

She flung back her head and tried to raise her arms to return the embrace. They were as high as her throat before she remembered she couldn't throw them wide. They were bound tightly before her.

'Ti'-Reine's young cousin, who'd been pressed into service as altar boy, was having a little trouble getting the proper swing on the censor. His arm was more used to the slingshot when he guarded against thieving blackbirds in the ripening wheat, his pace more used to a skipping run than the solid, solemn pace he'd been instructed to set. Occupied with these difficulties, he'd gotten far ahead, was out the doorless opening and halfway into the dusty road. Père Frontel called him back with a stifled shout. Then the priest prodded Jehannette in the small of her back with the butt end of his monumental cross.

She lowered her hands. She lowered her head, away from the blessedness of the martinets, the sky. She ducked into the shadow of the still-standing wall, then quickly past the faces lining the way before her. All the familiar, dear faces of Domrémy, of everyone she'd ever known, even of her family, staring at her as if they'd never seen her before. Staring in curiosity—and in horror.

There was no place left to look but down to her hands. She clasped them before her because the cords left her no choice. Another prod from Père Frontey and she walked down the stone church steps and between those two rows of faces, whom wonder and hostility had turned into strangers. The sin that had turned their village to a burned-out hull, these strangers watched it being flushed from their midst. "The inexplicable had explanation, the guilty, judgment." Père Frontey had said these very words in his sermon.

The molish priest had blinked his shortsighted eyes in surprise when her confession had revealed nothing to him. He was even more surprised when the communion he offered her didn't send her mad, jerking on the ground or foaming at the mouth, as the demon-possessed were supposed to do.

But there was still the swimming to come, and that seemed to satisfy him, to judge by the heavy self-righteousness in the step behind her.

The two files of villagers closed in after the small procession composed of no more than incense, altar boy, witch, cross, and priest, and followed it down the road. Before Jehannette had time for another lucid thought, another glance up to the martinets, another prayer to her Voices, the procession halted on the planks spanning the Meuse. Someone had patched the neglected bridge leading into Burgundian territory. The newly planed wood—that had better gone to repair the burned-out buildings of the village, she thought—was comfortable under her bare feet. The span went on, making its way to the island in the center of the river, where the ruins of the ancient fort crumbled, then forward to the other side.

But the procession stopped on the near side.

She sensed where her family was, heard her mother's muffled sobs. But she purposely avoided looking that way, into the grim faces of her father and her brothers.

Across the bridge, on the far bank, mirroring the people of Domrémy, thronged all the folk of Maxey. She caught a glimpse of Renard's red head. People had come from Greux, from other villages, too. There seemed to be so many people and so many strangers that she wondered if they hadn't come with Père Frontey all the way from Vaucouleurs. There was even a peddler with ribbons on a branched pole looking like some brave nobleman's pennant and a brew wife with mugs of ale. Who had money to buy? She couldn't imagine. All were come to see, if not a cure for their misery, at least something they could blame and control.

A wave of emotion stung her eyes. Jehannette knew what the people of this valley suffered. And, yes, in a way, she was to blame. Yes, Domrémy could be easier, the way a single God wanted it to be, if she were gone.

This was every person she'd ever known. The only person she didn't see, couldn't even sense, was the old hermit, the other priest, Père Michel. The scene seemed somehow incomplete without him. Out of balance, without him standing against Père Frontey. As if the river had but a single bank.

How she wished, now, that she had run up to the hermitage to counsel with him in the days while there had just been talk. Perhaps her Voices would have come to her on the lonely walk as well. In her pride, she had not. She saw now that La Pucelle, sacred as the calling was, was not a matter for a scrap of pride.

"Father!" she cried in her mind. He would know what to do. He would make all well. If he would just come . . .

But only Père Frontey answered her. He prodded her in the back again. She was meant to take off her girdle and red dress. He would not do it for her. She tried, but with her hands bound, the task was impossible. She managed to brush off her kerchief, but no more. Père Frontey squinted at her and scowled, but he let her struggle on—for the amusement of the entire gathering, Jehannette couldn't help but feel.

Eventually, he seemed to decide that the diversion had lasted long enough. He nodded to one of the men nearby, who came and undid her cords.

Jehannette twisted and rubbed her wrists, hoping to restore normal feeling to them. But the priest, as if he feared she might be working some spell with such gestures, prodded her again. She undressed clumsily and, when she bent to fold her garments neatly, Père Frontey kicked them carelessly out of her reach.

She stood then, before all these people, in nothing but her shift. And, tied around her waist, the woolen sash containing the caul with which she was born. She tried to be ashamed. More than anything, she felt she ought to be ashamed of the unmended holes in her elbows and at the hem. But she wasn't.

Perhaps because they didn't give her time.

The man who'd undone her cords approached with another burly soul. First they knotted the ends of two long ropes about her waist. The caul made a hollow sound. Then they shoved her down into a crouch. They were gentle enough, but their purpose was to bind her, hand to foot, right hand to left ankle and left to right. In this position, she was aware of the smell and warmth of her own body. The censor in 'Ti'-Reine's cousin's hand, swinging now just at the level of her nose, offered no competition. Besides that, it seemed to have blown itself out.

She knew she ought to be disgusted of this thing they were about to toss into the water for the general purification. She tried. Honestly, she did. But it was the smell of rich, new-turned soil. And she loved it. She knew there should be fear and hate. But there was only love.

Between the slats of the bridge she saw the water slipping

by. To her surprise, the sight did not terrify her. She did not have to close her eyes or look away from it. The idea of drowning—that terrified her, when she closed her eyes and imagined mouth, nose, lungs swimming with that water instead of air. But the water itself—how could it? The same God that had made her La Pucelle had made the water. And how could one snuff out the other before that first had run its own course?

Then—there was her father. And this was her father, who had made her, his daughter, as well. Jacquot d'Arc had shoved one of the other men aside.

"Ah, Papa . . ." she said, certain he would change his mind, now that it came to it.

"Not tight enough," he muttered instead. "The fool doesn't tie tight enough." And he tied—very tight, as if by grappling his daughter's hand to leg he could grapple her life to his. Then—other words came. They spilled from him, the river in spring flood.

"I had another family. In Champagne. Before I came here. Another family. Wife, my sweetheart from childhood. Four children. Then—then the soldiers came. Then I was not so fortunate. They killed them. All. Raping my wife and the girls first before my eyes. And I, I could do nothing, for I'd been run through and left for dead. They killed them. Left them stacked like sheaves of wheat in the yard. All but the oldest girl. Rossignole, I called her. I have not said it since that moment. Rossignole, because she sang like a nightingale, everywhere she went. She was the eldest. About your age, or a little younger. She looked like you, too, Jehannette. A little. The last time I saw her, she was riding away on the crupper of a soldier's horse. And still, she was singing . . ."

"No!" Jacquot d'Arc yanked at the two ends of his rope as if so doing could yank the memory from his mind.

"She was singing, my Rossignole, as she rode away. *Singing!* Go! Into the water, Jehannette. Go! Rather than lead the life I have seen for my Rossignole every hour since."

The side her father had tied was so tight, Jehannette felt the blood throbbing there, cut off with no place to go. She didn't think she could open her mouth or a cry would escape rather than any word. But still she tried to meet her father's eyes, to assure him that she understood what he was trying to say. That she forgave him, even if he could not forgive himself. That Rossignole, the sister she'd never met, forgave him, too. Forgave him that he was a man and could only give them life, not protect that life for them as he felt he ought.

But Jacquot d'Arc stood up and backed away. Her eyes could not turn up high enough to meet his.

"Toss her in. Throw her away," she heard her father say. As if he were the priest.

What, if anything, Père Frontey said she didn't hear. But suddenly, strong arms hoisted her into the air. She was up, over the bridge railing. She was midair. And before, even, she could suck good air into her lungs and hold it, the water swallowed her.

Water, Blood-Warm on the Surface, Cooler Below

———•—•———

Jehannette had not thought about her time in the water much, mostly because she had been so certain it would never come. When she had thought about it, there'd never been any terror.

"I can swim," she'd always told herself. Then she'd thought, Maybe I shouldn't even try. I taught myself in secret, down in the shallows beyond the willows. When nobody was looking. If I do swim, they're bound to condemn me for a witch. A girl who can swim, like any boy—that's monster enough.

So she'd come to no conclusion beforehand. Now, as the water—blood-warm on the surface, cooler below—filled her face, her body reacted instinctively. It tried to flatten out, to paddle arms and legs, to get her head above water. But she'd never tried to swim tied up in a knot before. The struggles of her arms and legs pulled the cords tighter. The one at her waist went taut as well. The round of the caul pressed into her belly.

Then she noticed that her parents' ring around her finger added to the prying at her hands. It seemed to want to sink, whereas the rest of her—beginning with the caul—the rest wanted to float. Her eyes had adjusted to the grey-green surroundings, streaked with sunlight through which floated flecks of mud.

Bubbles had stopped coming, even from the folds of her shift. There was no air left to make them.

She couldn't help herself. Her aching lungs began to draw in water like air. She thrashed, for she felt very near the surface. But thrashing only hurt her hands and her waist more and pulled more water into her lungs. She felt like the floating flecks of mud, like ash thrown on the surface. Her ears rang. She was fire, about to be extinguished. Like the altar boy's incense.

Then . . . then the light filtering though the water grew bright, sparked with magic as well as mud. The ringing in her ears turned to Voices. They were here.

"La Pucelle, La Pucelle," they gurgled.

"No," she tried to say—and swallowed water 'til there was no difference between throat inside and out, and all the way down hurt.

I'm not La Pucelle if I must drown.

And what happened to Jehannette? she demanded of them, only silently now, to the roar of their words. Am I not your Jehannette? Shall I never be little Jehannette again?

"Daughter-God. You are La Pucelle."

And then she couldn't tell if the tendrils gently sweeping her face were water grass or her own hair. The water, rather than trying to extinguish her, embraced her. Its slow current and her pulse were the same. The light was brilliant, filling her, without shadow, as if the water were all fire and part of her very marrow.

"Yes," she cried. "Yes. I am she. I am La Pucelle."

Water-fire burst from her throat and nose, leaving a stinging behind. Even her ears seemed to have burst, to sting and ring, and her caul-pressed belly as well. The stinging was so fierce she felt she couldn't pull air back in over those passages. She felt she'd rather die and the comfort . . .

Then the breath was forced in. Like wind, refusing to let her die. "Live," it said. "Live, and be La Pucelle."

Another force of wind.

Jehannette flickered her eyes. The wind had bristles, like bits of chaff caught on the threshing floor, encircling her mouth and hitting the wind-side cheek. Another force of wind opened her eyes and she saw—Père Michel's head framed in the aching perfect of blue sky. With martinets shouting "Noël" overhead. Père Michel bent toward her. Drops of sweat, of river water, beaded the grey hairs mixed with the black of his beard. High color flamed in his cheeks. She saw it all at once.

How he'd heard of her fate and run all the way. Concern pinched between his brows.

She thought he was going to kiss her. She closed her eyes for that and thought it a fine thing. If she couldn't kiss the whole world at once—as her chest ached to do—she'd kiss the whole world in him.

Then he moved back, unshadowing her face.

"She lives!" he cried, joy like lark song in his voice.

And she realized that he had breathed the life back into her. By a magic like the brewing of a windstorm.

"Jehannette," he said to her. Then, "La Pucelle."

And she said, "Yes," though everything from belly to head hurt to say it. She wanted to go on to say, "Keep it our secret," but breath abandoned her once more.

Flame, light, ringing Voice left her. She lay on the grass, wet, as if with her own wetness the river had overflowed its banks.

"Well, so. She lives." From a far distance, so far that it had no meaning to her world or life, she heard Père Frontey's molish voice. "So, now she's a proven witch and must be burnt."

Père Michel no longer crouched at her side. Only the ragged hem of his black robe swishing about his bare feet told her he remained near and had risen in her defense. His outer cloak lay on top of her, keeping the worst spasms of shock from gripping her rib cage. Closing her eyes again, she could hear the weeping of the village women—her own mother among them. She could hear the hum of insects and the high whistle of the martinets. But, in a sort of comfortable exhaustion, she remained above and beyond any of what followed.

"I must disagree with my learned colleague," Père Michel replied to Père Frontey's threat.

She didn't see, but she knew the hermit was busy making hand signs within the deep sleeves of his habit. She could feel the peace as it dropped over her, over the people and all living things about her. The world shifted toward balance again.

"But you saw her, didn't you?" Père Frontey insisted. "She floated. Like corkbark. Would you deny your own eyes?"

"Not at all. Nor would I deny the eyes of all these good folk, all witnesses."

"She floated. Against all nature."

"Truly. Against the usual. And yet—with Nature."

"Jehanne d'Arc here is a proven witch."

"People hereabouts call a daughter for her mother's name, not her father's. By tradition, she'd be called Jehanne Romée instead."

Père Frontey waved the difference away. "The name matters not. A daughter should submit to her father, as should every wife to her husband."

"Indeed, it does matter. For half of your hearers are women, sir, and they would not care to have their interests so quickly swept under the rug as easily as you do it."

Feminine murmurs from the crowd agreed.

Père Frontey said, "What matters is that she's a proven witch."

"What matters is that she's a proven vessel of power."

"She should be consigned to the flame—for the good of her immortal soul and for the good of all these folk."

"That is the point on which we disagree."

"What? Would you deny the word of scripture? 'Thou shalt not suffer a witch to live'?"

"They must mean an evil witch."

"A witch is a witch, anyone who works beyond the good power of God."

"Not so, as any here will tell you." Père Michel's whole body shifted with the energy of the spell he was working. "Our Mother River Meuse has shown us that this girl has power. That She accepts her as Her own and yet, gives her back to us at this grave time."

Murmurs ran through the crowd, murmurs that matched the sound of the river and the sigh of the wind overhead. The feminine murmurs supported now by the masculine.

"Blasphemy," Père Frontey exclaimed.

"Indeed not. As long ago as St. Elophe and before, this trial was known."

"To help people discern witches."

"To help them discern who among them was gifted with power from the earth. St. Elophe was so shown, before he worked the miracle of standing up to evil, picking up his severed head and carrying it in his arms to the top of yonder Mount Julian."

Clearly, Père Frontey was unfamiliar with this part of the tale, but he dared not admit it when the reaction of the crowd said that the people knew it well. Or at least, if they had never heard it, it suited their sense of things as they should be. Père Frontey moved in closer to his adversary now, until Jehannette felt the less-ragged hem of his robe brushing her other side. He, too, felt the safety of balance in this world, much as his own desire for power set him against it.

"Blasphemy" was all the counter he could think of.

"Indeed not. Is it blasphemy to accept the power of God, however it manifests itself?"

"The power of the devil, rather."

"If it's good, can it be a devil?"

"Good? Who here does not look at his field trodden and burned? Whose walls are not blackened? Who has not lost beasts? Or loved ones? God punishes you for your sins. Your heathen ways. Leaves you open to the power of the devil."

"Heathen ways?" Père Michel protested. "How can that be? Here, among such good people. Who here has not always tried to live the best life he could? Even Jehannette Romée has tried—you know her and her heart and you have instructed her. Who has not tried to live the life his parents taught him, and handed down to him in trust? How is this to be evil?"

Père Michel had stopped addressing his counterpart directly, but addressed the people in general, the people among whom good and evil was more evenly sown.

"Good folk," he said, "after such attempts on your part and when you have suffered such great losses, why would a loving God send you an evil power instead of a good? No, the evil comes from outside. And, just as the heavens send sun to balance the rain, so the earth sends a Maid to balance the evil men."

Jehannette felt something come and touch the hem of her chemise. And then something else.

Père Frontey continued to rant, that they should eschew all evil from their lives. No one heeded him.

One by one the people had begun to approach. They came

to touch her for the virtue, to help in rebuilding their lives, like a saint's relics. Like a saint's relics, she lay still and let them come until one touch out of all the others she recognized.

She opened her eyes and saw her father. Yet he seemed not to recognize her.

"You promised me," Jacquot d'Arc spoke to Père Michel as he knelt. "Long ago, before she was born. You promised me. When I first had my dream. You promised me you would drown her."

The old hermit replied, "I promised I would drown her if ever I saw the honor of your house in jeopardy. I did not see it then, and I do not see it now. In fact, I only see it rising, rising to the stars."

When he had straightened after the reverence, Jacquot d'Arc stood next to Père Michel and asked, "Will you take her with you, Father, when you go?" Clearly, for her to leave with a priest was better than riding behind a soldier on his horse's crupper.

"Yes," the priest replied.

"No," Jehannette struggled to say.

"Perhaps not yet."

Père Michel spoke as if translating for someone who couldn't speak the same tongue she had learned in her father's house. Then she realized that she hadn't spoken aloud, that she was as yet too weak to do so.

"A sign," whispered her Voices.

"A sign," she thought, very hard.

And Père Michel said, "She awaits a sign."

"Orléans."

"Something to do with Orléans. And a siege, as she forewarned Baudricourt."

"What is Orléans?" Jacquot d'Arc asked.

"A great town. In France."

"Yes," Jehannette said wearily as the martinets shot through the blue overhead and she closed her eyes once more. "I'll wait for the sign and then I'll go. To Baudricourt first and then—then into France."

Seventh Antiphon

The Oak Wood, Burst into Flame

The ancient oak wood around St. Gilles' well seemed to have burst into flame overnight. The nights were cool, mist smoked the standing stones at dawn, and the rains began to soak me, my bare feet and hermit's robes, to the skin.

A man of the Craft learns to embrace all the seasons of the Mother as they come. But as autumn had come in other years, those first few years of my calling, I'd tried to think of some hearth or other to which I could escape to, to avoid the death to come.

That had been a younger Yann le Drapier. I no longer felt that way, having spent many autumns and winters in the place of my calling. I'd come to see not only that it could be done, but that these seasons had blessings of their own equal to, though quite different from, the blessings of spring and summer. Autumn with its abundance of nuts, herbs and fruits made me feel rich and sleek and comfortable.

And some mornings I'd wake with the first glimmerings of winter's gifts at my doorstep. In the loneliness of those short, dark days to come, the stream of pilgrims would slow and finally freeze just like the streams of water. Then, then I'd feel old, old beyond my years, and wisdom would drape me like a cloak, just as foolishness possessed me in spring. It was on those days, in autumn and winter, that I felt the equal of my calling at last.

That year, I began to see Gilles de Rais reflected in the Saint's fountain at that time, his lovely dark head nimbused by the flame of the wood. So I was not surprised when, one day shortly thereafter, he appeared at the shrine in the flesh.

Gilles, of course, knew better than some pilgrims, and had left his horse outside the sacred precincts, proceeding the last way on foot. Still, I knew it was he and, without looking up from my task, greeted him.

"Merry meet, Gilles de Rais. You've come to celebrate the dead with me? Happy Samonias."

He looked about him, as if realizing for the first time what the season was. But he said nothing.

"So? What news of the world?" I asked him.

Gilles took a look at what I was doing and wrinkled his nose with disgust. Over a low bone-fire, I tended my cauldron. Ingredients to add as seemed well lay on a cloth before me: slugs, snails, puff balls, and one dead, dried newt. Gilles shifted a little to be upwind of the smoke and steam. I found the smell to be one of powerful richness, but he, I knew, would find it foul.

Still, he didn't complain aloud. He squatted down on his haunches beside me and took in the ancient stones, the fountain, wood, and all—as a man does the comforts of a familiar place when the world has hunted him with its strangeness.

"I may speak?" he asked presently.

"Of course."

"I won't break your spell?"

"This? No, not at all. This depends for its virtue on ingredients, little on the Craftsman's concentration."

Gilles nodded without much attention. Then he said, "Monseigneur Arthur de Richemont has been driven back to his own stronghold of Parthenay, fairly into the sea."

"That is so."

"Not by any *goddams,* mind you, or Burgundians, but by Charles' own men. Well, by La Trémoïlle's. That's what my hog of a cousin did, the moment he had hold of the purse strings. Turned his men against the *connétable,* the man closest to him in power at court."

"It was to be expected."

"And now Charles has named La Trémoïlle lieutenant-general, overriding the post of *connétable*."

"Also expected, I'm afraid."

"This is all your fault. You and your stupid magic." There was some anger in his voice, but more exhaustion.

"And how is it my fault?"

"Your stupid spell to get rid of Giac. That sheep's heart stuck with nails."

"It was a goat."

"Sheep, goat, what difference does it make? I had to work like a madman to keep you from being tossed in the flames for carelessly leaving such talismans around where anyone could find them. And me after you."

"Thank you for your consideration, milk brother," I said.

"Then, after all, it didn't work."

"It didn't?"

"No, it did not."

"Hamish Power and I set that spell to free you of Pierre de Giac."

"It didn't work, I tell you. We killed Giac, Richemont and I. Had him executed according to the rule of law."

"And so he's gone. Just as we planned."

Suddenly, light dawned in my milk brother's black eyes. It was as if they caught the gleam of the forest around us for the first time. Before that, they'd reflected nothing but his own inner thoughts. He stared at me, hard, across the fire. Then he looked into the fire, into my kettle, with a new respect.

"You mean to tell me—" he began, then lost the words.

"I am glad to see you have some care for your less-than-noble milk brother, after all. Or was it only care for your own skin?"

Gilles scratched at that skin as if it prickled. Eventually, he murmured, "And we put La Trémoïlle to his trough."

"And you are surprised now at how he feeds?" I asked.

"Charles' inheritance was divided in half by Burgundy before he was ever heir, in half again by England and now, with cousin Georges—a pox upon him!—in half again. How is any prophecy to come when eight times the forces fight against it?"

This speaking of parts turned my attention to my recipe once more. It amused me that my milk brother thought of men and battlefields as I thought of herbs and cauldrons. Gilles watched me and was not amused.

"I suppose you knew all this already?" he demanded.

I kept my eyes on the glowing, rainbow colors of the surface of my brew. "Folk come to me with news," I told him. "Hamish Power sends word to me, Pieronne, Lady Anne de Sillé. And, of course, I See things as well."

"So why have you stayed hermited away here all this time? Why don't you do something?"

His voice reached a fever pitch. He dragged a hand through the dark curls at his temple, then rubbed his goatee fiercely.

"You don't seem to like it when I do."

That silenced him. He continued to rub his chin. I decided I needed a few black hairs.

"Could I have a couple of hairs from your chin, brother?" I asked instead.

Gilles shrugged, drew his dagger, and provided them for me. I smiled my thanks.

"So why don't you do something?" he demanded again as the steam swallowed up the pinch of beard.

"What do you want me to do?"

"Set a curse on La Trémoïlle."

"Your own cousin?"

"I'd have more charity towards him if our blood were not so close."

"You've cursed him yourself, I suppose."

"Indeed I have."

I met his eyes and reminded him, with a glance, of the young ladies, his betrothed, who were the last people he'd asked me to hex. I had refused. He'd done the business himself. "I think you set a creditable curse yourself," I told him.

"But add yours to mine. For such a great monster as this, I cannot afford to misfire."

"Georges de la Trémoïlle is cursed enough. By his own character."

"Not enough for me."

"Give it time. Wait for La Pucelle."

"So where the hell is this Pucelle of yours?"

"She's coming."

He nodded toward the cauldron. "You've Seen her, too, I suppose?"

"I have. We sent out the call."

"That was over three years ago."

"She heard it. She didn't understand it, not at first. Now she does, but that took time. This summer I saw her struggle with it. An inundation of water—"

"You look into water, you must see water, I suppose."

"This water nearly killed her. But—it did not."

"I'm glad to hear it," he said sardonically.

I studied how the brilliant leaves at his back burned a halo about his dark head. "She is a fire soul. Like you, my brother. And of such intensity that water cannot put her out."

"I'm glad to hear it." He dredged up more sarcasm to keep himself patient.

"Now, finally, after this, she has come to accept the calling. She embraces it with both arms."

"So what is she waiting for?"

"Orléans."

"Orléans?"

"She will be called the Maid of Orléans. It's in the prophecy, in the hidden passages."

"Fine. Call her what you will. Only get her here—if she's to come at all."

"She must come and raise the siege of Orléans."

"Orléans? Orléans is not under siege." He jumped to his feet nonetheless.

I gave his pacing my own words. "It could be."

"Yes, yes. The *goddams* under the earl of Salisbury, pushing their way down from Chartres. Of course, that's their plan. And La Trémoïlle too busy besieging Richemont at Parthenay to care. And Richemont, besieged . . ."

He stopped pacing then and shot off the way he'd just come.

"What?" I asked him, never turning from my fire. "You will fight these English on your own?"

"I have Bricqueville."

"You and Roger de Bricqueville and the few hundred men you can command between you?"

"But the *goddams* must be stopped," he said. "If they take Orléans, they have the heart of France. Once they hold that bridge across the Loire, there is truly nothing to stop them 'til the Mediterranean. Fleeing to Spain will be the only option left for the Dauphin—for the King, I mean."

"That is so. That is why *she* must come."

"When she comes, she will find nothing left."

"She feels the turn of the year. Winter, she knows, is not a time for action, but for rest."

Gilles said, "But there are men—My dear brother, always with your head in the clouds—There are men like Salisbury, who have discovered they are stronger than the constraints of Earth. It is winter? What does that matter to them? A sleeve of ocean separates the island God gave them from us? What do they care? They build great ships to cross it. They know that if they move while other men sleep, by the time other men wake, they will hold the high ground. They will hold Orléans and its bridge and those of us who've been dozing— or fighting our own stupid, petty quarrels—might as well have died—died like the Earth in winter."

"Ah, you forget. Our Mother Earth but sleeps under Her blanket of ice and snow. Safe within her bosom, She holds the seeds ready for spring's blossoming. La Pucelle waits, to build up strength for future efforts. And this is whence her power comes, after all. From working with the Earth rather than against Her."

"So what am I supposed to do?" he asked.

"Well, I suggest you do the same."

"Wait? Wait around, sitting on my hands while the postern gate is stormed?"

"Go to your lands. Tend them. You've been warring endlessly. I have no doubt there is much in need of husbanding in the lands of Rais . . ."

And then I realized what I'd said wrong. By his face, I could tell he hadn't stopped by Champtocé after leaving Richemont at Parthenay. He could never go home, not as long as his wife, the lady de Thouars, was there—in want of a husband.

"Well, stay here awhile," I told him. "Celebrate Samonias with me."

And so he did.

Eighth Antiphon

A Single White Butterfly

———◆———

Gilles helped me stopper away my ointment for inflamed limbs against the cold months to come. We gathered in the end-of-year's bounty. Together, we hollowed out the turnips and other wild roots. We filled them with walnut oil, wicked them with reeds, and then Gilles hoisted me up to set them burning along the horizontals of the great old stones, to lead the dead back to their graves after their night of haunting.

"Do you remember—?" he asked when we stepped back and silently regarded our handiwork, ghostly in the misty night.

I knew before he said it what the sight reminded him of. It reminded me of the same thing.

"The courtyard at Blaison," I said. "That autumn your brother was born and the duchess of Orléans came in her *charet.*"

Gilles shivered involuntarily. "The serpent devouring an infant painted on its side."

"Which you, at three, attacked with madame la duchesse's tiny silver fork."

"Sometimes I wonder—" He stopped, his mind drifting back as the spirits of the dead drift.

"What do you wonder?"

"My brother's birth and the duchess's wish for him to live was the start of all of this. This fracturing of France into a hundred pieces."

"In part, yes, that is so." I had always known what the magic that long-ago night had brought. A black magic.

"I've always wondered—if I were simply to kill my brother, would all be set to rights? Maybe we need no Pucelle at all. Maybe that's what I need to do, and all this dying and destruction would cease. It'd be an easy enough thing to do. I doubt René would even complain as I slipped the bowstring round his sluggish neck."

I spoke carefully, as if treading on thin ice, knowing Gilles was certainly capable of such a deed. "Surely that is true, that the death of one man can save an entire land. That is how the great Sacrifice works. Every nine years—"

"And three years from this night, you will have had to find the new victim."

"That is so."

A wind tossed the rows of flames and sent a shiver down my back.

"Who will it be?" Gilles asked.

"I don't know yet."

"Well, there's always my brother. I volunteer René."

I laughed at the child still in this man. "Sire René is not of royal blood. Even though, in royal fashion, he owes his life to the chaos that surrounds us."

"Even though, being a lord, he will benefit from the outcome of this war."

"That, too. It is royal blood the Sacrifice demands, however, the ancient blood of Charlemagne and Clovis."

"So Charles is your man. By God, I doubt in three years he'll even be properly anointed and crowned."

"And his eldest son is barely out of leading strings," I agreed. "I don't think a long minority is what this kingdom needs to regain stability."

"Who then?"

"I don't know."

"You're not worried?"

"I didn't know I would have Charles' father until two weeks before Samonias last time. I meditate on the problem often, consider this option and then that. Uncles. Royal sisters, perhaps. Some substitute. The Land will provide. The death of the old King taught me that. Until that time, I simply do my best—as La Pucelle does—to be in tune with Her."

Gilles nodded. Another gust whipped the ghost lights and sent leaves scuttling against the old stones like the year's death rattle. We went on to speak of other things.

Come morning, we took auguries of the weather at this year's turn. As the French say, *Telle Toussaint, tel Noël* and *À la Toussaint, le froid revient et met l'hiver en train:* "As All Saints', so Noël" and "At All Saints' the cold returns and brings winter in its train."

And, when we drew it down, we dedicated the moon to Our Lady Huntress. Though it is a sacrilege to kill the Horned Ones within St. Gilles' sanctuary, each activity has its place.

———·———

Later, a weak sun returned after a few days of drowsy wet, which we'd spent huddled round the fire, talking, or simply dreaming to the images in the flames. Then Gilles helped me to make a sturdier thing of the dovecote I'd tried to form of lashed withies.

"I thought you wouldn't eat animal flesh," he teased. "You don't consider pigeons animals? Just look at their black eyes. They look unhappy enough about the prospect of the stew pot."

"I don't keep them to eat," I assured him.

Presently, as we worked, I suggested, "Perhaps it would be best if you went back to court. You are not forbidden Charles' presence, are you?"

"I'm known as a good friend and ally of Richemont, but—"

"But?"

"As long as my cousin keeps me his heir, he'd have to let me in, I suppose." Gilles chuckled, but not without bitterness. Then he grew more sober. "It's funny you should say so. I was just thinking of that very thing."

I didn't bother saying that, in the quiet and concentration of our work, I had heard his thought. I think he knew it.

"That is where she'll first come. La Pucelle, I mean." Gently, I urged him along the trail his meditations had set before him. "That is where things will begin."

We discussed this for a while longer amid the musty smell of feathers and bird droppings, the gentle rustle and cooing of those birds that were not out feeding. Gilles had me come and hold a joint with my left hand while he lashed it firmly.

Then he said, "Yes. I'll do it."

"I'll have you take one of my pigeons with you when you go," I told him.

"A pigeon? What would I do with a pigeon?" he demanded. "I'm not a bored woman who keeps a linnet in a gilded cage."

"No. But when the time comes, when you have something important to tell me and want to get the message here in a hurry, simply tie it fast to one of the bird's legs and let her loose. She'll fly straight back to me."

"Is it true? What magic is this?"

I explained to him how I'd been keeping touch with Pieronne on the Mont-Saint-Michel, Anne de Sillé in Champtocé, and Hamish Power in Tours by just these means between our infrequent visits to one another.

"Well, I will try it," he said. "Until Orléans is besieged."

"Yes, until La Pucelle comes."

And then, a day or two later, I watched him go, carrying the bird in a little withy cage. He went off through the oak wood, whose flaming colors the recent rain had dowsed.

And across his path flew a very strange thing for that time of year: a single white butterfly.

36

Dawn Over the Bois Chênu

The village of Domrémy had a lean Yuletide. The whole valley did, most of their crops having been burned in summer and the frost coming early to catch them at the other end. Her own hunger made Jehannette's limbs tingle with expectation, not limp and sleepy like others. She denied herself more than she needed to and thought that, if nothing else, they would do better without one more mouth to feed.

But still she waited.

When Père Michel came to knock on Jacquot d'Arc's door she was ready. That Thursday night a storm raged and the cohorts of the dead chomped on their bits and howled in the wind behind him.

Jehannette was ready. She'd made a costume of rags like scraps of shroud, but also like the tattered wings of a butterfly.

"You'll go in the flesh?" he asked her.

"Yes. That is La Pucelle's calling, not to lie abed while others fight."

Beneath a brave new crown of antlers, Père Michel nodded.

She turned to pick up her weapon and when she turned back, her father was there, barring the door.

"No daughter of mine goes out to fight at night," he said. But there was already defeat in his voice.

"I'm sorry, Father," she said. "I must."

She pressed past him as gently as she could. He didn't try to stop her more.

Her weapon was Grison's shin bone, the skin and muscle shriveling on it now. In her hands, on that night, it seemed the dead refleshed himself. She rode high on that broad back again where it gleamed white as the moon came and went through battered clouds. The sharp wind blew her to haste and everywhere, she and her mount shed prosperity like fresh dung.

When the cock crowed and Grison shrank down to a single bone again, Renard stayed a while on the field in the early light with her and Père Michel. They watched the others creep off to find their beds and then the three of them were alone.

"I should know better than to fight any team that has you on it, Jehannette," Renard laughed lightly. "Domrémy will win every time."

Jehannette was still panting with the exertion, with the flushing thrill of it all.

"Never mind, Renard. I shan't fight for Domrémy next year, and you'll have another chance to win."

"What? You'll come to Maxey? You'll fight on our side instead?"

"No. Something else." She looked away. The western hill of the Bois Chênu, jagged with its old forest, stood now clearly against the grey of dawn.

"I was afraid you were talking marriage again, Jehannette, and I . . ."

"You're promised to another. That's what gossip tells me."

"I am. I mean to bring her to my father's house before Lent. She's a fine girl."

"But she doesn't fight."

"No, she doesn't."

"It's just as well. Someone ought to keep the bed warm."

"I would hate for there to be rancor between us, Jehannette."

"No more breach-of-promise suits?"

"I was a fool. I . . ."

"And I ought to have been flattered when all I could see

was the obstacles you threw in my way and how you would steal from me the main source of my magic."

"You forgive me?"

"Nothing to forgive, Renard."

They shook hands. Jehannette looked away again, from the dawn in the east toward the west. She heard the last hunting cry of an owl and let the bitter cold hit the back of her nose, clearing her head.

"I won't be in this dear valley at all next year," she said.

The two men with her looked in the same direction, knowing she spoke with the force of her Voices, trying to sense them as well, but failing.

Then matins began to ring, first from St. Catherine in Maxey, and then from Greux. Their usual securing compass was missing its soul, for Saint-Rémy's bell lay still unmended.

"You'll be off soon."

Renard's statement was so certain, she turned to stare at him, wondering if he had indeed heard Michel, Catherine, and now Marguerite, too.

"Well, won't you? To raise the siege of Orléans?"

"Orléans?" Jehannette repeated.

"Orléans is under siege. Yes, that's definitely what we heard in Maxey from one passing through just before Christmas. One who ought to know."

"Then my time has come," Jehannette whispered. "I must be with the Dauphin before mid-Lent." She was able to see her breath now, in stiff white clouds of mist. "Thanks, Renard, for telling me."

"Not at all," he replied.

"Come, Father." She put an arm around the old hermit whose knee had not improved with a cold night's running, even when he had tried to keep pretty much to the edge of the fray, shouting encouragement to her. "It's time we were on our way."

At the edge of the field, she turned back to where Renard still watched her—her or the dawn over the Bois Chênu.

"God bless you, Renard."

Then she went on.

37

Naked Tree Limbs Encased in Sparkling Ice

January was a bitter, wet month, and the clearing didn't come until the end. All the time she watched for it, Jehannette knew her father was watching her.

Then, it came. That early morning when she went out to tend the chickens and found the air as clear and frozen hard as steel. The naked tree limbs, encased in sparkling ice, etched against the cold blue sky.

She broke the solid water in the hens' dish, gave them new, and found a single, warm egg amongst the cold straw.

Not Lent yet. But almost.

She hurried inside.

Jehannette heard her father's heavy tread enter the next room. She rocked back on her heels away from the clothing chest. Although she didn't turn, she listened hard, her heart pounding. Her father must have seen her, carefully secreting half a loaf and a few nuts into an extra cloak.

"You have sworn to me," her father said, "that if Jehannette runs off with the soldiers, you will stop her and drown her."

Her brothers were in that next room, finished with the morning chores and turning their hands to whittling. She could hear their nervous shuffle on the flags as they sat side by side and faced their father's inquisition.

"Yes, Father." Pierre, the oldest, spoke first, very soberly. "You did make us promise."

"So? Today's the day. You must drown her. Drown her at once in the Meuse."

"But we can't, Father," Jean interrupted impulsively.

"We already tried that," Pierre went on. "Or at least Père Frontey tried it."

"You saw how it was."

"The water spares her—for something."

"For this," Jean declared.

She felt rather than saw the glance he sent desperately back at his older brother.

"We must go back on our vow," Pierre said. "I'm sorry, Father."

Jacquot d'Arc exploded with an anger that made Jehannette flinch, even at a distance. "What? You would see your only sister dishonored?"

"No, Father."

"You would see her a camp follower, whoring with the soldiers?"

"She's not going to whore with them," Jean piped.

"She's going to fight with them," elaborated Pierre.

Another explosion. "Not only have I a whore for a daughter, I've two fools for sons. How long would she last? How long would any woman last? You fools don't know soldiers. All Domrémy suffered last summer—your bellies still growl from the hunger—all this was nothing. You're babes in the woods."

"She's not going with Burgundians, Father, nor the *goddams*," Jean said. "She's going with the French."

"Burgundians, English, French. They're all soldiers. There's not a pea's weight of difference between them. And if she fights with one side, she'll be captured by the other. You're damned fools if you think otherwise. Or if you'll let her disgrace . . ."

"I won't disgrace you, Father. I swear." Jehannette had stood now and faced him through the doorway. She met her brothers' eyes in turn over her father's broad back. But the older man himself wouldn't turn and didn't address her.

"I had a dream. You must drown her."

"Rejoice, Father, that you have true dreams. But I also have true dreams. I must do what I must do and the water, which has rejected me once, will reject me again."

"Like a witch." He barely dared to utter the words aloud.

"Father—"

She took a step toward the broad back, longing to hug it to her, though she'd never dared such a thing before. But Pierre gave her a sharp signal that she must not. She must approach no closer, she mustn't speak another word. Pierre could see their father's face; she could not. She did as her brother signaled her.

"I . . . I am an old man. You must do it. I . . . I cannot . . ."

Jehannette heard her father's voice crack. Such a hard, hard thing could not break without breaking other things along with it. Jehannette clutched at her own heart, feeling it go, too.

"Father," Pierre spoke in his careful, calming fashion. "Were she our sister, as she was when you made us swear, we would do as you ask in a moment. Were she still our sister."

"She is . . ." Jacquot d'Arc's voice and his daughter's heart cracked again.

"But she is not. In the time between, she's . . . she's become something else. Something bigger."

"La Pucelle," Jean tried to explain.

"I don't think we could drown her if . . . if we tried."

"A witch," their father muttered again.

"You know how she's always been. She can beat us both off with the end of her distaff."

"Cowards! She . . . is . . . your . . . sister."

Jacquot d'Arc swept to the corner of the room and claimed his ax. Jehannette steeled herself for a blow. Would it hurt worse than a soldier's crop? Flat edge or blade, it must. Her father's arm backed it.

"She must be your sister." The man's voice was a whisper. "Because she . . . she is my daughter. The only daughter . . . left to me."

His eyes met hers for one agonized instant. Then Jacquot d'Arc threw open the door and went up toward the forest to chop more wood than anybody needed.

As he went, she heard something she'd never heard before, in all the times he'd left the house so. She heard him singing.

Why, she hadn't even known he had a voice. But he did. Cracked with disuse it was, but deep and sonorous. The song was also something she didn't know. Something about a *rossignol,* a nightingale.

Or was it about the other daughter he had lost? Not Catherine. The one before?

When he was gone, Pierre and Jean moved quickly to her, hugging and slapping her on the back. Their words tumbled over each other in their haste.

"So this is it, Jehannette?"

"Good luck, then."

"Kill a Burgundian or two for me."

At the end of this speech of Jean's, Jehannette was aware that her mother was in the room, too. Zabillet Romée had been upstairs, taking advantage of the fine weather to air the bedding out the loft window. The two women looked at each other across the narrow, domestic space. Such incomprehension was almost too much to bear any love.

Jehannette saw grey at her mother's temple, just before it disappeared beneath her kerchief. Jehannette had never noticed it before and she couldn't endure the sight long.

Quickly, she turned to her brothers.

"You two will have to take brides soon," she said. "Bring home good girls to help my mother out."

"Oh, no, not me," Jean said quickly. "I'm going to join the army. Like you, Jehannette."

"You . . . you'll come with me today?"

"Not today," he said. "Later. When you've won a place of honor for me."

Honor is something you must win for yourself. You mustn't depend on others to gain it for you. I certainly wouldn't depend on you to win mine.

The words came to Jehannette's mind but she decided this was not the time for lofty preachments. It was time for action. She hugged them both once more, and saved the last for her mother.

While she endured that painful awkwardness, Jean said to

Pierre, "At least we won't have to worry about getting trapped up in the barn loft anymore."

"You'll kill your father, Jehannette," her mother said.

Jehannette said nothing, but picked up her bundle and, with one last glance around the comfortable hearth, her distaff abandoned by its side, turned to the door. In the yard she turned and waved to them once more, standing grouped in the door under the steep angle of the roof that had sheltered her since the day she was born. Then she went out the gate, shutting it carefully to keep dogs away from the poultry. She turned left, taking the road to Vaucouleurs.

The Arc house was the southernmost in the village. The road led her by every other landmark: the church still in the midst of repairs that would swing its facade around to face east instead of an old, barbaric west. The graveyard where Catherine lay. The old men, reduced to two, sunning themselves on the bench. 'Ti' Reine with her "chou-chou."

Jehannette noted it all but walked quickly as she said good-bye for the last time to the little village of Domrémy, tears blinding her eyes.

38

A Sharp Slant of Light Cutting the Forest Gloom

On her way to Vaucouleurs, Jehannette stopped at the hermitage of Bermont to celebrate Candlemas or, as Père Michel liked to call it in his strange, old tongue, Imbolc. He set the winter-dark trees all around the clearing with beeswax candles. Their fragrance and warmth, not to mention twinkling fairy light, replicated the purification of the Blessed Virgin, the first stirrings of the Earth toward spring, the readying of the bride to once more join her groom.

When it was time for her to continue on, Jehannette knelt on the damp, cold ground before the old priest and asked for his blessing. He raised the outer two fingers of his right hand, calling on the Stag, and gave it to her.

"Come with me," she said quietly when he was done.

"I'm getting too old, Jehannette," he replied. "And last month's Night Battle put the final twist on this old knee of mine. I'd only slow you down."

She looked at his twisted, cracked feet beneath the rough, black hem of his robe. Her knees were numb with cold, even through her heavy stockings, linen shift, and red wool skirt. But he would not give up contact with the Mother, even in the season of Her bitterest cold.

And this was the Mother that needed her. Jehannette understood that now.

But "Give your pain to another," she pleaded. "I know you can do it, and then you could come."

"Perhaps I will come. In a month or two, when my old

bones warm a little. But every person must carry his own pain and not seek to shirk it. Surely I've taught you this, if nothing else."

"Yes, Father."

"Someday, you will learn this, not just through my telling, but through your own experience. That trying to avoid your own pain only makes it bigger when it comes back to you, as it must, eventually, in the even balance of things. I've had a good life here. Better than most, I must thank Our Lady."

He stole a glance toward the ever-smiling wooden face within the shrine, then went on. "I've been blessed to see you, like old St. Simeon taking the Christ in his arms in the temple, and now I can embrace the pain that my joy must help me to."

"Simeon? Who is he?"

"Never you mind, child. Because contemplation of arcane Christianity has been my joy along with the mysteries of the ancient wisdom does not mean it must be yours. Yours is all the older way, and action. Always action. Go, daughter of God. Go."

His words echoed those of the Voices so closely, she knew they must have the same deep clearness as their source.

"Come with me," she repeated.

"When you come into France, there will be another, like me, who will find you."

"How will I know him?"

"His name is Yann. He was my pupil. Don't worry. He will know you. He saw your very birth, child, even better than I."

Jehannette considered this, doubtfully. Tears of fear pricked the corners of her eyes, but she refused to let them fall.

"Don't worry," Père Michel said again. "The power of your magic works better when you're alone. Remember that. For there are many who will try to put other goals before you. Goals that may seem so close to the one your Voices give you that even you may rub your eyes and blink before you see the difference. Remember, Jehannette—Only I shouldn't call you Jehannette anymore, should I? The leader of armies should be Jehanne. Or simply La Pucelle, daughter of the Bois Chênu."

"Come with me." She was pleading now.

"No, Jehanne. I would only slow you down. If you need me, I will know and I will surely come. But now—now, you don't need me at all."

Her task was to get men to do her will and she had failed in her first attempt. She had failed with one who loved her mission perhaps even more than she, one who had acknowledged her power long before she had done so herself. Even he had been able to resist her strongest threefold conjuring.

This did not bode well for the rest of the mission.

But her Voices conjured her and she was too weak to resist. "Go, Daughter-God. Go, go, go!"

She got to her feet and went, pushed by the sharp slant of light that cut east to west through the forest gloom and mist. Her peasant's sabots clattered over every exposed rock.

39

At the Rim of the Cauldron

A child could have taken the fortress of Vaucouleurs. Though the sun had already set behind the western hills into which the outpost pressed its back, its foot-thick doors stood open wide to catch the cool of the evening. For Citadel Vaucouleurs simmered on the hearth of Carnival.

Bright, brassy torch- and firelight smoothed the walls of seams. The music, voices, shouts, songs, and laughter of celebration rang off those walls as if they were hammered metal instead of stone.

The place was a great, deep cauldron. It simmered with the hot smells of the slaughtered beef, roasting whole on the spit, the fatty pease porridge, the buttered pancakes, sloshed wine and frothing ale. As a slick to all floated the odors of vomit, urine, and male flesh in the ripeness of festivity and lust. All the wonderful human ingredients that must be given up and forgotten with the purifying flames of Ash Wednesday, tonight they rippled through the warm air like sheets of heat.

Jehannette leaned against the lintel just inside the door to the great citadel hall, trying to judge the brew.

"A watched pot never boils," her mother always used to say. But Jehannette knew she couldn't wander off to some other task and hope to come back when the magic was done. She must be within arm's reach the instant that point came, to snatch the chance.

She stepped inside and began to walk slowly around the rim of this great vessel, watching, stirring. It seemed some ingredient was missing. She worked her nose, then her lips, trying to tell what it might be. A little salt? A little thyme? Would it take the rare luxury of pepper?

There was dicing and the squawks and flying feathers of a cockfight. Men danced, men coupled with men. Two others played shrill whistles, rarely the same note at the same time, accompanied by drums: the battle drum, yes, but also hides stretched over sieves, wooden spoons on pots, staves over the rough embossing of shields pulled down from the walls, slats of bovine ribs slapped together on the knee.

Sometimes no more than a quartet, sometimes the whole hall joined in a rowdy song of the season. Except for the graveling undercurrent of bass notes, they sounded like anything but an army. Somehow, this is where the battle must begin.

They didn't look like an army, either. Leather jerkins and riding boots had been given over to wild Carnival costumes made of whatever was to hand. Vaucouleurs' booty chests had been dug into for scraps of shimmering silk and wild, bright twists of velvet and brocade. The fabrics stood out against the brassy light as if the interior of the vessel were studded with gems: ruby, sapphire, emerald.

The citadel's carpentry had been raided for curls of blond, planed wood which some men wore head to toe. The local chapel had been raided, too, for chasubles, embroidered stoles, and altar cloths, all worn backward, of course, in honor—or dishonor—of the season. Holy vessels sat as crowns upon the mangiest heads.

Grandest of all was the Lord of Misrule who sat on the padded armchair on the dais, dispensing his topsy-turvy justice. He wore a white bishop's miter, backward. The tabs trying to hang down in his face and his constant gestures to shove them aside added to his ridiculousness. He wore a fine purple robe turned inside out so the badger fur shimmered in a sweep off the dais and over his knees. His scepter was a riding crop—and that was how Jehannette recognized him. He was the common soldier who had cut her across the face with that crop. Carnival had raised him to the top for the course of the festivities.

The brunt of most of his harsh sentencing was, of course, the commander of the castle. Robert de Baudricourt took the demands to fill empty horns, serve others the best cuts of meat as they grew brown, the cries to "Clean my boots" and even "Kiss my ass," all with good grace. The commander's face under a poor peasant's battered straw hat was broad, open, boylike.

This is a hopeful sign, Jehannette thought. He doesn't take himself altogether as seriously as he might—on this night, anyway.

Yes, her reflections went on. This is the time ordained when the world is topsy-turvy, all former rank and stations made a laughingstock, seen for the products of mortal weakness that they are. Whatever entered the brew at this time held great potential to remain new and different. It would remain so even after the world smeared ashes on its forehead and repented the deeds done this night in a month and a half of contrition.

Now is the time of the magician, to change one perception to another in the womb of the Mother's cauldron. This is an ancient time, more ancient than the Lent that follows it. Now is the time of Voices. Of Gods.

Mardi Gras is a time of Sacrifice, Jehannette realized. Her circuit of the room sensitized her to this wheel-about, helped her to see with the magicians' seeing.

We are used to thinking of Lent as the sacrifice, Mardi Gras as the compensation. But Mardi Gras is the time pulled out of grinding solemnity and everyday fact. And this time, fiercely claimed from lord and church, thoroughly warmed and soaked in wine, set with good food and garish apparel, this time was presented to the Gods on a shining salver. So might any lamb taken from the fold be presented, or the *bœuf gras* that enriched the day.

A few of the men, Jehannette noticed, had even gone so far in their head-over-heels revelry that they were dressed in women's clothes. This masquerade was grossly imperfect. At least one of them kept a beard and none of them managed to lace up their women's garments, wearing no linen underneath and flaunting great gaps of hairy flesh, front and back. The gowns were snug where the burly soldiers were broad, puckered where they were slender, and the feminine gestures and voices the men only sometimes affected were clownish and crude.

Jehannette also noticed where the gowns came from. It took a while to perceive the four or five women who served the assembly of thirty or more men. They were working in their shifts, some even with bosoms visible through open slits in the linen. The women seemed used enough to their position. When stray hands groped after breast or buttock, there were festive squeals, slaps that were only playful taps and often the prelude to something more.

Sometimes the "something more" occurred after a writhing, four-legged stumble beyond an inner door. Sometimes it did not, the congress taking place there among the winter-old straw to the cheers and encouragement of others—like the cockfight. Human and beast were also reversed at this time of year.

Jehannette's stomach felt uneasy. She folded her arms across her chest as she continued to walk around and turned from the sight of men and women copulating like goats in the field. The God and Goddess were in such couplings, she knew. But she also knew they could never be for La Pucelle, and she thought that just as well.

But, thought Jehannette bitterly, I see no Queen of Misrule. These women are not getting someone to take their sweating turns at the spit—of either kind. Nobody fetches them cooling quaffs of wine. The magic effect of this Mardi Gras mirror has its limits—and they are severe.

The men were singing yet another age-old song of the season:

Candlemas' flames ask
And St. Paul scolds:
Are the trees still standing?
Or is the summer wood cut and stacked?

Leeoo, laaoo.
Are the rafters straight?
Or do they groan under the weight of winter spinning?
And leeoo, laaoo.
Are there any virgins left?
Or have all the children been conceived?
Leeoo, laaoo, at Shrovetide.

If not, every man was lending himself to that work with a good will.

"Ah-ha, my pretty."

Jehannette forced her heart to beat again after the start that had nearly crushed it. She hadn't seen the man creeping up behind her until he clamped a meaty hand around her wrist. One of her bones seemed pressed into the other by the force of his grip. He seemed in no hurry to relax that grip, even when she tried to turn and face him, to give him a smile, warrior to fellow warrior.

"Skinny little thing," the man muttered through lips thickened by an oozing cold sore. "I can't believe you've been taken care of. Like the song says, 'child conceived'?"

"I'm La Pucelle," Jehannette explained.

"La Pu—Who?"

"La Pucelle. The Savior of the Land. The Maid."

"Now that's something I understand. The Maid. That's also something I can remedy right quick. 'Leeoo, laaoo, it's Shrovetide.' "

To her surprise, the man began to drag her by the same bruised wrist to a dark corridor that led off the main hall. The thought occurred to her that perhaps she ought to have set the glamour Père Michel had taught her over herself until she'd decided what would be best to do. But that was ridiculous. La Pucelle was meant to be seen—particularly by men-at-arms.

A dark corridor, however, with a single, minor man-at-arms she knew to be decidedly against the mission of La Pucelle. All power could be gone from her, she knew, as well as all the future of the land, in a matter of moments.

"Robert de Baudricourt!" she shouted. She meant to go on

in the words she had rehearsed to herself. "It's I, La Pucelle. Orléans is besieged. Did I not prophesy it? My time has come and now you must give me what my Lord requires."

But her captor hardly let her get the first syllable out before he clamped his free hand over her mouth.

As she'd already discovered from his use of her wrist, this man had big, chunky hands. Now she discovered that they smelled of hounds and a recent trip to the latrine. They also had grime etched into every crease and the man bit his nails. A fringe of rough scab set right into the quick circled the end of each finger and dug sharply into the softness of her cheek.

"No, *nenil,* don't go calling on my lord of Baudricourt." The words snapped like a cur in her ear and the stubble of his round chin was like brushing burs. "He plays to the Lord of Misrule, all right, this once a year. But the truth is, that man's the same as any lord. Always takes the best for himself whenever he sees it. The trick is—so I've learned—not to let him get first look. I saw you first—though what such a child such as you is doing in a place like this on a night like this, I can't imagine. I mean to keep you to myself."

Drink had obviously made this one eloquent. He continued to blow fermented breath at her as he dragged her far into the depths of the citadel. Her light-saturated eyes could no longer see more than the vaguest shadows of things, nothing by which to get her bearings. He was so tall, and he held her so tight, that her sabots hardly touched the floor at all. One of them dropped off with a clatter. There was no way for her to get purchase on the ground. All she felt was her wiry, strong body sinking into his paunch like a feather bed. Even through several layers of cloth, she didn't like the damp heat, the doughy quality of his flesh.

"You mean to go chasing Burgundians in such terrible shape?" she wanted to ask him. "I'd have you running up and down the castle stairs twenty times a day in full armor if I were in charge here."

But she wasn't in charge here, she had to remind herself. She wasn't even in charge of where she was being .carried.

The Carnival opposite of how things ought to be going. She didn't even have control of her voice.

She tried to work calming spells with her fingers, as Père Michel had tried to teach her, but she'd never been very good at that: calming was not her magic. Besides, the man kept tight control of at least one of her hands at all times to keep her from thrashing.

The size of the man's hand presented an additional problem. Not only could Jehannette not speak. His fat top finger crammed up against her nose so she could hardly breathe.

She knew this wasn't what her Voices wanted. It certainly wasn't what was best for the land.

She doubted it was even very good for herself.

40

The Close Overweave of a Mend in the Elbow

Had this soldier been one of her brothers, Jehannette never would have gotten away with it. Pierre and Jean would have been on the lookout for some quick and devastating move. But then, they knew their sister. And, in her presence, would not have let their minds get clouded with anything other than self-defense.

This soldier expected his prey to cower in the corner where he dropped her while he took the time necessary with the laces of his hose and his braies. The very last thing he expected was for her to spring suddenly directly at him, going for the eyes.

That was the first thing Jehannette did.

"Why, you . . . !" The man bellowed with rage.

Jehannette caught up his heel as he lunged at her so the lunge got overweighted. She slipped the only clog left to her under his other ankle. These things, and the drink, sent him toppling heavily to the ground.

Then she kicked him, hard. She kicked him where her brothers had made her swear very earnestly by St. Rémy that she must never, ever hit them there again if she hoped to have any little nieces and nephews. She'd sworn to them, but she'd never sworn to this man, so she did it. She only wished she'd been able to keep both of her clogs. But the man had very little protecting him in that spot and she struck keenly, without hesitation. It was enough. She leaped over his crumpled form, leaving her second clog behind.

Once she was running barefoot toward the glow and noise

of the hall, she knew he couldn't catch her. But the thought of reentering that hall again right away unnerved her. If there was one man unwilling to listen to her message in that crowd, unwilling to recognize La Pucelle when he saw her in a red peasant girl's kirtle, there were probably twenty. Though she still didn't feel his eyes on her, she knew she didn't have too long before the man behind her would be up and looking for vengeance. And if he was like her Jean, he'd gather up a Pierre or two first.

When a door presented itself slightly ajar on her right, she jerked in that direction and pushed through the low, rounded archway.

Jehannette was just as disappointed to find that the room had an occupant as he seemed to be to see her. She hoped to get off to a better start with this soldier, however, than the last one.

"Good evening," she greeted him.

"Who . . . who are you?"

"La Pucelle," she told him matter-of-factly, trying to sound like it and conceal the sober reality that she was out of breath and, yes, perhaps even a little frightened.

The room's occupant had been lying with his face in the bolster of one of three very cramped beds. He rose up on an elbow and stared at her, hard, as if the single weak lamp that lit the place shed nowhere near enough light.

She saw at once that he was young, hardly more than a boy. And that he'd been crying. He scrubbed at his tears—and then forgot them altogether.

"La Pucelle?" he repeated. "The one who prophesied the siege of Orléans? And brought the Burgundians to this valley last summer as a punishment?"

"That's right." Jehannette invited herself to sit down on the foot of his bed to catch her breath.

The young man reached out a tentative hand and touched her on the arm.

She laughed. "Don't worry. I won't fly away."

"You're real," he whispered in awe.

"Of course I'm real. Aren't you?"

"Well, the way the others talked about you, I couldn't be sure. I mean, some said you must be an angel, some a witch, some that you were simply mad and others that anyone who believed such nonsense must be mad himself. I heard the prophecy of Merlin myself, back home. In Metz." The thought made his lower lip quiver again, but he controlled it. "But I never thought . . . I never thought I'd actually live to see you."

"So, now you have."

"Yes." The young man breathed sudden courage. "Now I have."

Jehannette was busy studying the room hard, studying the way soldiers lived for some idea as to what she ought to do next. The space was windowless, fireless, cheerless, and cluttered. A flight of stairs rose out of it at the rear. This must be the base of one of the towers, and the men who slept here kept the watch of that tower in turn. They kept their arms here for the watch as well, instead of in the general armory. A buckler and sword hung from a post of two of the beds, as if up, out of the everyday mess of living. Oh, she wanted a sword herself.

"So? What . . . what are you doing in Vaucouleurs tonight— Madame—La Pucelle?"

She guessed her silence had begun to unnerve the young man. At least he felt he must say something if she would not, although doing so tripped up his tongue.

"I'm not sure yet," she replied.

"Is it time? Is it now? The salvation spoken of in the prophecy?"

"Yes." Just not to unnerve him, she added, "I think so. My Voices have brought me here. But they haven't quite told me how to go about it."

"Just go. Call to the men. They will answer. They must answer the call of La Pucelle."

"You must not have seen the last time." Jehannette thoughtfully fingered the cheek that had felt the Lord of Misrule's riding crop.

"No, I didn't. But I heard."

"This time he must listen to me. It's the third time. I . . . we don't get another chance. Baudricourt must not turn a deaf ear. Not again."

"I . . . I will go out with you," the young man offered.

It didn't sound like his favorite activity. But he would do it—for her.

Jehannette returned her gaze from the inanimate things of the room to this young face again. It seemed a good face, pale, sporting the merest powder of a beard on upper lip and chin, but glowing, truly glowing, with belief—in her. Such belief fired her.

"You're new here?" she asked.

"Yes," he admitted. "Only here a week."

"This is your first holiday away from home?"

"Yes."

"Mine, too."

"My mother would always make the best sausages for Carnival and—and I miss them. I miss her."

He didn't show any shame. He seemed to assume he could hide nothing from her.

"What's your name?"

"Jean."

"I have a brother named Jean."

He shrugged, embarrassed. "It's a common name."

Jehannette looked more closely at this Jean's possessions, the spare suit of clothes hung on the post opposite the sword. She'd glanced only cursorily at them before, her fascination all with the sword. But the thought of her brother at home made her look again. The hempen shirt had been tossed sloppily aside, inside out—though perhaps that was how he'd worn it, having worn it the other way until it stank.

This Carnival way of looking at things allowed her to see the tiny, even stitches that had put the garment together. She noted the tight weave, then the skillful, uniform spin of the threads. There was even the close little over-weaving of a mend in the elbow. She could never do work like that. But she knew what went into it. What love some sister—or mother—back in Metz had for this almost-boy, and the thought of it melted her insides, coating like wax.

Then she heard the heavy clomp of boots outside. Her attacker had begun to move again. She heard him trip over her first sabot, swear to no purpose, then swear in full earnest, "By Our Lord's Blood, I'll get that bitch."

The boots marched like anvils on down the corridor. The attacker ignored the door, but Jehannette knew she didn't have much time.

"Look, Jean of Metz," she said. "Will you lend me these clothes of yours?"

"My clothes?" Jean of Metz looked at the heap dubiously. He knew how they smelled. "Why?"

"For Carnival."

That made some sense to him, even made him laugh. "Of course."

"And your sword, too?"

This gave him even more pause. He reached around her and picked up the weapon, belt and all, considering them.

"It's not a very good one," he confessed. "I hope to win another, better one shortly. But how do you beat a *goddam* who has a better sword than you do?"

"You understand my position, then. For how am I to win with no sword at all?"

He saw her point. "Anything for La Pucelle," he said, and thrust it at her.

She took it and pulled off the scabbard. It was a poor sword, no doubt about it. She had never held a sword before, but her distaff was better balanced and she could see that this thing was chipped in so many places it could hardly hold an edge. Was Baudricourt so careless he wouldn't even let a new recruit pay a visit to his ironsmith?

"I'm . . . I'm sorry." Jean de Metz flushed as he must have read the disappointment in her face. "I told you it wasn't very good."

"Never mind." Jehannette forced as much cheer as she could into her voice. "We have to start somewhere."

She tossed aside the sheath, then her kerchief. Jumping to her feet, she asked, "Which way is east?"

Jean de Metz considered a moment, playing the twists and

turns of the citadel out in his mind, before pointing towards the door.

Jehannette grabbed the pile of clothes and tossed them in a heap on the middle of the floor. Then, starting at the door, she began to draw a circle around herself, sunwise, with the tip of the sword.

"Hey, stop that." Jean de Metz jumped to his feet and grabbed her hand. "What do you think you're doing?"

"Now you've done it," Jehannette said, feeling the building power spill from her with the contact as if the young man had overturned a goblet in the midst of pouring wine.

"Pardon." Jean de Metz looked guilty enough to have disturbed her. But he couldn't resist continuing, "Isn't it bad enough that I must go into my first battle with an edge hacked like that? Now you'll give me a point that won't even go through butter."

"Jean of Metz," she said, trying to make her eyes a sword as she looked at him. "After tonight, Robert de Baudricourt is a fool if he doesn't get his best ironsmith to rehammer this. He may even give you a new sword, with my magic."

41

The World Spun on Its Head

---◆---

Jehannette's words placated the young man somewhat. But still he stood by, watching apprehensively, while she sketched the circle and whispered the spell, as Père Michel had taught her. She honored the spirits in each quadrant, called them, welcomed them, and bade them be with her and help her with the work that must be done.

Then she bent to set the old blade down, and when she stood again, her fingers were already at the laces of her bodice.

Jehannette was vaguely aware of her companion's groan of discomfort. Then she knew that Jean de Metz had fled the room, shutting the door behind him. But it made no difference to her. She knew herself safe within the circle she had drawn. She could have done what she did in the midst of the Carnival hall, completely safe from harm—or from the effect of the men's reaction on her. No reaction mattered the tiniest bit except her own. And her own was a rushing, swamping, overwhelming sort of thing, answering to the magic of the spell upon her body.

The burden of the red kirtle slipped off her shoulders and pooled about her feet to the very edges of the circle: the blood she had ever failed to shed.

She stood for a moment in only her stockings and her shift, breathing deeply with anticipation. Around her waist, where the caul sash was, where the lacing had been tight, the shift was bunched and creased. It was wet with sweat from her time in the hall and with the soldier. This room was cold and a shiver caught her about the midriff. It spread from there to her toes, feeling the rough flagstones through her stockings, and to the crown of her head, where the hairs rose. It was a freeing, thrilling shiver.

Jehannette felt herself light as the vapor that escaped in puffs from her mouth into that cold air. Slowly, deliberately, she pulled the shift up over her head. The linen she had woven—rough as whiskers over the curve of her buttocks—sent other shivers through her when it reached her shoulder blades.

The shift pulled at her hair as it came over her head. She dropped the shift, shook her braid loose, kicked off her stockings. Then she just stood, conscious of her small breasts bunching in the cold, of the shivers. Of the caul and purpose of her birth. This body of hers seemed lighter and more formless than breath itself.

"Daughter-God." Her Voices were very close, but very quiet, like the whispers of lovers.

"Come," she invited them, urged them. "Come."

"Good, Daughter-God," they said, slipping over her skin, riding her ribs like leaves on a breath of air.

"Come," she begged. "Fill me. Make of this what you will. What must be."

The light was there. Even with her eyes closed, she could see it. It blinded her. The Voices sang, exulted, rang like a thousand bells. She felt them enter, then explode within her, just below her navel, below the caul. They began, slowly, to spread. Like thick smoke through still air, like blood through water.

She gasped, her throat thirsty, throbbing to take all into itself. Her throats, the one above, between her lips, and the one below, beneath the thin, disappointing cloud of pubic hair.

She gave a little cry of surprise and delight, then went limp and felt herself carried to a place beyond time or thought in a sort of cone of light above that troublesome body's head.

As soon as the Voices gave her mind room in the body once more, she stooped immediately. She found the hard shaft of the sword under her cast-off garments and used it to start a rent in her shift. She took the bottom foot or more off the hem with a satisfying rrripp! and spray of linen fibers into the air.

This strip she pulled snugly up between her legs, then wrapped the ends several times around the loins that had so disappointed. She wound it tight, giving her hips new shape, new purpose in the braies a man might wear. Then she returned the shift to her body, short as a man's shirt now, for she decided to leave Jean of Metz the careful stitches of his mother's handiwork as his own.

These undergarments hardly gave her more form. She felt herself a grub, uncovered by mischance under a stone. Twitching in helplessness, she felt blind, with limbs as yet hardly more than hairs, shelless, boneless, even organless, soft and milky outside, and to cut her in half would reveal only more milk within.

She began to work quickly now, as the Voices invigorated her, as cold became a spur more than a pleasure. If she were in a cocoon, she must hasten her birth as a butterfly.

But "butterfly" was more suited to the bright red she'd cast off, not this grey pourpoint she slipped on first, and the shadow-colored tunic. These were the colors of a moth. No matter. She began to feel herself transformed. And it was no mythical metamorphosis, but a change into the form for which she'd always known, in her heart of hearts, her every fiber held the potential. To be otherwise had always been like chopping off her own limbs, half grown.

Quickly she did up the tunic's buttons. She had never worked buttons before—her people didn't know them—but they were simple enough. They were made of the same fabric through which she pushed them, skillfully knotted around itself to make even, grape-sized balls.

When I get home, I'll teach *maman* how to—But, no. She would never sit by the fire next to her mother again, trying to cramp her hand around a tiny needle. She was changing, quite physically, from the body that had done that.

She had to roll up the tunic's sleeves twice at either wrist. It pinched in at the waist. Though she might have fit another half a Jehannette in that space at least, the slack grew less as she followed the buttons up. The chest of the garment, she noticed, had been stiffly padded with layers of linen, and neatly quilted to give the wearer the image of having greater muscles. The fabric tucked up against her tiny breasts, flattened them to the mere slabs of a man's.

This is the last time I shall consider how such things are made, she told herself, and fret that my fingers shall never be so clever. A warrior does not think of the needlework he wears. No man does, at all.

But it was not the last time, not quite. As she sat on the floor and grabbed for the rough-weave black hose, a hard lump of matching black tumbled to the floor with a thud. She picked it up and studied it. At first she couldn't imagine what it might be, a little thing stuffed with old rags about as big as her cupped hands, rounded. Then she saw the stitching, rude, wild stitching, and decided Jean of Metz must have made it himself, cutting off the top bit of his hose to accomplish it. Upon arrival at the citadel—away from mother or sister—he'd tried to augment his costume with a codpiece. No wonder he'd tossed this pair aside as useless!

Jehannette tentatively fit the thing where it ought to go on herself. Truly, it was too silly, and she tossed it aside. On her, the tunic was long enough that such covering was unnecessary. It was probably so even on Jean—unless he left the lower four buttons undone in exhibition.

But her mind ran along the same lines Jean's had. Someday. Someday, if perhaps I prove myself a great enough warrior, someday I may get a pair of hose supplied with a proper dandy's codpiece.

Until then, it was only a matter of getting to her feet again and pulling up the hose. They bagged abominably but were nevertheless very freeing to skirt-bound legs. The hand's width cut off the top didn't matter on her short figure. She tied them up to the laces inside the pourpoint. It took her two attempts to get the knack, for though forming a knot was simple enough, the hose pulled right through the first time when she twisted to tie them in the rear. She tied the back laces first and then managed better.

She strode about the circle, trying out the effect. She wished, for the first time she could remember, for a polished pot or a pond of water—something in which to admire herself. But reflections are for girls, she decided. A soldier had only to move to know how well he looked.

And moving was a pleasure. Such delight that it stung the corners of her eyes with very unsoldier-like tears. She swiped at such foolish incongruity.

There remained only one final act. She took the sword in her right hand, her thin braid in her left, pulling it around her shoulder to the front. Like any proper girl, she'd never cut her hair since she was born—except for that one winter when the lice got too bad. She'd always remembered that spring when the strands, too short yet to even tie back, had brushed her cheek in the sharp breezes. She'd loved it.

Now she pulled the braid tight and sawed at it—straight across the roots with the impossible blade. She didn't stop when the loose ends swung free, however. She continued to hack off portions where they brushed her ears and fell into her eyes. It was uneven, she knew, and the fringe in front got suddenly so high that the dark V of her widow's peak must be exposed. But what did a soldier care, under his—under *her*—helmet?

She was still only in stocking feet, but she didn't think that mattered. If worse came to worse, she could recover her sabots until some proper riding boots came her way.

That was enough for now, for she could hear Jean of Metz's voice raised just outside the door. He must have stood guard there all this time of her transformation, she thought, the dear.

"No, sir, I cannot allow you in," he was saying.

"But somewhere under this roof is a vicious doxy I mean to teach the lesson of her life." She recognized her assaulter's voice. "I've looked every place else and your room, boy, is the last place she could be. I certainly don't mean to let you have more than the crumbs of her."

"No, sir, I can't let you."

The soldier's voice grew keen, barely concealing an eager cruelty. "Do you mean to fight me for her, boy?"

Jean was quite willing to try—though probably incapable of winning a sword that way.

There was no time to waste. Jehannette—only she wasn't Jehannette at all, not anymore. La Pucelle was the only name for such a creature. La Pucelle unmade her circuit quickly, dismissing the spirits who had come and helped her perform the magic. She kicked the old red kirtle through the sacred boundary and into a dark corner to do so. Then she snatched up the sword and pulled open the door.

"Ah-ha," the soldier exclaimed, but any other words died in his throat the moment he looked closer.

Jean of Metz stood dumbfounded, too. La Pucelle pushed her way between them and strode down the corridor toward the light of the great hall.

"Robert de Baudricourt!" she shouted when she judged her position central enough. "The time has come."

The commander of the citadel ignored her, some fealty due to the Lord of Misrule occupying him and the loud mirth of most of the room.

With all her might, La Pucelle slapped the flat of Jean of Metz's sword across the nearest table. In one quick motion, she used it to sweep everything from that point to the end of the board off. Cutlery, crockery, metal plate, bones, and flagons crashed to the floor. La Pucelle leaped easily to the cleared space and stood, feet apart. The sword point, dull as it was, dug into the tabletop with the force of her vault. She yanked it out and swung it high above her head.

La Pucelle repeated her message into the silence she'd cleared as surely as she'd cleared the table, "The time has come, Sire de Baudricourt. France must be saved."

For one long moment, nobody in the room moved. Nobody spoke. Nobody blinked as they all stared at her in wonder.

To the side, retired to their cages, a pair of fighting cocks untimely set up their halloo, threatened nervously, standing their ground. They were aware, in their beasts' minds, that something very uncommon had just happened.

Later, Jean of Metz would bring her her red kirtle, neatly folded. She would stuff it in her sack when she really wanted to tell him, "Give it to some deserving maid. I won't need that again."

The cuttings of her hair, she would also see being carefully swept up. People would keep them as talismans.

For the magic of Carnival had now truly spun the world on its head.

La Pucelle had come.

Afterword

Margaret A. Murray's books *The Witch Cult in Western Europe* and *The God of the Witches* were the immediate inspirations for the Joan of Arc Tapestries. I am perfectly aware that no respectable scholar since the 1970s has taken her thesis seriously, but this didn't stop me from setting off on my quest. I write fiction, after all.

The longer I live in Joan's world, however, the more convinced I become that it did not hold to the uniform faith the Catholics who sainted her in 1920 would have us believe. In the European farm village where I lived as a child, there was more to do at Whitsun with hawthorne on the cow byre than with any biblical apostles and tongues of fire. I am certain this was even more the case six hundred years ago in the priest-neglected farm village, Domrémy, where Joan grew up. Now that I've begun to look for it, sometimes I find the events of her well-recorded life ring through the Christian gloss with such paganism that I get chills.

I am indebted to hundreds of authors besides Dr. Murray for my research. Particularly important for this volume were the studies of Carlo Ginzburg, *The Night Battles* and *Ecstasies: Deciphering the Witches' Sabbath*. I also relied heavily on the biography by E. Cosneau of *Le Connétable de Richemont* and a little book, hardly more than a pamphlet, by Pierre Marot that I picked up in Domrémy at the Joan of Arc House: *Joan the Good Lorrainer at Domrémy*.

Please note that for the dates in the headings I have used the Julian calendar, as the Christian world did in the fifteenth century. The new year began at Easter rather than in January as we do with the Gregorian calendar, so that the first three months of every year are counted with what we consider to be the previous year.